Recombinations

Recombinations

PERRI KLASS

G. P. Putnam's Sons/New York

Published by G. P. Putnam's Sons, 200 Madison Avenue
New York, NY 10016.
Published simultaneously in Canada by
General Publishing Co., Limited, Toronto.

The text of this book is set in Caslon.

Library of Congress Cataloging in Publication Data

Klass, Perri, date.
  Recombinations.

  I. Title.
PS3561.L248R4   1985   813'.54   85-9516
ISBN 0-399-13090-X

Printed in the United States of America
1   2   3   4   5   6   7   8   9   10

For Larry Wolff with love

Contents

I. *Endless Hot Water*

I. A Twenty-nine-Inch Waist

It is a pleasant place to work, Viatech, a new bioengineering company in Manhattan, staffed by fairly young biochemists and molecular biologists and geneticists. Anne feels lucky to be working there. The general spirit of the place reminds her of graduate school, with *New Yorker* cartoons hanging on laboratory doors and doughnut breaks every morning. As long as everyone looks busy, works on the assigned projects, the higher-ups are not particularly inclined to bother the junior research personnel, like Anne. The fields in which they are all working are new and wide open. Brilliant discoveries could easily come from educated messing around. Viatech provides the toys, the glassware and centrifuges and bottles of fetal calf serum. Though they have now joined the business world, the researchers at Viatech believe in the romance of science, of research. Scientists must be left untrammeled, not forced into patterns. The scientific world is full of legends: geniuses who broke every rule, geneticists with magic hands, eccentric professors who fed their lab animals on rotten vegetables. Scientific flair conquers all. Everyone believes these legends, Anne included, and the researchers are left pretty much to do as they please. And so Anne, and most of the others, find Viatech a very pleasant place to work.

Viatech is really the brainchild of one young man, Richie Grossman, a scientist who fell in with a group of investors who saw that in the technology of recombinant DNA there were for-

tunes to be made. They raised money, found a couple of distinguished professors to sign on as advisors, then hired some hotshots
and left them to play. Richie Grossman is himself slightly tentative
in the laboratory, but completely confident, even brash, when it
comes to handling potential investors, hiring and firing staff, even
deciding which projects are most likely to lead to valuable patents.
He acts as the liaison between the scientific staff and the businessmen; most of the researchers think of him as their boss, even
though he is actually nowhere near the top of the real corporate
hierarchy. Still, he is a scientist, he speaks the language the other
scientists understand. He is not a business school graduate in a
three-piece suit who talks about marketing and promotion and corporate image—concepts which Anne, like most of her colleagues,
find profoundly nebulous and completely devoid of interest. Richie
Grossman still has a lab of his own, in which a couple of the
brightest most junior employees are diligently doing research, always including Richie's name on their publications, and in return
getting first crack at some of the most exciting new materials.

There is no real pressure, from Richie or from anyone else, for
the Viatech employees to dress as corporate types. But every day
Anne comes to work dressed neatly and respectably, and she has
noticed that the other female researchers also tend to dress more
formally than the males. The men come to work in flannel shirts,
in teeshirts when it's hot, in sneakers and sweatsocks. Anne generally wears a skirt and a blouse, stockings and low-heeled shoes.
Sometimes a dress. In other words, the men look like graduate
students, and she and the other women don't quite.

Recombinant DNA technology means this: You can isolate a
single genetic sequence, the DNA which codes for a particular
molecule. You can play with it, alter its properties, learn its secrets. You can put that DNA into a completely different organism, and watch that organism turn into a little factory producing
your molecule. Anne looks at her plates, little round plastic petri
dishes full of soft nutritious medium. On this medium grow colonies of cells, mammal cells, bacteria, fungi, growing and dividing
in the warmth of incubators, waiting for Anne to come and test

them, to check what products they are making, how quickly they are dividing. This is her kingdom, her right and proper place, manipulating these cells which she cannot see without a microscope, manipulating their DNA which is too small to be seen even with most microscopes.

Anne's mind plays easily with the tiny threads of DNA, snipping pieces, knotting them together in new places. Anne's fingers move skillfully under the sterile hood, a big white chimney which thrusts down into her lab, a glass window in front of her face to keep her from breathing on the materials. She sucks fluid out of one bottle with a precision-calibrated suction pipet, injects it into each of a hundred tiny indentations on a plastic plate. She is happy doing this, precise and careful, and her mind leaps ahead to what she will find in a couple of days when she tests each of these tiny wells.

Anne likes Viatech, she likes coming back from the doughnut break, walking into the lab that she shares with one other junior researcher, hearing the hum of the machinery, smelling the vague combination of disinfectants and chemical solutions and coffee. She likes seeing herself in the polished metal side of a lab refrigerator, or in the shiny door of an incubator, wrapped in her white lab coat, her hair neatly pinned up. She likes the idea of disappearing into Viatech in the morning, putting on the lab coat, and then coming out again in the evening, leaving her lab coat behind, after a precisely bounded day of science.

A precisely bounded day of science and lusting after the laboratory technician and his twenty-nine-inch waist. He moves around the laboratory collecting dirty glassware, delivering clean glassware. He brings cages of mice from the animal room. He is not a skilled technician like the quiet Japanese woman who attends to routine scientific tasks for Anne and her labmate, he is just a sort of glorified errand boy. His name is Jason, and he wears a pair of twenty-nine-inch-waist Levi's to work every single day. Perhaps he has more than one pair, all faded to the identical soft uneven pastel blue. A twenty-nine-inch waist; he is a very skinny young man. Lately Anne has become aware of his hair, which is a little longer than most men's hair, just covering his ears. Brown hair, brown eyes, it must say on his driver's license, though the hair is very dark brown and the eyes are oddly light. Height and weight? Anne wonders. He is tall, maybe six feet, maybe a little less, and he is so very skinny. But not gawky; skinny with a graceful layer of flesh covering his bones. Skinny like a dancer.

She notices his hair and eyes, she wonders about his exact height, but mostly she watches his ass under those Levi's. She can see the rectangular tan label, with the Levi's insignia and down in the corner the information she read one day: W 29, L 33. Waist, twenty-nine inches; length, thirty-three inches.

They are friendly, Anne the researcher and Jason the technician, after a fashion. Between them is the constraint which comes from their disparate positions at Viatech, her potential contempt for him, near her own age but not a scientist, not anything in particular, a collector of dirty glassware, and also his probable contempt for her, the universal contempt of lowly support personnel for the "experts" and "professionals" whose great endeavors they support. Still, they are friendly. They say hello, they know each other's names. She sometimes uses his, she likes saying it. "Jason, my mice are reproducing behind my back. There seem to be more of them every day." But he does not use hers. Technically she is Doctor Montgomery, but no one at Viatech uses titles.

Anne's Ph.D. is in molecular genetics and her specialty at Viatech is gene expression. That is, she doesn't do the actual cloning, painfully meticulous work. By the time a project gets to Anne, someone else has done that. Anne takes the gene and puts it into different kinds of cells, working to develop the most efficient biological factory for making the product molecule which will eventually be marketed—a hormone which improves cell growth in the laboratory, for example, or a protein useful in diagnostic medical tests. It almost doesn't matter to Anne, that final purpose. Her puzzle is the molecule in itself, its idiosyncrasies, its preferences, its secrets. Her mind moves among her silent cell colonies, trying to bend them to her goals, to turn their complexity of biochemical reactions to her own uses.

In the moments during the day when Anne lets her mind relax, waiting for some reaction to happen in a test-tube, waiting for test-tubes to come out of the centrifuge, pausing between procedures, she automatically slips into a vision. She is watching Jason take off his Levi's and under them he is naked. She goes no further than that; over and over she watches him take off his Levi's. He takes them off slowly, and she watches, knowing that wonderful things are about to happen.

Generally this lust for Jason only makes Viatech more pleasant for Anne. Not only does she have her mice and her cell cultures and the morning doughnut breaks, she also has a mild daydream always in the background. If not for Jason, Viatech would have no sexual interest; she is not attracted to any of the other researchers. She is never attracted to scientists. The man she lives with works in a bank. She has begun to wonder if she is perhaps never attracted to bankers either. She has been living with this particular banker ever since he was a graduate student in linguistics. She liked him better then, though perhaps it is unfair to blame the banking for the changes. Perhaps, as he says, the ways he has changed are simply part of his growing up, and if she would grow up too they would not upset her. She should not get upset when he mentions getting married, buying a condominium, or even just buying a new stereo together. Or a car.

Still, better a banker than a scientist. Anne's banker has a thirty-two-inch waist, which certainly doesn't make him fat, just built on a somewhat larger scale than a lab technician with a twenty-nine-inch waist. Anne, of course, is not actually planning to set up housekeeping with Jason. Her most extreme wish is to watch him take those Levi's off and then to find out about those wonderful things she always senses in her daydream. But that is just a wish, not a plan. For one thing, there is her boyfriend the banker; she may not be completely pleased with his new so-called adulthood, but that doesn't mean she's going to strip the Levi's off someone she hardly knows. And besides, she has no reason to think that Jason would be at all interested. For all she knows, he is never attracted to scientists any more than she is.

Anne doesn't expect anything to come from her feelings for Jason. She expects to go on feeling lust and curiosity, a stable little self-indulgence in a generally well organized and satisfying life; that's how she has it catalogued.

She moves through her days at Viatech, piecing her DNA together, experimenting with different cell lines, adding other little bits of DNA that make the cells grow faster or produce more. She works all day with substances she cannot see, with liquids and media which are nothing to look at, but Anne has no trouble believing in what is there. The test-tubes and the culture plates, the pipets and all the other paraphernalia dance slowly before her in constantly interesting patterns. And when she wants a break, there is Jason to think of, and sometimes, to watch.

And she never really figures out what is special about the day she invites Jason out to dinner. She is not planning to invite him out, she has not been particularly conscious of him all day (no more than usual), she is not particularly reluctant to go home to Kent, and she has not extended her fantasy about Jason to include dinner. All that happens is that as she is leaving she meets Jason in the hall, also leaving for the day, and they ride down in the elevator together. They are alone in the elevator from the twelfth floor to the first floor.

"Leaving a little early today?"

"Yes," Anne says, then jokes feebly, "don't report me."

"Well, seeing as I'm just as guilty . . ."

"Yes," Anne says. "What to have a beer somewhere?"

He is plainly surprised. So is Anne. She stares up at the illuminated red number over the elevator door, watches it jump from six to five.

"Okay," Jason says. "Why not?"

It is cold out, even for March. They pull their coats close and bend forward a little into the wind which is blowing strongly in off the Hudson River, several blocks to the west. Anne leads them to a cheap Mexican restaurant about ten minutes from Viatech. It is not a Viatech hangout like the coffee shop and the Chinese restaurant near the Viatech building. As they are walking to the restaurant, she wonders about calling Kent but decides not to. He will assume that some Viatech business has come up, as it occasionally has in the past. He is not the type to get anxious, let alone angry, about something like that.

"I hope you like Dos Equis," Anne says to Jason, who has not asked where they are going.

"I love Mexican beer—and food," he says. He smiles at Anne, and on impulse she takes his arm. She has never touched him before.

After several beers, they decide to order some burritos and refried beans. Before the food arrives, Jason goes to the bathroom, and Anne takes out the barrette which has been holding her hair up in a knot. When Jason comes back he looks at her loose hair and Anne realizes that she is trembling slightly under the table. What are you doing, she asks herself, what are you doing to Kent, and for that matter to yourself? Then she tells herself firmly: Don't get your hopes up, probably you are doing nothing at all except having dinner with a nice young lab tech. Soon you'll be home with Kent. But she doesn't believe it, not anymore. The hair down on her shoulders may embarrass her, may make her feel both obvious and clichéd, but it also suggests that she may not be home with Kent right after dinner.

The burritos are wonderful and Anne and Jason both eat enthusiastically and among their heaping forks and the bits of tortilla with which they mop up the sauce, they are able to talk comfortably and without pauses. But as they finish their food, suddenly there is a pause.

"There's one thing," Jason says finally, and Anne is suddenly so sure that he is about to say, I have a lover, that she says, "So do I," before she realizes that what he has actually said is, "I have a girlfriend."

"I mean," Anne says, "I have a boyfriend." She and Jason smile at one another. "What does your girlfriend do?"

"She's a dancer."

"A professional dancer?"

Jason names the company his girlfriend dances with. Anne has heard of it. She wants to say: The two of you must be so graceful together. Instead she says, "Do you live with her?"

"Yes. Do you live with your boyfriend?"

"Yes," Anne says, and this time when they smile at one another there is an acknowledged complicity: Both of them should be home for dinner.

"My boyfriend is a banker," Anne says, aware that this conjures up no graceful images.

Anne and Jason finish what's left of their beers. Anne wonders if Jason is also unsure about what is going to happen next. The check arrives, Anne hands the waiter a twenty-dollar bill, and then they are out in the street, wandering slowly back in the general direction of Viatech. And Anne is thinking, he's going to say goodbye and thanks, he's going to go home to his dancer. Any corner now could turn out to be where he disappears.

And so it is Anne who brings them to a halt at the very next corner and they stand there staring at each other. She wants to say something definite, but all she can manage is, "Well?"

But it is enough. "Well," says Jason, "it seems we can't go to my place and we can't go to your place."

"Such complicated lives we lead," Anne says, too light-headed for a minute to make a helpful suggestion. Then it occurs to her.

"We can go back to the lab," she says. Jason offers his arm and she takes it and they are both giggling as they walk uptown back to Viatech.

Back in graduate school, there were lots of people who virtually lived in their labs, staying there till the bleary hours of the very early morning, heating up instant coffee and canned soup on Bunsen burners, napping at their desks or even on the floor. They lived according to the rhythms of their experiments and their experimental organisms. Anne was not one of the more extreme nocturnal lab types, but even so, there had been many nights when Kent, then a graduate student in linguistics, came by the lab to pick her up, they went out for a cheap Chinese dinner, and then he walked her back to her lab and left her there. As he walked away she would stare around her at the quiet lab and feel within herself a tremendous disinclination to start things going again. She would want to run after Kent and go home with him to sit around his room and drink tea and read an article or two from a journal of cell biology while he read some linguistics, and then to put down her teacup and slip smoothly and easily into lovemaking. "Living like real people," she and Kent called those nights she did not have to stay late at the lab; tonight we can behave like real people. But when she had to work late at the lab in the evening she usually ended up going back to her own room alone because the extra hours of picky work left her feeling unsociable and withdrawn and because all she wanted to do was shower and drop into bed.

And now when Anne remembers graduate school, one of the images that comes back to her most clearly is of herself alone in the lab after Kent has left, the sense of the big biology building around her, empty except for a scattered few graduate students, the evening and night hours ahead of her, and the certainty of weariness to come. And at Viatech there is less of this. The scientists do not work nine to five by any means; they straggle in between nine and ten and they often stay late, but by eight o'clock almost everyone is gone. Many of them do not live in Manhattan but commute to Westchester or Long Island or New Jersey; they have big suburban houses and families to go home to. They are not interested in behaving like graduate students for the rest of their lives, though when a project is close to completion, when things are going well, they sometimes revert to their graduate student selves, and spend every waking moment in the lab.

But it isn't only because the researchers don't want to stay that Viatech empties out by eight o'clock. It is also the official policy of the higher-ups to discourage them from staying too late, spending nights in the lab. It is very hard to handle security if everyone is coming and going at all hours. And security is important, as directive after directive reminds the Viatech staff. Security is important because, first of all, there is valuable stuff lying around. Thousands of dollars' worth of supplies could easily be carried out in a shopping bag. Second, there is the problem of what you might call industrial espionage. All Viatech personnel have to sign what amounts to a solemn oath not to reveal secrets to other genetic engineering firms. Unauthorized people are not allowed to wander around. And third, there is the issue of safety; various dangerous substances are in use at Viatech, radioactive materials, disease-causing bacteria. Everything has to be kept track of, checked over and over again at the end of the workday. There are government safety regulations to comply with, as well as Viatech's own regulations. And so, all in all, it is easier to run Viatech if all the researchers and technicians clear out in the evening.

To get into your lab at night, you check in with the night watchman. And once you are in your lab, no one is going to bother you. All this is going through Anne's mind as she and Jason are walking back to the building, waiting for the elevator, riding up to the twelfth floor, and even signing in with the watchman. She is picturing herself in graduate school, standing in her lab and wanting to be home in Kent's room. She is thinking about the Viatech security directives and the oath she signed about not revealing secrets. And she is thinking that after tonight she will have a real secret, even if it is not the kind Viatech had in mind.

She unlocks the door to her lab, turns on the bright overhead lights. Jason looks at her questioningly. "For the watchman," she says. "In case he walks by, he'll expect to see the light on in here."

"Where shall we go?" Jason asks. Anne wonders whether he is nervous (if they are caught, what will happen? will he lose his job? will she lose hers?), but he seems to be calm enough. Anne leads the way into a little room which opens off the back of her lab. She does not turn the lights on, but there is enough light to see by, coming in from the main lab. This room contains the big incubators where the plates of living cells are kept. The room is warm and the big silver boxes hum gently. Little red lights indicate that all is working smoothly. It makes Anne feel warmed and comforted that the room is full of tiny living things growing and reproducing in chambers of artificially high temperature.

Jason looks at her, then at the floor. She recognizes this as flirting, but virtuoso flirting done purely for its own sake; there is no question anymore of what is going to happen, no persuading to be done by either of them, and he is flirting only to smooth the way, to impress her, to show her he is enjoying it. Anne manages to smile. She does not feel capable of flirtation. She has expended all her initiative in getting them to this point and now she feels almost weak. Jason puts out his hand and strokes her shoulder and then draws her into an embrace. While he is kissing her, a very long slow kiss, a kiss which tastes faintly of beer and refried beans, Anne slides her hand down the concave of his long back, taking possession after all her long lusting.

He prolongs the standing and kissing; Anne has begun to tremble and she is sure she can feel an answering tremble in Jason. She imagines that there is a faint vibration coming from the incubators and that she and Jason are taking on this rhythm. Then he takes his mouth from hers and whispers in her ear, "Do you have anything we can spread on the floor?"

She looks around and sees a white lab coat, bright in the dim light, hanging over a chair. She spreads it on the floor and then looks up to see Jason taking off his Levi's. She is only mildly disappointed to discover that in actuality he wears white cotton underpants under them. He takes them off, and she unbuttons her skirt, still watching him. Wearing only his flannel shirt, he comes to join her on the floor, and she unbuttons the shirt.

"Wait," she whispers, and reaches for his Levi's, discarded in a heap. She rolls them up and tucks them under her head for a pillow.

2. Afterthoughts

Anne rides uptown on the subway, home to Kent. She is neatly dressed once more. It is not even nine o'clock yet. She rides uptown thinking of Kent, feeling guilty, thinking of Jason and feeling all sorts of things.

Kent: Anne and Kent met when they were both graduate students. They had a long, fairly casual affair, and then they moved in together; neither of them had ever had such a serious relationship before and they were nervous about letting it become even more serious. But the living together worked out well; they both finished their dissertations almost on schedule and they helped each other through the final typing and proofreading stages. So far, so good. Then they moved to New York. Anne had gotten the job at Viatech and Kent had not been able to find a job in linguistics. That was not terribly surprising, given the state of the academic job market. He would work at something else for a while and try to revise his dissertation for publication and after it was published he would apply for academic jobs again. That was almost three years ago. Kent shows no signs of revising the dissertation. The linguistics texts and foreign grammars sit on a shelf over his neat desk, but as far as Anne can see he never takes them down. All his life Kent has been fascinated by foreign alphabets. His hobby is acquiring new ones. He loves learning languages with alphabets all their own. Although his major field is Sanskrit, he knows a little Russian, a little Thai, a little Greek. And he knows Farsi, Persian.

He actually has learned one new language since coming to New York: Arabic. It is connected to how he got his banking job, a story he once loved to tell but now seems to be tired of.

When Kent had his job interview at the bank he now works for, his interviewer asked him, with bluff contempt, what good all those languages were going to do in the banking world. He looked again at Kent's resume. We do a lot of business with people who speak Arabic. The interviewer rooted around on his desk and produced a pamphlet printed in the distinctive flowing slopes and valleys of Arabic script. Fellow brought this back for me as a souvenir, he said. Could Kent read it?

Kent picked up the pamphlet, without much hope, and then realized that it was in Persian, a language completely unrelated to Arabic but written with the Arabic alphabet. He read off the first few sentences and began to translate. The pamphlet, a relic of the Shah's regime, was about family planning. Kent's interviewer roared with laughter and said, That's just like that guy's sense of humor. On that note the interview ended, and Kent was subsequently offered a job which included some correspondence work with banks in Arabic-speaking countries. And so he has taught himself Arabic, which has given him a great deal of pleasure. It was almost the only thing he had liked about working at the bank for the first six months or so. That and telling the story of how he had been hired. Anne was sorry he was so unhappy, but bothered that he was not spurred into working on the dissertation. His sense of helplessness annoyed her but now she is even more annoyed that he is happy and moderately enthusiastic in his work. He says it is because he has been promoted very fast, given more interesting things to do, because he now works with more intelligent people. Anne suspects that Kent has become enamored of the idea of being an executive, of living life like an executive. In short, she suspects him of having switched fantasies.

Anne rides uptown on the subway, going home to Kent, to the little apartment near West End Avenue where she lives with Kent, thinking about Kent. This is Kent, this is our history together, this is what I do not like.

What is Kent's fantasy these days? Kent is a responsible citizen, surely he does not waste his time in the kind of lecherous fantasy that Anne so enjoys. And look how her irresponsible fantasies have been rewarded. She tries, for the first time ever, to imagine Jason in some other context, life with Jason, life *as* Jason. What is it like not to have a "field"? What is it like to work to support yourself and to choose the job only for that reason? Anne, moving from the world of graduate school into the warm welcome of Viatech, has had little to do with people who lack vocations. And here she is, condemning Kent for making his bank into a vocation, for refusing to look at it the way Jason looks at his lab tech job. She is being unfair to Kent and she knows it. She doesn't really want to think about Kent.

With Jason, Anne has no history at all. Only someone in a six-or-more-year relationship can understand the light feeling that gives her.

And why is Anne running all this through her mildly dazed brain? Is she about to drop Kent and take up with Jason? Has Jason even so much as suggested that someday they might once again go into the incubator room together? No, she is merely speculating as she rides uptown on the subway, as she goes home to Kent after her tryst (if you can call it that) on the incubator room floor with Jason. And here she is, neatly dressed again. And here it is, not even nine o'clock. Every few minutes the memory of Jason starts again, and all her speculations disappear in a flush of embarrassment and pleasure. Jason, on the incubator room floor, was dynamite. Somewhere in some fair and just corner of her mind she resolved early in the evening that she would make no direct comparisons, that direct comparisons would be meaningless and anyway impossible to make. But that was before the fact. There are, it is true, none to make, but that is only because the comparison has already been made and it would be silly to bother spelling it out. In short, there is no competition. And it is precisely *that* which is embarrassing Anne as she sits on the subway, grateful for the loud noise which protects her anonymity. It is the memory of her own surprise and then her own demonstrativeness; Anne has always thought of herself as silent-but-sensuous in bed. Now it appears that on laboratory floors, at least, she is capable of being wild-crude-and-noisy.

The other memory which embarrasses her is the memory of Jason afterward, when they finished dressing and were checking to see that the room was in order. Jason took her hand just before they left the little room and smiled at her and then looked down as though he were suddenly shy.

"That was really something," he said, without looking at Anne, and then he kissed her lightly on the mouth. And after that, it seems to Anne, they did not once look at one another directly; they left the building and he walked her to her subway stop and touched her arm as he said good-bye. Anne wishes suddenly that it were Friday; she does not want to see Jason again immediately. She has to think about how to behave. And how can she think about how to behave tomorrow at work when she has to decide immediately how she will behave toward Kent when she gets home?

Kent is a monogamous creature. Anne has always thought of herself as another monogamous creature. Anne has never been unfaithful to Kent, or at least not since the two of them began to take their relationship seriously. Way back at the beginning they both had other lovers but those drifted away as Anne and Kent became solidly coupled off. Why is she even thinking about telling Kent? Does she just want to hurt him? Does she want to shock him into changing his ways?

Experimentally Anne tries putting herself into the future and imagining Jason in the past. It is three years from now; she is telling a good friend (her good friend Charlotte, her only scientist friend): Remember that good-looking lab tech we used to have in our lab (surely Jason will have drifted on by then), the skinny one with the brown hair? Well, one night three years ago he and I struck some sparks off each other on the floor of the incubator room. I've never told Kent.

Or perhaps it is five years from now and she is telling Kent (surely the statute of limitations has expired): The only time I've ever been unfaithful to you was one crazy night more than five years ago when I messed around a little with someone at work. We were both drunk, it was kind of a passing impulse. We thought better of it right away. (Do these little lies make Kent feel better about the one truth that is finally being told?)

With only two stops to go, Anne thinks rather desperately about how she will act when she gets home. Act natural, of course, is the obvious answer, but should she act natural, meaning a little irritated, a little distant, as she all too often is these days, or should she be sweet and loving . . . and lure him into making love to her? Anne is a little horrified to find that the idea is rather appealing.

Kent, it turns out, is not alone. Of all people, it would have to be Anne's cousin Louisa who happened to stop by earlier, who was invited by Kent to stay and wait for Anne and have dinner, who waited with Kent for almost two hours and then finally helped him prepare and consume the chicken that was in the refrigerator. And she is still there, a cheerful witness to Anne's lack of considerateness.

"Well, look who's finally here," she calls archly, as Anne lets herself into the apartment. "And just what have you been up to, may I ask?"

Kent himself does not look angry, only a little weary, which is natural after several hours of unadulterated Louisa (while Anne was off adulterating, of course). Anne drops into a chair as if weighted down with immense weariness.

"God," she finds herself saying, "I'm sorry, I feel really bad about not calling, but I've been in the most god-awful meeting since four o'clock this afternoon. Nonstop, this incredible interminable meeting, and I lost all track of time. I was just waiting for it to be over."

"Did you get any supper?" Louisa asks, concerned and maternal.

"They sent out for sandwiches." Anne wonders if she carries the scent of Mexican food about her. This is an unwelcome thought, and it brings more unwelcome thoughts. "What I'd really like to do is just get in the shower," she says.

"I should be going, you're so tired," Louisa says.

"First tell me how you are," Anne says, but as she speaks she removes her shoes and stretches her feet luxuriously, just to remind Louisa that this is not an invitation to stay another hour.

"Oh, Kent can fill you in. He's just been listening to me go on and on."

"About what?"

"I've met the most wonderful man," Lousia says, and pauses for Anne to exclaim, Oh, not a new one, or perhaps, Oh no, Louisa, you aren't in love again, are you? For Louisa is able to be quite sincere about each new love and at the same time able to enjoy Anne's reactions.

"Oh no, Louisa, not again?" Anne obliges.

"This time I'm really in love and he is too. Anne, we have so much in common it's amazing."

Anne thinks abruptly of Jason and how little she has in common with him. To cover the thought, she turns away and pretends to yawn, and at once Louisa is on her feet, assuring Anne that Kent will fill her in on all the details about the wonderful new man.

Kent politely sees Louisa to the door, then comes back and sits on the arm of Anne's chair. He strokes her head and she says cheerfully, "So, Louisa is in love."

"Yes," Kent says, "Louisa is in love again." They exchange a smile full of amused affection for Louisa.

"Poor Louisa," Anne says, but she says it with lightness; this love will not work out and Louisa will be sad, but she will find a new one fast enough.

"Don't feel too sorry for her," Kent says, "she's happy," and Anne wonders, in her guilty sensitivity, if there is an inference to be drawn from that sentence, an unspoken emphasis on the "she."

"I'm going to take a shower," Anne says. "It's been a long day."

One of the blessings of the apartment Anne and Kent share is its shower, which is ferociously strong. And the hot water never gives out. Stepping under the shower, Anne is instantly soaked in a familiar and reassuring way; water streams through her hair and drums loudly on the bathtub and Anne feel herself relax. She leans her shoulder against the tiled wall and turns her face into the flow of water. After a few seconds of the stinging heat she has to turn away. Wet and relaxed, she admits to herself that the real reason she wanted to take a shower was to wash between men.

As Anne is rinsing off, Kent pushes aside the shower curtain and joins her in the shower. He wraps his arms around her and they stand together under the water. "Hi," he says into her ear, pushing aside a loop of wet hair. "I thought I'd come visit."

Anne allows her whole body to be soaped a second time; at first she is not quite pleased by Kent's presence, feeling that she was not really ready for him, but then she becomes aroused and begins to enjoy the combination of hot water and soap and hands. They each revolve once under the shower, washing off all the soap, then they hastily dry each other off and adjourn to their bedroom, where Kent goes some way toward lessening the severity of the comparisons Anne had been making on the subway. They lie in bed and read for a while, get up to brush their teeth, turn out the light. Anne finds herself, after the euphoria of her adventure with Jason and the vaguely mindless sensuality of her interval with Kent, a little bit confused and disturbed.

"What was the meeting about?" Kent asks.

Anne answers almost before she has time to remember what meeting he must be referring to; some responsible segment of her mind has apparently thought it all out. "That ridiculous Richie Grossman," she says. "He wants us to take on this project, which everyone else thinks is too risky. It turned into an endlessly long fight, and it just went on forever." Anne is filled with admiration for the cleverness of this reply; it is almost as though she herself had not thought it up. The issue is indeed in the air at Viatech, and may in fact generate meetings in the near future.

"I'll get home early tomorrow," she says, wondering if she is promising that she won't sleep with Jason again—but that's ridiculous, to expect it to happen again tomorrow, same time, same place.

Kent wraps his arms around her and she enjoys the familiarity and comfort of this post-sex, pre-sleep embrace. When he actually speaks, he deals her one of those shocks which make you believe in the presence of extrasensory perception between longtime lovers. "Remember in grad school," Kent says, "when you used to have to work late at the lab?"

"Yes," Anne says; the familiarity of the embrace is now a little frightening. How can he have picked up her own recollections from earlier in the evening?

"And we would eat Chinese food?" Kent goes on. "And I would walk you back to your lab?"

"Yes," Anne says again, "yes, I remember."

"Those were good times." He pauses. "Anne? This is silly but I feel—we aren't losing each other, are we?"

Anne tells herself that he can only bring himself to ask the question because things have gone so pleasantly between them this evening. It is a question which reflects general trends, not her specific and recent infidelity. It even occurs to her that Kent's joining her in the shower, making love to her, was planned to lead up to this question and at the same time to ensure that her answer would be the one Kent wants to hear. And perhaps that should be her answer, a dishonest bewilderment at his asking such a question. But it is only her guilt over Jason which tempts her to take this easy way out. She forces herself to answer more honestly, as she would probably have answered any other night. "I don't know," she says. "I hope not." Between them now is the silence of their mutual admission. Kent tightens his arms around her as though to leave no room for anything at all between their bodies.

Although they do not fall asleep like this, neither of them actually says anything else. Entwined, they both grow drowsy, release each other without speaking, and fall asleep, both toward the middle of the bed. Anne is relieved to be falling asleep; she is afraid to think about Kent and afraid to think about Jason. She knows that in the morning she will be hurried and Kent will be hurried and that her next real opportunity to think will come when she is in her lab at Viatech. But then it will not be merely thoughts of Jason which will trouble her. Jason may come along in the flesh. Falling asleep, Anne thinks of Jason in the flesh.

3. A New York Career Girl

Anne's family: Anne's life is a structure of tiny memories, of course, but it is broken, intersected, and divided by a single event so large that it is sometimes difficult even for her to focus on the tiny evocative bits from one side or the other.

Anne's parents were both high school teachers, though fortunately neither of them taught in the school Anne attended. Her father taught English and coached the tennis team (Anne has never learned to play tennis) at a high school one town away, in the Chicago suburbs, while her mother was a guidance counselor who in her spare time read copiously about adolescent psychology in professional journals and popular psychology books. Anne as an adolescent was always prickly, always resentful. (If Anne had allowed herself, would she have said, You worry about other kids all day, never about me? Would she have said to her father, I would have learned tennis if you had really pushed, but you didn't care enough? These are the sorts of obvious things you work out with an analyst, Anne supposes.) They were both conscientious people, heavily involved in the affairs of the town in which they taught—school board meetings, hirings and firings, fund-raisers, football—but it was not the town they lived in. The town they taught in was too expensive for them; they had bought a house in a more middle-class suburb, where Anne grew up and went to school.

The house Anne grew up in was small and neat; her parents were not people who accumulated clutter. They had not really been expecting a child, Anne thought. They had married right out of college, and they were married for fifteen years before Anne was born; probably they had been convinced they would have no children. Together they had built an equilibrium, their neat little house, the two of them together in the evening, reading, grading papers, talking about the school where they both worked.

And then Anne was born and her mother conscientiously gave up her job and spent eight years in the neat uncluttered house, watching her daughter, often with a rather puzzled look on her face, as if to say, Is there something you want me to be doing? Anne never quite penetrated that bond her parents forged before she was born; they loved her, of course, but they always turned first to each other, then, smiling, to Anne, as if she were a tremendously welcome guest, and they, in the warmth of their domesticity, would do all they could to make her feel at home. Is that really how it was? Does she remember her childhood correctly, this sense that her parents were a tight functional unit all by themselves, devoted to her but never really including her?

Anne had parents who thought often and seriously about people she never knew, about the well-heeled college-bound students they were responsible for, and Anne, when she hit adolescence, lost no time in transforming herself into the other kind of student, the kind who made rude noises when college was mentioned. Actually, of course, she sometimes thought she might kind of like to go to a good college. But what better way to attack an English teacher and a guidance counselor than by talking about how much you hate school, and how much you don't want to go to college.

When Anne was fifteen years old, both her parents were killed in an automobile accident. Anne was given the choice of which family to live with while she finished high school. She chose between her mother's brother's family, Louisa's family, who lived on a farm in Minnesota, and her father's sister's family, who lived in yet another suburb of Chicago. Since Anne had grown up in a similar suburb, she was briefly tempted by the idea of the farm; this was the era when farm life had a sort of hip halo around it, images of whole-grain bread and making patchwork quilts on winter evenings around a log fire. But though she did not know her Minnesota cousins well, she was fairly sure that whatever their life might be, it was not hip romance. So she chose Aunt Letitia and her husband, Uncle Douglas, who was a professor at the University of Chicago. And as she sorted this out and made this choice, intermittently calm in the tumult of family gatherings and sudden outbreaks of tears and hysteria several weeks after her parents' death, Anne was conscious, even then, of a very particular regret. This regret, which has grown stronger and clearer ever since, is as follows: Anne lost her parents at a terrible time, terrible not because she was particularly close to them, but because she had not yet left behind the miasma of resentment, rebellion, hostility, and self-absorption which had immersed her for the past year or so. She had hardly been aware of her parents, except as obstacles. She lived to pull away from them, to prove to them that they did not control her, to lure them into trying, to scare them into making the mistake of questioning her. She knew, and she was always to tell herself that they knew too, that this would not last forever. Now when Anne talks to her parents, which she does very rarely and always without expecting to, what she tells them is, You would like me if you knew me now, and please believe that I would like you too.

Anne holds on to a few members of her extended family, or they hold on to her. Her Uncle Douglas and Aunt Letitia. And her cousin Louisa, who has left the farm and come to New York. Sometimes Anne thinks she holds on and allows herself to be held on to partly because of these feelings about her parents. She will not let anyone else slip away ignored and mocked and unappreciated. When Anne was fifteen, she got to choose between two homes, and she carries with her the belief that it is possible to choose in this life. But maybe Anne also believes that the most important things are the ones you don't get to choose, the family connections that are there whether you like them or not.

Anne's cousin Louisa came to New York two years ago, one year after Anne and Kent. Louisa is a receptionist in a large company that manufactures and sells office machines. Back in Minnesota, she had taken a secretarial course and worked for various Minneapolis firms. At the age of twenty-five, after the dissolution of an engagement which had already been announced to the family and written up in the paper, she had decided to come to New York and, as she herself put it, start over.

Louisa is attractive in a sort of un–New York way; she is soft and round and blond, small and plump and giggly. She shares an apartment with two other women. Men take Louisa out in the evenings, often men she meets through her job, they take her out and bring her home and go to bed with her. She falls in love, she hopes it will last, she loses one and starts hoping for the next. It seems to Anne that Louisa is trying to live a life patterned after the stories she reads in the magazines which she pores over every month, studying with equal seriousness the newest diets and the rules for making a casual date into a serious relationship.

She takes to heart the rules which reinforce her natural tendencies, rules which assure her that careful attention to the likes and dislikes of your love object will gain his heart. Sometimes Louisa comes across articles which advise her to play emotionally hard to get, but this is beyond her power. She has a tremendous capacity for a certain kind of love; that is, when she has a serious lover, she devotes herself to him completely, learning to bake the desserts he orders in restaurants, sending him frequent perky greeting cards. She sends him tiny bottles of aftershave and jars of fancy jam. Some men like this treatment, but few can survive it for long. And so, most of the time, Louisa is searching for her next serious romance and in the meantime going out on dates. If there is no special man to buy cards for, there are always Anne and Kent, or the family back home in Minnesota, or her roommates.

Louisa has advanced, during her two years at her office machinery firm, to a position of some authority. That is, in many ways she is the one who keeps the office running, because she has a tireless memory for details and is on good terms with everyone. The chores which secretaries often resent, shopping for presents for the boss's children, serving coffee and doughnuts at board meetings, are pleasures for Louisa. Her boss has often said, to

Louisa's delight, "We ought to import some more of these Minnesota secretaries."

The completely disarming and lovable side of Louisa is just this: She is delighted with her life, and she believes deeply that it is the glamorous life of a true New York sophisticate. It is precisely for this that she left Minnesota. Cheerfully, she discusses all the details with Anne, even with Kent, sure that as fellow sophisticates they will be interested but unshocked. In fact, Anne and Kent have been shocked so repeatedly by Louisa that they probably don't see her quite clearly anymore; they have come to view her as a caricature of what she actually is. And so Louisa is in love again.

The next morning she phones Anne at Viatech.

"Something terrible happened last night."

"Last night? You mean after you left our place?" Anne asks, alarmed.

"Yes," Louisa almost whispers. Anne wonders if she can detect intimations of tears in Louisa's voice.

"Louisa, are you okay?"

"I'm okay. But I can't talk about it now. Someone might hear."

"Listen," Anne says, "why don't you come have lunch with me today?" Louisa works only fifteen blocks from Viatech, but she and Anne have never been in the habit of meeting during the day. Anne has been unwilling to see their friendship extend its boundaries, but here is Louisa, sounding upset, and here is Anne, feeling herself eager to comfort. They agree to meet at a soup-and-salad place near Viatech.

Just as Anne hangs up the phone, Jason comes into the room. No one else is there; it is doughnut-break time. Anne wonders if Jason has deliberately sought her out, has perhaps noticed that she was not in the crowd around the coffee machine in the lounge. She wonders what he will say. It does not occur to her that he will do what he actually does, which is to come over to her, put his arm around her shoulders, and kiss her passionately, pressing her backward into the little telephone niche. After a minute, his hands unbutton her lab coat and begin to move over her sweater. Anne is, of course, alert for the sound of the door opening, but she is otherwise completely given over to his mouth and hands.

Finally they pull apart a little and he says, "After work?"

"Is there anywhere we could go? I mean, there'll still be people here. And I don't want to get home too late."

"If I find somewhere for us to go?"

"I'll be here till five o'clock," Anne says. "Stop by and tell me."

"Okay," he says. He leaves the room without kissing her again, and she wants to call him back. Quickly she buttons her lab coat, aware that her nipples are pointing visibly through the sweater, aware that if he doesn't find someplace for them to go after work, she will be desperately disappointed. Safe inside her coat, she joins the doughnut-break throng, which is already beginning to dissipate. There are no doughnuts left, but she gets a cup of very strong coffee from the bottom of the urn.

Anne's morning goes quickly. When Jason is in the room delivering things to Anne and her labmate, she does not even have to look at him to be perfectly aware of his every move. And now, finally she knows that the awareness is not only one-way. He is, after all, trying to find a place for them to go and make love after work. Anne is thrilled all morning by this, her secret. Although once, making neat notes in her hardbound lab notebook, she finds herself writing, "Just what is all this anyway?" This is the sort of comment she often makes in her lab book as a way of bringing herself up short when she feels she has been pursuing an unlikely lead, but this time she suspects it has nothing to do with the perfectly reasonable list of cell counts above it on the page.

She disciplines her wayward mind, she makes herself repeat and then write down from memory a complex genetic arrangement she was reading about the night before. An intricate sequence which has only just been worked out: what turns the gene on, what turns it off, how it regulates itself in the presence or absence of several other factors. It is so elegant it takes her breath away, when she finally has it diagrammed to her own satisfaction, another irrelevant scribble in her lab notebook. She stares down at the diagram, absorbing the logic, the perfect coherence of this submicroscopic system. And she is conscious of a sudden not completely unfamiliar wish that she were a post-doc somewhere, or a junior professor, someone who could seize on whatever problems she found most fascinating, without worrying about their market value, without reporting, however indirectly, to businessmen.

At lunch, Anne finds a perfectly normal Louisa, carefully made up, dressed in a wool dress and a corduroy blazer, her short blond hair held back with a plaid ribbon band. As they collect their soup and salad on bright red plastic trays and find a table, Louisa chatters about what a nice place it is and how lucky Anne is to be able to take blue cheese instead of diet Italian. And then, once they are seated, their trays covering almost the whole butcher-block surface of the table, Louisa's face collapses into misery and quickly into tears; the paper napkin is soon lightly marked with the flesh tones of her makeup.

"It's going to sound so silly," Lousia says, trying to keep her tone light.

"No, it isn't. Really, I'm sure it won't sound silly. What's wrong?"

Louisa's story, it turns out, is about Jim, the man she is currently in love with, the one she met about three weeks ago, after he had just transferred to New York from Chicago to work for her firm. The two of them have a lot in common, Louisa says. They are both from the Midwest, they both grew up on farms. Jim is new to New York, and Louisa has been showing him around, and they have both been enjoying themselves tremendously. Together, Louisa and Jim have been visiting museums, restaurants listed in guidebooks (the one at the top of the World Trade Center, for example), and also restaurants Louisa has discovered, whose virtue lies in not being listed in guidebooks. They have been to a Broadway show and an off-Broadway show and to a movie at a revival house. And they have been sleeping together several nights a week. And Jim has told her that he thinks he is falling in love with her.

And then, last night after Louisa left Anne's apartment, she went home to find an old flame sitting in the living room, talking to her roommate Cara. The old flame was a young professor of physics at NYU, and Louisa had met him at a party and they had

had a brief fling almost a year ago. She could not quite believe in him as a match for herself, because she thought he was a little bit weird and not totally presentable. Anne, recalling the physicists she has known, is inclined to believe that if Louisa had found one who was only a little bit weird and unpresentable, she had been doing pretty well.

Anne, who is accustomed to Louisa's intricate succession of relationships, is able to follow all this without difficulty. There are two main men in the story, Jim and the physicist. Louisa is now serious about Jim, as she was never serious about the physicist. And last night the physicist turned up. And Louisa slept with him, she confesses, her eyes filling again as she says it. Because, in the most melodramatic way possible, Jim came by later last night, unannounced, to find Louisa in bed with the physicist.

"You mean he actually walked in on you?" Anne asks, unable to believe it. Could such a bedroom farce scene happen in real life? Maybe to Louisa.

"No, not as bad as that," Louisa says, and then, irrepressibly, she giggles. "That would have been really something, wouldn't it? That would have been even worse." She thinks a minute. "That would have been the worst. No, he just came and rang the bell, and I was, you know, in bed, except we were all finished, and I was just getting up to get us some wine. So anyway, when I answered the intercom, he said, 'Hi, honey, it's me,' and I didn't know what to do, I couldn't think of anything, so I buzzed him in."

"What about the physicist?" Anne asks.

"I didn't know what to do," Louisa repeats. "I just left him there, you know, in my room. I kept thinking maybe I could go out with Jim for a while or something. He never did that before, just came over without calling. I guess he was thinking of us as being more, you know, closely involved." And suddenly she is crying again, and Anne is searching in her shoulder bag for tissues to supplement the napkins.

"Even so," Anne says firmly, hoping to stop Louisa's tears, "it was bad manners for him to come over without calling first. I mean, you might just not have been in the mood to see him."

Louisa's bewildered expression indicates what Anne already knows: When Louisa is in love with someone, she is never not in the mood to see him—except of course if she happens to be in bed with another man. "So then what happened?" Anne asks.

"Well, Jim smiled, he was so happy to see me, and we were sitting in the living room and talking and I knew he was expecting me to offer him a drink and then we would go into my room, and I looked at him, and I felt so bad because of what I had done to him. I mean, after just last week he said he was falling in love with me. I felt so guilty. I couldn't pretend, I couldn't just sit and wait for him to find out. So I just told him."

"What did you say?" Anne asks, curious about the details, wondering why she should be hearing this story today of all days.

"I started to tell him, but then I couldn't, so I just said, 'There's someone here,' and he looked at me and I could tell he understood. He said, 'You mean with you?' and then I started crying and he didn't say anything else for a while, and then he said he guessed he'd better go, and finally he said not to cry, but he said it angrily, and he said maybe he should have expected it, but he hadn't thought I was so liberated as all that."

Anne is, of course, a little bit amused by Jim's choice of words. She is sorry for Louisa, she is even identifying with Louisa, but still, Louisa *would* pick a man who used "liberated" as an insult in that peculiarly ridiculous way. Louisa is no longer crying. In fact, she is now consuming her clam chowder between sentences. Anne has finished her own minestrone and is eating her salad slowly.

"So did he leave then?" Anne asks.

"Yes, and he said, 'Good-bye, it's been nice knowing you,' and then I just said, 'Oh Jim, I'm so sorry,' and he said he guessed he hadn't been in New York long enough for this."

"Oh yes," Anne says sharply, afraid Louisa is going to cry again, "in Chicago no one ever cheats on anyone. They aren't liberated enough."

"And then he left. And I just sat in the living room and cried, and then Yuri, you know, the physicist, he came out and he'd heard it all."

"What did he say?"

"Well, he said he was very sorry, he hadn't meant to make any trouble for me, but I knew I could just not have gone to bed with him of course, so it wasn't his fault at all. And I could see he was very uncomfortable, so finally I told him he should just go home, I wanted to be by myself.

"So he left. And I woke Cara up and told her what happened. She made me drink a glass of whiskey, and she tried to tell me it would be okay, but I could tell she was shocked at me. You know, Cara is engaged to Mike, and they would never be unfaithful, she hasn't even thought about another man since she and Mike got involved. And she knew I was in love with Jim."

"Louisa," Anne interrupts, feeling a little impatient with the virtuous Cara, "why did you go to bed with the physicist?"

And now suddenly Louisa seems ashamed, and specifically ashamed to face Anne. She seems almost afraid to answer the question, afraid that now Anne will immediately condemn her. But she also feels bound to answer. She fumbles for a minute, wiping up bits of chowder with a piece of bread, then dropping the bread uneaten into her bowl. "To be honest, Anne," she says finally, "I feel really silly telling you this. I think it was because I was with you and Kent. I mean, sometimes it just seems to me that you two have everything. I mean, together the way you are. I just wanted to be with someone after I left you there together. I was going home thinking how much I wanted to be with Jim, but also just to be with *someone,* and then Yuri was there and I knew he wanted to. And also—I don't know if I ever told you this, but Yuri was just wonderful, you know . . ." She lowers her voice, looks even more self-conscious. "It's the worst thing I've ever done," she says.

"Oh, Louisa," Anne protests, "it was just a little bit dumb, that's all."

Louisa shakes her head. "It wasn't just dumb. It was what Jim said, I must have become some other kind of person if I can do a thing like that. I mean, I'm in love with Jim, I was in love with Jim and I did it anyway."

"Louisa, that happens," Anne says, aware that it is herself she is defending.

"I didn't think it happened to me. I don't think it happens if people are really in love with each other. I mean, if they're good people. I don't see myself as that kind of person. In a way, I think it's only fair that Jim found out. I don't deserve for Jim to love me."

Anne realizes that Louisa is dead serious. She feels uncomfortable in the presence of Louisa's self-reproach, and yet, strangely, she also feels jealous of Louisa for being able to take it so seriously; how can Louisa feel that she has committed a major betrayal when she and Jim have only known each other for three weeks while Anne, after all her years with Kent, takes her own infidelity so lightly? She almost wishes that she could feel with some of the depth that Louisa is now feeling.

"Louisa," she says again, "these things happen. Even to good people."

Again Louisa shakes her head, condemning herself.

"Louisa," Anne says suddenly, in a different, urgent tone, and Louisa looks up, "listen, Louisa, yesterday I did the same thing you did. I went to bed with someone. So you don't need to be jealous of me and Kent. I did the same thing."

Louisa is looking at her with genuine astonishment.

"When I got home yesterday and I said I was at that meeting? I was really with this man."

Louisa continues to stare, and then asks the most inappropriate question Anne can imagine: the question Louisa would naturally ask. "You're in love with someone else, not with Kent?"

"No, Louisa, that's the whole point." Anne is already a little horrified that she has told Louisa. She had been planning to tell no one at all. She also suspects her own motives; has she told Louisa really to comfort her, or just to establish her own superior sophistication on this particular issue? "I'm not in love with this man. I hardly know him. I'm just attracted to him. I just want to go to bed with him."

"You mean you're going to—again?" Louisa asks.

"Yes, in fact, probably today."

"And you don't—don't you feel funny about it? I mean, about Kent?"

"Yes," Anne says. With some relief, she knows that it is true. "I feel very funny about it. But I'm still going to do it." And then, when Louisa does not say anything, Anne says aggressively, "So you don't need to think of Kent and me as the ideal couple."

"But how can you do that to Kent?" Louisa asks, unable to stop herself. "How do you think he would feel if he knew?"

There is a silence. Anne wonders what she can say. A few minutes ago she was half jealous of the intensity of Louisa's feelings, and now she is almost grateful that Louisa is reacting this way; it gives Anne's behavior the seriousness that she seems unable to give it herself.

"I don't know. Pretty terrible, I guess."

"Why are you doing it then? Why are you going to do it again?"

"I don't know exactly. Maybe because I'm so attracted to this other man. Does there really have to be a simple reason?"

"Who is it, anyway?" Louisa asks, and Anne finds herself reluctant to name Jason, or describe him.

"Someone at work. And speaking of work, I have to be getting back," she adds, looking at her watch.

Louisa looks at her own watch and exclaims; she will be late unless she runs all the way back. Still, she remembers to ask Anne whether they should leave a tip even though they carried their own food to the table; in the end they each leave fifty cents for the people who clear the tables. Anne is ashamed of herself for baiting Louisa, ashamed because Louisa is genuinely thoughtful, unwilling to stiff waiters even when she is in a hurry. They leave the restaurant together and before they part on the sidewalk, Louisa gives Anne a quick kiss on the cheek.

"Thank you for coming," Louisa says. "I needed to talk."

Again Anne is faintly ashamed of herself. Louisa usually has this effect on her because Anne can never be quite natural with Louisa, can never keep from finding her comic, and yet, Louisa is sincere.

"We'll talk again soon," Anne says, and then Louisa is walking away quickly in her high-heeled shoes. Anne, whose shoes have very modest heels, and whose comings and goings are not so strictly monitored, stands for a minute in front of the large glass window of the restaurant, watching Louisa's retreating figure.

4. Assays

The project Anne is working on at Viatech is not very interesting from a theoretical point of view, but involves a great deal of practical cleverness. She is trying to work out a way to simplify a very complicated and expensive enzyme assay. There is this enzyme, this protein, which figures frequently in lab experiments, because it is produced in certain mutated cell lines, and Viatech would like to patent a process for measuring, that is, assaying the concentration of this enzyme in a sample of fluid. But it's complicated; they haven't been able to find a way to measure the enzyme directly, so they've ended up cloning a gene for another protein to which the enzyme binds—and then they measure the "bound" second molecule. The problem is that this binding process is not one hundred percent; for some reason no one understands, a certain amount of the enzyme won't bind to the special marker molecule.

Anne has been assigned this particular problem to work on, as has the other researcher in her lab. They should actually be working together, but he is a priggish and grasping man who believes firmly that he, working alone, will solve the problem, and he wants the credit. When the two of them had their first formal meeting to discuss the assignment, this man, Arthur Schenk, lectured Anne at some length about the foolishness of what he called "teamwork science." With that inauspicious beginning, they did in fact try working together—but Anne soon realized that Arthur was unwilling to discuss his ideas with her, and so without ever really talking about it, they are working more or less independently, and probably repeating each other's experiments and wasting lots of money—but it's a fairly minor project, and no one seems to have noticed yet.

Minor it may be, but Arthur obviously dreams of making his reputation with this project. He gets on Anne's nerves with his secretive ways, his assumption of superiority. The sight of him fussing around at his lab bench has come to irritate her. He is a fat man from Georgia, in his mid-thirites. Anne is actually relieved not to be working with him. She considers it quite likely that she can solve the problem working by herself, and she is cynical enough to leave none of her notes lying around the lab. Sometimes Arthur comes to her lab bench and hovers around, reminding Anne irresistibly of a blimp, asking if she has a bit of a particular chemical she could spare, his nervous little eyes sneaking glances at her setup.

Anne finds it hard to believe that this untouchable creature has a wife and two children in Westchester. She does not find it hard to believe that he could be a competent geneticist; he fits her image of the nonhuman scientist. She even feels a little sorry for Arthur Schenk. But she looks forward to leaving him in the dust with a brilliant solution to the assay.

Unfortunately, no brilliant solution has presented itself. Anne has merely been following all the most obvious pathways, trying to put the marker molecule DNA into different kinds of cells, looking for problems with the marker. She hasn't really been getting anywhere, and she is beginning to wonder whether the problem might not be intrinsic to the original enzyme, the target of the assay—maybe some of it just won't bind. It is during the second week of her affair with Jason that Anne experiences, one morning in the lab, one of those lightning moments of inspiration which are so important in the popular picture of how science works. Not that it would have seemed like such an impressive moment to anyone expecting the discovery of penicillin, or the cracking of the genetic code. But that morning, Anne is sitting on a stool, aimlessly drawing little diagrams of the assay, jigsaw-puzzle-like representations of one molecule locking onto another, when it hits her: There is actually a possible way to double and triple the assay, to add a second and even a third molecule which bind the enzyme, though somewhat less efficiently, to pick up little bits of enzyme that won't bind to the major marker. If you could pick up enough little bits, you could come really close to an accurate assay—and Anne sees a way, she thinks. She needs a whole array of new materials, she needs to set up a new and different group of processes.

If she is right, if her idea is good, the assay will pass from her back to the cloners, and she can be rid of this project, which is starting to bore her a little. What she will do is try a very rough version of it on her own. She opens a drawer and reaches for a pile of requisition slips, thinking with automatic resentment that this new supply-requisitioning system of Richie Grossman's is a pain in the ass.

Ever since Viatech was founded, up until two weeks ago, supply requisitioning for simple, nonregulated materials other than biological supplies has followed a straightforward pattern. You went down to the stockroom and asked them for what you wanted and they gave it to you and made a note on your page in the loose-leaf binder. But two weeks ago Richie Grossman announced that all supplies must be requisitioned on little forms made of carbonless carbon paper so that one copy can stay in the stockroom and the other be returned to the requisitioning researcher, who is supposed to file it away, but who in fact invariably throws it out. And instead of going down to the stockroom themselves, researchers are urged to give their completed forms to lab techs like Jason who can then bring them the supplies. This new system, Richie claims, will "expedite record keeping" and "relieve the traffic flow problem at the stockroom."

No one is happy with this system. First and foremost, many of the researchers need to see materials before they know what they want. Now everyone is supposed to fill out slips giving exact details of the materials needed, thumbing through catalogues to find precise sizes. "That turkey Richie Grossman," Anne's friend

Charlotte grumbles, "he thinks science is like a chemistry experiment in high school. First you think up your hypothesis. Then you make a list of all the materials you will need, and you write at the top of your list, 'Materials I Will Need.' And neatness counts."

So the researchers are not happy, and they take revenge by throwing away their copies of the requisition slips. Except of course for Arthur Schenk, who complains as loudly as anyone else about the new rules but surreptitiously saves his slips in an empty bottom drawer—not a file, just a casual, almost accidental pile in a drawer. Anne enjoys explaining this to Charlotte, and in fact a couple of times when a tech has come in and distributed materials and carbons of requisition slips, she has hung around Arthur's bench and made idle conversation while he sweated it out, unable to put away his new slips, afraid she would notice that he wasn't throwing them out, and also afraid that from his new materials Anne was deducing the path of his experiments.

But in fact, Anne is now herself a little nervous, as she contemplates her new idea. She is worried that Arthur will see the off-the-wall things she is ordering and will start wondering what she is up to, will perhaps catch on to her inspiration. Probably he doesn't have the imagination, but still, she would be happier if he had no idea what she was doing. Anne grins triumphantly to herself; she is, after all, a particular friend of the lab tech. She fills out her slips, tucks them carefully into her pocketbook, and spends the rest of that morning winding up a series of uninteresting experiments.

Toward noon Charlotte comes into Anne's lab.

"How about roast beef sandwiches at the luncheonette on Eighth Avenue?"

"I can't today," Anne says. "Tomorrow."

At twelve-thirty Anne puts on her jacket and takes her pocketbook and leaves the building. In the elevator she says hello to various Viatech people, all on their way to lunch, and refuses an invitation to join one little group. She walks west, toward the Hudson River.

Viatech has several floors in a building on the West Side of

Manhattan. These floors were formerly occupied by a company that made veterinary medicines, and so the basic laboratories were already there. The veterinary medicine company has moved to Connecticut, where it is doing very well. Many people think that it is crazy for Viatech to be located in Manhattan, where the rents are so high. But Richie Grossman says that all the disadvantages of New York City are counterbalanced by the advantages. Richie likes being in the middle of things. From seminars at the Rockefeller Institute and Columbia, Richie or his agents pick up ideas for new avenues of research. Richie makes contacts with hospital administrators at Mount Sinai and Sloan-Kettering, with academic researchers at NYU and Einstein. Definitely, in his own way, Richie Grossman is a genius, even if he thinks like a high school teacher when it comes to lab work.

Viatech is only a few blocks from the Hudson, and the building where Anne finally stops is literally on the river. It is a large and dingy warehouse. She goes in a small door and finds Jason waiting for her. Together they go up in the cavernous service elevator which smells of stale tobacco smoke. On the very top floor there is a door painted a bright shade of purple with a silver border. Jason produces his key and they go in.

A very close friend of Jason's is converting the top floor of this building into a nightclub. He and his backers have great hopes, Jason says, they talk about waterfront chic and gentrification and they spend every evening painting and fixing up the place. During the day there is no one there since all the people connected with the project are holding full-time jobs, hoping that this little nightclub will make them rich and independent, dreaming, Jason says, of cocaine and pictures in *People* magazine. And so Jason has the key.

The nightclub-to-be encompasses several rooms, but generally Anne and Jason stay in the largest, where a small dais has already been built for the musical groups. In this room there is a mattress on the floor, because, Jason says, his friend sometimes works very late and spends the night there. It is a narrow single mattress, and the first time Anne and Jason used it, it was completely bare. The second time Jason brought a fitted sheet printed with cartoon cats.

He and Anne go there at lunchtime or at five o'clock almost every day. And every time they come back to the room he puts the sheet on again. Anne has thought of buying a plain sheet or a sheet with a pretty print, but she has decided that the pattern of this whole affair, including the pattern of the sheets, is out of her hands, and she will just let it happen.

So this time when they come to the nightclub it is almost a routine: Jason gets the sheet and puts it on the mattress while Anne wanders around the room looking to see if any new renovations have been completed since yesterday. The walls are being painted with red enamel, but it seems to Anne that the painting is going very slowly; she cannot understand why they don't get the whole place done at once.

"Her ladyship's bed is ready," Jason calls, and Anne goes to join him on the mattress. They start out with a quick and energetic fuck, over in about ten minutes, and then they rest for a while, warming up for a more leisurely reengagement. Anne is continually impressed by how dependable Jason is about being able to repeat so quickly; true, he doesn't always come a second time if they only have their lunch hour, but he doesn't really seem to mind that. Anne is embarrassed to find that she cares about all the things she has always heard are unimportant: She likes it that Jason can get it up twice in a row, that he has a large penis.

As they rest in between quick-and-energetic and slow-and-leisurely, Anne asks Jason what the nightclub is going to be called. "Well," Jason says, "Sidney wants to call it Sidney's."

"Very catchy," Anne says. "Maybe even Chez Sidney, or else Studio Sidney."

"It may yet work," Jason says, and Anne is aware, as she has been before, that even though he makes fun of the nightclub, Jason wants it to succeed. Not just for his friend's sake either, she suspects, but also because the whole idea of a sudden jump from nowhere to fame and fortune appeals to him. Jason wants to believe that opportunities are all around and that someday he will simply walk into one. She strokes his thick hair and he begins to kiss her, not touching her with his hands, focusing everything on their two mouths until he is erect again and she is reaching for him.

And after that, as they are getting dressed a little hurriedly, Anne tells him that she has some requisition slips in her pocketbook and she wants him to get her the stuff but not bring it into the lab when anyone else is there. Could he bring it after five o'clock? Sure, Jason says, and teases her: She is only sleeping with him to get him to do her favors like that, she is a cold, calculating, ambitious woman. Anne wants to answer in kind: Yes, and I decided, coldly, calculatedly, and ambitiously, that sleeping with a lab tech was the logical way to advance my scientific career. But she doesn't say it; she is not really sure how he feels about his job, and about hers.

He does as she asks, bringing all her new supplies to her lab a little after five, after Arthur Schenk has gone home. Anne hides chemicals and equipment in a little cabinet to which she has the key, locks the cabinet, and allows Jason to pull her into the incubator room and press her against the wall for a few minutes, although she rather regrets this, since it makes her want to go right back to the nightclub with him and she has to get home. Tomorrow, they agree. After work, Anne adds, thinking of her lunch date with Charlotte. It's just amazing, Jason whispers, as they leave the incubator room, it doesn't wear off, it just gets worse.

"What gets worse?" Anne asks, dishonestly; she knows.

"You know what I mean."

And in fact it has gotten worse and worse, or better and better, from another point of view. Anne's mild obsession from afar has turned into a fierce obsession. She is almost unwilling to think about the way things are going; every day or almost every day she gets Jason on the mattress in Sidney's, and then she goes home to Kent and waits for the next day. She is behaving like a crazy person, she sometimes feels, or at any rate, like a bad person. She loves Kent, for whatever it's worth; she has never thought of the word *love* in connection with Jason. But that seems to have nothing to do with anything. She finds herself being kinder and kinder to Kent, but it is a distant, gutless, guilty kindness. Sometimes she looks at Kent and feels that with Jason she is escaping from a life which was going dead, and other times she finds herself fighting the attraction to Jason and feeling imprisoned by it.

Certainly, it is with almost insane excitement that she seizes on this new scientific idea, on the suspense of thinking it through, on the intrigue of keeping it from Arthur Schenk. It is a great relief to feel her mind sharpening, to sit across from Kent and think about enzymes and assays, lock-and-key formations clicking in her brain. It is wonderful to lie on the mattress with Jason, stroking his back after sex, and think happily about the afternoon's experiments ahead. She almost feels entitled to Jason; working so well all day in her lab, she deserves some physical release. She is on her toes, she is dancing, her mind sees all the steps ahead, she is sure and confident. This is real, this cleverness, this thinking, and Kent and Jason shrink together and merge into a different category, two versions of something which is at least temporarily much less real to her.

Arthur Schenk definitely becomes aware that something is up. Anne watches him watching her. She is busy over her bench, using reagents and solutions in containers labeled according to some code of her own. Her former line of experiments seems to have been discontinued. She is more scrupulously careful than ever not to leave her notebook lying around. Arthur is nervous, but he presumably tells himself that Anne has no chance of finding a scientific possibility that he, Arthur, has overlooked. Arthur is, after all, not to mince words, a fine old Southern sexist.

Charlotte also has no use for Arthur Schenk. Months ago, she told Anne he looked like an inflatable beach toy. A puffy stomach and a head full of hot air. She does not take kindly to sexist scientists; she is much harsher about them than Anne. This is partially because Charlotte is eight years older than Anne, which makes her in some ways a woman scientist from another era, a role model, a crusader. Charlotte did not have an easy time in graduate school. Before coming to Viatech, she taught for four years at a state university in the Midwest, and she did not have an easy time there either. She does not talk about it a great deal, but Anne has come across enough trouble herself from sexist scientists to be able to imagine what it must have been like eight years earlier.

Charlotte is understandably eager for Anne's brainstorm to work out into a solution to the problem of the assay. She actually goes over the idea with Anne, the two of them drawing molecules on napkins at the luncheonette on Eighth Avenue where the roast beef sandwiches are so good. After lunch they crumple up the napkins and carefully carry them to the garbage can. "Mata Hari," Anne mutters, and Charlotte says, "Well, you can't be too careful. That bag lady over there may be in the pay of Arthur Schenk."

In fact, over the next few weeks, Anne's idea seems to be working out. As far as she can tell, her assay is approaching a much higher level of accuracy than any of the three binder molecules could reach alone. As she hoped, enzymes which won't bind to one will bind to the others—or so it seems, from the very crude preliminary tests she can carry out with her makeshift setup.

She does not deceive herself about her own motives: She wants to be noticed and perhaps given an opportunity to take on something bigger and more important, she wants to move up in Viatech, and, of course, she wants to puncture Arthur Schenk, the blimp, and watch the air leak out of him. But there is also the very particular pleasure of feeling that each of her experiments has a definite meaning, that she is no longer casting about for leads to follow, or following unpromising leads for lack of anything better to do. She can already see the shape of her final report. The work she is doing now does not actually require great brilliance, but she is conscious all the time of the underlying cleverness of her idea, and that makes even the routine work very pleasant. She has known periods of work like this before, and she knows enough to realize that this one will not last forever. These interludes of logic and purpose occur only every so often, when a project is nearing completion, when she is actually tracking down an idea of her own instead of finding information that everyone knew would be there as soon as someone bothered to look for it.

"Poor old Arthur," Charlotte says triumphantly, as Anne sketches out her progress several weeks after her original brainstorm.

"Yes," Anne says, "it's going to work, isn't it?"

"It's going to put you on the map," Charlotte says. "Richie will have to give you something important." They are both thinking about the rumors that Richie Grossman is going to take on some mysterious and risky piece of work. No one seems to know what it is, or rather, a number of people claim to know what it is, but their theories are wildly different.

"I may be the one to develop the Richie Grossman anticancer miracle drug," Anne says. "I only hope that when he steps up onstage to get his Nobel Prize, he remembers to thank me."

"You're thinking of the Academy Awards." Charlotte is smiling, but her mind is somewhere else. "And you know what?" she says. "After you produce this perfectly brilliant piece of work, if you get half the recognition you deserve, if you get something really interesting to do, what do you want to bet that Arthur will be going around telling people you slept with someone to get it?"

"It's time you knew," Anne says, thinking it really is time Charlotte knew, but somehow not the right moment to tell her, "I've been having a passionate affair with Richie Grossman, and in a tender moment, he whispered this idea in my ear. You know Richie, he may not be much in the lab, but when it comes to ideas—"

"His mouth is quicker than his test-tube?" Charlotte suggests.

"Yes," Anne giggles, "but that isn't saying much. It's a pretty pathetic test-tube."

5. In Translation

Charlotte is secretive about her own life. When she does talk about it, she does not exactly discuss it. She recounts it in neatly polished anecdotes, each leading to a logical stopping place, each complete with moral. These anecdotes have been presented to Anne one by one as she and Charlotte have become friends, almost as though Charlotte is providing necessary background material. Not that Charlotte discusses only the facts and events of her own life; the odd thing is that her stories include all her own emotions, as dispassionately described as a case history. It took Anne some time to understand that this is, in fact, the result of prolonged psychoanalysis; Charlotte is accustomed to seeing her own emotions as bits of evidence which eventually lead to a conclusion. She is thus a professional when it comes to describing her own life.

Charlotte was born in London, right after the end of the Second World War. Her parents were Jews from Dresden. Her father taught chemistry in a London high school and carried out his own experiments in a small laboratory he set up in their apartment. Her mother helped her father in the laboratory and kept his records just as she had done in Germany. Charlotte's mother, despite all the years she spent as her husband's lab assistant, was not at all interested in chemistry. She was a dedicated reader of English nineteenth-century novels in German translation; after five or six years in England, she tried one in the original English and was very disappointed: She had imagined a language unbeliev-ably rich and evocative and the real thing didn't measure up. She went back to her German translations and the fabulous English prose she had imagined before she actually knew English. Still, she named her third daughter for Charlotte Brontë.

When she first told Anne all this, Charlotte said, "My mother is going to love it when she finds out that I have a friend called Anne."

"Why?" Anne asked.

"Charlotte Brontë had a sister called Anne, who was also a writer."

"I thought she had a sister named Emily."

"Yes, and there was also a less talented sister who wrote two novels and died of consumption at an early age."

"Thanks," Anne said.

When Charlotte was eleven, her family moved to America and settled in upstate New York where her father had a job teaching chemistry at the State University. The two older daughters went to that university, lived at home, and eventually married and set-tled nearby. Charlotte was different. She was an excellent student in high school, went away to college, studied chemistry, and mar-ried a graduate student in chemistry at Yale—in short, a man who was all her parents had wanted: Jewish, hardworking, a talented scientist. In fact, the marriage lasted only two years. Charlotte's husband was fanatically jealous of every moment of Charlotte's time. He resented the time she put in on her own research, and he said she was just doing it to compete with him. He was jealous of the other younger graduate students with whom she worked. They, of course, were all male, and he was always insinuating that she was attracted to one or another of them. And there were other reasons why Charlotte found it impossible to live with him. He preferred to live in what she considered complete filth and squalor, and he made fun of her if she tried to clean up. She was unable to survive in the mess he created. Charlotte presents the list of rea-sons for their incompatibility whenever she mentions him. These are the conclusions she has reached. These are her excuses for her failure.

In fact, she did fall in love with one of the other graduate students. She did not, however, betray her husband. This is another of Charlotte's set stories: the end of my marriage. Always the same details. Acting on rather obscure principle, she waited until the man with whom she had fallen in love had gone away for the summer before telling her husband that she wanted a divorce. He was agreeable, even pleasant about it; whatever he had been looking for in a wife, he had not found in Charlotte. He offered to leave her the apartment, but she insisted on moving out and she rented a single room which she kept fanatically neat and orderly. The other graduate student came back at the end of the summer and he and Charlotte began an affair. Her ex-husband finished his dissertation that year and left Yale to begin a very promising career. Charlotte stayed on and finished her own graduate work. The affair with the other graduate student petered out and was not, apparently, replaced by anything serious; it is the last affair Charlotte mentions when she tells the story of her life, and she mentions it perhaps to give her ex-husband his due, to admit that in the end his suspicions were not unfounded.

After she finished her dissertation, she got the job in the Midwest, the only woman in the chemistry department, which she stuck out for four years. To escape she came to Viatech, bought a small co-op apartment on the East Side and began going to an analyst twice a week. The little episodes that make up Charlotte's story lead to this conclusion: She is happier now, she says, than she has ever been before. The happiness includes the apartment, which is expensively furnished with antiques and Japanese prints and a very elaborate stereo system, as well as the job at Viatech, where she feels competent but not pressured. The happiness also includes the insights into herself acquired in analysis, a new and more peaceful relationship with her parents, a couple of solid friendships, but not, at least as far as Anne can tell, any lovers worth mentioning.

One Friday night she and Anne go out to celebrate the continued successful development of Anne's new line of research. The evening out is Anne's suggestion; she knows Charlotte is too tactful to issue such an invitation to Anne who is so nearly married.

"Honestly," Anne says, "you wouldn't believe how big a deal it is if I want to go off with a friend on Friday night. I mean, what do Kent and I usually do on Friday night? Maybe we go to a movie, usually we just sit at home."

"And instead here we are in a setting of wild excitement and shameless decadence," Charlotte says. They are in a Hunanese restaurant in Chinatown, drinking their tea and waiting for the soup.

"Yes, I know," Anne says, "that's what makes it so ridiculous. How can he think it's a betrayal for me to come down to China-town with you?" Actually, she is being completely unfair to Kent, who did not mind at all that she was going out with Charlotte for the evening. She is just saying these things to bring up the issue of men, and of betrayal.

"He just irritates me sometimes," Anne says. "And I feel guilty about him too."

"Why?" Charlotte asks. "Just because you get irritated at him sometimes?"

"No," Anne says, accepting the opening. "Because I've been sleeping with someone else. I've been being unfaithful to Kent."

At this dramatic moment the soup arrives. The waiter ladles it from the big bowl into their two small bowls. Anne is remembering her lunch with Louisa; now more confessions, more bowls of soup.

"I didn't know that," Charlotte says. She considers for a minute. "Is it someone I know?"

Now, suddenly, Anne is ashamed. "It's one of the lab techs," she says. "His name is Jason."

Charlotte considers. "The thin one, right, with the beautiful brown hair?"

"And the beautiful ass," Anne says and shrugs, knowing her grin is sheepish.

Charlotte grins back at her. "I don't think I ever noticed," she says. "I'll look more closely next time I see him."

They both eat their soup. Anne waits for Charlotte's next question, wondering what it will be. Do you love him? Is it serious?

Does Kent suspect? But Charlotte asks a much more intelligent question: Where do you and this lab tech *go?* So Anne begins to explain about the warehouse that is being converted into a nightclub.

"DISCO LOVE NEST FOR SEXY SCIENTIST," Charlotte says in *Daily News* headlines, and they both start laughing.

They finish the soup and the Hunan pork arrives, followed by the spicy eggplant. Perhaps because she is more comfortable now that she knows that Anne's relationship with Kent is not perfect and smooth, Charlotte has begun to talk about her ex-husband. She has just seen an article by him in a chemistry journal. He is continuing to do good work, continuing to be a promising younger (if no longer a promising young) chemist. He and Charlotte have not kept in touch. Anne has trouble understanding how after two years of marriage there could remain no friendship, no goodwill, not even curiosity. She tries to picture herself simply losing Kent. Not losing him in the sense of moving out, ending the relationship, but actually losing him, not knowing his address, his job, how he is looking, who he is sleeping with.

"Well, you know," Charlotte says, "my father thought my husband was the Nobel Prize chemist of tomorrow. For my father it was probably a way to fulfill his own ambitions vicariously, marrying me off to someone who would be an important scientist someday as my father never was."

Again Anne can hear the conclusions Charlotte has reached with her analyst, not so much in the statement itself as in the way it follows automatically at that point in the story.

And what Anne thinks is that she never ever wants to be psychoanalyzed. She doesn't want to know why she is a scientist. She prefers to believe that she does what she does because it is the single most fascinating thing in the world. Literally, the secret of life, she thinks emphatically, as if she were saying it to some bearded doctor who had other ideas.

"Don't your parents want to marry you off again?" Anne asks, hinting around at the question of Charlotte's sex life.

"No," Charlotte says. "They haven't really forgiven me for

screwing up the first marriage. It was such a golden opportunity and I wasted it. They take for granted now that I should live alone. It's sort of convenient for them with my sisters married, because I think they plan to come and live with me eventually, when they're very old."

Anne is shocked. Charlotte sounds resigned. And yet she has never claimed to be deeply devoted to her parents—how can she talk calmly about having them come to live with her?

"Could you stand that?" Anne asks.

"Oh, I guess I could stand it," Charlotte says. "If it was just my mother, I would even like it."

Anne is marveling at Charlotte's frankness, no doubt the result of all that analysis—the calm preference that her father should die before her mother. And yet apparently she would not consider it possible to tell her father that he was not welcome to move in. If my parents were alive, Anne thinks, I would not want them to move in with me, would I? But then immediately her treacherous mind proposes the bargain: If you could save their lives, would you have them live with you? This kind of equation tortured her for years; nowadays she almost never tests herself this way, but it is still somewhat raw, the memory of the years when it was also her response to any pleasure, any reward—to assure herself that she would gladly give it up to have her parents back.

A large family is being seated at the round table next to Anne and Charlotte. A fat mother, a thinner bald father, and four plump children. The parents are giving instructions: Each child may choose one dish. The father assigns: You choose a beef dish, you choose a pork dish, you choose a chicken dish, you choose a shrimp dish. Several children speak at once: But I don't want to choose the chicken dish, but what if I want to eat all of the one I choose, but why can't we have two shrimp dishes? The father announces in a voice loud enough to be heard all through the restaurant that if there is any more arguing they will all go home immediately. The children shut up and the parents look satisfied.

Anne is conscious of the privilege of being an adult. She thinks suddenly of the very occasional trips to Chinese restaurants she made with her parents when she was growing up, of the incredible treat of spareribs and sweet-and-sour pork. And she remembers herself about fifteen, the year of her parents' death, briefly and self-righteously vegetarian. She remembers sitting with her parents and some friends of theirs in a local Chinese restaurant, watching them divide the spareribs. Anne had refused them with tremendous disdain, but then waiting for the vegetable chow mein she had ordered, she found herself watching the others bite into the glistening barbecue-pink meat, furious with them, furious with herself. "I have to make a phone call," she had said abruptly, and had gone to the phone in the back of the restaurant, and half an hour later her seventeen-year-old boyfriend had come in his car, and she had abandoned the table, her parents, the remains of her chow mein, walking purposefully out of the restaurant, feeling avenged for the spareribs.

How many episodes like that are there, not forgotten exactly but rarely remembered? Anne wants to say to Charlotte, God, I don't ever want to be analyzed, how can you stand it?

But Charlotte is talking. "Oh well," she says softly, "I may have screwed up my marriage but at least I didn't go and have children." She is watching the family at the next table.

"Do you ever want any?" Anne asks, thinking about herself and Kent. They used to talk about having children one day but they rarely mention it anymore.

"No," Charlotte says, "I don't think I do. I'm getting to the point where if I did want one I'd have to think about doing it soon. But I don't really feel the need. Maybe it's because of my sisters, they did nothing but have children, one after another. And you know, they think they're happy, I shouldn't go around saying they have miserable lives." She thinks for a minute. "What it really is is that I can't think of anyone at all who has children and still has a life I'd like to have. I'm probably just too neat and too accustomed to having things my own way."

"I can't think of anyone either," Anne says, after pausing for a minute to try, "anyone who has children and a life I like. That's a good point."

At the next table, the egg rolls have arrived. Two of the children think they taste funny. The smallest child pushes her egg roll away from her and knocks over the bottle of soy sauce and it spills on the tablecloth. Her mother slaps her and confiscates the egg roll.

The atmosphere of the restaurant seems to Anne to have been completely poisoned by the bad will and sourness emanating from the family group. She and Charlotte finish their tea and pay their bill. They go uptown to a bar near Charlotte's apartment.

The bar is crowded and the drinks are strong. They eventually get a booth and are able to leave the Friday-night-hunting ambience around the bar itself. The atmosphere is thick with evaluating glances and overly casual conversations. Anne, a little bit drunk, confides in Charlotte that Jason has a big penis and that she likes that very much and is ashamed of herself for liking it. "Well," she explains, "not exactly ashamed of myself for liking it, just for caring. You know, I feel like I'm being some sort of exploiting sexist manipulator. I mean, men can't help how big they are, right?"

"Oh, for Christ's sake," Charlotte says, "why should you admit you like his ass but then be ashamed because you like his prick? He can't help the size and shape of either one, can he?"

This strikes Anne as very wise and yet somehow beside the point. She tries to think of exactly what the point is. "You know, all those articles and sex advice books, they always tell you that women don't care, that the man's skill and that sort of stuff matters more."

"Yes," says Charlotte, "and what about all those articles that tell women that no matter what they look like, if they just make the best of their good points and develop interesting personalities, men will be attracted? All the same brand of bullshit."

"That's just it," Anne says, relieved because she thinks she suddenly sees her own point. "I wouldn't like a man who only cared about what a woman looked like, you know, how big her breasts were or something like that. I want men to be like the men those articles are talking about, I want men to fall in love with personality and individuality. And here I am, I mean, with Jason—I feel like I'm not playing fair."

"Okay," Charlotte says, "so tell me what he's really like. The hair I've seen, the ass I'll take a look at on Monday, the prick I'll take on faith. Is there anything else to him?"

Anne considers. She tries to think of an appropriately light answer, but, in her drunken seriousness, she is suddenly feeling very guilty. She should not have told Charlotte about Jason. Now Louisa and Charlotte both know; it is somehow triply unfair to Kent that all these people should know she is cheating on him while he is completely ignorant of it. It seems to her terrifyingly likely that somehow it will get back to Kent. She feels guilty and trapped and confused.

"Oh," she says, in a bad imitation of an offhand tone, "Jason really isn't very interesting." Is he? Anne tries to think of a new subject for conversation, but can get no farther than her own lab. "He doesn't interest me half as much as Arthur Schenk." This is, after all, a favorite joke between Anne and Charlotte; she offers it as a substitution for more talk about Jason. Charlotte accepts it.

"Poor Anne, wasting away with love for Arthur, while he ignores her."

"He certainly isn't wasting away," Anne says.

"Wait till he finds out about your research," Charlotte gloats. "He'll waste away then, all right."

Anne is suddenly light-headed, laughing so hard she ends up coughing into her napkin.

"You are drunk, my girl," says Charlotte.

"Nonsense," says Anne, "it's just my consumption acting up again."

6. Boys

It is really time to talk a little bit more about Kent, this shadow figure whose supposed jealousies Anne manipulates so unfairly when she talks to Charlotte; this ex-linguist now banker; this man whose anatomical details have been implied by comparison to those of Jason; this man with whom Anne lives, with whom she is, at least theoretically, in love. It is time to talk about him directly, not through Anne's self-justifying descriptions, not through her suggestive remarks about Jason. And it is an appropriate time, because the weekend after Anne and Charlotte go for dinner, Anne and Kent make good on an old promise and spend two days upstate with some friends. They are Kent's friends, really, and they have a summer house on a lake which they insist is beautiful in the spring. As things turn out, it's a little cold that particular weekend. But first, about Kent.

Kent has always given the impression that he is extremely self-sufficient. He is self-sufficient emotionally, or at least so he seems, but more important to Anne has always been his self-sufficiency in matters of everyday life. There is nothing that Kent needs to do that he cannot do. It is not just that he is a competent cook, that he understands cars and electricity and ironing, but he can also paint or remove paint, sand floors or lay carpet, force African violets to flower, type eighty words a minute. In his reactions to the little problems of life, Kent is careful and deliberate. He considers for a moment before he tackles anything: What kind of paint is necessary? Which tools? Can this shirt be washed in hot water? And as a result, he rarely makes mistakes, he almost never ruins things, he doesn't have accidents. And Anne has always found this immensely attractive. She has tried to learn from him and especially to apply his patterns to her work: It seems to her that if Kent were a scientist he would be a perfect scientist. He would think things through before he started a project, he would figure out the best way to arrange his experiments, he would order the most useful equipment—he would never just plunge ahead and then find himself at the end with unusable data, unusable because the experiment was not carefully planned, because certain variables had not been controlled. Also, Anne, like many other scientists, has a profound respect for people who are "handy" in the lab, who can solve technical problems by rigging up a new piece of apparatus from a couple of pieces of glassware and some rubber tubing and a scrap or two of Plexiglas. Anne does not have this talent, and she is sure Kent would.

But Kent's hobby is not cars or cooking or gardening or carpentry. Those are all small challenges of living which he meets with calm competence. His hobby is hiking and camping, and this, of course, adds a romantic gloss to his more domestic self-sufficiencies. Kent likes to take a small tent and a pack and go off for three or four days, and supplement his freeze-dried packaged food with things he finds in the woods, and drink from streams, and if the weather is good leave the tent rolled up and lie outside so he can look at the stars before he goes to sleep. Kent has hiked and camped all over the U.S., in the Rockies, the Appalachians, the Sierras, the Green Mountains. Anne has gone with him on several short trips and enjoyed herself, but without ever losing self-consciousness; she worries over every move—Will the fire really light? Will she be able to sleep? Is there any more toilet paper? It seems to her that Kent, on the other hand, is more at ease and less self-conscious when he is camping than he is at any other time. His general competence fits so well into camping, where everything is a small challenge to be met. And perhaps this is what lets him enjoy the camping so wholeheartedly while she, Anne, is always just a little bit dutiful about it; she knows she should love being outdoors and waking up to birdsong and hot cocoa and another day on the trail, and she does like it, really she does, but always with a vague sense of duty. She would never go if she weren't going with Kent, and she knows that he would go, has gone many times, all on his own.

And what does he look like? He has straight dark blond hair and a dark blond beard; in graduate school they were both a little shaggy but now they are kept carefully trimmed. He trims them himself: another self-sufficiency. He is only a little taller than Anne, and solidly built, a thick chest, muscular arms and legs. With clothes on he is quite attractive; naked he sometimes looks a little bit beefy (perhaps unfair; maybe it is just muscle), though people who find beefiness attractive would find him good-looking. He does not move particularly gracefully, but his deliberateness prevents him from seeming awkward.

Languages were another sort of competence for Kent. It was always a strong satisfaction to him to be able to read a completely alien alphabet and also to know all the exceptions to every rule of grammar. He enjoyed the detail and also the reward of the whole, of an understanding which had to be constructed piece by piece but finally revealed pages of meaning. And now he is a banker. And perhaps he has been trapped by his own deliberateness. That is, since he is a banker, he must feel himself a competent banker who wants to be a competent banker. He needs to take pride not only in doing his job well but in shaping his life to fit the job. He takes pride in what he calls, perhaps revealingly, being an adult. As far as Anne can see, Kent's self-sufficiency has here turned into closed disapproval, disapproval of Anne and of all the ways in which she is not, by his standards, an adult.

How does Kent feel about science, about Anne's science, to use her own type of phrase (as in, "My love life is confused but my science is going well")? When they were both in graduate school it was tacitly agreed between them that he didn't understand the language of her work any more than she understood the various languages of his. Sure, she passed a French exam in graduate school (translating a scientific article with the aid of a dictionary, a technical dictionary, and all those cognate words), and sure, he took a biology course back in college (to fulfill a science requirement— dissecting frogs and growing bacteria colonies in petri dishes and watching color films about food chains), but neither pretended to any real knowledge of the other's subject. Sometimes people expressed surprise that the two of them could maintain a relationship when they were in such completely different fields, but in fact, if they wanted to talk about their work, the general obsessions of graduate school gave them plenty of material: Qualifying exams, publications, teaching assistantships, and so on were common ground in form if not in substance. Neither of them ever felt the need for a lover with whom it would be possible to talk shop late into the night; in fact, they watched with some amazement the many couplings within their respective departments.

It would be fair to say that Kent has a little of the typical attitude toward science of those who study the humanities: On the one hand, he feels superior because science and especially technology are so removed from any of the beauties he finds in life (perhaps it would be different if Anne studied nature or animals or plants). On the other hand, there is a sort of bewildered respect that Anne uses computers or radioactive materials or even very expensive microscopes, that she cuts open rats and mice. And Anne, in her turn, has perhaps a little of the typical mixture of feelings of the scientist for the nonscience scholar: a tiny contempt because there are no real *facts* to discover, because sometimes languages and literature seem an awfully ethereal thing to spend your time on. And then a much larger share of respect. Scientists generally take great trouble to make it clear to themselves and to others that they respect and admire the humanities; they are afraid of fitting an ugly cliché about scientists who have no feeling for anything but science. Nonscientists, on the other hand, are frequently much more willing to express a distaste for technology, for the study of science. Both groups in some unstated way seem to agree that the humanities are "higher." But of course Kent would never express any distaste for science.

See how Anne still thinks of him as a linguist. In fact, now he is doing something which Anne doesn't want to know about at all, something with no subject as far as she can see. He is like the business people at Viatech, who are essentially despised by the scientists. They have no real skills. They do nothing you can point to and say, There is cleverness, there is achievement, there is genuine worth. Anne's prejudices are rigid, enforced by the prejudices of all her colleagues.

Kent seems to be losing his identity as a linguist. And now Anne is sleeping with Jason who has no professional identity in particular. And now Anne's research is going well, though she has not told Kent how close she feels to a triumph on her project. And now they are planning this weekend trip.

These friends, the Saltzbergs, who have their summer house in upstate New York, are people Kent has known since he was in college. More specifically, they are a woman he was once romantically involved with and her husband who has also become a friend. The romantic involvement was short and unimportant, Kent says, and Anne believes him. The woman, Margie, comes from a very wealthy family in California, and the summer house was in fact a wedding present from her parents. Her husband, Alan, is not from a wealthy family and he does not make a great deal of money—he works as a legal-aid lawyer. Margie herself has no job; she used to teach at a private school in Manhattan, but she gave that up four years ago when their son, Curtis, was born. In fact, Margie Saltzberg was one of the people Anne thought of when she and Charlotte were talking about whether they knew any women with children whose lives were appealing. Margie's life seems completely without appeal to Anne: the job she used to have, the fact that she gave it up, even the apartment in the area of Brooklyn which is just undergoing gentrification. Anne doesn't dislike Margie, though she has never grown particularly fond of her. Under Margie's small blond cheerfulness, her superficially haphazard but actually well organized domesticity, Anne always senses something a little bit off, perhaps nothing as strong as actual mental imbalance, but at least a warp in perspective. Margie's points of emphasis are somehow unpredictable: What will she take seriously? What will she not permit? Her husband, Alan, seems to be a much more straightforward creature, a gentle, well-meaning man chasing endlessly after post–women's movement ideals of male perfection. He is embarrassed that his wife stopped working to have a child, he talks about "shared parenting," he cultivates his own sensitivity, he is very careful about his language, careful to use "he or she" instead of just "he," and "woman" instead of "girl." He is a Jewish boy from Long Island, Alan Saltzberg, with dark eyes and curly blond hair.

So as the five of them sit in Alan and Margie's car, driving upstate, the only two with dark hair are Anne and four-year-old Curtis. Curtis is sitting in the backseat next to Anne, and Kent is on her other side. Anne likes Curtis better than she does either of his parents.

"How's your work in the laboratory?" Alan asks Anne.

Before she can answer, Curtis pipes up with, "Atoms. Molecules."

"Where did you learn about those?" Anne says, trying to keep any patronizing amazement out of her voice.

"In school," Curtis says.

"That's terrific. I work with DNA—did you learn about that?"

"Anne, for heaven's sake," Margie interrupts from the front seat. "We're talking about *nursery* school here, do you realize that?"

Curtis says, "My teacher says we have genes."

Anne wants to hug him. "Yes," she says. "Exactly. You must go to some wonderful nursery school."

"And do you remember what genes do?" asks Alan.

"It's hard to explain," says Curtis, finally looking defeated.

"It certainly is," Anne says.

"Why don't you ask Anne to tell you what genes do," Alan contributes, gently pushing to make this into an educational experience.

"Okay," Curtis says. As far as Anne can tell, he is still genuinely interested. She wants to answer him in a way that will make things clear, expand his interest. She has no idea what to say. She feels confused and somewhat inadequate.

"Genes are the molecules which parents put into their children," she begins, and already feels hopelessly stupid, "the messengers—they carry a message which tells your body what to look like—for example," she says, falling back on the most obvious, "there are genes for things like what color your eyes should be, what color your hair should be. And they come from your parents, that's why people look a little bit like their parents, but of course everyone has genes from two parents, all mixed up together."

"Well, if you understand, Curtis, you can explain it to me," Margie puts in, meaning to be funny. But Curtis is concentrating. Finally he says, "Yeah. I have brown hair, but I forget. Mommy has blond hair and Daddy has blond hair . . ." He looks confused. "I forget," he says finally, in a low voice.

Anne wonders what to say. Two blond people cannot have a brown-haired child in theory, she could say, but your mother dyes her hair and that doesn't affect her genes. Anne can just imagine some poor overambitious teacher trying to explain dominant and recessive genes to a class of small children and coming up against the distinctly non-Mendelian effects of Clairol.

Margie changes the subject, suggesting what she refers to as a pit stop. They pull in at a gas station and Kent, Curtis, and Alan go off together to the men's room. Margie gets the key to the women's bathroom, but comes back after a minute saying it's too filthy to use and she'll wait. She and Anne stand and watch the cars going by on the road.

"Actually, Curtis is in a gifted children's group in his nursery school," Margie says abruptly. "That's probably where he heard all that stuff." Margie suddenly bends forward from the waist, bouncing up and down so her fingers touch the pavement by her toes on each bounce. The blond hair bobs rhythmically, one beat behind.

She talks calmly as she bounces. "I started going to the gym to get back into shape after Curtis was born. It's really good for you."

"Yes, you look like you're in really good shape," Anne says, feeling falsely polite—but why? Margie does look good.

"Well, you know, staying home all day it's easy to let yourself go. You have to be careful. I wonder what's taking the men so long?"

"Maybe that bathroom was dirty too. Maybe they've gone into the woods." Anne gestures at the scrubby grass behind the gas station.

Anne and Margie both seem tired by the effort of conversation. Margie starts doing stretches again, bending backward this time.

The males return and everyone stands around for a minute. Alan picks Curtis up and tosses him into the air a couple of times while Curtis shrieks and Margie mutters to Anne, "He'll get carsick." Then everyone gets back into the car and they set off.

Anne finds she is thinking of a car trip she took with her parents one summer when she was just hitting adolescence. Things were a little tense as they drove out to Minnesota to visit her cousins, Louisa's family. Anne sat in the back and sulked because her friends back home were going to the pool and she was stuck going to visit her stupid cousins. Her parents, up in the front seat, were fighting about something or other, as people do on long car trips to visit relatives. For a long time Anne could not think of her parents in a car, because of how they died. Now she thinks of them, stiff and silent in the front as she sat stiff and silent behind, and she wants to animate that sullen child, to make her reach forward and stroke her mother's shoulder, melt the anger in the car into conversation, with the three of them looking out their windows and talking cheerfully about the flat country going by. Instead she touches Kent's shoulder, and then allows herself to be drawn into Curtis's license plate game, competing to find the numbers in order, then the letters, as though helping him create a happier memory.

Curtis eventually begins to feel carsick, thus demonstrating to Anne that she has been being too hard on Margie in her thoughts. It seemed to Anne that Margie was deliberately crushing Curtis's fun, but in fact Margie was right. They stop the car at a McDonald's and buy Curtis a Coke, and soon he feels better. The license plate game continues, mostly Alan and Curtis now. Curtis interrupts it to ask if he can go swimming when they get there, and Margie, in a tone which makes it clear that they have already been through this, tells him that it will be too cold for swimming.

"Wading?" Curtis asks.

"We'll see. If it isn't too cold."

Anne hopes the weekend isn't going to be difficult; she has been looking forward to it as a chance to rebuild something between Kent and herself. She has pictured the two of them walking in the woods, making love in an unfamiliar bed.

Anne takes Kent's hand and smiles at him. One of the reasons she has looked forward to this weekend is that she knows Kent will appear to good advantage against a background of woods and lake. In his old jeans and his faded red plaid flannel shirt, almost too warm for the day, Kent looks familiar and pleasant.

For a moment Anne imagines Kent and herself driving a car that belongs to them—perhaps on their way to a summer house that belongs to them? Why not; if she is prepared to imagine a car, why not a summer house? Curtis wriggles beside her, and she adds an intelligent four-year-old child to the picture. Is this what Kent wants? Is this what he means by being adults? Is there anything so terrible about the picture she has conjured up? She imagines the neat and well-thought-out packing for the weekend which Kent has tucked away in the trunk of their car. The careful competence of his driving. And, never fear, he would play license plate games with his child for hours, and probably there would be in his manner none of the overeager attentive fatherhood which grates on her in Alan. For a few minutes it almost seems possible.

Curtis and Margie are having a rather prolonged argument about whether he can go for a walk first thing to find out whether his birds are back in the same place. His birds are robins who lived in a certain tree right near a particular field last summer. Margie is explaining that she will have too much to do right when they arrive, she will not be able to go for a walk with him, and no, he can't go alone. Kent offers to go with him to see if the birds are there.

And soon after that, Curtis recognizes the drive-in bank which marks the beginning of the town right near their summer house, proud of himself for remembering from last year, and soon after that they are there.

7. At Pooh Corner

While Kent and Curtis go to look for the birds, Anne sweeps and brushes away cobwebs, Alan carries in bags of groceries, Margie sets things up in the kitchen. Finally the three of them sit in the living room, drinking red California wine. The summer house has a living room with a fireplace, two bedrooms, and a sort of half-room which serves as a dining room opening off the kitchen. The house is comfortably furnished and smells vaguely but pleasantly of damp and mildew.

"So," Alan says, refilling his glass, "how are you really these days, Anne? We didn't get much of a chance to talk in the car."

Anne is aware that this is meant as an invitation to unfold her innermost secrets. "Oh," she says, "I'm fine." Alan and Margie wait. "Things are going pretty well for me."

"How's your job?" Alan asks.

"Oh, fine," Anne says. "Really fine. I'm doing okay."

"That was a terrific explanation of genes you gave Curtis," Alan says. "Do you ever think you might like to teach?"

"Not really," Anne says quickly, then, remembering that Margie was a teacher, "I really don't think I have the talent for it."

"Anyone can teach," Margie says.

"Well, you just say that because you *have* the talent, honey," Alan puts in, a little hastily. "It just seems easy to you. But don't you think Anne might make a good teacher?"

"Sure," Margie says, then directs a genuinely warm and

friendly smile at Anne, who finds herself smiling back, the two of them united in humoring Alan.

"And I think you'd find teaching very rewarding," Alan continues.

Anne decides to give him the courtesy of a straight response. "I'm afraid something happens to people who do science," she says, rejecting the word "scientist" as too technical for this context. "You get so used to the really basic stuff, you just come to take it for granted. It's really hard to remember back to what it was like not to know the elementary concepts and that makes it hard to explain to people who don't know them. At least for me."

"Well, it might be a really valuable experience for you to get back to those basics and think about them," Alan says.

"I don't see why," Margie says. "If she's got beyond them and she's doing important work, why should she go back and learn the alphabet?"

"I don't know if I'm doing important work, exactly," Anne says to fill in space, afraid that Alan is hurt.

"What's important is that you find it satisfying," Alan says.

"Well, I guess I do," Anne says. Then quickly, "And you, how's it going with you?"

"Oh, my job's pretty much the same as always," Alan says. "But just as you were saying, the main thing is that I find it satisfying."

"Yes, I can imagine," Anne says.

"And of course Margie and Curtis are just doing great, you can see that. You know, I think the thing about having a kid is, really, you learn more from him than he does from you."

"Yes, I'm sure," Anne says.

"Margie's thinking of going back to teaching in a year or so when Curtis starts first grade."

"We'll see," Margie says, directly to Anne. "I might also think about doing something else."

"Like what?" Anne asks, relieved to be talking to Margie, a person who can be asked straightforward questions free of sensitivity-group jargon.

"I'm not sure, I was thinking I might like to lead exercise classes, like the ones I take. But then I was thinking, I like working with kids, at least I like them better than overweight middle-aged ladies, so maybe I might become a gym teacher."

"I was always terrified of my gym teachers," Anne says.

"When I was teaching fourth grade, I used to get just as restless cooped up in the classroom all day as the kids did," Margie says.

"I think when you were doing it you enjoyed it a lot," Alan says. "I think you've just begun to feel this way sort of in retrospect. Being a gym teacher couldn't be as rewarding as really *teaching.*" It is clear from his voice that they have had this conversation before.

"Kent seems like he's doing well too," Margie says.

"Yes, I think he is," Anne says. "He's really happy to be here for the weekend. You know how he loves being out in the woods." Anne has a sudden lunatic urge to tell them about Jason, to break the forced and boring conversation with a confession. If she told them, she would have to tell Kent. Perhaps she and Kent could enjoy being cool about it together in front of the Saltzbergs. But of course that can't be done unless she tells him first. She doesn't tell Alan and Margie, of course. Instead, she looks at Margie. If Kent had married her, presumably he would now have the car and the child and so on, not to mention the summer house. And Margie would have Kent for a husband, not Alan. Of course Anne takes into consideration that Margie probably likes Alan's constant need to reexamine everything and turn it into a sort of domestic encounter session. Probably she would find Kent too isolated. If Margie shows some contempt for Alan, well, doesn't Anne herself show some for Kent on occasion? Perhaps every woman has that kind of contempt in her, and perhaps no man recognizes it.

"I hope Curtis finds his robins," Anne says.

"It's amazing, the things kids remember from one year to another," Alan says. "I mean they forget all sorts of important things and then they remember little details . . ."

"Well, so do grown-ups," says Margie.

As if on cue, through the open door comes Curtis's voice.

"Kent found them! In another tree. I thought they didn't come back. But Kent found them!" Curtis bursts out.

"They were just a little way off," Kent says.

"We heard them, he recognized their song," Curtis explains, awed.

Anne can see the adoring look in Curtis's eyes when he watches Kent. She thinks of Kent taking time and trouble to find Curtis's birds, and she is touched.

Margie announces that it is time to start making dinner. Everyone offers to help, but she tells Kent and Anne to go take a walk, so they do, leaving her husband and son to help her. Down by the lake it is beginning to feel cooler. Kent and Anne sit together on a tree trunk. The pale beach is splotched with dark detritus.

"I thought it would be all swept clean after winter," Anne says.

"There must have been storms this spring," Kent says. The lake is a dark gray-green. Anne traces the curve of the shore around to her right, loses it a little on the far side where it is complicated by islands, picks it up again, and follows it the rest of the way around. Occasional brown patches suggest people's private docks and beaches. There are other houses visible, all dark and closed and sleeping in the off-season sun.

"Lord," Anne says, "imagine having this just sitting here waiting for you, like a different life you can just step into whenever you want." She is thinking about the different views, different smells in the air.

"I don't know. It seems to me that one of the problems with owning a place like this is you come here and it isn't really a different life. I mean it's just a house, you know, a kitchen, a bathroom, a living room—"

"I guess," Anne says. He means, she knows, that it isn't a complete change the way camping is.

"That was wonderful, that you found Curtis's birds."

"Well, city kids. All they know about wild things is from books. It's really something when they see a bird behave as if it has rules to follow, you know, like coming back to the same place every year. Otherwise they don't believe there's any logic in nature, no organization, no rules." He sits silent for a minute, then grins. "Of course, it might have been a different robin family from last year. But no point in destroying a child's faith."

Anne smiles at him and he puts his arms around her. The air has become quite cool and his arms feel warm and strong, and she finds herself kissing him with an altogether unusual sense of pleasure, as if she is finally in the middle of some long-cherished fantasy and it is as wonderful as she had hoped it would be. And the pleasure is not just sexual either, it is more generally sensual. The smell of his hair, the taste of his mouth, the firmness of his fingers moving in her hair, all give Anne a profound thrill. In fact, she finds herself shivering slightly, and Kent pulls her closer. She is slipping off the tree trunk a tiny bit; she can feel that she is depending on his arms to hold her in place and this increases her sense of floating in the cool tree-scented air of the moment. There is a loud noise, a crow, and little noises of the water moving, and then there is Kent whispering in her ear that he loves her, and she is able to reply with complete sincerity that she loves him too. They are smiling at one another, pleased with what they both understand has been happening between them there on that tree trunk, when they hear a high-pitched voice calling Kent's name. Curtis stumbles around a rock farther along the shore, sees them, and relaxes with evident relief. Kent and Anne move apart and Curtis runs toward them with a somewhat weary step.

"Is dinner ready?" Kent asks cheerfully. "Is that what you've come to tell us?"

Curtis considers for a minute, as if he is not sure, then nods. "Dinner," he says.

"Well then, back we go," Kent says. "You want a ride?"

"Ride?"

"Piggyback," says Kent, and Curtis lights up, and Anne helps him wriggle up from standing on the tree trunk to clasping Kent around the shoulders with his arms and around the waist with his legs.

At the house it turns out that Curtis was not in fact sent to find Kent and Anne, that he wandered off by himself and that he has only just been missed. Alan is about to start off hunting for him and Margie is calling his name in the area around the house when he returns, triumphantly carried on Kent's back. Curtis is scolded, reminded that he is not supposed to go down to the lake alone, doesn't he remember that from last year?

"I wasn't alone!" he protests. "I was with Kent."

"We want to be able to trust you here," Alan says, "and we can't do that if you won't follow the rules." He kneels down, takes Curtis's hands, looks him in the eyes. "Do you know the rules?"

"Do not go down to the beach alone," Curtis mumbles.

"It's probably silly," Margie explains, "because he's much too sensible to go in the water alone, but until he can swim . . ."

"No, sure, of course," Anne and Kent say together.

Actually, dinner is ready—spaghetti, with butter sauce for Curtis, who is a picky eater, with tomato and mushroom sauce for the others. When complimented on the sauce, Margie insists that it came out of a jar.

"Oh, but honey, you did a lot of things to it. It doesn't taste like it came out of the jar at all," Alan puts in.

After dinner Anne and Kent do the dishes and Margie and Alan swing into a putting-Curtis-to-bed routine. Curtis is taken to the bathroom, his toothbrushing supervised, he is dressed in blue pajamas with feet, and then brought into the kitchen by his father.

"Kent, how would you feel about reading Curtis a story? He wants you to take my place for one night."

"Sure," Kent says. In the living room everyone listens to Kent reading aloud a chapter from *The House at Pooh Corner*. Curtis demands that Kent carry him to bed, piggyback. Curtis is sleeping on a cot in his parents' room so Anne and Kent can have the room he usually sleeps in. Kent carries Curtis away and Anne, Margie, and Alan sit more or less in silence; perhaps all of them feel they have already had enough three-way conversation.

Even when Kent comes back conversation is slow, and finally Margie brings out a Monopoly set, a fixture of the summer house, with its air of being somewhat decomposed; the paper is peeling away from the board in the corners, the title deed cards are bent and creased to the softness of much-used bookmarks, there are almost no playing pieces left and Anne uses a button, Alan a dime. Kent, of course, is made to be banker. Anne remembers Monopoly from her childhood as interminable, usually ending in a fight or loss of interest, rarely in a victory for one of the players. She is quite surprised by how quickly things move once the four of them start playing. In fact, after an hour or so, it is quite clear that Margie is about to win. Her hotels imperil passage along all four sides of the board, Alan is mortgaged up to his neck, and Kent and Anne each hold a few scattered properties with a house or two.

Margie does win, and the others tease Kent a little about losing when he really is a banker, and Alan and Margie decide to go to bed. Anne feels a tremendous sense of relief that at least one evening is gone, and without any trouble. But what trouble is she afraid of? Is something wrong between Alan and Margie? Is it something between herself and Kent? She thinks of the lovely moments down on the tree trunk near the lake and hopes that she was not deceiving both Kent and herself by allowing those lovely moments.

In fact, when they are in bed things do not go well. The bed itself is not comfortable; it is a single mattress on which Curtis usually sleeps; it can be opened out into a double mattress, but when it is opened out it is quite thin and all the ridges and coils of the frame can be felt. Kent will sleep well anyway, Anne knows; Kent can sleep in a sleeping bag stretched out on the rocky ground. Anne is a pretty sound sleeper herself, but the bed irritates her, and particularly when Kent rolls on top of her and begins to make love to her; she has an especially sharp ridge sticking her in the back. She does not tell Kent or try to move. She is not going to enjoy the sex, but will set herself to fake it for Kent's sake, a generous martyrdom. And so she does, moaning just loud enough so he will think she is trying to keep her voice down because of the people in the next room, just loud enough so he can be titillated by the possibility that the people in the next room can hear anyway. And for a little while after his orgasm, she feels free of her guilt and resolutely tries to stay free of contempt, though, of course, successfully faking sexual pleasure, when all you are really feeling is back pain, does conduce to contempt. Perhaps all martyrdom conduces to contempt.

In the middle of the night Anne is awakened by the cold. It is a slow awakening, she was dreaming that something was wrong with her feet, she was dreaming that she was shaking, and then she is awake and aware that her feet, down in the bottom of the bed, are so cold that they hurt, that she is in fact shivering all over. She curls up into the fetal position. She pulls her head under the blanket. She thinks about getting out of bed to search for her socks, to find a sweatshirt, but stepping forth into the room seems as impossible as diving into ice water.

"Kent," she whispers, shaking his shoulder, from which comes a mild and ineffective warmth, "Kent, aren't you cold?" He wakes up immediately, awake and alert, and considers. "I'm freezing," he says, "I'm absolutely freezing."

Kent the brave, the man who by choice sleeps in the open and bathes in icy streams, finally summons the nerve to leap out of the bed and forage for socks and warm shirts. They keep putting on clothes, and when they finally try to sleep again, they are wearing almost everything they brought for the weekend.

"I wonder if the others are okay," Anne says, as they huddle fully clothed under their blanket.

"They probably have all the extra blankets, selfish pigs," Kent says, and suddenly Anne is liking him, loving him, once more. He falls asleep and she lies awake, trying to think systematically about Jason, about herself and Jason, about herself and Kent. Sometimes it is clear to her that the thing with Jason is a very small thing and that Kent will of course understand that. She can wait until she and Jason are through with each other, which will surely not take long, and then she can tell Kent about it and he will shrug and say, Oh well, as long as I'm the one you love, and that will be that. Two flaws in this theory (the scientist always keeps an eye out for flaws in too-convenient theories): Number one, if it could happen with Jason, why couldn't it happen with someone else, and if she tells Kent about it, will that be tantamount to a promise never to do it again? And number two, the second flaw in this theory, is that it is patently insane; Kent will never ever, not in a million billion years, take it that casually. The best she can hope for, realistically, is that he will be angry for a while and then calm down and eventually they will leave the whole thing behind them. And then some of the time it seems to her that once she tells Kent, that will be the end of everything for the two of them. He will never forgive her, he will never feel the same about her again, she will have sacrificed the most important relationship she has ever had, and for what? For Jason? For honesty?

That, of course, is the problem. There is no real reason for her to tell Kent about her affair with Jason. Traditionally, those who commit adultery may feel guilty about their sins, but they don't feel they ought to come out and admit them to the injured parties, do they? In fact, surely the classic adulterer is trying desperately to conceal the infidelity. So here she is in an enviable position; Kent apparently suspects nothing.

But no question: She almost feels guiltier about not telling Kent than she does about sleeping with Jason in the first place. Is this just sensitivity-group silliness, Alan's ideals of honesty in relationships, telling people things they would perhaps rather not know?

Of course, there is an interpretation of the impulse which would credit Anne with much less lofty motives: Does she want to tell Kent because she wants to hurt him, maybe even because she wants to end the relationship? And so she lies awake in the uncomfortable bed, feeling oddly bulky because she is wearing ordinary clothes and yet is in bed; between her and the sheets are a turtleneck, two flannel shirts, and a sweater, not just a nightgown. She lies awake and agonizes and finally she falls asleep.

8. Sweat and Cookies

In the morning it is still very, very cold and the sky is gray. Alan and Margie are apologetic at breakfast, ostensibly because Kent and Anne didn't know to look for spare blankets in the bottom drawer of the dresser in their bedroom, actually because they feel responsible for the weekend, the weather. Curtis corrals Kent into playing with his Lego bricks and Alan goes off to join them, perhaps a little jealous of how Kent is sharing the parenting, as Alan would surely call it. Margie and Anne sit over second cups of coffee at the table. As Margie talks about her exercise classes, Anne again has the impression that something is off.

"Do you like the way your own sweat smells?" Margie asks.

"I guess so—I mean, while I'm moving I do. I don't like to go on smelling of it for hours."

Margie nods. "I like the smell of my own, but I hate the smell of other people's."

This time Anne nods, unable to think of a response.

Far from sweating, Anne is near shivering though she is wearing two sweaters and three pairs of socks. She and Margie go and sit on the couch with blankets wrapped around them. It is much warmer sitting like this, though Anne begins to feel that moving from under the blanket would be as impossible as getting out of bed seemed the night before. Through the window she can see the day getting darker and grayer, and she wonders aloud if snow is a possibility. Margie tells her it isn't cold enough for that, and in fact, Anne can see that though the others are wearing extra sweaters none of them is as cold as she. In addition, she is beginning to cough a little, and she comes to the conclusion that her sense of freezing and her general lassitude must mean that she is coming down with something, at least a cold, maybe something worse.

The three males are building red and white structures in front of the fireplace. Curtis is mostly interested in watching what the others build, and Kent and Alan are competing for his approval.

Speaking very softly, so the males won't hear, Margie says, "It's really amazing how when you have one child and four adults, everything centers around the child, you can't forget for a minute that it's there."

"Yes, I suppose," Anne says. "Does that bother you?"

Margie shrugs. "It's *my* child, I would think it would bother you more. Being invited for a weekend of baby-sitting."

"Oh, come on. I like Curtis."

Anne starts coughing again and Margie goes off to make her some tea. Alan abandons his son to Kent and comes to sit beside Anne and tell her that she and Kent really should have children of their own, look how good Kent is with children.

"Maybe someday," Anne says.

"It's just so amazingly rewarding."

"Yes, it must be."

"Let me ask you something, Anne. Are you worried about your career, is that why you worry about having kids?"

"Well, I guess that's part of it." Anne tries to think of language that will be acceptable to Alan. "I mean, that's only one aspect, I also worry about how big it is as a commitment and a responsibility." With Alan, one must talk fuzzy.

Sure enough, she has hit the mark. "I can certainly understand that, Anne, I know exactly what you mean. But in the end, that's part of what makes it so rewarding. Nothing can really be rewarding if you haven't made a commitment to it."

Is Alan some moronic messenger of God, sent to lecture her about Jason, Anne wonders suddenly, smiling to herself. But Jason is definitely rewarding—or is great sex perhaps not what Alan means when he says rewarding?

Anne nods.

"I mean, I know your work is important to you, Anne."

"Well, I just find it so rewarding." Surely Alan can tell when he is being teased.

"Yes, I can tell that you do."

Anne is impressed. Are there no limits? Margie appears with tea and lemon, and Anne drinks gratefully, and then, at Alan's insistent prodding, talks to him a little about her work. On balance, she would rather talk about genetics than about having a baby, but it seems to her that both subjects are reduced to such a simple level by Alan that neither is very interesting. He outlines for her the ways he has read that recombinant DNA will save lives, prevent birth defects, he encourages her to claim credit for each philanthropic possiblity.

"Someday maybe," she says finally, "someday we'll have the technology for all that, I guess. But we're a long way away."

"Oh, technology," Alan says deprecatingly. "You already have the main idea, the main discovery, right, and that's the important thing, not the technology."

"No really, that's backward," Anne says, getting unfairly irritated. Unfairly because why on earth should he be sophisticated about these things? "The point about recombinant DNA, the discovery, if you want to call it that, the main idea, is all technology. The whole theory is in the technology." Her voice is perhaps too loud and emphatic; Kent and Curtis are looking at her and Alan seems a little uncomfortable.

The cold day moves slowly. After lunch, it begins to rain. Curtis draws pictures with crayons, lying on the floor in front of the fireplace. The grown-ups decide against another game of Monopoly and end by drinking more red California wine and admiring each completed picture Curtis makes. Anne is bored, but it is not a terribly unpleasant boredom. Once again wrapped in a blanket and feeling a little bit sick, she drinks her wine and feels tranquil. Around four o'clock in the afternoon Kent announces that the rain has stopped and that he is going to go for a walk. Curtis is by this time taking a nap in the bedroom and the other three adults are a tiny bit drunk. Kent puts on his jacket and goes out, and Anne huddles closer under her blanket and feels herself on the verge of sleep.

Alan decides that it would be a good idea to go out to the woodshed and bring in enough logs for the evening. Margie puts on her shoes and jacket to go help him and suddenly Anne is eager to be out in the air too, if only for a minute or two. The three of them carry in quite a bit of wood, and then go out behind the woodshed, where the trees begin, and stand there breathing in the cold air.

They go back inside and begin to make dinner. Margie arranges pieces of chicken in a pan and pours barbecue sauce over them while Anne and Alan make a salad. It occurs to Margie that she should go wake up Curtis; if he naps much longer, he will have trouble falling asleep for the night. A minute later she is back, looking frightened. Curtis is not in his bed, is apparently not in the house. For a few minutes the three of them search the house again: He must be there. But Margie discovers that his shoes are gone, and also his jacket, and the next minute Anne and Alan and Margie are all outside calling Curtis's name. How long has he been gone? Since they went out to get the wood? Did he wake up and find the house empty? Did he go out only a few minutes ago while they were all in the kitchen, did he put on his shoes and his jacket and perhaps go out to play a joke on them? "Curtis! Curtis!"

Before they have quite pulled themselves together to cope with the fact that he has not answered, Kent comes out of the woods behind the house, looking confused.

"I heard you calling," he says. "What's up?"

Anne explains, as quickly as she can, and then suddenly Margie breaks in.

"This is your fault," she screams at Kent, "he went out to find you! The big hero woodsman, I suppose you think it's good for a little kid to be wandering around alone in the woods when it's getting dark! You had to go off alone . . ."

Alan, looking a little horrified, puts his arms around Margie and turns her face into his shoulder. "She's just upset," he says.

Anne, and perhaps everyone else, is suddenly sure that that is what happened, exactly what Margie said.

Kent is organizing the search; within ten minutes all four of them are moving off in different directions. Anne is following the curve of the lake shore around to the right; there is a trail along the lake which Alan thinks Curtis might remember from last year. He himself is following the lake around in the other direction while Kent and Margie pursue trails back behind the house, away from the lake. Margie did recover from her moment of fury and apologized to Kent, who assured her that he understood, but the force of Margie's words is still in Anne's mind; she wants to find Curtis partially for Kent's sake. She is wearing a poncho which Alan found for her in a closet; it is made of bright orange plastic and catches on bushes as she moves, so since it is not raining just now, she finally takes it off and carries it rolled up under her arm. In one pocket of her jacket is a cellophane-wrapped package of Oreo cookies and a small box of raisins, and in the other is a little plastic flashlight. Every few steps she calls Curtis's name, and between the shouting and the speed with which she is moving along the trail, she is soon panting for breath. She is hot and sweaty, and thinks briefly of the conversation she had with Margie about sweat earlier that day. Suddenly she imagines what she knows Margie and Alan must be imagining: Curtis drowned in the lake, the little blue parka floating helplessly in the cold gray water. Curtis eaten by a bear—are there bears around here? Wolves? Surely not.

"Curtis! Curtis!" she shouts across her own panting, and is overcome by coughing. She has to stop for a minute and almost immediately her sweat begins to feel cold on her skin, she is shivering, perhaps feverish. So she goes on again and finds that to be warm she has to keep moving fast enough to feel overheated. "Curtis! Curtis!" The trail has veered away from the lake and is circling behind one of the dark closed-up houses. Could Curtis possibly have walked this far? Should she turn around and go back, see if one of the others has found him, try a different trail? But she goes on, afraid that he is somewhere just ahead. "Curtis! Curtis!" She does not really see any of what she is passing, the newly green trees bowed down with water from the afternoon's rain, the desolate beach of the empty house. And it is getting darker. Could Curtis have walked this far?

She doesn't even know exactly how she expects to find him: Will she see his blue parka? Will he come running out on the path in answer to her call? Or will she stumble suddenly and look down . . . ridiculous. He is only lost, he is not unconscious or eaten. She goes on, almost running to keep warm, stopping to pant and shiver. She must not think about animals, she is scaring herself for nothing, and not only on Curtis's behalf either. After all, she is out here alone and it is getting dark and she is no hero woodsman. That was what Margie called Kent. Kent is out there somewhere searching for Curtis, and that comforts Anne a little—surely Kent will find him? Or else Margie will; Anne doesn't really believe in her own efforts or in Alan's. She can't even move quickly along the trail without gasping for breath and coughing, she is half frightened to be out here alone.

And in fact, when she first hears the cries, her response is fear. It sounds like some animal, high-pitched, wailing. Then she realizes it is a child's voice, repeating over and over her own call: "Curtis! Curtis!" And in fact it is Curtis; she rounds a corner of the trail into a small clearing and there he is. It is actually a shock to come upon him, blue parka and all, sitting on a rock and howling his own name into the gloom. And his first reaction to her, as she comes bursting out of the woods, is fear, his cries turn into a scream and he pulls back. Then he recognizes her, runs to her, clasps her around the waist, and begins to cry in earnest, with a force which shakes both his body and her own.

For a minute Anne is panting too hard to say anything.

"It's okay, Curtis," she says, when she can talk. "It's okay. I'm here, Curtis, I'm here now and you're okay. We can go home."

He doesn't seem to hear her; his crying gets louder instead of softer. It begins to verge on real hysteria, he is shrieking and pounding his head against her. She half carries, half drags him to the rock where he was sitting and she sits down herself and manages to pull him into her lap, thinking that she will hold him and calm him for a minute before they start out for home. She hugs him as tightly as she can and rocks him and finally he grows quieter. "I'm here, it's okay, everything's okay now," she keeps repeating. She pulls out the package of cookies, takes one out and holds it to his mouth. While he is eating it she locates a tissue and wipes his nose, thinking that this must be something Margie does all the time, a classic maternal gesture. Curtis responds to it as to something familiar; he becomes a little calmer and she gives him another cookie. With one hand he still clutches Anne around the neck, but with the other he accepts one cookie after another, and then he eats all the raisins, which Anne takes out of the little box and pops into his mouth one by one, first zooming each one around like an airplane. Curtis is almost smiling. Anne silently blesses Kent for thinking of the food.

When everything is eaten, Anne hugs Curtis close and says, "Well, ready to start for home? Your parents are sort of worried about you." She starts to get to her feet, but Curtis screams and she drops back down again. "What's wrong, honey?" Anne asks, using the term Alan and Margie use, for Curtis, for each other. "Don't you want to go home? It isn't really such a long walk. We'll be there soon. If you like, I'll carry you for a way."

"No," Curtis says, close to tears again. "I can't."

"What can't you do? Go home?" She tries to keep her tone light.

"I can't go back in there!" He points to the woods around the clearing.

"Oh, Curtis, but I'm here with you. We'll go together all the way."

"I can't," he say firmly.

"We just have to go a little way. It's only trees, you know. They won't hurt you." Is this what she should be saying?

"But it's raining," Curtis says. It has, in fact, begun to drizzle very lightly. "You can't go in the forest when it's raining."

"Why not?"

" 'Cause a tree could get struck by lightning and kill you. You can't ever go into the forest when it's raining."

"But, Curtis, this is just a tiny little rain. There isn't any thunder and lightning. And if we stay here, we'll get all wet, don't you want to go home and see your mommy and daddy and put on dry clothes?" Her own clothes are wet with sweat; she is holding Curtis tight to keep herself from shivering with cold.

"We have to stay here," he tells her, calmly, but with the force behind it which suggests hysteria. "We just have to wait right here, that's all."

"But it's almost dark," Anne says, hoping to scare him into going home.

"You can't go into the forest when it's dark," Curtis says, his voice rising.

Okay, Anne decides, better sit for a while, let him get a little colder. She thinks guiltily of his frantic parents, wonders if she should simply pick him up and carry him off—but she isn't at all sure she can carry him the whole way home, especially if he struggles. She arranges the plastic poncho over their heads so there is some shelter from the light rain, and Curtis, rightly accepting this as proof that the question of moving has been shelved, snuggles up to her.

Anne feels very sick; she is cold through and through and she is also sweating, her arms ache from propping the poncho in place and her knees ache from Curtis's weight. She has an inexcusable wish simply to get up and walk away into the forest; surely he will have to follow? But she cannot abandon this four-year-old child who has been so thoroughly terrified, can she? And anyway, if he didn't follow she would have to come back to him and then it would probably be twice as hard to get him to move. She starts to cough.

"Are you sick?" Curtis asks.

"Yes, I feel really sick. That's why I'd really like to go back to the house. It isn't good for me to be out here, I'm cold, and you might get sick, too. Please, Curtis, aren't you ready to go back to the house?"

"No," he says, but without that firm undertone of unreason.

"Please, Curtis, aren't you cold?"

"Yes."

"Well, there's a nice warm fire at home. And other things too. Can't we go back there?"

"No, we can't go in the forest."

"But I'll carry you. Piggyback."

"Piggyback?"

Anne doesn't press him for a verbal agreement. Instead she stands, hoists him up onto the rock they have been sitting on, trying to keep the poncho wrapped around him, and offers her back. After a minute, she feels his arms around her neck and she reaches back and helps his legs around her waist. Without further discussion she sets out for the trail on which she came. Curtis is immediately heavier than she had expected him to be; she is sure she will not be able to carry him the whole way. Perhaps he seems so heavy because she doesn't feel well. But the important thing is to get started. As she enters the trees, she hears a noise of uncertain protest from Curtis, but she pulls gently at his hands to keep them from holding her too tightly around the neck and keeps going. It is hard to walk with the extra burden; the moss and the leaf mold are slippery, and she knows she is allowing her forward momentum to carry her, which is probably dangerous; she will run into something or trip. She pauses to take out the flashlight; it is not really completely dark, but she cannot quite see where she is stepping. The wavering beam on the path is only a partial help, but it is comforting. And at least Curtis is not protesting.

Inside her own head Anne is chanting to herself, counting steps, telling herself to keep going and she'll get there, hoping there is no ambiguity about the trail. It seems to her that she is going back much more slowly than she came, and how long did it take her to come?

"Stop, stop, stop!" Curtis is screaming, drumming at her with his heels, and she does not know how long he has been screaming, she was concentrating so hard on one step after another. She comes to a stop.

"What is it?"

"I have to go to the bathroom," he says through tears.

And so she lets him down and helps him pee. Anne is fairly inept about helping him, naturally, and is wildly relieved that he only has to do what in her childhood was called number one. She helps him tuck his little penis away and zip up the little fly, but then when she tries to get going again he is unwilling to climb on her back.

"I'm tired. I don't want to ride anymore. And I'm cold."

"Me too, Curtis, but if we keep on going we'll be home soon, really we will."

"No!" he screams, and begins to cry, and Anne wants to hit him and slap him and shake him. She is shocked by the violence of her own reaction to his immovable irrationality. Again she is tempted to walk away and leave him to follow. The world has shrunk down to cold and sweaty wetness and a feverish feeling in her head, to dark wet trees and coughing, and she has trouble believing that not so very far away there is a little house with food and light in it, that there are other adults somewhere in these woods.

"Hello!" she screams, as loud as she can. "Is anybody there?" There is no answer, and suddenly, overcome with fury at Curtis's sniffles, she grabs him up in her arms and crashes forward along the trail. She cannot hold the flashlight in position, carrying him like this, and he is struggling. After a few steps she comes to a halt; he is wriggling and screaming and hitting at her with his hands and his feet, and in fact she cannot carry him. With a sort of vague detached surprise she realizes that the will of a four-year-old child is not completely subject to control by an adult. In the back of her mind she has been assuming all along that if she was ready to force him he could be forced, that a child that size is in the end in control only because adults allow him to be. But there it is: She cannot carry Curtis if he doesn't want to be carried.

She grabs him by the shoulders and shakes him a little.

"Curtis, we have to go home. We have to keep moving. You can walk or you can ride on my back, but we have to go home."

"I can't," he says, almost begging, and her anger is mixed with a certain sympathy. She isn't sure she could keep going either if she didn't have to play the adult for Curtis.

"Curtis, you're doing so well, you're being so brave. Just a little farther to go and we'll be there. Please come on, get on my back again."

And she manages to get him up there, though he doesn't feel very secure to her; either he isn't high enough or he isn't holding tight enough, but she keeps moving. He is crying now but at least he isn't fighting her, they are moving.

And then she hears voices, "Curtis! Curtis! Anne!" some distance ahead.

She stops because she cannot move and shout loud enough at the same time. "Here!" she screams. "Hello! We're here!" Curtis has slid off her back and is standing clutching her around the waist. "It's okay," she tells him, hugging him, "they're coming. We'll be just fine now, you'll see."

It seems to Anne that it takes a very long time for the others to reach them. For a few minutes she isn't even sure the voices are getting louder and she is worried that they are on the wrong trail. She shouts and shouts and finally she is sure they are coming closer. And she hugs Curtis, who has retreated into complete silence. She feels fondly toward him now, she feels they are almost companions. And now there are noises of bodies moving along the trail and shapes coming dimly into view, and then Alan and Kent are running toward them and all three adults are talking at once. Curtis is in his father's arms and Anne is in Kent's. Curtis is not crying, and neither is Anne, and neither is Alan, though there is some feeling that everyone is on the verge. They set off along the trail, Alan carrying Curtis who clings to him, eating Oreos from the store Alan was carrying. Kent and Anne follow, Kent shining a flashlight ahead to light Alan's way, trying to keep his arm around Anne. But it is very hard to walk two abreast on the trail, and in the end she walks a little behind him, holding his hand. They are not moving very fast, it seems to Anne, but in fact they are back at the house fairly soon. She and Curtis must have covered more ground together than she realized.

Margie comes running out to grab Curtis, and finally someone is crying, two people in fact, because Curtis cries too. Margie hurries him into the house, warm dry clothes, comfort, while Kent does the same for Anne. He rubs her with a towel, rough and almost unbearable warmth, he wraps her up in a blanket, puts her down on the bed, patiently rubs her hair dry and even brushes it back into place.

"He wouldn't come," she tells Kent. "He wouldn't come back with me. That's why I couldn't bring him back."

"Sure," Kent says, "I understand. He must have been pretty scared. You were wonderful. I love you."

He wraps his arms around her, kissing her still-damp hair, and she sees that watching Alan and Margie, terrified that they had lost their son, has made Kent feel some phantom terror of losing her. Perhaps because she was also out there in the dark woods, he imagined himself suddenly bereft of Anne, his lover, his love.

And then what she thinks, very suddenly, is this: Of course I have to tell him about Jason.

9. Sick Sex

Anne is home sick for three days after she and Kent get back to New York, She is, in fact, sicker than she has been in years. She lies in bed and blows her nose and coughs almost constantly, her head feels enormous and full of scratchy dried leaves, and when she senses a new spasm of coughing coming on, the dread of it makes her tighten up all over, which only makes the coughing more painful. Kent puts a little hot pot by her bed along with tea bags and packaged soup mix, also, with his usual thoroughness, several cups, spoons, napkins, and a big jug full of water. He buys her copies of ten or fifteen magazines and leaves them in a glossy pile.

Anne and Kent's bedroom is small and very easily feels cluttered; the paraphernalia of her illness, all those magazines, the hot pot and tea bags and things seem to fill the room. It has only one window, and Kent and Anne tried to brighten the room by hanging blue curtains with a tiny white flower pattern, but it is just a small dark room with flowered curtains.

Their bedroom is usually kept very orderly through Kent's natural habits and Anne's forcing herself not to be too much of a slob. She knows Kent doesn't like it if she leaves clothes lying around and she tries hard to be neat, so hard she almost thinks it has become habit for her too. Anne spent her early adolescence fighting with her mother over the state of her room; she knows she is capable of extreme squalor, but she also knows some of that was developed deliberately to spite her mother. When she started living with Kent and became much neater than she had ever been alone, she would think occasionally of her mother, welcoming her into these clean pretty rooms.

Sick, Anne thinks constantly in a sort of confused dreamlike way that as soon as she is well she will be telling Kent about Jason. She no longer bothers to picture one scenario after another, she just reminds herself again and again, like a person almost asleep trying to commit to memory some terribly important and easily forgotten task to be done the next day. The other thing she keeps thinking about is the time she spent in the woods with Curtis. Sometimes, in her confusion, in the strange intensity of the fever and the heavy calm of the cough syrup, she is sure that her adventure in the woods held some sort of a message which she must now decipher. What sort of message? Don't ever go hiking. Don't ever have a child. Don't ever leave Kent. No, something much more complicated, something much more elusive. Don't ever think you can really make other people move. Don't try logic when you can plead. Always carry cookies. But all these are half-rational guesses at something which she will never be able to identify logically. To think there is a message in the first place is too illogical.

Anne knows that Kent is not just taking predictably competent care of a sick person. Of course he would never be a less than perfect nurse, but now Anne's sickness is being treated as the convalescence of a wounded hero. There is a special eagerness to serve her which is part of her reward for having found Curtis, recompense for those hours she spent coughing out in the woods. All the way home in the car on Sunday Anne lay stretched out on the backseat, her head in Kent's lap, while Curtis was held on Margie's lap in the front. Anne felt a little silly, as if she were playing invalid, but the fact was that when she had woken up that morning she had felt feverish and dizzy and she had not been at all sure she could manage the ride back. They stopped once on the way and Margie brought Anne a Styrofoam cup full of hot tea which she drank while the others ate their Howard Johnson's ice cream.

Anyway, her first day home in bed she feels too sick to talk to anyone. The second day she is perhaps a little better and in need of distraction, and she calls Viatech, talks briefly to the secretary about her health, and then asks to be connected to Charlotte's lab.

"So what's up with you?" Charlotte asks. "Weekend just too active?"

"You could say that. I'm sick ."

"I can hear it. You sound terrible."

"I'm lying here reading *Playboy* magazine because I can't concentrate enough to do anything else. How about a little sympathy?"

"Poor child."

"Speaking of boys . . ."

"Yes? Were we?"

"If you see Jason—"

"Your tech?"

"—would you just tell him I'm sick and I'll be out for a couple of days? But bring it up casually so he doesn't know you know, okay?"

"Sure," Charlotte says, "don't worry about it. Listen, you get well and come back here so you can finish the stuff you were doing. I can't wait to see Arthur's face."

"It's really almost done," Anne says. "I basically think I'm ready to tell Richie Grossman about it."

"Well, hallelujah. I shall look forward to your return. Do you want visitors?"

"No, I don't really think so."

"Just you and the playmate of the month, huh?"

"Let me tell you, the playmate of the month happens to be very intelligent. Her interests include classical music and parachute jumping."

"God," Charlotte says, "how can the rest of us hope to compete with that?"

Talking to Charlotte leaves Anne feeling at least temporarily better. And she has sent a message to Jason; frankly, she doesn't completely trust his discretion in her absence: Would he ask about her, why she isn't there? Would he ask the wrong person or ask in the wrong tone, somehow make someone suspicious? After all, of the two of them it is obviously she who has more to lose, if only in terms of reputation, should their affair become general knowledge at Viatech. Sexism and double standards to one side, as they may not be completely in this case, there are the different prestige levels of their jobs. Even if she credits her colleagues with a reasonable degree of liberalness about the sexes, she is under no illusions about what you might call their class prejudices.

Anne lies back in her bed and tries to formulate her experiments, put her cells and enzymes through their paces. But her mind is sludgy. Her molecules will not dance for her. She knows they're out there, waiting for her, her own little piece of work, her tiny corner of clarity. Be patient, she tells herself, be patient and wait, your mind is blocked for now. Read a magazine.

That same day, Tuesday, Anne has a visitor. Kent has called Louisa and asked her to stop by and cheer Anne up. At first this seems to Anne to have been a rather unexplainable gesture on Kent's part, but after five minutes with her cousin, she understands: Louisa is really very comforting and soothing to a sick person, and somehow she single-handedly creates the impression that a whole family is out there, worrying about Anne, wondering every few minutes whether Anne is feeling any better.

Louisa bustles in around suppertime with a bouquet of pink-ridged carnations and a box of chocolate-covered cherries and an enormous card. Anne coos over the picture on the card, a chicken in a hospital bed with a thermometer in its mouth—"Sorry to hear you're one sick chicken . . ." Anne opens the card. "Hope you get well eggs-tremely soon!"

"I'll put it here on top of the dresser so you can see it," Kent says.

Louisa sits on the foot of the bed. Kent goes off to make tea.

Louisa chatters on about sickness, about how Kent is taking such good care of Anne. Anne suddenly remembers what Louisa said at the soup-and-salad restaurant about how watching Kent and Anne together made her feel alone. Maybe it isn't really a good idea for Louisa to see Anne sick in bed and lovingly tended by Kent: If Louisa got sick, who would be taking care of her? Her roommate? Her current lover? Surely whoever it was would not be doing it with Kent's loving thoroughness. Anne wonders who Louisa's current lover is, anyway.

Anne is accustomed to getting news of Louisa's life in fairly disjointed installments. She feels a little guilty for not having called Louisa to follow up on the crisis Louisa was going through when Anne last saw her, but of course that was right at the beginning of Anne's affair with Jason, and then she got so involved in her work and Louisa never called. So what with one thing and another it has been more than a month since she talked to Louisa.

"What's going on with you?" Anne asks.

By now Louisa could be back with the Midwesterner, or she could be serious about the physicist, or she could be involved with someone completely new. Or, of course, she could be between lovers.

"Well, Jim said he didn't want to see me anymore, and I was sort of seeing Yuri, you know, he was calling and all and I have a pretty good time with him, but it isn't serious or anything."

"So you're back with Yuri now." The physicist, Anne remembers.

"Well, we're sort of seeing each other. But you know, I kept thinking about Jim and how well we got on together and how much I must have hurt him."

"So what did you do?"

"I just couldn't talk about it with him. I wasn't brave enough. Finally I wrote him a letter."

"You did?" Anne cannot help trying to picture the stationery, probably bought especially for the letter—hearts? flowers? Snoopy?

"What did you say?"

"Oh, just how I loved him and I still love him and I understood if he hates me because it was so horrible what I did to him, but I tried to tell him that I wasn't really like that, and I apologized and told him I would always treasure the memory of our time together."

"And did he respond?"

"I only mailed the letter last Friday. I don't even know if he got it yet. And I haven't seen him at work this week. I don't see him most days." Louisa pauses, leans closer to Anne, whispers, "Was it okay to send a letter like that, do you think? I really do want him back."

"Sure it was okay. What can you lose?"

They both hear some sounds from the kitchen. As if suddenly reminded by this evidence of Kent, Louisa leans even closer, breathing in germs with complete indifference, and whispers in the most noiseless of whispers, audible only because Anne knows more or less what to expect, "What about you?"

"You mean my quote-unquote affair?" Anne's whisper is pretty soft.

"It's gotten serious?" Louisa whispers, round-eyed.

"It isn't the least bit serious." It is hard to whisper with a bad head cold; the effort leaves Anne almost breathless. "It's just sex."

"And Kent doesn't know?"

"No."

"Oh, Anne. How *can* you?"

And at that moment Kent himself reenters with a pot of hot tea and clean germless cups for Louisa and himself. Anne looks at the two of them, sitting on her bed drinking tea.

Would Louisa think Kent was good in bed? Anne's imagination falters before the task of figuring out what is good in bed according to Louisa. Baby talk? Sex-manual sophistication, a new position for every day of the week? Or just strong silent macho stuff?

"So what's new?" Kent asks Louisa.

"Not much. Same old job, same old life. My roommate Cara is getting married to Mike this weekend, though. That's pretty exciting."

"Are you going to be a bridesmaid?" Kent asks.

"No, her sisters and her best friend from high school are. Now, don't make fun of it, you two," she goes on, having intercepted a glance, "*you* may be too liberated to believe in marriage, but lots of other people aren't. Cara's been dreaming about this wedding for months."

"Do you have someone to take over her room?" Kent asks, practical as always.

"Not yet definitely, we probably have to run an ad. For a while it looked like one of the girls I work with would move in with us. But I think she's going to move in with her boyfriend."

Anne is naturally tempted to say, Oh, are they too liberated to believe in marriage? but she doesn't. She shouldn't tease Louisa about this; probably even Louisa is not exactly enthusiastic about finding someone new to live with, about judging some stranger in a quick interview and then inviting her to come share the bathroom for the indefinite future. Probably it makes the domesticity of Anne and Kent seem that much more desirable. Probably it makes Anne seem that much more unworthy and ungrateful.

The telephone rings and Kent picks it up. "Hello? Yes, one second."

He hands the phone to Anne, who has a sudden premonition.

"Hi, it's me," Jason says. She was right. "I just wanted to see how you were."

"Oh, I'm okay. Well, I'm sick." She feels desperately stilted. Kent and Louisa are not looking right at her, but neither are they bothering to make it obvious that they aren't listening; clearly neither of them thinks this a particularly private call. What can she say? What will sound normal? "Did you hear from Charlotte?" Make it sound like she is talking to a friend of a friend. Invoke a woman's name, make it sound like he's her property.

"Yeah, sure. Are you coming back soon?"

Can Kent and Louisa hear? Doesn't Jason realize that Kent is in the room?

"Well, I hope so. You know, I've been working on that project, it's been going so well, I really want to get back and finish it." There, if anything will remind him that they are not in private, that should. Kent and Louisa are now talking quietly, but they could just be doing that to be polite.

"Is that the only reason you want to come back? Your project?"

"Thanks for calling," she says, perhaps too firmly; does it sound like a dismissal to the two people sitting on her sickbed?

"Hurry back," Jason's voice says into her ear, dropping a little in volume and in tone, "I miss you."

"Okay, good-bye," Anne says, and hangs up, angry at him but

also suddenly aroused. "Someone from work," she explains unnecessarily to Kent and Louisa, wondering how she can respond like that to Jason when she feels so sick, so completely unable to move or think clearly. Perhaps because she cannot smell anything, she cannot taste anything distinctly, even her hearing seems to be clouded, her eyes feel itchy . . . perhaps she just wants to feel something intensely.

Anne sees that Louisa is looking at her, and when Kent goes out of the room again to put up more water to boil, Louisa leans forward and whispers, "Was that . . . ?"

Anne nods.

"See, he does care about you," Louisa hisses. She nods her head with satisfaction, and Anne feels extremely irritated.

"He misses me," she whispers back. "He misses me because with me out sick he doesn't have anyone to fuck during his lunch hour."

Louisa shrinks back slightly from the word, which bothers her most in its literal context. Anne leans back into her pillows. The two of them wait quietly for Kent to return, and when he does they leave the conversation up to him, which means that very soon he is giving Louisa a full account of the search for Curtis and the heroism of Anne.

After Louisa has left, Kent straightens up, carrying out the used cups and the remnants of cold tea, bringing Anne a fresh box of tissues. He asks if there is anything he can do for her.

"Come to bed," she says, meaning to suggest only that he has already done more than enough, that his presence is worth a hundred tiny sickroom favors.

"Are you up to that?" he asks, smiling at her.

"Well, if *you* can be romantic about such a mess of dirty tissues and germs . . ." Of course, she doesn't really know whether she wants him. That is, she knows she wants him, but she also knows that it is only as a substitute that she wants him, and she feels bad about using him this way. Even so. Even so. Surely a sick person has additional moral leeway?

A few minutes later he is in bed beside her, naked, his hand sliding up her leg under the flannel nightgown in which all day she has felt sick and sexless.

"You just lie still," he whispers, though nowhere near as softly as she and Louisa whispered, "you lie there and I'll take care of everything."

In fact it is a shock after the dulled and drugged sensations of the day to suddenly feel something so fiercely. He raises the nightgown, moves his lips down over her breasts, down her belly, whispers, "Your skin is so hot," and even though she knows it is fever, she somehow feels that it is also the metaphorical burn of desire. She is almost immediately ready for him, but he holds them both back, teasing her, perhaps pretending consideration for an invalid, while she laces her hands into his hair and pulls upward, squirming, almost losing patience with his gentle licking when what she wants is something ferocious.

Finally she gets what she wants, and it takes all the vague delirium and fever of Anne's day and makes them into something intoxicating. It is a million miles away from that calculatingly unenjoyed episode up at the summer house. It is terrific. It has additional significance, though neither Anne nor Kent knows this at the time, because it is the last fuck before Kent knows about Jason. The last fuck of their innocence, you might call it, or rather, of Kent's innocence, since surely Anne has been beyond lost innocence for a long time now, has in fact been actively guilty.

10. The Moment of Truth

On Thursday Anne is dressed up. Back at Viatech, but she is not really dressed for Viatech. Nor for Jason, though of course she will see him. She is costumed for the confession which she knows, getting dressed in the morning, that she will make that evening. She is wearing a long red dress, not floor-length but only a few inches above her ankles. The yoke is decorated with heavy black embroidery which is obviously intended to be ethnic, perhaps Balkan, but is just as obviously the product of a fashion designer. The dress was an extravagance of two years ago, when it cost more money than Anne usually spends on an article of clothing. Anne has worn it only rarely. It makes her a little self-conscious, so much red. And yet, at the same time, she knows that when she wears it she feels curiously immune to the scrutiny of other people: They may be looking at her dress, but they aren't looking at her. Only after she has put it on does she make the connections: red, scarlet woman.

The familiar questions—why does she sleep with Jason, why is it important to tell Kent about it—don't trouble Anne much on that particular day. The dress is her concession to the occasion, and everything is decided. Her mind is purified by sickness and resolve. She has come vaguely to the conclusion that Kent will accept her confession in the moderately casual spirit in which the crime has been committed.

It is good to have her mind in working order again, to stare down at her petri dishes, down at her lab notebook, and inside her head watch molecules rearrange themselves. There are answers to be found, however elusive they may be. She is humming as she settles down in front of the sterile hood to begin playing with her cell cultures.

As for why she sleeps with Jason, well, Anne feels and has felt for some time that other people do not seem to act from the same motives that she does. Or perhaps it is just that characters in books and movies do not. A fictional character might be regularly betraying a good man like Kent for any of several reasons. She might feel trapped in her marriage or her serious relationship, and be chasing a feminist freedom. But would she be doing it out of a relatively uncomplicated lust?

When Jason comes up to her that day at work, steps up behind her and puts his hands on her shoulders, Anne promptly goes weak in the knees. Presumably they are alone in the lab; she turns her head and checks. Jason slides his hands down onto her breasts, whispering in her ear that he missed her. She turns and faces him, smiles.

"I missed you too," she says, but lightly, no husky sexual accents.

"Lunchtime?" he asks.

"No," Anne says, determined to behave herself, at least for today—what if Kent should ask her tonight when she had last . . .

"Why not?"

"I just don't . . . I'm not feeling very well. I'd probably give you my sickness. Let's leave it for today."

"Okay," Jason says. "See you tomorrow."

He leaves the lab, passing Arthur Schenk who is just coming in. Anne turns her attention to her work. Really it is done. All that's left are some details. She is ready to show it to Richie. But she feels that she owes Arthur a word of warning. She tells herself this is silly, he would never give her a warning if he thought he was about to humiliate her. Resolutely, she goes in search of Richie Grossman.

The morning break is about to begin and Richie is standing by the coffee machine nibbling at a jelly-filled cruller. Richie arrives early for the doughnut break every day; he does not have to worry that anyone will think he is shirking, and he gets his pick of the doughnuts. Richie has a mild weight problem and he loves sweets.

"Hiya, Anne, I understand you've had the plague."

"Nothing special, Richie, just smallpox."

He gives a loud laugh. "Sure someone didn't inoculate you for a private experiment?"

"Listen, Richie, I have something to show you. Can you make time to come by the lab?" Her voice has dropped; a few other people have begun to cluster around the coffee machine, mixing their customary morning combinations of coffee, non-dairy creamer, sugar or Sweet 'n Low.

The very formal reporting procedure for the end of a project is used only after the project has been completely finished off, packaged into its most attractive form. When some project or other is nearing completion scientifically, the researchers just make an informal appointment with Richie, or in some cases an intermediate personage, show off what has been accomplished, accept advice.

"Not today," he replies, also in a soft voice; everyone recognizes that these little conferences are to be kept private. "I really don't have a free minute. Will tomorrow be okay?"

"Sure."

"We'll say right after lunch then?" Richie carries appointments in his head. "I'm looking forward to seeing what you've got. Let me get you a cup of coffee," he goes on, a little louder, ending their private conclave.

Anne ends up having lunch that day with Charlotte and several other people at the Chinese restaurant where half of Viatech eats every day. Conversation at the table is shoptalk, naturally. There have been reports in the newspapers that several of the new genetic engineering firms are in financial trouble; the expected boom in profits and revolutionary developments has not quite materialized. This is not news to the Viatech people, who also know that their own company is doing quite well, perhaps because it is small to begin with, not predicated on enormous breakthroughs, perhaps because, you have to admit it, Richie Grossman knows his stuff. Still, there is a kind of nervousness palpable at the table; these are people who have been accustomed to seeing themselves as on the scientific frontier, and it is disconcerting to read in the newspapers that the frontier may be something of a flop. Disconcerting even though without the newspapers recombinant DNA and genetic engineering would never have been seen as such an immediate source of supercolossal scientific advances to begin with. Everyone at the table knows that the whole thing was blown up by the newspapers, and any current disappointment simply reflects the inability of research to move as fast as speculation. Still, it is a little frightening. It reminds them all that their jobs are extremely specialized, and surely all specialists feel a little frightened at threats to their specialty. They console themselves by repeating to one another that at least Viatech is doing well.

Working in her lab during the afternoon, Anne thinks of the tiny size of the breakthrough for which she is now responsible. No newspaper article could make it sound even faintly important. Even Anne herself would not claim it as anything but a clever (and lucky) piece of biochemical maneuvering. Scientists tend to forget that they are often pictured by nonscientists as hovering always on the brink of some major step forward, moving with clear intent and direction toward some very definite and very important goal, like the cure for cancer—until one of them finally succeeds.

Arthur Schenk putters on over in his corner. He has several new test-tube racks set up and he is painstakingly labeling his test-tubes with indelible Magic Marker. Anne can see that after he labels each tube he makes a notation in his lab book, putting down the Magic Marker, picking up his black pen. She feels sorry for him. Finally, when she is taking off her lab coat to leave, she turns to Arthur, on impulse. He has put away his lab book, every bit of his equipment. He is changing his lab coat for a sports jacket, a would-be academic tweed which doesn't quite make it.

"Listen, Arthur?"

"Yes, ma'am?" The courtesy sets her teeth on edge.

"I think I'm sort of on to something. Anyway, Richie is coming by tomorrow after lunch; if you like, I mean, if you're curious, you can come listen too."

"Well, thank you," Arthur says, looking absolutely confused. Anne nods and says good-bye and leaves, unable to face his confused expression, his ugly jacket, his soft swollen stomach. She cannot really feel gleeful, but now at least she has been scrupulous about professional courtesy, and Arthur will know that something is coming.

She is home before Kent and she starts cooking dinner. She cuts up vegetables for ratatouille, and then, as it is bubbling on the stove, suddenly adds a great quantity of soy sauce and hot red pepper. She puts down the wooden spoon, not even stirring it, and goes to stand in the living room, wondering why she did that. What will the soy sauce do to it? Will it even be edible, or did she put in too much hot pepper? Not that she and Kent don't both like hot food, but there are limits. What was she thinking of? Of the red pepper which tonight she is going to throw into Kent's life? Was she trying to suggest something about experimentation and variety? She doesn't understand her own messages. She goes back into the kitchen, seeing Kent's touch in everything: the row of hooks he put up to hang pots and utensils, the orderly spice rack, the cabinet which didn't close properly until Kent fixed it. She takes a package of chopped meat out of the freezer and throws it into her bubbling pot of what used to be ratatouille. Kent, naturally, would have remembered to leave some meat out to defrost in the morning if he was going to cook dinner. As Anne stirs her frozen red lump of chopped meat, watching little bits of it brown so she can scrape them off with her spoon, she reminds herself that Kent has a sense of proportion, after all. He will understand that Jason is not exactly important. Carefully, she protects her red dress from spatters as she knocks the block of meat back and forth.

She thinks about Kent and herself as graduate students, sleeping together, studying together, falling very gradually in love. Would that fondly remembered Kent, the linguistics graduate student, have minded if Anne had had an affair with someone else? Or would he have pardoned it as an essentially frivolous act? And will the current Kent, the banker, be more inclined to treat it as a weighty adult matter? Anne suspects she is trying to set things up in her mind so that if he takes it badly it will be a character defect on his part.

She leaves the pot on the stove over a very low flame, and when Kent comes home, she pours a little wine for each of them. They sit in the living room, together on the couch, Kent complimenting her on the dress, asking about her health. He is still wearing his shirt and tie, the pants of his suit. In fact, they look like two adults, she thinks—is this a picture which is somehow very pleasing to Kent? There is something odd and datelike about the two of them, dressed like that, sipping wine. She can almost imagine that he is someone she doesn't know well, someone to whom she is about to reveal a certain fact about her life. Enough preliminaries, it is time to tell him.

"Kent, listen."

"Yes?"

"There's something I've been meaning to talk to you about, I mean, maybe it isn't very important, it's a little bit embarrassing, but I wanted to tell you."

She watches his face, feeling clumsy, wondering what he expects after that introduction.

"Okay," he says.

"The thing is, it's sort of embarrassing . . ." She looks away from him, fixes her eyes on the Brooklyn Museum poster of *The Peaceable Kingdom* on the wall, announces to it, "I've been sort of having an affair with someone at work." She doesn't turn to look at Kent, it seems too much the act of a voyeur when she has been thinking about this scene for so long, when she knew what was coming and he didn't. At least allow him privacy for the first minute. She goes on: "It's absolutely unimportant, I mean to me . . . I mean it isn't anything serious, but I felt really bad about it being a secret." No, that's wrong, it sounds like she expects him to condone it and let her continue. Well, doesn't she? Is it possible that she expects to continue, having confessed and been absolved, maybe to continue it while pretending to Kent that it is over, having reached some kind of bargain with her own conscience?

Finally Kent says something. "How long has this been happening?"

"About a month," Anne says, though in fact it's been longer, and she turns and looks at Kent and sees that he is angry. Which was, after all, to be expected, and probably it is easier to have him angry than hurt, but still, she is frightened. Kent is rarely angry.

"And how many times?" he asks, with a sort of sarcastic curiosity.

"What do you mean?" she asks, thinking that he cannot mean what she thinks he means.

"How many times have you screwed him?" The same sarcastic tone.

"Don't be silly."

"How many times?" His voice has more anger in it.

"I don't know, I really don't." Her voice now has some anger, some exasperation in it. "I didn't count."

"Five? Ten? More than ten? More than twenty?"

"What is this, a multiple choice test?"

"Goddamn it, how many times?" The loudness of his voice shocks her. He is almost shouting.

"I don't know!" And then, as he seems to move toward her threateningly, "Maybe about twenty. Something like that." And to her relief he settles back down, shaking his head, as though in disbelief.

"Jesus Christ," he says softly. "You've really been busy." She understands that he was hoping she was talking about one or two infidelities, that this number has floored him even more than the original confession. She should have lied, she thinks.

"I'm sorry," Anne says helplessly, "I know it sounds more serious than it was."

"Then why the fuck were you doing it if it wasn't serious?"

"It was just . . . stupid. I mean, it was sexual but that's all."

"Oh, that's all. It was just sex."

"It was just someone I was attracted to sexually, that's what I mean, not even someone I like very much."

"And do you mind my asking who?" The sarcasm is back. Anne is cursing herself; how could she ever have imagined telling Kent, how could she ever have thought it could be a small thing?

"It's someone I work with. He's just a lab tech."

"Named?"

"Jason." That is the hardest thing of all to say. It is followed by a silence during which she can see Kent looking at her dress and she knows he is thinking that she wore it for Jason's sake. He doesn't say that, though.

"I'm sorry," she says again.

Kent explodes. "You're sorry! You're fucking sorry! You screw somebody every single day for a month and it isn't important and now you're sorry!" He is really shouting now.

"It wasn't important. I'm not in love with him." She is not shouting yet.

"Then why the fuck did you do it? Aren't I important?"

"Yes, you are, that's the whole point. That's the difference between you and him."

"Oh, thank you very much. That's supposed to make it all much better? I'm so important that you jump into bed with any unimportant man who comes along?"

"Only with one. I was just attracted to him, it was just silliness, I know that." She is hesitating between raising her voice and starting to cry, not that it is a conscious decision, just that she can feel both impulses within her.

For a minute she is afraid that *he* will cry, but instead he gets up and begins to pace around the living room. His tone is fairly normal when he speaks. "I can't exactly believe this, Anne. I mean, I know there have been things wrong between us for a while, and I was trying to figure out how to make things go better, and all the time you're just . . . doing this."

Finally she does begin to cry. "I'm sorry." She remembers her feeling from early in the day that her own motivations are somehow not those of other people. Kent has reinforced this, making her feel that if he had cheated on her it would at least have been for love of someone else. He finds her motives the most offensive thing of all. She was right, she is somehow off, she is not quite connected to other people.

"And now what?" he asks her from across the room.

"I won't anymore, I promise." She realizes that the promise is being offered sincerely and she feels a sharp pang at the thought of Jason, wishing she had at least gone with him at lunch for one last time.

"And that's supposed to make it all all right?"

"What else do you want me to do?"

He comes across the room, bends toward her, grabs her shoulders. "I guess I want you to stop wanting him." She is silent. "But that isn't all, I can't stand the idea that you're capable of something like this. Do you think I sleep with other people?"

"No."

"I never have while we've been together, in case you didn't know."

Anne gets up, folding her arms across the heavy embroidery of her dress. She walks a few steps, turns, sits on the arm of the chair. She wants to be angry but her words come out as still tearful.

"Okay, you're a better person than I am, I admit it. And I'm sorry, I know I did something stupid. And I'll stop." Then her anger comes. "I can't promise I'll stop wanting him, I don't know if you're so goddamn virtuous that you never even want anybody else. I'll stop sleeping with him and that's all I can do. For God's sake, I'm telling you about this because you *are* the important thing and I hated lying to you." But of course, she is wondering why she really told him. She doesn't want to stop sleeping with Jason. And yet, there is a tremendous relief in having finally told Kent. She believes that when he has forgiven her and they have both calmed down she may yet be glad she did it.

"I'm sorry, Anne, I can't accept this," Kent says, and his calm tone startles her as much as his words. She holds herself more tightly. "I can't accept that our relationship means so much to you and yet you could still go and do what you did. I don't want to just pick up and carry on from here."

"What are you saying?"

"You know perfectly well what I'm saying. I'm saying that when two people have such different ideas about what a serious relationship means, then they shouldn't be having one and that's all there is to it." And with that he stomps into the bedroom and slams the door.

Anne, left on the arm of the couch, thinks confusedly of her strange dinner still bubbling on the stove, of following Kent into the bedroom and trying to talk some more. Is he packing his things? She cannot take it in. Then suddenly her head feels somewhat clearer and she realizes one thing very distinctly: There was some relief in Kent's manner when he said what he said. He is relieved to be so firmly in the right. If he ends the relationship now, he will be using her affair with Jason as a pretext; he was really very ready to end things. She has given him the opportunity to break up with her and remain morally above her. She is positive of it. She even wonders if she has been playing to it all along. So why are they actually breaking up then? Is it really something as silly as "adulthood" and banking? Are her perceptions and her sense of what is important so very different from everyone else's? Would she be a better person if she could honestly say she had slept with Jason because she loved him, or alternatively if she were really sure that living with Kent had changed drastically for the worse? She feels guilty and bewildered and terribly, terribly sad.

She goes to the bedroom door and knocks. Kent opens it. He has not been packing after all, only changing to his usual evening khaki pants and workshirt. Anne swallows. "I made a very weird sort of ratatouille tonight. I don't know if it's even edible. But we could try."

Kent looks at her for a minute. "I was serious before," he says.

"I know." She feels herself starting to cry again. "But we can still eat dinner, can't we?"

And so they do, not talking to each other very much. When they do talk to each other, they are carefully polite and inconsequential. Anne sees ahead of them a night in bed, neither falling easily asleep, each apologizing for any unintended brushing against the other. An accurate prophecy, as it turns out.

While they eat dinner, she watches his neat, careful table manners, how he pours water without spilling a drop, how he never tries to lift too much on his fork. The weird ratatouille, as it happens, is delicious.

II. *Singles*

II. A New Life

The clock radio woke Anne up with a burst of the soundtrack from *The Big Chill*. She fumbled with it, pressed the wrong button, and the station changed; she had a religious sermon. She found the right button, clicked off the sound altogether. Then she lay for a minute in the still unfamiliar narrowness of the bed. She had been sleeping in the bed for just three nights.

She met Louisa, exiting from the bathroom as Anne entered, and they both nodded but said nothing. Anne found herself in the bathroom among the elaborate paraphernalia of her new roommates, blow-dryers, hot combs, quantities of jars and bottles. She herself did not yet feel sufficiently at home to leave any of her own possessions in the shared bathroom except her toothbrush; everything else she carried back and forth each time. She felt that she was in a college dormitory, that another girl was about to appear at another sink beside her.

Anne had moved through her life with Kent assuming, without much attention, that that life would probably go on forever. But her life in Louisa's apartment felt different to her from the beginning, felt like a time which would soon be behind her, almost as if she were already remembering it even while it was happening.

She dressed quickly, choosing a neat skirt and blouse so that she would feel comfortable facing Louisa in the kitchen. Louisa was not only dressed much more snazzily than Anne but was also in full makeup. She was making instant coffee and toasting half an

English muffin, and Anne accepted the remaining half with a cup of coffee.

The other roommate was also in the kitchen, but she was no- where near dressed yet. Felice, almost six feet tall and disconcert- ingly thin, leaned against the wall in a long black satin robe, her eyes still gummy with sleep, languidly chewing her Tiger's Milk protein-rich bar. She ate one of those bars for breakfast every day, and said they gave her enough energy to skip lunch altogether. Felice would move as slowly as possible until the last minute, when she would dress rapidly and run out of the house, and, according to Louisa, arrive at work late. Louisa was fond of Felice, but con- sidered her a little odd.

Only Anne and Louisa made breakfast conversation. The kitchen was nowhere near as neat or as welcoming as the one Anne had shared with Kent. This kitchen had the distinct look of a room for which no one felt responsible; you could almost sense the division of shelves in the refrigerator.

Anne and Louisa left together for work, swinging their shoul- der bags. They went down in the elevator, walked together to the subway. The air was fresh and pleasant, the beginning of a new day. On the crowded subway, Anne watched Louisa, who seemed to carry within herself a certain perpetual professional crispness. Anne was early to work thanks to Louisa's extraordinary punctu- ality.

She unlocked her cabinets, took out her lab book, some of her pieces of apparatus, handling them, and carrying herself, with some of Louisa's infectious professional manner. She put on her lab coat trying for a crisp sense of uniform, buttoning it carefully before she stepped away from the locker. But when she went into her lab, there was nothing she could sit down and begin to do with calm efficiency. There was no telephone with buttons to push, no list of appointments, and no one to watch her in action. Her con- ference with Richie Grossman the week before had gone very well; even the day after her confession to Kent, she had been able to enjoy Richie's approval. He was enough of a scientist to under- stand that she had not only solved the problem, but had solved it in a fairly nonobvious way. He had been congratulatory and had hinted at rewards to come. And poor old Arthur Schenk had also muttered a compliment or two, and ever since, he had treated Anne with a reserve which she suspected might include some deference, along with a great deal of resentment.

In the usual way, though nothing official had been announced, everyone at Viatech knew that Anne had pulled off a coup. Charlotte was openly triumphant. Other people took trouble to speak to Anne, noticing her as someone worth cultivating.

It was of course very good that her work was going well. It had softened the almost unbelievable speed with which her life with Kent had dissolved. The comfort of her moderate celebrity at work, the sense that she was spending her days to good purpose, had helped to get her through the week after her confession. She moved out on Sunday, the day after Louisa's old roommate had gotten married and gone away on her honeymoon. So Anne and Kent had lived together for a number of days after Anne's confession, but after the first night, Kent had slept in a sleeping bag on the living room floor. This had not prevented a sudden sexual encounter late one night when they had been dividing up books. They had both been near tears, and they had not shared a bed afterward, but it seemed to have healed something between them; after that night they were able to be friendlier toward each other.

Arthur Schenk arrived while Anne was still staring vaguely at her lab book. She was almost glad to see him; she was glad that the scenes and the characters of the Viatech part of her life had not changed. It was reassuring, given the total upheaval in everything else. Arthur put away his sports jacket, fussed with his lab coat. Anne decided to go hunt up Charlotte. In the corridor she passed Jason, who was pushing a metal cart. He smiled at her, and she smiled back, and they both moved on. She had not slept with him during the past week; she had told him that she was in the process of breaking up with her boyfriend and she couldn't quite handle sex with someone else for a little while. In fact, the real reason she didn't want to go back to the warehouse with him was that she had decided that the only way she could cope with the breakup was by recognizing that Jason really had very little to do with it. She had to hold on to her certainty that Jason had provided an excuse for a breakup which she and Kent really wanted for other, more important reasons. But enough. Now she would bring Jason to her new room, they would have the comfort of a bed.

Charlotte was very busy at her lab bench; perhaps inspired by Anne's success, she had become increasingly involved with her own work over the last week. Still, she pulled up a stool for Anne and asked her how things were going. Charlotte had been acting as if she considered it her responsibility to support Anne through her crisis. She was also clearly not quite sure of Anne's motives; Charlotte wanted to make it into an escape from a constricting relationship, a search for personal and sexual liberty. And Anne, trying resolutely to be fair, refused to cooperate. She confined herself to generalities, which were, in fact, the closest she herself could come to understanding what had happened: Things just weren't working out, we had grown apart. She sensed that Charlotte was ready for an increased closeness, a fellowship of escapees from long-term relationships, and she was not sure she wanted to be part of that.

"Things are going pretty well," Anne said, "I just have to get used to living with roommates."

"Are you thinking of this as a permanent setup?"

"No," Anne said, "I should probably get a place of my own eventually, but right now I don't feel up to apartment hunting. I'm just glad this slot was here for me to fall into."

"And Kent's keeping your old place?" Charlotte and Anne had gone over this before; Charlotte seemed to feel that Anne was in some way being cheated.

"I didn't want it," Anne said, a little sharply. "I never liked it all that much, and frankly I don't think I could stand to live in it, you know, with Kent's ghost. But I think he'll keep it. At least I'll always know where to call him."

"Don't. You have to break the habit of talking to him or seeing him."

"Charlotte, the rules for you and your husband are not necessarily the rules for everyone in the world, you know. I don't want to just lose track of Kent."

"Nobody said you have to lose track of him. He isn't going to run away. But you can't just stop being lovers and start being best friends."

Back in her own lab, Anne forced herself to pick up her work and was rewarded by becoming absorbed in it. Arthur went out for the doughnut break—it took daily doughnuts to maintain that physique—and, just as Anne had hoped, Jason came and found her in the lab. Perhaps the smile she had given him earlier in the morning had been warmer and more inviting than the other looks she had sent his way over the past week. He was, however, cautious; he did not try to touch her or kiss her.

"Hi," he said.

"I was wondering if you'd like to come visit my new apartment."

She realized that she was nervous. She wasn't eager to go back to the mattress in the warehouse; that was too bound up in her mind with cheating on Kent. She wanted what she had wanted all along from Jason, but she wanted it in a comfortable clean room. And she wanted to make it clear that one phase of her life was over and another beginning, with new people, with old people in new contexts.

"I think that would be really nice," he said. "I probably can't stay, though."

"It's a single bed anyway," Anne said.

At eight-thirty the bell rang. She heard his voice fuzzy on the intercom from downstairs. She buzzed him in. Louisa was out on a date. Felice was in her room, playing reggae records on her stereo, the volume turned up loud. Louisa also had a record player in her room, but Anne did not. Kent had kept the record player, since it had been his originally. They had left their property in a rather unsettled state of division; much of it had stayed with Kent in the apartment on the understanding that Anne would come back later and take some. And Anne had the satisfaction of knowing that the collection of things she had brought with her to her new room was completely hers.

Anne's new room was small and square and cell-like. The bed

and the dresser and the table and chair had been left behind by Cara. There was a small mirror on the wall, and Anne had hung nothing else. Louisa had insisted on loaning her a bedspread: pink strawberries and a white ruffle. Anne was wearing tight faded jeans and a white cotton blouse with a low drawstring neckline, and examining herself in the long mirror in the bathroom, had thought that Jason had never seen her in jeans, only in work clothes. Jason was dressed the way he dressed every day, Levi's and a button-down shirt. But to see him standing there in the doorway of this new apartment changed everything. He was someone who had come to visit her. She was someone who had dressed for him.

As he walked into the apartment, he moved to the reggae music, and she watched him. He moved so beautifully. He smiled at her and took her into his arms, but to dance, not to kiss. She found herself moving in response to his signals, they were holding each other close and dancing to the beat of the reggae. It felt alarmingly public.

"Show me your room," he said into her ear.

They sat on the floor, leaning against the side of the single bed. Jason produced a joint and Anne was suddenly absurdly flattered, as if he had brought a good bottle of wine to dinner, or perhaps a corsage for her. She went to the kitchen to get matches and a saucer to serve as an ashtray, and then they smoked in silence.

Anne was enjoying sitting on the floor and smoking, she was enjoying the feel of her own tight jeans. They made her feel like she was a sixteen-year-old at a party. Jason put his arm across her shoulders and she leaned into him, fitting herself into the warmth of his arm. Jason pulled away for a minute to go turn off the overhead light and turn on the bedside lamp. The lamp was very dim, as Anne had already discovered; she didn't think Cara had done much reading in bed.

Only after the joint was absolutely and completely gone did Jason make any overt sexual move. And all he did was to move his hand down from her shoulder and begin to trail his fingers over her breast. Anne could hear both of them breathing. She closed her eyes, hoping she would start to want him as intensely as usual.

She imagined herself at sixteen, during her first year with her aunt and uncle. She remembered a party, the air heavy with marijuana and cigarette smoke and herself sitting in a circle next to a boy, his arm around her shoulders. She had just met him at this party, she thought he was very good-looking. Periodically he would fill his mouth with smoke, press his lips to hers, and blow smoke into her mouth. Anne thought this was extremely sexy. She hoped the boy would offer to drive her home. She had not yet found out how her aunt and uncle would deal with her having a boyfriend, and she was surprised to find in herself no eagerness for a confrontation, none of the excited, almost giddy daring which, when her parents had been alive, would have made her kiss this boy good night on her own front porch for an hour or two. And while she was thinking this, the boy beside her had begun to caress her shoulder, very tentatively, his hand moving slowly down her back. And Anne had gotten up and left the circle and gone to call her uncle, saying, Please come pick me up, I don't feel well.

Jason was kissing her gently on the ear. It was pleasant. It was mildly arousing. Finally he reached with his other hand and pulled her shirt loose from the waistband of her jeans in the front and put his hand up under her shirt to cover one of her breasts with sudden warmth. And that was not mildly arousing but wildly arousing. She had begun to move in his embrace, she unbuttoned his shirt and made an attempt on the fly of his jeans, but she could not unzip it; his sitting position, the tightness of his pants, his erection, all made it impossible for her to move the zipper. They would probably have ended up fucking on the floor if they had not both been aware that for the first time they had a real bed, and almost conscientiously they climbed up. It was a lengthy and pleasantly stoned encounter, Anne and Jason pausing to change positions, trying to change positions without pausing, Anne giggling when Jason momentarily lost her in one overly acrobatic twist, her giggles changing to throatier noises when he found her again. They came, not at the absolute peak of their mutual intensity, but when they were both definitely slowing down, and then they lay for a long time amid Louisa's strawberries and ruffles, pleased with themselves and with each other.

Anne became aware that there were voices in the living room, Louisa's and a man's. Jason had noticed it too; he turned his head and looked into her eyes, grinned, but seemed to be waiting for something.

"You want to meet my cousin? My roommate?"

"I thought you said she was on your boyfriend's side."

"Louisa doesn't have it in her to be rude to anybody's date. And that's how she'll see you."

They dressed, took turns combing their hair in front of the mirror. Then, more than a little self-conscious, she opened the bedroom door and led the way out, wishing her bedroom wasn't so close to the living room.

There were in fact three people in the living room. Louisa was wearing a shiny blue dress with thin strings on the shoulders, no sleeves, slits up the sides, and high-heeled blue sandals. The man beside her on the couch was dark and somehow unkempt, despite his own fairly formal clothing. Anne was conscious of the jeans that she and Jason were wearing, the smell of dope which she was sure still clung to them a little. She felt for a minute like the teen-age daughter of Louisa and her date, smoking dope and making out with a boyfriend while the parents were out of the house, misgauging their time of return and emerging sheepishly from her bedroom with the boy in tow, hoping they would overlook what had obviously been going on.

Her own parents, Anne was suddenly sure, would have managed to ignore it, to smile and welcome the boy, to wait until he left the house, everything very polite. And then what? She had a somewhat dim memory of her mother coming to her room late one night—had her parents come home to find a boy there, or had Anne been out all evening with her seventeen-year-old boyfriend?—sitting down resolutely on her bed. But then, for all her professional training, she could not say what she wanted to say or ask what she wanted to ask, and she ended up saying, Are you all right? And Anne, disarmed, had said, Yes, really, I'm fine, and her mother had smiled.

Louisa was smiling at her now, but not with relief or discomfort; Louisa was delighted to be meeting Anne's date and showing off her own. The other figure in the living room was Felice, wearing skintight scarlet overalls and a silver leotard. She was in full makeup, that is to say, she looked ready to step out on a stage, and she was drinking a bottle of celery soda.

"Well, look who's here," Louisa said in a tone of cheerful welcome.

"This is Jason," Anne said abruptly, wondering whether she had told Louisa the name of "the man at work" or whether Louisa would just think this was some random male.

"Hi there, Jason, I'm Louisa."

"And this is Felice," said Anne. Felice waved her bottle.

"This is Yuri," Louisa said, presenting the man beside her. "We've just had the most wonderful dinner, but I can't tell you what we ate because I'd pronounce all the names wrong. I was just so glad Yuri was there to order for me."

"The waiter was not French," Yuri protested. "What did it matter if you pronounced the names wrong? He knew you were an American." Yuri had a faint but detectable accent.

"I can't help it," Louisa said to Yuri, "I just get embarrassed in these really elegant places." She turned to Anne. "It was such a beautiful place too, you should have seen it."

"It sounds like you really went somewhere special," Jason put in, when no one else seemed disposed to say anything.

"Yuri chose it," Louisa said proudly.

"Louisa, you are too easy to impress," Yuri told her. "It was just a decent French restaurant."

"Then someday," said Louisa, undaunted, "you have to take me to a place that you think is special."

Yuri smiled at her with genuine fondness, or so it seemed to Anne; she was prepared to give him a little credit for that. It had seemed to her possible that he was just a somewhat unpresentable, somewhat lonely man who had happened across Louisa and discovered that in return for fairly simple dating behavior she was willing to sleep with him. But maybe Yuri liked Louisa, even if he didn't quite understand what she was.

"I think I better be going," Jason said softly, and Anne got up to see him to the door. He said good-bye to everyone and everyone said good-bye to him, and at the door, out of sight of the others, he put his arms around Anne and kissed her for a long time. And then he left and she stood in the hallway for a minute, feeling still a little stoned, feeling that this new life of hers was full of pleasures. Then she went back into the living room and saw the three of them sitting there, and she thought: Oh no, I am among strangers.

12. Gossiping

A telephone call from Kent. Anne was in the living room of her new apartment talking to Kent on the phone. She had taken Charlotte's advice and not called him, and now he had called her. It was after supper; Anne had eaten frozen eggplant parmigiana with Louisa, at Louisa's express invitation, and had then been sitting in her bare little room, wondering how to spend the rest of the evening, wishing Jason were coming again.

"Anne? It's me," the voice still so familiar, she wondered if it always would be.

"Hi. How are you?" She thought of saying, I'm glad you called, I thought about calling you yesterday, it's good to hear your voice. She didn't say it. Suppose he had called about a matter of business, think how silly she would feel.

"It's good to hear your voice, Anne. I feel sort of strange living here alone."

"I can imagine. I feel sort of strange here too."

"Alan called. I told him." This was a subject of constant mutual interest for Anne and Kent: who knew, who had been told.

"What did he say?" And that too of course.

"Oh, he was sort of upset." Kent sounded a little amused. "You know him. He said he was sure we could find a way to work it out, two really fine human beings like us." That was a little close to the bone, close to something which had probably crossed both their minds many times. To avoid remembering, they took refuge in laughing at Alan, which of course only consolidated them as a couple.

"Did he say anything about us being honest with each other?" Anne asked.

"Naturally. And he also said it was important to confront the really major issues."

"I guess we did that all right," Anne said, ending the joke. For the last several days she had found herself near tears every so often and now again she felt ready to cry. She held the phone tight and kept the tears back and waited for Kent to say something.

He was also silent for a little while. She thought of him sitting in their apartment, in his apartment, holding the phone. Finally he said, "Tell me how you're doing."

"Okay," Anne said, "really okay. Living here is very easy in a way, it isn't lonely, I feel sort of distracted. You know, I can't brood on my sorrows so much because there's Louisa and then there's this other roommate, Felice." Actually, she was saying all this so Kent wouldn't feel uncomfortable about keeping the apartment and most of the things in it while she set out into the world with her suitcases and a cardboard carton or two. He hadn't really believed that she preferred it that way; he, like Charlotte, had thought she was getting the worse deal.

"And Jason?" Kent said. It was a shock to hear Kent say the name, which had been mentioned only one time between them, a shock to realize he remembered it. Anne wondered if Kent thought they had already reached the stage of friendship where they could gossip with one another about their separate sex lives; she was quite sure they were nowhere near there yet. She thought it more likely that Kent was asking the question as a test for himself, a way of demonstrating to himself just once more that things were really over with Anne.

"Oh, okay." Anne was flustered, then angry at him for bringing it up. She said deliberately, "He was over here last night." She was sure that it would bother Kent to think that other people were now allowed to see Jason as her lover.

Sure enough, the next thing he said showed he had been thinking along precisely those lines. "Anne, did anyone know about you and him?" Kent seemed unable to say the name a second time. "I mean, before you told me?"

"Louisa did," Anne admitted. She felt a bit ashamed of this, but then, perversely, since she and Kent had actually broken up, officially because of her affair with Jason, she no longer felt it was a very bad thing to have told other people about the affair before she told Kent about it. She was sure that Kent would not like the idea, but she hoped he would remember that now that they were broken up he had no right to make her feel guilty about it. She decided to edit out the fact that she had told Charlotte as well— since Charlotte was someone Kent hardly knew, since her life didn't really touch his.

"Louisa," Kent repeated.

"Yes, I told Louisa about it. If it's any comfort, she was on your side all the way, she thought it was terrible for me to be doing such a thing to you." Anne felt the brittle quality of her own attempts at light speech.

"Terrific," Kent said, obviously also trying to be light but coming off as bitter.

Anne considered the possibility of asking about *his* love life, but she didn't think there was any friendly way to pursue this line of conversation. She hadn't really faced the thought of Kent with a new girlfriend and she skipped over it again, allowing herself a fleeting and contemptuous prediction: someone who worked at the bank, always dressed professionally, always neat and adult, the new-image girlfriend for the new-image Kent.

"Alan invited me to have dinner at their house," Kent said after a pause. "I think we're going to find out about having friends who invite one of us at a time—you know, it's another one of the classic things about divorce."

"Well, Alan and Margie are really *your* friends," Anne pointed out. She had no desire at all for her own separate invitation to dinner, with maybe a young man one of them wanted her to meet. Or at the very least with a long and very "honest" talk about what had gone wrong between her and Kent and how she was doing now on her own. "It's very rewarding," she could hear herself saying inanely to Alan, over and over.

"They think of you as a friend too, especially after you found Curtis in the woods."

"What did you tell them was the reason we broke up?" Anne asked. By common if unspoken agreement, Anne and Kent were generally not telling people that the reason they had broken up was that Anne was sleeping with someone else. Neither of them wanted to cast Kent as the furious cuckold, which was odd, Anne thought, since that was in fact the role he had chosen to play. Still, it seemed more dignified for both of them to keep that relatively private. But Anne assumed Kent would confide in his really close friends, and she thought the Saltzbergs, or at least Margie, might fit into that category. And if he had told them, Anne wanted to know it. She wanted to know what people knew about her.

"Just that things weren't working out. He didn't ask if there was, you know, how shall I put it—"

"Someone else."

"Exactly, he didn't ask if there was someone else. Margie will, though. And if it's okay with you—"

"Sure, go ahead and tell her. I don't mind." It was a little absurd, Anne thought, to be gossiping like this with Kent about the details of their own separation. She tried to summon up the willpower to end the conversation, but she knew she couldn't do it. She wanted it to drag on for hours, wanted to hold on to Kent across the wire. She did not want to go back into her room, to try to read—to let aimlessness and boredom send her knocking on Louisa's door for the talk about Jason which she had sensed coming since the night before. After Jason had gone home, Louisa and Yuri had disappeared into Louisa's room. Anne did not really want to be asked for her opinion of Yuri now, and she didn't really want to hear Louisa's opinion of Jason, and yet she could imagine herself knocking on Louisa's door, sitting down on Louisa's bed. In fact, it seemed almost inevitable—as soon as she got off the phone.

"So what else is new?" Anne asked, exaggeratedly casual accents to make it a joke.

"I've started learning Hebrew," Kent said.

"Hebrew? Are you planning to change your religion?"

"It's very easy if you know Arabic."

Anne was thinking that if only he had started learning a new language a few weeks ago maybe none of this would ever have happened. She dismissed the thought, silly, trivial.

"Are you studying it all on your own?"

"Yes, but I may take a class. I don't know, I've been feeling a little bit at a loss in the evenings, you know."

"Yes. I know." Silly of her not to have thought of this: Kent, feeling lonely, would not plunge into some unappealing love affair. He would not hang around at the houses of his coupled-off friends complaining about Anne. He would start studying a new language, maybe start taking classes. But he wouldn't take the classes as a way to meet people, he would take them to learn the language. Anne was impressed.

There was another pause. It had been a conversation full of pauses, the two of them taking comfort even in the faint breathing noises: contact, connection. Anne waited for Kent to find the strength to end the conversation. He said nothing. She surprised herself: "I guess it's silly for us to just sit over the phone all night," she said.

"Yes, I know. It is. I just——" His voice broke slightly.

"Me too," Anne said, and began to cry in earnest.

"Anne!" Kent said suddenly, excitedly, and she was terrified; he was about to take the risk, propose that he come over, tell her it was all a mistake.

She cut him off: "Now I'm crying. I can't talk. I'll talk to you soon." And, amazed at herself, she hung up the phone. She was sure it would ring again immediately, he would call back to continue the conversation—but he didn't. He had more self-control than that, of course. And Anne went into the bathroom and washed her face and stood a minute until she was sure the tears were over before going to knock on Louisa's door.

13. Dormitory

Felice's life was dominated by her ambition. Felice wanted to be a fashion model. Louisa explained to Anne that Felice fit every one of the body measurements that models were supposed to fit: height, weight, chest size, leg length, all the rest of it. She was from a small town in New Jersey where she had passed through high school in theatrical makeup, in clothes too high-fashion to be considered attractive, in spike heels which had emphasized the height that made her so ineligible as a prom date. She had borne it all with serenity, carrying within her always the certainty of her vocation. She had finished high school, moved to New York, enrolled in several modeling courses, put together an extensive and ever-changing portfolio, and found a job in the secretarial pool of an advertising agency.

Felice was twenty years old. She spent every penny of her salary and more; checks arrived regularly from her parents in New Jersey who owned a hardware store and rarely ventured into New York.

"I have to make the investment now," she had explained to Anne, displaying four new pink jars which together contained a revolutionary skin care and rejuvenation program. "It's all going to pay off later. It would be silly to be stingy at this point, just when it's really important."

According to Louisa, Felice was chaste in her devotion to her calling; her evenings were spent with her clothes or her pink bottles or her beauty books, and all this effort was not in any way aimed at admirers, dates, lovers.

"You mean she never goes out?" Anne asked.

"Oh, once in a while. You'll see. There are these really weird *old* men who take her out sometimes."

"How old?"

"You know, like fifty."

"And does she sleep with them?"

"No, never. She just has dinner or goes to a show and then comes home."

Everything Felice did seemed to Anne to have an odd sort of decision about it. She never hesitated; even her most bizarre combinations of clothing were apparently thoroughly rehearsed in her head, and she wore them confidently, as if cameras were clicking all around her. Louisa was heavily influenced by this certainty of Felice's; for all that Louisa found Felice a little bit strange, she never doubted for a minute that Felice would eventually succeed in her chosen profession and she used this future success of Felice's to justify all current eccentricities. Louisa, it seemed, had also dreamed of being a model when she had been an adolescent, she had read magazine articles on the life of a model, articles which forever ended her own dreams by revealing those lists of ideal measurements which fit Felice as surely as they totally failed to fit Louisa. Anne herself had never dreamed of fashion modeling; that presumably reflected the difference, or one of the differences, between her own vaguely hippy adolescence and Louisa's wholesome high school career.

Anne, like Louisa, was infected with Felice's sense of destiny. There was something comforting about Felice's single-mindedness. It even made Anne feel more of a scientist, as if she were responding to the example of someone for whom a chosen career dominated every moment of the day. Felice, in the end, was fun to live with, and, though she was much younger than Anne or Louisa, Anne never felt the least bit protective of her the way she sometimes did of Louisa. Felice was someone who within her obsession could take care of herself.

Anne was fascinated by Felice at dinnertime, chomping down her meal, a tablespoon of store-bought tabbouleh, a small pineapple yogurt, and three bell peppers cut carefully into slices. Felice devoured her food and then left the room, sometimes with the announcement that she couldn't bear to sit and watch the other two eat poison.

Anne had, without meaning to, been absorbed into Louisa's evening meals. Louisa shopped for two and cooked for them both, allowing Anne to pay her for the food but never allowing her to help with the preparations, insisting that it was no more work to cook for two than for one and that she enjoyed the company at supper. Anne knew that Louisa was trying to nurse her through the separation. Not that Louisa could cook. She joked about how she would have to learn before she got married. She claimed to have two or three company menus she could prepare, but otherwise she relied on frozen food and things that didn't really take any knowledge—minute steaks, hamburgers premolded into patties. Anne and Kent had eaten a great deal more erratically; Anne could not remember the last time she had had such a succession of "balanced" meals, nor such a succession of tasteless ones.

Anne remembered her own mother as a rather erratic cook, surprisingly so, given her generally competent and organized approach to life. It had occurred to Anne that her mother's style of cooking had probably developed during all those years that she and her husband had spent without children. It was a cooking style which suited them both, a great deal of meat, very simply prepared, often grilled almost black, accompanied by anything at all—sometimes by an odd assortment of vegetables (an ear of corn and some radishes), sometimes only by French fries from the diner. When Anne moved in with her aunt and uncle, she began, for the first time in her life, to eat carefully planned balanced meals, several things arranged on the plate, each representing important nutrients. Her Aunt Letitia was a better cook than Louisa, but still, Anne sometimes thought she recognized this sensation of having gone from unpredictable and interesting meals to the four basic food groups incarnate. When I live with people who really matter to me, Anne thought, we eat eccentrically. But when I move in with my quote-unquote family, with my relatives, it becomes much healthier and much less interesting. And she felt somehow relieved to have identified a pattern, even if it made no particular sense.

When Louisa went to answer the phone, Anne contemplated sliding her minute steak into the garbage. What stopped her was less a feeling that it would be wasteful than a suspicion that Louisa would somehow discover it.

Louisa came back from the phone, radiant. "Jim wants to see me tomorrow night," she reported.

It turned out that Jim had a proposal for Louisa. Not a Proposal, not marriage, but a proposal. Louisa came back from their meeting around eight o'clock and promptly knocked on Anne's door. Anne had just washed her hair, wishing that the shower produced a spray as intense and satisfying as the shower in the apartment she had shared with Kent. She was sitting on her bed in a large teeshirt and a pair of underpants. Louisa, in a tan linen suit and a light pink blouse with a ruffle up the front, sat in the chair and looked puzzled. Jim's proposal was this: He wanted to start "seeing" Louisa again, but he wanted it to be on the clear understanding that they were both "seeing" other people as well. He wanted, he told Louisa, to "play by her rules." He was not willing to accept promises that this time she would be faithful, he was not interested in being the only man in her life. If she wanted a relationship of that sort, she could count him out. He had decided to adopt New York customs.

Anne's reaction was complicated. On the one hand, she still thought Jim sounded like an A-number-one turkey. On the other hand, there did seem to be a disconcerting perspective from which he and Louisa paralleled herself and Kent. Suppose Kent had made that same proposal when she told him about Jason?

"So, what do you think?" she asked Louisa cautiously.

As usual, Louisa managed to be just a tiny bit unpredictable while still being utterly true to herself. "I really think that since I'm the one who destroyed his trust, it's up to me to help him learn to trust again."

What all this country-cousin sincerity added up to, Anne reflected, was that Louisa was going to manage to get Jim back and also keep Yuri, and she was going to do it all with a sense of noble self-sacrifice. She, Anne, had meanwhile managed to lose one of her two men—and she felt guilty into the bargain. Obviously she had managed things wrong.

"And are you going to be involved with other people?"

"Well . . . I don't want to hurt Yuri's feelings."

"And besides," Anne said, "he's good in bed, right?"

Louisa just nodded and looked worried. "I can tell *you*," she said, "I can't talk about this very easily, but that was sort of a problem between me and Jim."

"Really?"

Louisa nodded again. "I fell bad about it because I know it shouldn't be important, but it sort of was."

"For heaven's sake, why shouldn't it be important?"

"Well, I have so much in common with Jim, it seems silly to make a big thing out of one little problem."

"What is he, impotent? Or just not very good?"

"Oh no, he isn't impotent." Louisa paused. She didn't seem to know what words to use. Finally she said, "It's sort of the opposite."

"The opposite of what?"

"Of impotent. He just . . . it's all over very fast. Sometimes before we, you know."

"Oh, right," Anne said. She wondered if giving it a name would make it easier for Louisa to talk about it. "That's called premature ejaculation."

Louisa accepted Anne's scientific authority. She seemed relieved to have the "problem" taken so seriously, given a name.

"I mean, I don't even know if he knows it's a problem. I mean, he always has orgasms, so I don't know if he thinks there's anything wrong."

"He probably knows it's a problem. He'd probably be relieved to discuss it. You could help him, you know, help him satisfy you other ways and that would make him feel better about it." Talking to Louisa, Anne felt shy about using any of the words or phrases that would have come naturally talking to Charlotte or to any other friend. Instead she was talking like a sex manual.

Louisa, on the other hand, did not seem the least bit ill at ease. She seemed fascinated. "Do you really think he'd like to talk about it?"

"Louisa, he has to know that things aren't perfect in bed, doesn't he? I mean, he must realize that you don't have an orgasm or whatever." Or whatever what? Anne was not sure what she meant, but Louisa was nodding.

"Well, sometimes I pretend to. And I'm not really good at talking about sex with men."

"I know what you mean," Anne said. Actually, she had never been as embarrassed talking to a man as she was talking to Louisa.

"What about Jason? I mean sexually?" Louisa was evidently determined to get some sort of return for her frankness.

Anne decided to try to be the swinger Louisa evidently wanted her to be. "He drives me crazy. I think he may be, sexually, the best I've ever had. It's just phenomenal."

"And Kent?" According to Louisa's rules, Anne knew, the man you stayed with for years should be "the best"; it was in fact for this reason that Louisa was so concerned about Jim's problem—how could she picture the two of them eventually settling down together if she couldn't even pretend that he was good in bed?

"Kent was fine. Sometimes better than fine. But I think maybe I changed sexually, you know, during my time with Kent, and Jason somehow just fit in with the changes." She wondered why she was trying to explain this to Louisa. She had not really tried to explain it to Charlotte, with whom she could discuss Jason in a simple locker-room sort of way.

Charlotte would never ask, as Louisa did next, "But doesn't it make any difference to you whether you're in love or not?"

"Look at you, you aren't in love with Yuri, are you?"

"I don't think so," Louisa said, in such a way that Anne was sure that if Jim had not suddenly reentered the picture, Louisa would have been about ready to declare herself in love with Yuri. Anne felt suddenly very impatient. She said something which under normal circumstances she would never have said to Louisa; she might have said it to Charlotte, to amuse her, or to some man or other who deserved it, to irritate him.

"Louisa, do you know why men made up all that nonsense about how much difference it makes to women whether they're in love or not? In bed, I mean. A man is a lousy lay, a woman doesn't enjoy it, everyone pretends that the problem is that she isn't in love. Men just can't stand to admit how much difference their own talents make."

Louisa was smiling a gently patronizing smile. "Are you trying to shock me? I know you aren't serious."

Anne, who had in fact been trying to shock a little, who hadn't been entirely serious, felt suddenly that she believed every word she had said.

Louisa kicked off her shoes, gray high-heeled pumps, and massaged one foot. Then she stood and reached up her skirt to peel off her panty hose. She dropped them in a little rolled-up heap next to the shoes.

"God, that feels good," she said, "those are too tight for me." Then she took off first her blazer and then her skirt, putting each down neatly on the table. In her ruffled pink shirt and her white nylon slip—a riot of femininity—Louisa sat down again. The single bed, the two of them half-undressed, even the feeling in the air that boys were being discussed, compared, analyzed, again gave Anne the strong sense that she was in a college dormitory.

"I think you really do care about Jason more than you realize," Louisa said thoughtfully.

Anne shrugged. She was not willing to let other people talk her into making Jason a grand passion—not Louisa, not Kent, not anyone. "He's okay," she said, deliberately callous.

"Now, I don't think you mean that the way it sounds. Are you worried that he's only interested in you sexually, is that it?"

Anne was, not for the first time in her life, left a little breathless by the progression of Louisa's thoughts. "I was just telling you, Louisa, that's why I'm interested in him. Why should he be different?"

"Is he involved with someone else?"

"He lives with his girlfriend." Anne felt defensive; she saw before it actually appeared the sympathetic understanding expression on Louisa's face. Anne pushed on, "It's probably better that way, don't you think? It makes it much less likely he'll get emotionally involved with me."

Suddenly, unaccountably, Louisa got up and came over to the bed. She sat down beside Anne and opened her arms and Anne found herself, her head on Louisa's pink shoulder, giving way to the tears that still took her over periodically. Louisa said nothing, only hugged her and patted her back and sat there smelling of perfume.

"I'm getting you all wet," Anne said finally, realizing that her hair, still wet from being washed, was trailing down into Louisa's ruffles. Louisa produced a Kleenex and Anne gratefully blew her nose, then wiped her eyes on the hem of her teeshirt. "I'm sorry," she said.

"Don't be silly." Louisa did not seem the least bit bothered by Anne's tears. "Here you've been giving me advice and helping me when you're the one going through a bad time."

"Hey in there!" Felice called from the hall outside Anne's door. "Can I come in for a minute?"

Felice wore white silk pants which ended just below her knees and a tube top of red and gold fibers. On her feet were red spike-heeled sandals with thin gold ankle straps. Her shoulder-length dark hair was swept back with rhinestone combs.

"Going on a picnic?" Anne asked before she could stop herself.

"That's exactly what I wanted to ask," Felice said, pivoting expertly to show them the rear view. "Is this effective country clothing, or does it look too city?"

"Aren't the heels a little high for a picnic?" Louisa said, seriously.

"But still, they're sandals," Felice argued.

"It looks very comfortable," Anne said, suddenly missing Kent more distinctly than she had in days. He would never be able to appreciate this without having seen it, and she would never be able to describe it so as to do it justice.

"Are you going on a picnic, Felice?" Louisa asked.

Felice seemed taken aback. "Huh? Oh no, I just wanted to see if these pieces would work together for a picnic look."

"God, you're so tan already," Louisa said.

"Sunlamps and bronzing gel," Felice said absently. She was examining her face in Anne's small mirror. "The thing is, you have to imagine these colors under direct sunlight," she said, more to herself than to her audience.

"You're so lucky to be tall and thin," Louisa said, with easy generosity. "You can wear just about anything, can't you?"

"Yes," Felice said. She seemed distant and rapt, as if disclaiming responsibility for some terrifying talent. "Most kinds of clothes look right on a long figure."

"You're lucky," Louisa said again, and Anne realized with a rush of affection for her cousin that Louisa was not at all interested in any of this. She was interested in clothes and dressing nicely, but in a personal, small-scale way. She was taking part in this conversation only for Felice's sake. Anne wondered whether Felice's professionalism was real, that is, whether the ridiculous things she said were at least the right ridiculous things to say.

"Thanks," Felice said in a dreamy voice, and drifted out of the room.

"She's already planning her next outfit," Lousia said softly. "Well, I guess I should be getting along too. I've taken up enough of your time telling you my troubles."

"No, really, I've enjoyed talking to you. I'll be interested to see how things work out."

"You mean with Jim."

"And Yuri."

"Oh, Yuri. That could never be important."

"Physicists," Anne said, her tone suggesting that there was no more to be said.

"You're a scientist too, so don't go being superior." Louisa gathered up her various articles of clothing, kissed Anne on the cheek, and went off to her room.

Perhaps, Anne thought, I should change the way I dress. There are times when any change is good, just for the sake of change, and perhaps there is progress to be made as well.

14. Second Generation

There were a number of similarities that Anne and Charlotte had detected in their pasts. Both Anne's uncle and Charlotte's father were scientists. And both had been married to women who were distinctly not scientists, though Charlotte's mother had been much more involved in her husband's work than Anne's aunt. Further, Charlotte and Anne were the only children from their respective family groups to go into science. Charlotte's sisters had never had professions. Anne's two cousins, older than she, had both moved to California, where the girl was a real estate dealer and the boy a somewhat itinerant carpenter.

Anne and Charlotte were therefore both "favorite children" in one sense. True, Charlotte was counted a failure for not having married and reproduced, and true, Anne was only a child by late adoption, but still, the bond was there. Anne's uncle was clearly disappointed in his own children, clearly eager to keep up ties with Anne, who was spending her time doing something that he considered worthwhile. Charlotte's father grilled her occasionally about her lab techniques, about what journals she was following. He enjoyed correcting her, but it was clear he also enjoyed hearing the language of his own profession coming from the mouth of his daughter. She knew that he boasted about her to his colleagues. Anne knew that her Uncle Douglas did the same.

But given this parallel between their lives, Anne and Charlotte were conscious of a very distinct divergence. When Anne had left her uncle's home and gone to college, as she had gone further into genetics and therefore learned more and more about the hierarchy and the patterns of academic science, she had come to realize that her uncle was a fairly distinguished man, not the world's most famous physicist, not a blazing star, but a very respectable and respected man, a man worth studying with, a man who regularly produced "good science." Charlotte, on the other hand, had always assumed that her father was a very important chemist, but when she began learning the ropes, just like Anne, she discovered that her father was pretty much a zero in the eyes of his world. His very occasional publications were in unimportant journals and were nothing but exhaustively fussy detail work of no interest to anyone.

Anne and Charlotte felt that there was something significant about being second-generation scientists. It was an important parallel. Anne had wondered, Would she have gone into science if her own parents had lived, if she had never gone to live with a scientist uncle whom she had ended up pleasing so thoroughly with her choice of career? That has nothing to do with it, she told herself, but not Charlotte. Charlotte would have been too interested. Charlotte was too ready to consider the implications of scientist fathers, scientist uncles. And then, they had both grown up watching women who in one way or another rejected science. Charlotte's mother, of course, did not openly express anything but admiration for the research she helped along, but for her what mattered were her children and the books she read.

Anne's Aunt Letitia had dissociated herself much more thoroughly from her husband's work. She went so far as to make fun of it occasionally, to him and to other people. She was, Anne had decided in retrospect, a somewhat cynical and even perhaps abrasive woman. Anne sometimes found herself identifying with her aunt, even though in her choice of profession she had so allied herself with her uncle. When she found in herself what she suspected was an entirely inappropriate detachment, when she felt an inner callousness which had to be hidden, Anne thought of her Aunt Letitia. During Anne's adolescence, Letitia had not held a job. Instead, like Charlotte's mother, she had ranged herself with the forces of culture. She had patronized the symphony, chamber music concerts, art museums, and so on, always alone or with a female friend.

More recently, with all her children long gone, Letitia had decided to go into business. With two other women she had set up a boutique which sold elegant and expensive lingerie. They had done fabulous business from the start, and now had branched out, putting together a glossy mail-order catalogue of their lace-trimmed goodies. Anne's aunt had just sent her a copy, along with a little note inviting her to choose anything she liked within reason. Neither her Aunt Letitia nor her Uncle Douglas seemed an easy person to live with; Anne thought that either would have done better married to someone more compliant—someone with a personality more like Charlotte's mother. And yet, Aunt Letitia and Uncle Douglas survived together, perhaps partially because their ostentatious lack of interest in each other's interests gave them the necessary freedom. And they had even blossomed over the past few years. To go with her new business, Aunt Letitia had taken to expensive suits and fairly elaborate jewelry. And her manner had gone from disconcerting cynicism to a businesslike hard-bitten humor. In the meantime, her husband had also found a new interest. He had decided to write a book for nonscientists about the physics of space travel; he thought it would find a ready market in the enormous numbers of people who went to see space movies. It was not exactly his field, and he had never written anything except scientific articles for scientific journals. It had taken him over two years to research and write the book.

A few weeks after the catalogue came for her aunt, Anne received a note from her uncle, along with a Xerox of an ad for his book in *Publishers Weekly*. The book was finally on the point of publication and her uncle would be in New York to do publicity sometime in the near future and he looked forward to seeing her. The note had been sent to the old apartment; Anne had not yet told her aunt and uncle that she had moved. She had not told them that she no longer lived with Kent. They knew Kent; he and Anne had spent several vacations in Chicago during graduate school.

When Kent called to tell her that there was this letter from Chicago, he suggested they have dinner together. Anne suspected he was testing himself, proving that he could see her and then let her go without pain, and she was sure that he was rushing things. They had been living apart for less than three weeks, and already he thought he was ready for casual friendship. They ate in a would-be French restaurant on the East Side, not far from Anne's new apartment. The place was somewhere between quiche-and-salad and continental cuisine, uninteresting food, but Anne and Kent drank quite a bit of the house wine. Anne told him about Felice and all her outfits. Kent was a wonderful audience; his laughter recalled to Anne the laughter she had suppressed at each of the moments she was describing to him. By the end of dinner, Anne and Kent were both nearly hysterical.

Kent asked for the check. There was a pause. Then Anne said in an irritated tone of voice, "This is the thing I never understood about breaking up with someone."

"What is?" Kent asked. His voice was tender, maybe a little bit suggestive.

"How all your feelings are supposed to change overnight. Doesn't it seem that whenever we see each other there'll always be this feeling of why not just jump into bed for old time's sake?"

"Well," Kent said softly, "why not?"

Anne nodded. "I know," she said. "I've known all evening. But it still doesn't make sense." She pulled out her wallet and they split the check.

Anne was grateful that neither of her roommates was in evidence when she took Kent to her room. She watched his glance flick over the bedspread and was overwhelmingly glad to have him there, to have him noticing the strawberries and probably guessing immediately that Louisa had picked out the pattern. They made love, awkwardly at first because of the combination of familiarity and newness, but they got past the awkwardness and had a good time, though there was some sense that they were trying to impress each other. The real rush of familiarity for Anne came afterward, lying in his arms. Kent was familiar, his arms were familiar, only the room which was supposed to be her room was strange. Kent began to talk about his Hebrew classes; he had found a Zionist organization that offered Sunday morning classes down on Third Avenue. The classes were designed for people who were planning to emigrate to Israel. Kent was pleased with the whole setup. He was already fairly comfortable with this completely new alphabet, and he was delighted with the grammatical structure of the language.

"Anne?" Louisa knocked on the door and started to turn the handle.

"I'm not alone!" Anne shouted, panicking absurdly. Absurd or not, Kent had also reacted as if they had been caught; he was getting dressed even as Louisa apologized profusely and released the door handle. Anne dressed too. It was a convincing demonstration of how much things had actually changed, the fact that Kent was now going home for the night. Jason had also gone home after they made love, Anne reflected. She had not spent the night in bed with someone in a while. She remembered how she and Jason had gotten up, dressed, sauntered out into the living room. Now Anne was embarrassed to be producing Kent. Sure enough, Louisa was on the couch in the living room, and sure enough, Yuri and Felice were there too. It really was a parody, if not a direct repeat.

"Kent!" Louisa squealed, her delight at seeing him and her surprise both clear in her voice. Kent went over and kissed her cheek and then, to Anne's immense relief, said he'd be going. Anne let him out; he left without a kiss or even a word of affection.

"Anne, I can't believe it, I never thought for a minute you had Kent in there with you," Louisa began.

"Well, why the fuck not?" Anne tried to sound humorous but knew it came out irritated. "I lived with the guy for years, didn't I? One fuck more or less isn't going to cause any earthquakes."

"Very true," Yuri put in, looking at Anne with amusement and perhaps some lasciviousness too.

"See?" Louisa said to Yuri. "I told you Anne is very honest."

Anne wondered why on earth they had been discussing her and

what they had been saying. And what did honesty have to do with anything? Louisa's thought processes seemed so often just tantalizingly beyond the very edge of the comprehensible.

"You see, Louisa, I was telling you so. Your cousin is realistic. She is a scientist." He paused to smile at Anne, but she couldn't tell whether he was smiling at her to reassure her that he didn't mean what he was saying or to reassure her that he did. "She does not confuse relationships and sex."

Louisa was clearly embarrassed. Anne was more than a little embarrassed herself. Felice, who was not in the least embarrassed, came to the rescue.

"It seems to me," she said, in that voice which could only be from New Jersey, "it seems to me that it's really dumb to think that has anything to do with being a scientist."

"Scientists," Anne said, loud in her relief, "are generally very lousy at dealing with people." She felt she owed Yuri a poke. "Physicists are generally the worst, except maybe for mathematicians."

Yuri grinned at her. "Maybe it is true," he said. "Maybe scientists feel they have better things to do."

"What could be better, I mean more important, than your relationships?" Louisa asked. "I think that's a terrible thing to say."

Again Felice put in a statement. "Relationships aren't all that important to a lot of people," she said. "They just don't go around saying it. Especially not in front of the people they're having relationships with." This was said to no one in particular. Anne could not figure out whether Felice was coming to Louisa's defense or, in fact, stating her own credo. Felice, after all, was the one who didn't get involved with men.

"I did not mean to cause any offense," Yuri said seriously, taking it as a reprimand. Then he was teasing again. "I was speaking theoretically."

"Oh, you scientists!" Louisa moaned at him, picking up her cue.

Anne reflected not for the first time that she really couldn't see Yuri's appeal. She watched him, sitting on the couch, tickling the back of Louisa's neck. There was something vaguely distasteful about him. He was not a person Anne would have wanted to touch. Or to have touching her, that slyly proprietary neck-tickling. It was hard to believe that he really scored lots of points for sexual peformance.

It occurred to Anne, suddenly, that Louisa might be trying to compete with her. She felt foolish for not having thought of it before. When Anne had been living with Kent, Louisa had visibly enjoyed telling both of them about each new man, each new love. Even though all her stories had been couched in the most senti-mental language imaginable, Louisa had still been allowed to feel herself the adventurous one, the woman with the sophisticated sex life. Anne, for all that she might have been an object of envy, was solidly settled. She never had a new story to tell—at least, not until she had Jason. And now Anne, like Louisa, was on her own and liable to pop out of her bedroom with either Kent or Jason or maybe even someone else. Did Louisa feel threatened?

Well, she'd better get used to it, Anne thought, I may be em-barking on a very promiscuous period. The thought surprised her, even shocked her a little. And yet she felt she would have been re-ceptive, right at that moment, to any reasonably attractive man. Her pre-Kent past was not full of one-night stands. She would al-ways have said if she were not with Kent she would probably not have a wildly active social life; she would have predicted herself at most involved in one friendly and fairly casual affair. That had been her pattern before Kent. In fact, that had been the origin of her relationship with Kent.

Yuri and Louisa continued to banter in their odd unharmonious way. Anne listened, trying to decide whether Louisa's heart was in it. She looked over at Felice, tan pants that seemed to be made of burlap, very wide gold belt, canary-yellow silk blouse.

Why did she stay in the room with the three of them, Anne asked herself, why sit around taking stock of Felice's clothes and analyzing Louisa's relationship with Yuri? Anne knew why and knew she was reluctant to admit it: She did not want to go into her room and read. The evening was almost over; everyone would very soon go off to bed, together or alone, but still Anne couldn't face the remaining interval between evening and sleep. She could read, she could write a letter, she could wash out some clothes. But she couldn't, really, she had to stay in the living room and ward off loneliness. It had not gone away yet, the loneliness of not living with Kent. The evening was menaced by empty spaces which would somehow have been full if Kent had been in the apartment. Not because she and Kent would necessarily have been talking to each other or doing something together, but because there would have been a sort of domestic serenity in the air. She knew that she ought to go into her room and construct her own solitary serenity, but she found herself unable to abandon the sound of other voices.

Yuri was asking Anne a question, the same blend of complicity and suggestiveness in his voice as before. Was it flirtation? Was it something more? "Have you ever had a scientist for a boyfriend?" he asked.

"No," Anne said, automatically bringing out one of her stock lines, "I'm never attracted to scientists."

Yuri laughed and raised his eyebrows, and Louisa, delighted, put a fine mock severity into her voice and said to Anne, "That isn't a very polite thing to say."

"No, I told you, your cousin is a very realistic person. She watches herself as if she were trying to figure out the laws which govern her. And so she watches, she accumulates data, she comes to a theory: She is never attracted to scientists. And she will stay with that theory, unless of course"—he shot Anne a very distinct knowing leer—"unless of course she should come across some piece of information which conflicts with her theory."

"Well, I think that's terrible, talking about relationships and who you fall in love with like some sort of scientific experiment," Louisa said. She was still teasing.

Anne ignored her and answered Yuri. "I've gone even further than that. You think I've just been observing correlations, but I've gone as far as cause and effect."

"Ah, well then, perhaps your theory is unshakable," he said with fake courtesy.

"What on earth do you two mean?" asked Louisa, who was perhaps finally beginning to detect the undercurrents. "Correlations! Cause and effect! Whatever are you two talking about?"

"She means," Yuri translated, before Anne could, "that it is not just that she has noticed that the men she is attracted to are not scientists and that, as it happens, when she meets a scientist she is not attracted. That is not the whole story. She has also established to her own satisfaction that it is specifically the scientist in a man which makes him unattractive to her." He turned to Anne. "I have not distorted your meaning?"

"No," Anne said, feeling bored with the conversation, irritated with herself for getting drawn into it. "That's what I meant."

I5. Pink Ruffles

Louisa was giving a dinner party. Anne had been listening to her plan it for more than a week, listening but not registering the details. She had agreed to come and to invite Jason, and he had accepted, and beyond that, Anne nodded and murmured as Louisa talked about chicken Kiev and seating arrangements, and Louisa's words made a pleasant enough background while Anne thought about other things. Her work, for example. She was really coming to the end of this old project. A week or two at the most and she would have no excuse for working on it anymore. And yet she was reluctant to leave it. She knew that her reward for the good work she had done was to be a part of a very big project just gearing up; Richie Grossman had not even settled yet on the complete roster of researchers. He had been hinting about it and calling people into his office for conferences—Richie enjoyed managerial intrigue, Anne thought. Anne understood some of the details of the project—office rumors were active—and she felt very unenthusiastic. It would drag on for years and years, and very likely lead to nothing at all, it was an attempt to compete with much bigger companies which might easily leave Viatech far behind. It involved an ambitious attempt on several different lines of antibody production, attempts to produce synthetic versions of the specific substances made by the human body to fight off disease. The project would mean working closely with heaven only knew which scientists, and she rather glumly felt that it might irritate her and bore her and, if it went wrong, make her look bad without giving her enough scientific independence to make herself shine even against a lackluster project.

Louisa was giving a dinner party and it was the hottest day they had had all spring. It had been a fairly mild June so far, but that Saturday seemed to carry in it a foretaste of the muggiest dog days of summer. Anne sat on Felice's bed, the two of them listening to the sounds of Louisa's energetic preparations; all day she had refused their help while she cleaned and cooked.

Felice had resolutely refused to invite a date to the party, insisting she had no one to ask, so it was just Anne and Jason, Felice alone, and of course, Louisa and Jim. The party was in fact, Anne suspected, some kind of formalization of Louisa's rather confused relationship with Jim; why else would Louisa be going to so much trouble to make dinner for her roommates and a couple of boyfriends? But Louisa was unsettled because she was in love with Jim, yet still carrying on with Yuri, because everything seemed to be drifting and no one had called out that it was time to stop, break up, or to pledge true love, promise fidelity, get married. She was in love with Jim, but frequently even her Friday and Saturday night dates were with Yuri. This dinner party, Anne thought, was some equivalent of bringing Jim home to meet the family. He would come to dinner and then he would be her official boyfriend.

"Have you met Jim?" Anne asked Felice. Anne herself had rather actively avoided it, and perhaps he had also not wanted to be shown off—but then why had he agreed to the dinner party?

Felice shrugged. "He has very thick arms," she said.

Felice's room was total chaos; clothes and magazines and cosmetics and makeup brushes covered the floor and even the bed, except for the little corner where Anne sat. Anne wondered, did Felice sleep among her possessions or did she dump them off every night and then reaccumulate them over the course of the day. Felice herself was idly considering a set of fingernail decals. It made Anne feel cheered and comforted to watch her, proof that life was not so serious.

"Want to lend me a dress to wear tonight?" Anne asked, without really thinking about it.

Felice did not seem surprised to be asked. She considered Anne carefully for a minute, then removed from her closet a pink dress made of gauzy chiffonlike material. It had a very low neckline with a ruffle around it that fluffed out over Anne's breasts, then it went in at the waist and finally there was a tier of ruffles at the bottom. Anne was surprised that it fit her; surely it could not also fit the incredibly emaciated Felice. Anne stared at herself in the full-length mirror. It was a very pink dress, by no means pastel. To Anne it suggested the South, garden parties. It turned out that she and Felice wore the same size shoes, and Felice insisted that Anne borrow a pair of high-heeled white sandals. Then she arranged the front of Anne's hair in a small tight bun on one side of her head and teased the back part so that it fell in wisps over Anne's back and shoulders. Last of all she produced tiny pink rosebud earrings which dangled from the ears on tiny gold chains.

Felice stood back and regarded her handiwork. "Things that are tight on top but loose from the waist down are good for you," she said. "Also, the weight of the ruffle gives the skirt some shape so it doesn't just seem to be following your ass. And your face can handle having some of the hair pulled away from it. It would be better if you'd let me do your makeup."

"No, really," Anne said, "I wouldn't be comfortable with a lot of makeup on. This is enough for me to try and carry off."

"Okay," Felice said, "the important thing is for everyone to develop their own individual style."

Anne thanked her enthusiastically for the dress and the shoes and the hairdo and the earrings and the advice, and escaped to her own room where she spent a little while regretting the impulse that had led her to ask Felice. She was half convinced that she was about to make a terrible fool of herself. Anne was to be aware all night that she was absurdly conscious of everyone's clothing, everyone's appearance. It came from her own self-consciousness; she knew she didn't look normal, she knew everyone must be noticing the way she looked, so, obsessively, she noticed them back. First, as she came into the living room, before Jason and Jim had arrived, she noticed Louisa. Louisa looked sweet and round and whole-some. She had on a flowered dress, little blue and yellow flowers against a light green background, round puffed sleeves and a blue sash, like a child's party dress. Her blond curls were held back from her face on either side by enameled barrettes. Anne thought, She really is dressed to present her boyfriend to her family, you can see her, hoping they'll approve, hoping they won't be too hard on him. And then she remembered herself with Jason, coming out of the bedroom and feeling like Louisa's delinquent daughter, and thought, Well, we all have to be all things to each other.

Next to Louisa, Anne felt large and extremely ostentatious. You bring the guy home to meet the family, she thought, and the family turns out to be more than a little weird. She reassured herself with the thought that Felice would surely be even more osten-tatious. And taller, if not exactly larger.

Felice came into the living room where Anne and Louisa were sitting, waiting with a rather palpable nervousness for the guests to arrive. Well, Anne thought, if Auntie Anne is weird, Auntie Felice is from another planet. Poor Jim. Felice wore one of her skintight jumpsuits, this one with a tigerskin print. It ended right above the breasts, and around her neck was an enormous gold col-lar. There were similar wide bands of gold around her lower arms, her gold sandals added at least four inches to her height, and two gold knitting needles protruded from the tight bun of hair on the top of her head. She looked like a warrior from some comic-book tribe. At any moment she might pull a needle out of her hair and charge. Watch your step, Jim. The three of us, Anne thought, would make quite a group photo. "At Home With the New York Career Girls, or, Finding Your Own Style."

Anne was tremendously glad to see Jason. She kissed him and hugged him and checked out his clothes; she had warned him that people were going to dress up for this party and he had risen to the occasion with, of all things, a blue-and-white-striped seersucker suit. And he looked wonderful; he had the height and the grace to carry it off. And they looked good together too, Anne thought with some relief; the dress would look less silly.

Last to arrive was Jim, a young balding egg of a man, pink

around the ears and hairline, in a dark suit and striped tie; his clothes were neat and subdued and fit him correctly.

"Good to know you," he said to Anne when they were introduced.

They had drinks, they had dinner, Louisa bustling around with such energy that everyone perhaps felt a little embarrassed just sitting passively and eating. But they sat around the living room, balancing their plates in their laps, sawing away with their forks at the chicken Kiev. The food was not exciting, rather plain baked chicken with melted butter inside, salad, meticulously sliced morsels of French bread. But Louisa made a tremendous production of bringing out platters and replacing forks that fell and filling wine glasses, and loyally, Anne exclaimed over everything she tasted.

And so did everyone else; there was, in fact, very little other conversation. Louisa seemed almost feverish; it was impossible not to notice when she suddenly skidded to a halt in front of you and thrust out her plate of bread rounds. Impossible not to say, What fantastic bread. Anne found herself looking angrily at Jim, thinking, Ask her to marry you, for heaven's sake.

Louisa perched for a minute beside Jim, took up her own hardly touched plate and nibbled at a bit of chicken. Jim looked at her fondly, and then, under the same compulsion that was guiding them all, told her the chicken was delicious. So why don't you ask her to marry you if you think it's so delicious, Anne thought, still angry at Jim, as if his indifference to Louisa were forcing all this unbecoming effort.

Anne herself felt stiff and strange in the pink dress. I do not belong here, she was thinking, thank God I do not belong here. First she wanted to be alone with Jason, all these other people gone, their fancy clothes in a heap on the floor. And then she thought of herself in her lab, away from everyone, including Jason, and that seemed even more attractive. She let herself indulge in idle resolutions: She would approach this new project with an open mind, she would work hard, she would do a lot of reading in the scientific journals, she would shine, she would think brilliant thoughts. She stared across the room at Felice, who was eating one piece of lettuce at a time with great concentration and large definitive bites.

Jason and Jim were making rather limp conversation about movies, Anne was making her resolutions, Felice was chomping her lettuce and thinking God only knew what, and Louisa was starting around with the wine bottle again, when the doorbell rang and everyone looked up with relief, as at a somewhat belated off-stage signal which might help the evening move forward.

Louisa went into the kitchen to talk on the intercom, and reappeared looking tragic.

"It's Yuri!" she hissed at Anne, as if everyone else in the room couldn't hear. "Oh, I wish he wouldn't do this, he just drops by without even calling." She looked imploringly at Jim. "I'll just ask him in for dessert," she said.

Anne wondered whether Louisa was in fact too good-hearted to turn an uninvited guest away, or whether she was just a little titillated at the idea that both her lovers would be sitting in her living room, staring at each other.

In fact, invited or not, Yuri proved something of a blessing to Louisa's dinner party. He marched in, brown jacket, pants a slightly different brown, unusually hideous green-and-gold tie. His gestures were all a little burlesque, as if he appreciated the silly situation in which he found himself and was determined to play it up. He kissed, noisily, on the cheek, first Louisa, then Anne, then, ignoring the threat of the golden needles, Felice. He settled down on a chair beside Felice, announced himself delighted to have coffee and dessert, introduced himself to Jason and Jim with a rather overdone simulation of pleasure at making their acquaintance. And then a few minutes later, as Louisa dashed around collecting plates, refusing all offers of help, Yuri gave the party what it sorely needed, its first really general conversation. Meanwhile, Louisa whirled more frantically than ever, shaking her head violently at Anne when she got up to carry in her own plate, virtually snatching away wine glasses and napkins and the knives which no one had used because you can't really cut food when the plate's on your lap. This is my party, mine, Anne imagined that Louisa was saying, everybody out of my way, this is my exhibition.

And Yuri, deliberately and cheerfully, was starting a conversation. "Anne," he said, "I want to ask you something."

"What?"

"I was wondering, how does a person get interested in the sort of thing that you do?"

Anne noticed that everyone in the room was listening. Yes, definitely, everyone else had also been feeling the need of a group conversation to make the party seem a little more successful. Everyone was ready to go through the motions. Anne couldn't think of anything particularly fascinating to say.

"Oh, it just sort of happened, I guess."

Yuri laughed and addressed the room at large.

"She doesn't think it is worth trying to explain to a group of people who are not scientists. I think scientists must be the most arrogant people in the world. They don't believe that other people can understand anything about them because they think that if other people really understood what the scientists do, they would be doing it too."

"Well, maybe that's how *you* feel," Anne said, smiling, feeling hostile. "I've noticed in the past that lots of physicists don't really believe there is such a thing as a non-physicist."

"And do you believe there is such a thing as a non-biologist?" Yuri asked.

"I'm grateful that there is such a thing. I really have very limited patience with biologists." Jason smiled at her. She wondered whether he or anyone else in the room believed what Yuri had said, that she was contemptuous of them. She didn't quite understand why Yuri was attacking.

He continued to attack, explaining her again to the room at large. "What she means is, non-biologists are very relaxing for her because they are so simpleminded, I think."

"That is *not* what I mean."

Louisa made a fast circuit of the room, cake plates, cake forks, fresh napkins, back out to the kitchen. There was an awkward pause, during which Anne felt the need to make some comment about how pretty the plates were.

Jim, across the room, spoke up. "Just what is it, exactly, that you do?"

"I work with recombinant DNA," Anne said.

Jim nodded. "And do you really think that a nonscientist is incapable of understanding your work? Take a person like me, I read a lot of technical material in my job, and I don't usually have trouble with it. Can't you explain what you do?"

"Sure I could," Anne said. She wasn't sure whether he was trying to help her out or whether he too was somehow antagonistic. She was aware that everyone was looking at her, aware of the pinkness of her dress, the ruffles.

"You know what DNA is, right?"

Jim nodded. "The genetic code."

"Well, yes, but what it actually *is* is a long molecule made of little pieces strung together—and the whole point is the order. I mean, there are only four kinds of those little molecules, so the reason you have so many kinds of DNA, coding for so many proteins, is the order of the little pieces. And recombinant DNA is the technology to do manipulations. You make your own molecules by cutting up DNA and sticking pieces together. And then your molecules can replicate just like regular DNA. So you could in theory take a gene that contained a harmful mutation right out of someone's DNA and replace it with a healthy normal gene and make the ends all seal up. That's all, it's just the cutting and gluing technology."

She felt embarrassed. She had taken refuge in the kind of promises that the newspapers publicized: genetic surgery. Had she suggested that that was what she did all day, cut out people's bad genes and give them new clean ones?

"What about mongoloid babies?" Felice asked. "Isn't that genetic?"

"That's different," Anne said, "they have whole extra chromosomes."

Felice looked blank but not particularly concerned. They were all dutifully trying to help the party along, Anne thought, dredging up things they had seen or read somewhere, determined not to let go of this rather unpromising topic.

Jim spoke up again. "What about the possibility of taking out

the gene for normal intelligence and putting in a gene of superin-
telligence? Or cloning a genius?''

At this opportune moment, Louisa appeared, bearing a large
carrot cake on a platter. More slowly than before, with a rather
heavy-footed dignity, she circled the room allowing everyone to
take a piece, and replying to all compliments by saying, I didn't
make it, it comes from the bakery.

As Louisa finally settled down with her own piece of cake, several voices picked up the conversation again: Wasn't there some
story about the cloning of a man? What about those test-tube
babies? Do you really believe that intelligence is genetic? Anne
was no longer central, to her great relief. She felt slightly guilty;
why shouldn't she be willing to talk about her field? Hadn't she
proved Yuri's accusation, wasn't she proving it now, sitting there
and thinking that the way these people talked was miles away from
scientific reality? So what if they didn't even understand the difference between test-tube fertilization and cloning—why should
they? She looked over at Yuri and he smiled at her, triumphantly
and just a little nastily.

Jason had to go home right after they finished dinner. Anne was
disappointed to see him go, unhappily aware that he had been
doing her a favor by appearing in public as her boyfriend, that she
could have him only for a limited amount of time, for a dinner
party, for an evening in bed—but not necessarily for both.

Louisa seemed to have run down at last, sitting on the couch
with a rather dazed look on her face, her carrot cake untouched.
Felice and Anne and Yuri and Jim all helped carry the last round
of plates and forks into the kitchen. Felice went off to bed. "You'll
see," she whispered to Anne, "neither one of those two is going to
leave the other here with Louisa, not if it takes all night."

And in fact, Anne found herself sitting in the living room
drinking one last cup of coffee with Louisa and Jim and Yuri. She
was uncomfortable and would have gone to bed herself if Louisa
hadn't been giving her such worried, imploring looks. Anne
wanted to take off the silly dress and comb out her hair, brush her
teeth and put this awkward and pointless evening well behind her.

Well, she thought, you could hardly say that a new dress had transported me into a life of glamour and delight. Here I am, looking stupid, alone at the end of the evening, watching two unappealing men try to wait each other out for my poor cousin. So much for inspecting Louisa's young man. What it had been instead, she thought, was a chance for the marriageable daughter to show off her housewifely skills to both her young men. I could open up the floor for bids, Anne thought: Take her, she's a treasure.

"Louisa," Jim said, getting to his feet, "can I talk to you for a minute, please?"

Louisa gave Anne a final anxious look and followed him into the kitchen. Anne was not pleased to be left alone with Yuri. She didn't see why he should have singled her out for persecution, but she felt there were unpleasant undercurrents she didn't want to identify. He's up to something nasty, she thought. She hoped Jim would get Louisa.

"It was a good enough explanation of recombinant DNA that you gave," Yuri said suddenly, as if he had been sitting thinking of that all along, not of who would end up in bed with Louisa. "A little bit simple perhaps."

"And according to you, that just shows my contempt for all those people, that I tried to make it simple, right?" She spoke, to her own surprise, with very genuine hostility.

Yuri laughed. "I will tell you what your problem is," he said. "It is not a problem that you feel this contempt. It is a problem that you object to feeling it. If you could accept these feelings, you would have no problems with it."

"That's what you do?"

"Yes, of course. I admit that for me the world is divided into those people who can understand at all, on any reasonable level, what the things are that I spend most of my time thinking about—and the other people who cannot."

"Then I'm one of the ones who can't," Anne said. "I don't have any talent for physics." She meant that to put him on the spot.

But he just nodded. "Yes, all right, you are one of the ones who can't." Then he grinned at her. "But still, to be fair, I make an exception for people who study other branches of science. Shall we say I respect them without quite understanding what it is I respect."

"Thank you," Anne said.

Louisa came back into the room. She went up to Yuri and said softly, pleadingly, "I'm going to go with Jim now, please don't be upset or anything, he takes everything so seriously."

Yuri looked at her for a minute. Then he nodded. Louisa turned and almost ran for her bag and a jacket. She didn't say good-bye, just disappeared out the door.

Anne felt suddenly kinder toward Yuri. He had behaved with reasonably good grace, he had made things a little easier for Louisa. She assumed that she herself should now say good night and get out of the way; surely he would want to go home, he would not want to sit there with someone who had witnessed Louisa's rejection.

"So this is what you do, then?" Yuri said. "You work with this genetic surgery?" His voice was not absolutely steady and Anne felt sorry for him.

"No, not at all. I just put that in because it's something people have read about in the newspapers." She ignored his smile, which was clearly meant to suggest that she knew perfectly well that she had just proved his point, and went on, "I'm going to be working on antibody production as a matter of fact."

"And how do you use recombinant DNA to produce antibodies?"

"Well, in theory, you take a gene that codes for the antibody you want and you put it into some fast-growing prolific little cell and then you clone the cell and it just goes on making more and more antibody for you—it's like turning the cell into a factory."

"Ah, now we are back to the newspapers."

"Oh, cut it out, for God's sake. It must be after midnight and you keep expecting me to explain things *and* defend myself against all sorts of vague charges when whatever I say, you just claim it fits in with all your accusations." She was not really angry. This conversation was no longer bothering her at all, and she wondered again why it had upset her before when he had dragged her into a similar discussion with everyone else looking on.

Still, she knew she ought to say good night. But she didn't feel right saying it so abruptly, walking out on him right after Louisa had walked out on him. She was not at all surprised, really, when he put out his hand and began to play with the ruffle on her dress and then almost immediately slipped his hand under the dress and began to stroke her leg. He was not one of your slow step-by-step seducers; he immediately put his other hand on her breast and covered her mouth with his own.

Anne was surprised at herself for not pulling away. Until he had actually reached for her, she had not been aware that she was at all attracted to him, though she had been aware that a pass was at least a vague possibility. She was accustomed to thinking of him as someone who was completely lacking in appeal, and she certainly hadn't noticed her opinion changing—but now she was responding to him very strongly. She was, in fact, about ready to hop into bed with him. He grabbed her hand and pressed it to his crotch, where, no surprise, there was an erection.

"Come on," he whispered wetly into her ear, "let's go in your room."

Anne wondered why she was finding all this so very effective. Perhaps it was partly the direct sexual heat, the speed with which he was pushing things along. Perhaps it was just that she was in the mood to fuck someone, and here was someone, cutting right through all the possible preliminaries. Or had the preliminaries been that odd conversation at dinner? Had the challenge been partially a sexual challenge? And presumably her rather strong emotional response had been an acknowledgment of the sexual current between them, even if she hadn't seen it at the time. And never mind that she wasn't sure she liked him, that at moments she found him repulsive, never mind all that; at this particular moment she wanted him and he was there for the wanting.

"We can't," she said, finally, belatedly, pulling away from him. She was breathing hard.

"Why not?" His hand was back on her breasts. "Don't tell me

you don't want to?" Even his leering voice was not repulsive to her right at that moment.

"You know why not. Because of Louisa."

"Louisa! Louisa just went off to sleep with someone else. How can you talk about Louisa?"

"You can go sleep with someone else if you want, just not with me. I can't sleep with Louisa's lover, it might upset her." But even as Anne was saying this, Yuri was moving his hands on her thighs, and she wondered: How much would Louisa really mind? Would she even have to know? Yuri was whispering that she would never know, he would never say a word and certainly Anne wouldn't, and anyway, it was Jim that Louisa really cared about, and couldn't Anne feel how good it would be, couldn't she see how much they both really wanted it? He started to pull her dress up over her head, and she was suddenly terrified that he was ready to fuck on Louisa's living room couch.

"Okay," she said, "let's go in my room. But I think this is a mistake, I think we'll be sorry." Her tone did not even convince herself, and Yuri just laughed. He helped her to her feet. In the high-heeled sandals she was as tall as he was. He held her ass and lifted her against him.

"Or we could just do it standing up," he murmured, and Anne thought again, He is really unappealing, he is lecherous in all sorts of ridiculous ways, can I really want him?

But she did, no question about it. He followed her into her bedroom, closed the door behind him, and immediately returned to the task of pulling her dress over her head. Anne, trying to forget everything and concentrate on what she had wanted and was now going to get, was unable to rid her mind of two insistent thoughts, Number one, this really *is* a mistake, if not because of Louisa then because of me, myself, and two, well, I did say I might be beginning on a promiscuous period.

16. Sidney's

The warehouse where Anne and Jason had gone before she broke up with Kent was finally to become a nightclub. Jason told Anne that he was going to the opening night.

Anne pictured to herself Jason and his girlfriend all dressed up. Would Jason wear the seersucker suit he had worn to Louisa's dinner party? And the girlfriend? Anne and Jason had become better friends during the last few weeks, and she was interested in the details of his life as she had not been in the past. He came over a couple of nights a week, they got high together, made love, and lay around talking. These evenings were, for Anne, a refuge from the rest of her life. She and Jason did not take each other seriously. They gave each other pleasure and they were gentle with each other, but there was no intensity in their relationship except for the physical intensity, which still flowed between them. Evenings with Jason were relaxed and sensually intoxicating, while the rest of Anne's life at this point seemed tense. At work she was suddenly very conscious of being watched, of needing to prove herself. At home she faced bland food and the emotional minutiae of Louisa. The only thing for Anne to really treasure and look forward to was the time with beautiful naked Jason. And she had a feeling that he felt the same, that he looked forward to their evenings together as much as she did. They talked about themselves in a spirit that was neither passionate nor troubled. They were getting to be better friends, that was all.

Anne knew that Jason's parents lived in a small town near Boston. His father was a civil servant, his mother a housewife. Jason himself had started college in Boston but had not liked it much and in the end had quit to follow his girlfriend to New York. They had met while he was in college; she was studying dance. She had moved to New York for her career, which was going very well. Jason's own ambition, Anne had learned, with some surprise, was musical. He wanted to make a living as a jazz pianist. He seemed to know some of the right sorts of people, these friends of his who were involved with the new nightclub, for example, but there was no sense that he was ever given a chance to play. He insisted that he spent most of his spare time "fooling around" on the piano he had at home, but Anne had begun to wonder whether fooling around was his modest way of saying practicing, or whether it was in fact an accurate description of what he did. He seemed to be averse to any practical conversation about how he could make the jump from amateur to professional; when she asked him about auditions, club dates, how did it work, he led the conversation away from the subject. She couldn't help comparing him with Felice, who was obsessed with the mechanics of making it. Anne came to believe that Jason was very unwilling to put himself to any sort of test.

This, of course, was none of Anne's business. It was not up to her to change Jason's life for him. She was relieved to find out that at least in theory he had an ambition; she was willing to accept almost any specialty. She was happy to change her image of Jason to include a mind full of musical tones, harmonies, rhythms, fingering patterns. It made him into a person wtih "content." Strangely enough it was Yuri who had started her on this line of thought. She had found herself persistently bothered by what he had said—by his statements about how she saw nonscientists—and she had found herself repeatedly arguing with him in her mind, offering examples of this or that nonscientist whom she deeply respected. And so she had been led to make her own division. Those she had offered as objects of her respect had included, ironically enough, Jason's girlfriend. A professional dancer had content. So did Kent as a linguist; she found she still preferred not to pass judgment on Kent as a banker. She hesitated over Felice: Did she have content or was she the apotheosis of non-content, the trivial raised and glorified? It was not really a serious debate in Anne's mind, more a sort of defensive amusement, but it was affecting at least a little bit the way she looked at people. She was glad to move Jason solidly into the content category, taking on faith that he genuinely had some expertise when it came to playing the piano.

The argument went on only in her mind because Yuri was no longer on the scene. For this Anne was deeply grateful. Going to bed with him the night of Louisa's dinner party, she had expected to feel bad about it the next morning, and she had been right. They had sex, Yuri went home, and Anne went immediately to sleep. The next morning she felt more than a little revolted by the memory of him and of her own eagerness. In retrospect, the sexual images of him did not turn her on. She was not sure why she had been so aroused and she was positive that she did not want to repeat the experience. There was a curious sense of danger about it as well, a feeling that this was the sort of thing of which she might be capable nowadays, hopping into bed with a man who did not appeal to her in general but for a certain moment happened to excite her sexually. She could envision other such mornings-after, when all she wanted was a very thorough shower, when she dreaded seeing the man again for fear he would assume that they were now lovers of one sort or another. Fortunately, Louisa and Jim seemed to have come to some sort of agreement and Louisa had once more broken up with Yuri. Yuri had then called once to speak to Anne, choosing a Friday night when Louisa was, predictably, out. He had asked Anne if she wanted to go have dinner with him that weekend. She had said as firmly as she could that she didn't think it was a good idea for them to see each other. When he pressed, she went on to say that it had been fun, that night, but she would rather leave it at that. So he had disappeared, but she still found herself continuing to argue with him mentally.

Her sex life now was just those evenings with Jason. She and Kent had not repeated their encounter. They did not even talk on the phone very often and Anne was aware that she was waiting, tensed, for the news of a new girlfriend. She knew that in a certain sense Kent still existed in her life, she frequently pictured him living in their apartment, the apartment where there had once also been space for her. When he had a new girlfriend, she assumed, that picture would dissolve. She wasn't sure exactly how important it was to her, that mental connection to Kent.

For the same reason she was wary of placing too much stress on the connection she was developing with Jason. She watched herself closely for signs that she was falling in love with him, watched herself so closely, she hoped, that she prevented it from happening. She tried not to think about him all the time; on nights when he wasn't with her she made herself fantasize about a string of other men. For instance, a brilliant biochemist with longish thick blond hair with whom she jointly won the Nobel Prize; she danced in his arms at the celebratory ball in Stockholm and he whispered in her ear, When can we get away from this nonsense and be alone together? Better if he wasn't a scientist; she took a leaf out of Jason's book: a world-famous ballet dancer, same blond hair—he sat in the audience watching her make her Nobel speech, himself a center of attention. This was an amusing conceit, a pleasant fantasy, and intermittently sexy.

Anyway, the fantasies were a bulwark for Anne against letting Jason become too important. She could picture their relationship going on indefinitely and in much the same way; she wasn't sure whether she herself wanted more, and she felt it would be silly to ruin what they had by deciding that it wasn't enough. And what they had was really extremely pleasant, she liked Jason very much as she came to know him better.

And she was becoming curious about Jason's girlfriend. Did she really know nothing, suspect nothing, about Anne? The question seemed to trouble Jason. He thought about it for a while, then he finally admitted he wasn't sure. He had never told his girlfriend about Anne. They had both been unfaithful in the past and they had fought about it and in the end stayed together.

Anne was aware that she did not even know his girlfriend's name. Jeannette, Jason said, a little surprised, as if he thought he had told her before. Anway, he sort of thought Jeannette might suspect him of being involved with someone else. He sort of thought she might not mind too much this time.

Why, Anne asked, wouldn't Jeannette mind too much? He didn't seem to want to talk about it. Anne asked if something was wrong between him and Jeannette, and he said he didn't know, maybe, it was hard to tell. Anne, taking one more step, asked if he thought Jeannette had another lover and Jason laughed. "I only wish," he said, and Anne was more confused than before. She pushed; what did he mean?

Well, Jason said, old Jeannette wasn't really big on sex these days, not very likely she had another lover. She's just not into it.

Is she into women, Anne asked on impulse.

Jason looked slightly surprised. Well, he said, she has been, but lately she just wasn't into anyone. Of course, she was into her own body, he added, all dancers were, but lately it wasn't in any sort of sexual way.

So there was one reason he wanted me, Anne thought. Not, perhaps, a terribly flattering reason, but at least she shouldn't bother worrying about the comparisons he might be making, comparing her body to some perfect dancer's body. Jason didn't seem eager to discuss his girlfriend. Instead, they talked about the nightclub.

And unexpectedly enough, Sidney's was a success. It was quite warm, Jason reported to Anne; the air conditioning wasn't very effective. But the whole place clicked; the music was exciting, the air was alive, people looked glamorous against the red walls. Sidney's got written up in newspapers and magazines, customers began to turn up who didn't look familiar to any of the people running the place.

Jason was intoxicated by the success of Sidney's. He talked about it whenever he was with Anne. It was a miracle, a success story, proof that everything can change overnight, that smart and ambitious people can become rich and important and even glamorous. Finally Anne asked him when he was going to play the piano at the nightclub. Jason looked troubled. Sidney's could afford people with at least small "names," he said, he didn't want to presume on his friendship with the owners to make them take on an unknown. He'd start somewhere else, come to them only when he had a little following of his own. Anne, thinking of Felice and her single-minded determination to become a model, was sure that this was the wrong attitude. Not only was Felice willing to exploit her friends to further her career, but Anne suspected that most of Felice's friends were chosen only for their potential usefulness. Of course, Felice really believed in herself; she was sure that the minute she was given a chance, she'd be the most super of supermodels.

Felice, in fact, had been very impressed when Anne had told her about Jason's connection to the new nightclub. When she learned that he was a friend of *the* Sidney, she credited him with more importance in her scheme of the universe, a scheme in which people were ranked according to whether they could help Felice become a model and whether they would be useful to her after she had become one.

Anne was astonished by the speed with which all this moved; Sidney's opened in the middle of June and by the beginning of July it was an accepted success. Anne, of course, had never been there, unless you counted her various visits to what you might call the incipient Sidney's, the proto-Sidney's, the hours she had spent on the mattress, surrounded by debris and half-painted walls. Jason reported to her, a little sheepishly, that Sidney was always teasing him to bring "that girl" for whom he had lent Jason the key to the place. Sidney was curious.

"Terrific," Anne said, "we could go there and do our usual routine. We could be the new floor show." She didn't really like the idea of *the* Sidney being in on all the details of her affair with Jason. And she didn't really like the idea that Jason spent so much time at the nightclub. He seemed thinner, if that was possible, and he seemed very far away. And yet he seemed to need Anne badly when he did get to see her; after they made love he would hold on to her and press her to him in a way that was quite new between them, and he would want to talk about some of the very basic things they had never discussed before—their backgrounds, their childhoods, her relationship with Kent—though not his with Jeannette—her roommates, people at Viatech. He stayed later, talking and hugging her and making love again until it was very late at night, so that she really wondered how his girlfriend could not suspect.

Anne felt that though his friends' success had given him hope, it had also made him insecure. Until now his circle of friends had been boys with ambition, people who talked about one day hitting it big. But now a couple of them had actually hit it big. And it was clear that anyone who didn't make it didn't really have what it took. And so Jason was insecure. And since she herself was newly insecure at Viatech, and since all was not well at home with Louisa, Anne was glad of the emotional calm he provided by allowing her to comfort him. It seemed a very balanced exchange.

17. Work and Play

The problem for Anne at work was that she was suddenly being watched very closely. After sharing the lab with Arthur Schenk for such a long time, she was accustomed to keeping her own counsel about her work, to moving along at her own pace, and, in fact, to keeping her results a secret. But now she had been pulled into this project and there were regular meetings of Richie and his "team," and Anne, the youngest member of the team, felt constantly on the spot. Richie had, in fact, asked her if she'd like to move into another lab, one she could share with one of the other people on the team. But Anne didn't like the idea of working under someone's direct supervision, so she told Richie she'd rather stay where she was. Everyone accepted that, since, after all, scientists are a superstitious lot, attaching supernatural properties to certain laboratories, certain pieces of equipment. It is perfectly acceptable to say that you can get good results only working in your own lab, with your own particular incubator or centrifuge, the same way you believe in one particular brand of cell culture plate—like a musician who needs a specific music stand, an athlete who needs a certain pair of socks.

The other three researchers Richie had assigned to the project had a lot in common. All were in their late thirties. They had extensive publications, excellent academic credentials; their training dated back to an era when hotshot young geneticists were more or less expected to go into academics. They regarded themselves as something of an elite at Viatech, and the younger staff agreed;

all three of them had worked with a number of pioneers in the field. The younger staff also realized, although this was seldom said, that none of the three had exactly fulfilled his potential. They did "decent work," but they were not the shining successors to their distinguished teachers. Other students of these same teachers did much more important work, by and large students who had actually gone into academics and stayed there. This was rarely put into words because the younger staff were aware of it as their own future: They might do work that was very important from a commercial point of view, even very clever from a scientific point of view, but basically most of them believed that the really stunning advances would come out of the universities. Of course, you never could tell; Anne was surely not the only one who had one sort of fantasy or another about those parties in Stockholm. There was no reason why a fabulous breakthrough could not emerge from a genetic engineering company.

Anne knew more or less why Richie Grossman had included her on that team. He was hoping for a flash from her, an inspiration, a clever way around a problem. He had great faith in that sort of science—he was not capable of it himself, but he found it very attractive. It did not appeal to him nearly as much when people saw logical avenues branching out from a problem and explored them one by one. And though he knew that was really how most of the research at Viatech was accomplished, he kept his belief in bright ideas, in quick leaps. It was perfectly true that her last little project had been solved by a nonobvious and lucky solution. But she couldn't summon up inspiration on demand. And, even if she had an idea, she would not be allowed to work it out herself. She would have to present it at one of those damn meetings . . . no way here to do what she had done the last time, secretly assemble materials and follow her own whims.

At the meetings of the team, Anne was generally quiet. She made herself contribute to the discussion every now and then, usually seizing on some point which could not be too controversial, which could not tread too heavily on anyone's toes. The scientific head of the team was Mark Riskin, a large man who was completely bald on the top of his head, but with curly black hair on the sides. He wore blue jeans and tight workshirts which made his large stomach look even larger. His sense of humor was much in evidence at meetings and made Richie uncomfortable because it was so often sexist. Richie stole nervous glances at Anne whenever Mark chose some highly sexual analogy to illustrate a scientific point. Actually, Anne rather liked Mark. Of her three teammates, he was the only one who didn't seem suspicious of her, the only one she believed would genuinely welcome any progress she made. He seemed to be completely without personal vanity and his scientific vanity was so obvious and honest that no one could object to it. A good-natured egotist, he seemed to have no real life outside the laboratory.

The other two men were Henry Madison and Peter Chang. They both belonged in the category of Viatech workers with wives and children out in the New York suburbs. Henry got on Anne's nerves; he was the pickiest scientist she had ever worked with. He was a neat, small, unremarkable man, scrupulously clean-shaven. Peter Chang was the only one who ever gave Mark Riskin a real argument during meetings. He rarely accepted criticism of his work without a fight and he often criticized other people's, not, as Mark did, with gleeful one-upmanship, nor, as Henry did, to teach some fussy lesson, but rather with dogmatic determination to show that the other person's basic approach could be logically proven to be wrong. The right approach, invariably, according to Peter, could be derived from something he himself had been saying a little while before. Richie Grossman sometimes had to mediate between Mark and Peter; Anne, usually a little bored at these meetings, could not help hoping there would be a real knock-down drag-out fight.

No, she was not really happy at work these days. Mark sometimes dropped into her lab, Richie greeted her in the corridors with special warmth, Arthur Schenk regarded her with jealous hostility, and the whole thing left her tired. She didn't believe in the project. At meetings she volunteered to take on some of the little experiments that seemed to her technically interesting, she pushed through the days in her lab and got her results, but she wasn't happy. When she left work and stepped into the heat of the evening, after the air conditioning of Viatech, she felt a strong relaxed settling-down all through herself.

Charlotte gave her a pep talk almost every day. You have to speak up at meetings, you can't be the only female in the group and let them do all the talking. Charlotte also delivered the promised invitation to dinner and Anne accepted, but only on condition that they not discuss Anne's project at Viatech. Anne said she just wanted to put it out of her mind for an evening. Actually, of course, she put it out of her mind every evening. She didn't even take home the articles that the other people on the team recommended; she read them at work. That was perfectly acceptable, of course, to sit around reading a scientific article, it showed you were "keeping up on the literature," but all the same, it was something most people did at home. Anne always had before. She spent her evenings these days reading thrillers and talking to Louisa, who was always ready to talk about the troubles she was having with Jim. Also, Anne had begun to go to the movies alone in the evenings. She went mostly to the first-run Hollywood pictures, and when she thought back on them she could hardly remember one from the other.

The night before she was to have dinner at Charlotte's, Kent called. She hadn't talked to him in a while. They made rather stiff conversation about work for a couple of minutes, and then Anne asked, "How are your Hebrew lessons going?"

"Oh, fine," Kent said. Then, without apparent connection, he added, "Anne, I'm sort of seeing someone. I mean, sort of involved with someone."

"Congratulations," Anne said lightly. "That's terrific." There was a pause. Anne felt a little light-headed, now that the announcement had actually come. "I'm really glad, Kent," she added. Then she stopped, afraid that if she showed too much enthusiasm he would think she was patronizing him, or be hurt that she was relieved to have him taken care of. "Well, who is she?" Anne asked.

"She's someone I met in that Hebrew class." Kent sounded embarrassed. "She's a girl who—her parents are Zionists, they've just emigrated to Israel, you see, and they asked her to take Hebrew lessons and then come visit them later on—they're paying for it all, you see, and she's doing it because she thinks it means a lot to them."

"How old is she?" Anne asked, and was suddenly certain that longtime-lover ESP had been operating, that she had asked the question Kent least wanted to answer.

"That's the thing. I mean, she's nineteen."

Anne thought of all her images of Kent's possible new girlfriends in the banking world. Tailored suits, sleek hairdos, M.B.A.'s. It was hard to imagine all that on a nineteen-year-old. "Well," she said, "that's something."

"She says it's just typical of her," Kent went on, with fond amusement, "that her parents pay to send her to Hebrew classes and she ends up getting involved with the only person in the class who isn't Jewish."

"I see," Anne said. "Should I ask how involved you've gotten?"

"Well, we haven't really known each other very long. But it's not—I mean, I think I really care about her. Of course, she *is* so young."

"And she *is* going away."

"What do you mean?"

"I thought you said she was going to Israel?"

"Oh, that's just for a couple of weeks. She'll be back for college in the fall."

"She goes to college?" Perhaps she was an incipient business administration type after all.

"Sort of. She's at Barnard." He paused. "She's mostly interested in writing poetry, though."

"Oh," Anne said, unsure of the right response. "Is it good?"

"Well, actually, I haven't seen any of it yet," Kent said.

Anne, who had been prepared to discipline herself into kindly feelings toward Kent's new girlfriend, whatever she might be, was dismayed to find herself taking a dislike to the idea of this nineteen-year-old poetess.

"And you," Kent went on, "are you still carrying on with that Jason?" His voice was quite cheerful and gossipy.

"More or less," Anne said. "Listen," she said, "I'm really glad you've found someone you care about." It didn't sound right. The sentiment was somehow off and the tone was stiff.

This phone call left Anne feeling abandoned. She had thought she was thoroughly braced for Kent's new girlfriend, whoever she might be, but in fact she found herself thinking almost constantly about Kent and the nineteen-year-old, eating together, sleeping together, making plans to go away for the weekend together. She could not form a satisfactory mental picture of the girl, though she was inclined to imagine someone small, willowy, spiritual. Anne tried to stop herself from dwelling on these various thoughts, though in fact they did not actually cause her pain.

The problem, of course, was that she had no new connections which could take the place of Kent. The trouble was not the sexual place, not even the romantic place, because those had grown less prominent anyway by the time she and Kent broke up. What she needed were deep connections to other people, connections which involved complicated knowledge and intense interest and all the rest of it. Charlotte was a possibility, though Anne was not sure how deep she would ever be allowed to penetrate into Charlotte's life. Still, an invitation to dinner was in itself a new milestone in their friendship.

The dinner that Charlotte served Anne was chicken breasts, stuffed with salmon mousse and served in a green sauce made from fresh dill, accompanied by asparagus and small round potatoes—the whole effect was really very stunning and very unlike Anne's idea of home cooking. She thought of Louisa and the frozen hamburger patties and felt almost dizzy with the wonder of Charlotte's life. Anne wondered whether Charlotte cooked for herself like this every night.

"That's about the only thing I miss about being married," Charlotte said. "It was an excuse to take more trouble over the food every day without feeling you were being some sort of hedonist."

"Did you cook like this for your husband?"

"I didn't know nearly as much about cooking then as I do now," Charlotte said, "it was mostly more basic stuff, but it was pretty good."

They finished dinner, concluding with homemade strawberry tartlets, and Charlotte cleared everything away into the kitchen and refused to let Anne help wash up, saying she would take care of it all later. Charlotte steered Anne back into the living room, poured her a cognac, and settled her on the couch. Charlotte herself took up a position in a very large armchair which surrounded her comfortably and made her look small.

Anne was beginning to feel drunk. They had gone through a full bottle of wine with the dinner, and she had a feeling that she had put away more than half of it. Charlotte's living room felt cared for and luxurious, but Anne wasn't sure it felt comfortable—the furniture was polished and elegant, the bookshelves were almost oppressively orderly, and there was an enormous gleaming stereo system.

"Oh, for heaven's sake," Charlotte said, "look at you, sitting on the couch with your knees together as if you expect to be scolded any minute. Take your shoes off and make yourself comfortable, for heaven's sake."

Hesitantly, Anne kicked off her shoes. Then she boldly swung herself around on the couch, leaning back against the armrest and drawing her feet up.

"Better," Charlotte said, "there's no need to act like you're visiting some elderly relative."

"Look," Anne said, "I can't help it if I'm impressed by your apartment. You should see the one I'm living in. It looks as if it had been furnished in fifteen minutes by someone with a budget of thirty-five dollars."

"That's the explanation. This took longer and cost more."

"It makes me jealous," Anne said. "Seeing someone who knows how to take care of herself. I've been feeling lately that I really don't."

"It's just because you're coming out of a couple," Charlotte said. "Learning to do things for yourself takes a lot of time. With me it was literally years before I accepted that I was worth the

same effort I would make for my husband or for the two of us together." Anne heard, somewhere off in the distance, the voice of
the analyst. "In some ways," Charlotte continued, "I think I was
just waiting and waiting for the next man to come along, you
know, the next serious man. Only when I began to accept that
there never would be one did I begin to make myself a permanent
place to live."

"Do you really think that? That there's never going to be another one?" Anne's voice was casual, her curiosity was not. She
also felt a slight grope of panic in her stomach at what Charlotte
had said; was that what Anne had to learn to accept too?

Charlotte hesitated, as if she had said more than she meant to
say. Anne decided to push. "You really don't think you'll ever be
seriously involved with someone again? Why not? Are you against
it in principle?"

"Oh, no. But you know how it is, you watch yourself, you see
your own patterns." Anne was reminded of Yuri's remarks on the
subject of scientists. Charlotte continued slowly, "Some people,
wherever they go there are involvements waiting for them and
usually involvements of the same sort. Look at your cousin. And
then there are other people, like me. Involvements don't come
along for me and I don't have the talent or the interest to go looking for them."

"I have this feeling," Anne said abruptly, "that you're keeping
something a secret. You're involved with someone, you have been
all along," Anne said. She didn't know why she was so sure; she
hoped it wasn't just drunkenness.

But Charlotte nodded. She wasn't looking at Anne.

"A woman?" Anne asked.

Charlotte nodded again.

"Someone you're genuinely in love with?"

And Charlotte nodded again.

"Then why don't you ever—I mean, tell me about her." And
indeed it did seem to Anne that she had known all this for a while.

"Well," Charlotte said, and considered. Finally she said, "Well,
for one thing she's married."

"Oh, I see." Anne wasn't sure exactly what she saw.

"She's a doctor. They live in Connecticut, she and her husband. And her children, she has three children."

"When do you get to see each other?"

"She comes to New York every two weeks. She's affiliated with a hospital uptown. She stays here for two nights." Charlotte still sounded strained, as if she were forcing herself to answer.

"That's tough," Anne said, then wondered why she had said it.

"It's very hard. But there's no other way to manage things. She doesn't want to leave her husband and I don't even think I want her to—especially since either she'd end up with the kids, which I couldn't handle, or else her husband would fight her for custody, which she couldn't handle. Anyway, I'm not sure she really wants to move to the city full-time, I don't think either of us wants to live together . . . at least this way we see each other and things are stable."

"And how long has this been going on?"

Charlotte left a pause. "Four years." She took herself up on that hastily, "I know, it's amazing. You wouldn't think something this part-time would go on that long. But I know I couldn't stand to lose her—she's the most important thing in my life."

"And you don't get involved with other people—you're faithful to her?" It had certainly been a seductive dinner. Anne wondered what her reaction would be if Charlotte made some sort of pass.

"Yes, I'm faithful," Charlotte said. "I know it's a little absurd, with her spending twelve of every fourteen nights with her husband, but I don't seem to get interested in anyone else. I think that when I fall in love I'm the monogamous type." She paused, then finally looked directly at Anne and said, "Of course, I may not be qualified to judge that. She's probably the only person I've ever really been in love with." She left another pause. "And she's the only woman I've ever been involved with at all." Charlotte and Anne were both quiet for several minutes. Then Charlotte got up and put on a record. The sound poured out of the giant speakers, filling the room, until Charlotte touched a dial and it became background music. Charlotte returned to her chair and smiled nervously at Anne. "So now you know all," she said. She poured them each a little more cognac.

Anne sensed that these revelations had been difficult to make. The story of Charlotte and her doctor could not quite be packaged up like the story of Charlotte and her husband. Anne did not understand Charlotte's life, neither the cooking nor the apartment nor the love affair, but she wanted to understand it. That was the difference between Charlotte and all the other people currently prominent in Anne's life; Anne did not necessarily understand their ways of doing things either, but she didn't really care to. Charlotte seemed to hold some sort of relevance, some sort of possibility of guidance. Perhaps it all came back to the question of content; Charlotte was surely someone with content to spare.

Anne let her thoughts drift a little, carried on the music. When she finally spoke, it was to say, "Three children."

"What?" Charlotte sounded startled.

"You told me once that you couldn't think of any woman you knew who had children and also had a life that you envied."

"Oh," Charlotte said. "Well, I don't envy her her life. Most of the time she lives in this incredibly dreary town in Connecticut and she feels guilty about coming into the city for two days. She feels that she's abandoning her children to come spend time with me."

Anne, who had been developing a mental picture of the doctor as a supremely assured creature, now made some revisions.

"But maybe I'm being unfair." Charlotte was perhaps playing shrink to her own thoughts now. "Maybe it's just that her life doesn't include me as much as I might like it to, so I run it down."

"Is she happy?"

"No. But she functions, she gets things done. And she doesn't really complain." Charlotte still seemed very stiff. Anne wondered if she discussed this affair with her analyst; it sounded as if she wasn't used to talking about it. "I have all these fantasies," Charlotte said. "Of the two of us going away together, even for a week. Sleeping someplace that isn't my apartment. You can't imagine what it's like, something that goes on for four years and always in exactly the same setting."

"You couldn't take even a short trip together?"

"She'd feel guilty," Charlotte said. "As I said, she feels guilty as it is. Enough," she said, very definitely.

She changed the conversation to Anne's roommates, and Anne told her about Louisa's troubles. Louisa and Jim had decided to be monogamous again and things were not working out well between them. Louisa, with a querulousness that was, as far as Anne could see, competely new, complained that she didn't believe he really loved her, that she saw no future for their relationship. Anne couldn't decide whether Louisa was really exceptionally, deeply in love with Jim and therefore more demanding than usual, or whether Louisa was having trouble convincing herself that she was sufficiently in love with him and was therefore generally dissatisfied with the relationship. One way or another, she talked about him constantly, agonized over whether to call him, endlessly analyzed everything he said to her. Anne was a little tired of serving as confidante.

"She probably read one of those articles that tells women to have children now, before they're too old and all the children come out retarded," Charlotte said, "or maybe she found wrinkles when she looked in the mirror and decided that life was passing her by, or maybe she heard about some old schoolmates who got married."

"Who knows," Anne said.

"And it may wear off—she may read an article about how married women wish they were single and free again."

"I hope so," Anne said. "I think I prefer her in the single-and-free mode."

"Especially now that you're such a single-and-free type yourself."

"I don't ever want to get married." Anne said, with the sudden seriousness which occasionally comes to the almost drunk.

"Good," Charlotte said. "It's not a healthy ambition."

18. Gift Shops

Anne began to talk about moving. She mentioned it to Louisa, who seemed a little hurt. Anne assured her that it was not that there was any problem with the apartment, that she had never meant to stay long, that she had to get out on her own. Louisa seemed unconvinced. Anne mentioned moving to Felice, who didn't seem terribly interested. She mentioned it to Jason, who did. She told Jason she would find a place where she would have room for a double bed. He told her that he wanted to be able to spend the night with her, and she was touched. She mentioned it to Charlotte every so often, and Charlotte was encouraging. The only thing that Anne did not do was start looking for a place. She did not even read through the ads in the paper. It was too overwhelming to think of empty rooms somewhere out there, of all the decisions to be made. She waited for resolve to well up inside her.

One thing did take a turn for the better, though it was not without dangers. At work she finally had an idea, a test which she thought might save a lot of time if they could work out the details, which might predict for them the results of what would otherwise be a long and everlastingly picky chain of experiments that Henry Madison wanted them all to undertake. Anne made her suggestion, which she had carefully written out for herself before the meeting, but which she delivered without looking at her notes, pretending it was something she was thinking out as she went along. Peter Chang suddenly became a fierce partisan of Henry's line of research. He suggested that Anne should consider carefully whether her suggestion was actually aimed at discovering anything or just at avoiding work. He suggested that the test she had in mind would by no means answer the same questions as Henry's series of experiments. He suggested that she was trying to use machinery instead of logic. This last charge offered a clue to one source of his hostility: The test Anne had proposed would involve the use of a device which measured fluorescence in different substances. You could add a fluorescently "labeled" compound to a mixture of cells and then use the machine to see how many cells had taken it up. It was not a terribly complicated procedure, but not everyone at Viatech was comfortable with it. The company that manufactured the machine had sent an enthusiastic salesman to give a series of talks on how it was to be used. Anne had gone, and she was sure she remembered seeing Mark Riskin there too, but Peter Chang, it seemed, had stayed away. An unwillingness to learn new techniques, a distrust of new techniques you haven't learned, can of course be signs that a scientist is past the productive prime, and perhaps as a defense against this suspicion, Peter spoke particularly harshly about Anne's suggestion.

Anne did not feel up to combatting this onslaught of criticism. She didn't feel so strongly about her idea that she was willing to fight for it single-handedly. If no one wanted to support her she would let it go. She knew this was wrong, since she did suspect she was on the right track, and she knew that Charlotte would have called her a coward and a self-defeating traitor. Fortunately, Mark Riskin leaped in on her side, happy to argue with Peter, and also to show off his own superior knowledge of fluorescent labeling techniques. Anne sat back and let him do the fighting. Richie Grossman took his part; Richie was always happy to see an expensive piece of equipment used, and Richie had a stake in Anne's cleverness, since he had put her on this team. Between them, he and Mark pushed Henry and Peter to the wall. Mark Riskin was a very fair-minded person; when the meeting was over, he went up to Anne and made it clear that he remembered where the idea had originated—he had not meant to take it over by pushing for it so heartily. And so Anne had at least for the moment assumed a position of some prominence, and also some peril, since at least one member of the team would obviously be only too pleased to see her idea fail to work out. Henry Madison, though it was his experimental approach which had been at least temporarily scrapped, did not seem to be holding a grudge; he had quickly assumed his usual role and was now picking tiny holes in everyone's fluorescent labeling methodology.

She felt better at work; at least her brain was functioning. Surely it was time to get the rest of her life functioning, to move out, to leave Louisa and Felice behind. Charlotte agreed, surely it was time. Jason looked wistful and again said something about being able to spend the night together.

"But what about your girlfriend?" Anne asked.

"She won't mind. I'm going to tell her about us anyway one of these days."

"Be careful. That's what I did, tell Kent about us. I didn't know how much he'd mind."

"Yes," Jason said, "but she isn't really like my girlfriend at all anymore. We're just friends, really."

"But you live together?"

"Friends who live together." He smiled, looking a little cornered.

"You share a bed?" Anne was glad she could say that so lightly, as part of teasing him.

"Friends who share a bed." Jason was smiling. "We know each other pretty well, we're very close in a lot of ways. The only thing is, we aren't really lovers. I mean, sometimes we have sex but it's more when one of us needs to feel close to someone else than because we really turn each other on. You know what I mean?"

Anne nodded. She suddenly did feel a little jealous.

"With you, though," Jason said, seeming now a little shy, "the amazing thing is how we really do turn each other on. I mean, even after all this time."

They were lying naked on Anne's bed in what was evidently a resting period between two turnings-on. Anne just smiled at him.

Jason continued, still shy, "But I think lately you and I have also gotten closer. I feel like I know you a lot better than I used to."

"Yes," Anne said. Not only did she feel she knew him better, but she also liked him better. She was very fond of him, really. She too thought with pleasure of the day when she would have an apartment with a double bed and they could have their nights together. But in the meantime, she was not actually hunting for an apartment.

One day her uncle's book arrived in the mail, along with a note saying that he was coming to New York at the end of the next week. Anne found she was excited about seeing him. She tried to read his book and was disturbed to find it bored her and sometimes annoyed her. It was about the physics of space exploration, illustrated with a large number of photographs, *2001*-type material, psychedelic universe formations. Some of the book was history: the important advances in physics, engineering, and astrophysics that made the space program possible, and the further developments that grew out of discoveries made through the space program. Though Anne herself did not know much more about physics than the supposed common reader for whom the book was written, she could feel the patent simplification, the endless search for a homey metaphor. Other sections of the book were devoted to future uses of space, and Anne considered that there was an unappealing emphasis on space warfare, presumably to cash in on science fiction movie fans. Laser beams, satellites, space fortresses. The prose was almost gleeful, though Uncle Douglas took care to include a few dutiful statements about the terrible consequences for humanity.

The publishers had great hopes for the book. Anne's uncle was coming to New York to do two talk shows. Anne tried to make herself believe that as a scientist she had become a snob, that she was simply unwilling to read any science that was not written only for the initiated. She argued in her mind that lots of people would find her uncle's book diverting, fascinating, even inspiring.

When he arrived, she told him she had enjoyed the book very much and was impressed with the handsome presentation his publishers had given it. Her uncle seemed pleased by this; he was a man who measured his own prestige carefully. A large, tall man with thin features and short dark brown hair, a little bit military in aspect perhaps, but not in an unpleasant way, he seemed in general pleased with the world. He had bought, he confided to Anne, the most expensive suit he had ever owned for these TV appearances. His wife had picked it out for him. "She's the professional, after all," he said.

Uncle Douglas produced the gift Anne had finally chosen from her aunt's catalogue—a pale lavender camisole, lace-edged around the top. Her aunt had thrown in a matching pair of bikini underpants. Anne grinned as she unwrapped the pink-flowered tissue paper and held up the items.

"You have some special someone to wear those for?" her uncle asked.

She was sure that her uncle was much too far out of the normal male mainstream to understand what it was that men saw in fancy underwear for women. And she was sure that he understood even less the other aspects of his wife's sales pitch; don't buy elegant lingerie just to please your man, buy it because it's luxury you owe yourself.

"So, how about it?" her uncle persevered. "Have you replaced Kent yet?"

"Did Aunt Letitia give you instructions to find out?" Anne asked.

"Yes, as a matter of fact. And she wants to know why you two called it off."

Anne was sure that her uncle, left to himself, would never have thought to ask about such a matter. Anne could not believe that her uncle had ever devoted much attention to human relationships, his own or anyone else's. It was not that he felt himself above such things as gossip and romantic intrigue, just that he didn't really notice them.

"Tell Aunt Letitia that I'm playing the field these days, okay?"

"Sure," he said. He asked about her work and she outlined the project for him, struggling to use as many technical terms as possible, because she knew it pleased him to hear that she spoke a scientific language.

It was good to see him, good to be with someone who had known her for a long time, who had known her at different ages, even if she did wonder how much he had really noticed her before she went into science. It made her feel a little more securely anchored in herself. Sometimes, now that Kent was gone, she felt she had no past at all; she had lived through so much of the recent past seeing it reflected in Kent that without him she felt she had lost it. And the longer-ago past was unsettling too—it was not part of other people's picture of her and so she sometimes felt she had lost that.

Whatever problems there might be between her uncle and herself, problems going back to her adolescence when he was so distant, or new problems which came from her real feelings about his book, it was still clear that he was someone she loved and someone who loved her back. He was the man who had filled her own father's place, the man who had paid her expenses and worried about her and eaten dinner across the table from her every night when she was fifteen and sixteen and seventeen, until she went away to college. He was a connection of the sort that could not be disputed. True, he was not a connection like most people's fathers, because once upon a time she had actually chosen him. She wished that he had simply been a fact of life, that her own choice had not entered into it at all. That would add to the texture of the connection.

His last day in New York, a Saturday, Anne and her uncle planned some sightseeing. She was pleased, waking up, tucking into her shoulder bag a map of the city and a guidebook that belonged to Louisa. She asked him where he wanted to go and was surprised when he said the Metropolitan Museum of Art. He'd heard that they had a very good museum store, he wanted to buy Aunt Letitia a present there. Anne found this touching, though she thought her aunt might in fact have preferred some expensive item of clothing from a Fifth Avenue store. Still, she led the way to the museum, which she had visited only rarely herself; she now felt like a tourist. They stood for a minute in the enormous entrance hall, enjoying the marble coolness. The museum was crowded already.

It pleased Anne when her uncle asked if she would mind skipping the museum itself. She was relieved to find that he had not in fact been reformed into a more conventional admirer of culture. She wanted to feel that she knew him. In the shop he ended up buying some gold jewelry, reproductions of ancient Egyptian ornaments. Anne rather doubted that it was her aunt's sort of thing; Aunt Letitia liked her art European and from the last four or five centuries, and she liked her jewelry modern. Still, no doubt she would appreciate the thought.

As they left the museum, Anne suggested a walk through Central Park, ending up perhaps at the Museum of Natural History. She thought her uncle might at least like to see the planetarium. But he pointed out that Chicago had a perfectly good science museum and he never went; why should he come all the way to New York to do something he wouldn't bother doing at home?

The Empire State Building? The Statue of Liberty? But of course he had done those on his other trips to New York. Anne was aware that she was enjoying this. It emphasized how much the two of them were family. If he had been a friend or just an acquaintance, he would have been enthusiastically deferring to her every suggestion or at least trying to be subtle about turning them down. No, it was because they were family that Uncle Douglas felt free to be his difficult self.

It turned out that what he wanted to do was go to the United Nations, he had never seen it. To Anne's surprise, her uncle did not seem eager to take the guided tour.

"Conference rooms," he said. "I know what conference rooms look like."

He prowled around the lobby and finally suggested they go down to the gift shop. Anne was very amused by this tour of New York, one entranceway after another, one gift shop after another. Her uncle paused with genuine enthusiasm before the pendulum which was powered by the rotation of the earth.

"Good stuff," he said to Anne. "Good for making people realize that it's all one planet, right?"

She nodded. They went on to the gift shop, where he browsed with much more enthusiasm than he had shown in the museum shop. He bought another piece of jewelry for his wife, a string of wooden beads from Africa. He hesitated for some time over a salad bowl made of teak from Thailand, and finally bought that too. Then he told Anne that he wanted to buy her something. She protested, but then decided that as long as she was going to get a present, she would just as soon help choose it. She picked out a pair of earrings from Burma, little globes of filigreed silver.

They walked back uptown to Anne's apartment and drank the canned iced tea that Louisa kept in the refrigerator. Anne was glad that both her roommates were out. She felt that all morning there had in fact been some undercover communion going on between Uncle Douglas and herself. She was grateful for the eccentricity of his method of sightseeing. She was grateful for the earrings he had bought her because she was family; presents for Anne, presents for his wife.

"I'm going to be looking for a new place to live, I think," she said suddenly.

He looked around the living room with curiosity as if to see if its deficiencies were easily apparent.

"I only meant this to be temporary," Anne went on, "I really don't think I could go on sharing like this." She supposed that if she told him that living with two roommates interfered with her work he would be sympathetic. Instead she said, "I think I'd like to try living alone."

Unexpectedly, her uncle said, "What did go wrong with Kent anyway, if you don't mind my asking?"

Anne reflected that it was still very hard to answer this question—there simply was no easily understandable answer. "It's so hard to say—not just any one thing. We grew apart, I guess, and then things happened which brought it all to a head."

"I always thought," her uncle said, still more unexpectedly, "that it was a mistake for him to stop studying languages. I don't pretend to understand why anyone would want to study them, but he seemed to like it, wouldn't you say?"

"Yes," Anne said. "And he was good at it."

"Proves my point. He was a fool to stop."

"But, you know," Anne said, coming to Kent's defense, "he couldn't get a job here."

"So, why'd he need to be here? You didn't have any children. You weren't even married. He could have gone anywhere, at least for a little while."

"Yes," Anne said, abandoning Kent's defense, "I know." She considered for a minute. "Actually, that was a problem. I mean, I minded him giving up what he loved, and I minded him not loving it enough. He gave it up so easily."

"You're better off without him," Uncle Douglas said definitely. "And don't be in a hurry to find someone new, if you'll take my advice. Get on with what you're doing."

On Monday Jason came into Anne's lab as she was getting ready to go out for lunch.

"I'd like to talk to you," he said.

For a minute she thought, He wants to break up, he wants to end it, and she felt an urge to put off the conversation at all costs. It started in the lab, Anne thought, and it's going to end in the lab. Just when things were going so pleasantly. He's probably told his girlfriend, and she's making him end it, not like me and Kent, they're going to stick it out.

"So how're you doing?" Jason asked.

Anne shrugged. She wanted him to get to the point. But he didn't say anything, so she threw in what had become her stock conversational phrase these days. "I'm thinking about moving. I have to find a new place. I just can't seem to get myself off my ass and start looking for one."

"Yes," Jason said, "that's what I wanted to talk to you about, as a matter of fact."

He's tired of that stupid apartment, Anne thought, that narrow bed. Or maybe just tired of me.

"I wondered if you might like to move in with me for at least a little while, at least until you sort of get your bearings and figure out where you want to live."

Anne was completely taken aback. "What about your girl-friend?"

"Actually, we've sort of talked that out. I mean, we're really just friends now. She isn't my girlfriend at all. And now she knows all about you."

"Where is she living?"

"Well, see, my place is really just a studio. And there's another studio right next door which we've been renting so Jeannette could use it to practice in. She's just going to live in there."

"In the next apartment?"

"Well, we're still pretty close, me and Jeannette. I mean, I want to see her a lot, I don't want to lose touch with her. And I think she feels the same way. So this is very convenient. Why, would it bother you?"

"I don't know," Anne said. "I guess not. I mean, considering what the situation's been all along. I wouldn't have much right to resent her, would I?"

"Does that mean you'll move in?" Jason sounded elated.

"I don't know. I'll really have to think about it." Anne was bewildered. How had she gone from being sure that Jason wanted to break up to discussing calmly whether she should move in with him? Did she really have so little grip on what was going on be-tween them? It seemed to her now that either conversation had been equally likely when he came into the lab.

"It could be just very temporary," Jason said. "I think the place you're living in now is really getting you down. This would be nicer, I bet. And you'll like Jeannette, really you will."

Anne giggled. "That seems like sort of a strange way to invite a woman to come live with you, to tell her how much she'll like the woman who used to live with you but now lives next door."

Jason grinned at her. "It might all be a little strange, but I bet it would be fun." His voice got softer, more insinuating. "We *do* have fun together, Anne." He put his hand on her knee.

"Unfair," Anne said, "you're trying to seduce me into not thinking about this rationally."

"Fucking scientists."

"Yes, exactly." Actually, she was terrifically flattered by the invitation. And tempted too—it would be such an easy move, and it could be so temporary. The cons were what? One, not having her own bedroom, but the one she had now was not really a refuge. Two, the possibility of genuine weirdness with Jeannette and all that. Three, the possibility that the magic would wear off Jason if they tried living together.

But then, on the other hand, the pros. One, getting away from Louisa and Louisa's apartment. Two, tremendous sexual possibilities, Jason all night every night. Three, perhaps most important, the chance to get a really close look at another pattern of life. On her own now, she felt she should be making choices. Louisa and Felice offered an unappealing pattern. Charlotte's was an appealing one, but a pattern Anne felt she could never emulate. This would be a sort of absurd move, out into the unknown, but there was no permanence about it. And why cling to her present arrangement? The idea of moving out on a whim, moving into Jason's place, made Anne feel adventurous and light-hearted.

"Think about it then," Jason said.

"You're sure you want another roommate so soon?"

"Look, don't make a big deal out of it. If it doesn't seem to be working out, you can move." Jason seemed a little bit hurt. "And if you want to check the place out first . . ."

Anne considered. It felt right not to look at it, younger, more daring. "I don't know," she said.

"Look, you give it all some thought and then let me know."

"No," Anne said, suddenly. "I don't need to. I think it sounds like fun. I'd like to try it."

"Far out," Jason said, with the irony the phrase demanded, but also with genuine pleasure.

"Far out," Anne repeated, and they both laughed.

*

The next little piece of Anne's life felt from the beginning like an experiment, a silly and self-absorbed patch of time which fascinated her and amused her and sometimes left her frightened, as if it were completely out of her control. She made it into a story, telling it to herself as she went along, keeping track of herself as firmly as possible.

III. *A Mattress on the Floor*

19. Weird Living Situations

Jason borrowed a car to move me from Louisa's apartment to his. Louisa insisted on helping me pack. The result was that all my clothes were neatly folded and there was extra room in my suitcases, into which she insisted on slipping two baby-blue towels and a matching washcloth. She decided that I really could not go so dowerless to my new home, and she would in fact have given me a sheet or two as well but I didn't know the size of Jason's mattress. Louisa had also, with her usual cheerful efficiency, found someone to move into my room the very next day. After I had carried my suitcases and my cardboard cartons to the front door to wait for Jason, I went back and looked at the room I had lived in for almost two months. The room looked neat and antiseptic, waiting for its new tenant.

Jason and I took everything down in the elevator and put it in the back seat of the borrowed car. Louisa came down with us to wish me luck in my new apartment and tell Jason to take good care of me. She hugged me and stood beaming on the sidewalk as Jason and I got into the car and drove down to the Village. I almost expected to see shoes tied to the bumper and a JUST MOVING IN TOGETHER sign.

There was no elevator in Jason's apartment building, which was made of dark brick and had a generally sooty appearance. I liked the way it looked after all that modernity I had been living in recently. Jason's studio was on the third floor, and we took turns carrying things up and guarding the car. I carefully did not let myself look around until we had everything up the stairs. Then I looked. It was a corner of the building; two of the walls had windows, two windows each. The other walls were not at right angles and there were actually five of them, since they shaped into a little recess at the back of the room. Jason's bed was a very large mattress on the floor pushed into the corner where the two windowed walls met. It was covered with a dark red spread, meticulously distributed so that the little edge that lapped out onto the floor was even all along. I suspected that Jason had straightened up for me; the whole apartment looked unnaturally neat. Back in the little alcove, along with the sink and stove and refrigerator, was a small round table and two unmatched chairs, one with a woven cane back and bottom, and one that was just plain dark wood. There were brick and board bookcases along one wall, containing a good many books and also a good many other things, papers and odd objects like a harmonica, an ornate clay hash pipe, some empty flowerpots. But the largest and for me most unexpected object in the whole apartment was the piano. It shouldn't have been unexpected, of course. I had just never quite pictured myself living with a piano. It was a fairly battered black upright with scarred sides, as though people had been trying to carve their initials into it. Sheet music was piled on the top, paperweighted down by a small brass vase with no flowers in it.

I liked Jason's room. I liked his piano and the posters on the walls, none of them framed, posters from concerts and art exhibits. I did notice that none of them seemed to be for dance events, and I wondered if those had all gone next door with Jeannette. Jason showed me that he had cleared out two drawers in the dresser. I stuffed my clothing in, hung things up in the closet. Then I arranged my books on a shelf which he emptied off for me. It felt particularly reassuring to see my books properly and comfortably established; I already felt more at home than I ever had in Louisa's apartment. I showed Jason the set of baby-blue towels that Louisa had given me and he showed me the bathroom, which was small and dark, but with one of those nice old bathtubs raised up on four curved claws. I hung my baby-blues on the towel rack next to Jason's white towel. I put my toothbrush next to his. I was standing in the bathroom when I heard him start to play the piano, a happy rag, a welcome. I came out and stood watching the grace of his long back swaying on the piano stool, his slender arms reaching out to the end of the scale and then drawing back in. He smashed a finish, twirled himself around on the stool, and got up, coming toward me, holding out his arms.

"That was nice," I said, and found I was almost in tears. I felt I had come to a magical apartment where everything would be strange and musical and beautiful.

"It was for you," he said, and I remember thinking, Perhaps we are in love with each other after all. He began to kiss me and I wanted him every bit as badly as I had that very first time in the incubator room. He drew me down onto his king-size mattress and I looked up past his shoulder to the windows. We undressed each other as quickly as we could and went at it, enjoying all that mattress area after my measly single bed. I looked happily around the apartment and felt serene and secure. We took a cool shower together to wash off the sweat of the move and the sex. It was like we were children, the apartment was our toy. Ours to arrange and play in. And always the sense that we might be discovered by patronizing and indulgent but uncomprehending adults.

Jason produced bread and cheese and fruit and we ate at the little table and drank from a big jug of white wine. We talked a little about Jeannette. He told me that he played the piano sometimes for her to practice; they propped open the doors to the two studios so she could hear the music. Sometimes they even pushed the piano from one room to the other, but it was an old piano and motion had a tendency to knock it out of tune. I was glad that Jeannette did not use the room we were in for dancing.

That evening I called Kent. I hadn't told him I was going to move, and it didn't seem fair to leave it for him to find out from Louisa over the phone next time he tried to call me. But I was reluctant. I don't think I was afraid to hurt him exactly; it was more that I was afraid he would assume things about Jason and me that I didn't want anyone assuming, though I was no longer sure whether that was because I didn't want them to be true or because I wanted them to be true but was afraid they never would be.

I lay on the bed and pulled the phone over next to me. Jason hung about discreetly in the remotest part of the room, over by the sink and stove and refrigerator. Kent, as I had expected, did not seem terribly surprised by my news. I gave him my new address and phone number. I asked after his new girlfriend, and he told me that things were going well. I wondered what that meant, of course; were they "in love," was she going to move in with him, was he planning to propose marriage? But of course I suppose Kent must have wondered the same things about me and Jason; after all those protestations about how he wasn't important to me, now I had moved in with him. Kent mentioned that he had seen my uncle's book in a bookstore on Fifth Avenue. There had been a big display, blow-ups of some of the photographs and a pyramid of books. He had bought one, he said, and I felt touched because of course he had only bought it because it was my uncle.

"I hope you like it," I said.

"Did you know that Margie and Alan split up?" he asked me.

I was shocked. "Oh, that's so terrible," I said. "What happened?"

"I don't really know. I just called there the other night, and Alan was alone, and he told me that Margie had moved out. He seemed pretty unhappy."

"Maybe it was just a fight and she's already back," I suggested.

"He didn't think she'd be coming back. But I haven't talked to either of them since. I don't know where she is."

"That's so terrible," I said again. Alan and Margie were hardly my favorite people, but the idea of a married couple with a child splitting up seemed to me an entirely deeper level of horrible than my own breakup with Kent. And poor Curtis, I thought, that poor little boy. It seemed world-shaking. Kent promised he would call and tell me if he heard anything else about it.

After I hung up I explained it to Jason, who also thought it was terrible, two married people, a child. It occurred to me later that all of us, the recently broken-up childless, were exclaiming over Alan and Margie to excuse our own failures, our failures at keeping our relationships alive and our failures to feel sufficiently strongly when they died. When I agreed with Kent or Jason that the Alan–Margie split was truly tragic, what I was really saying was that I had been entitled to take my own troubles more lightly because there was no marriage, no child.

Life in Jason's apartment was a tremendous success from the beginning. We could not walk in to work together because of the need for secrecy, but we took the subway uptown together and then separated, taking different routes to Viatech. For the first time I became really conscious of how much pleasure Jason got from the secret, a pleasure which was partially due to all the scientists at whose beck and call he spent his days. Not that they were terribly rude to him; Viatech wasn't like a corporation where higher-ups treat their subordinates with a certain condescending formality for the sake of company protocol. Executives may have to remind themselves constantly of their own exalted status by acting superior to underlings, but I don't really think scientists are like that. After all, as far as I can see, the work most executives do is not very different from the work most secretaries do, except that executives rarely have demonstrable skills like typing ninety words a minute.

Anyway, scientists know that the work they do is essentially different from the work that anyone else does. A few of the enlightened even know that most people regard the work that scientists do as completely devoid of interest. My cousin Louisa would say sweetly that she liked a job where you got to work with people. Alan would say the same thing, but he would phrase it in a sillier way. He would allow science if it was meaningful, the old cure-for-cancer rationale. And in the end perhaps they would both have a point. I don't think I would like a job the whole point of which was "working with people." I don't think I could find it satisfying, a job which had no deeper reality than its effects on a series of people, whether it was solving their legal problems or convincing them to buy office machinery. The accusation that Louisa and Alan would have been making implicitly—scientists don't really care about people, scientists like to escape into their laboratories—is not without a certain truth, I suppose.

All of this was leading up to the suggestion that the way senior people at Viatech treated Jason was not a deliberate attempt to establish their higher status but simply an inability to see him as real. He wasn't a scientist, he was a function. He was just the personification of the services he performed. But whatever the reason, he didn't like this kind of treatment, which was only natural. Of course I think he got quite a kick out of the knowledge that he was intimately involved with one of the Viatech scientists, that that barrier was being broken every night, and broken with a vengeance. And I suppose we both got a certain thrill from the idea that we were playing out some very tame version of Lady Chatterley and her lover. Silliness.

I should say a word about the work I was doing during this period. Ever since I proposed the idea to develop a test using fluorescent labeling techniques, Henry Madison had been happy to fuss around telling people that they weren't being careful enough about the fine points of measuring and recording when they used the fluorescent materials, but Peter Chang was still disgruntled. It was clear that he was hoping the whole thing would be a washout. Richie Grossman (it must have been he) had meanwhile been spreading rumors that I had come up with another whopper of a brilliant idea, which was not at all the case, and other scientists at Viatech were coming to treat me with a deference that I found highly uncomfortable. I could just see the slight change which would eventually come about when one of my ideas didn't work out and everyone started treating me like someone who had shown great potential but seemed to have fizzled. I knew that my idea was really very ordinary and that Richie Grossman was pushing me for reasons of his own. Charlotte said I was downgrading my own abilities, she quoted studies which proved that women always tended to underrate themselves. I countered that the women in those studies were probably rating themselves quite accurately, their judgments just seemed off by comparison to the men who were giving themselves ratings much higher than they deserved. Typical, I muttered, take the men's ratings as correct and compare the women's ratings to them. Typical.

Anyway, Richie was supporting me, pushing my ideas. Mark Riskin was treating me as a colleague. Henry was forever showing up in my lab to point out that there were four tiny inconsistencies in the report I had written up on what I was doing. Peter was irritable, though he seemed to blame me less than he blamed Mark, who was an opponent nearer his own stature. I was enjoying working with the fluorescent materials. I liked the idea of the tiny cells glowing yellow in the dark of their chamber. When you work with such tiny things, bacteria and then individual molecules of DNA, which are unimaginably small, there is a certain tendency to become detached, to stop regarding them as quite real. I mean, you never look through a microscope and actually *see* your double helix of DNA, you just work with tubes and plates and other little containers and you know what's in there but it almost seems an act of faith. And then you do your various tests and that's another act of faith, believing that because something reacts in a certain way that proves it's this or that or the other thing. But occasionally you will find yourself trying to visualize your materials, and fluorescent labeling provided me with very satisfying images, glowing lights, tiny galaxies. Things were going quite well at Viatech.

And living with Jason was fun. It was never serious, really. In the evenings we lay around on the big bed and read and drifted into sex as often as not. We went out to eat or put together somewhat haphazard meals. We went to a lot of movies, sometimes a concert. Jason was not interested in going to Sidney's. I suspected he was bored with it, and he also seemed to have had a falling-out with Sidney himself. I wondered if he had finally asked for a chance to play the piano at the nightclub and been turned down.

And then there was Jeannette. Jeannette had at first seemed like an obstacle to my living with Jason. I think I was expecting her to be elegantly, classically beautiful, like the photographs of dancers that you always see, smooth hair pulled back tightly around an ethereal face, perfect controlled graceful body. Well, she had the body, of course; she was fairly tall and thin and the muscles of her arms and legs were amazing. But her face was perfectly round and freckled with a small turned-up nose that was far from ethereal, and she had frizzy sandy brown hair. She was nice. She seemed eager to like me, afraid of imposing on my life with Jason. What I finally decided about Jeannette was that she was genuinely socially weird—and I mean this as a compliment. Jason would have liked to be weird that way, and he tried to pretend that it seemed completely natural to him, the setup with Jeannette and me, but really I'm sure he was tickled to death about how brave and new it was. I was a little shocked and tentative about the whole arrangement. But Jeannette took it in stride. Jeannette took everything in stride. In her own studio she had a single mattress on the floor, a phonograph, some dance posters, and a couple of cartons full of everything else. She was essentially a calm and serene person, she took straightforward pleasure in the music Jason played on the piano, in the small amounts of food she would allow herself, in the things she bought for herself which all ended up in those cartons. There may have been something slightly daffy about her at times, but that added to her appeal. After my first few days in Jason's apartment, after I had met her and gotten to like her, I made it clear to Jason that I had no objection to seeing quite a bit of her, and she began coming over for dinner almost every evening. Sometimes we would prop open the doors of the two apartments and Jason would hammer at the piano and Jeannette would go into her own room and dance. I was at first shy about going in to watch her, but she made me welcome, and so sometimes I sat on her bed and watched. Mostly she did exercises, which were very beautiful to watch since her body was completely at her command. But I liked best when Jason improvised and Jeannette danced to the music. I would have expected that it would make me jealous, but it didn't.

I wish I could describe just how good I felt waking up those summer mornings on that big low mattress, looking at Jason's glorious hair on his pillow, bopping off to Viatech as if it were all light comedy. And going home in the evening to take off my work clothes and put on jeans, with sometimes a fuck midway if Jason happened to be paying attention, and then investigating, was there anything to eat in the house, should we go shopping, should we eat out, was there a movie? It was all so light-hearted, as though our lack of a common past, of those years and years of learning to live as a couple, had miraculously freed us from all the wrangles and decisions that go with communal life, shared apartments. There was the hot summer and the taste of Jason's sweat, of course, and the street noises coming through the open window.

He said it first, after I had been living there for almost two weeks. He said it very easily, it was late in the evening, we had made love and we were naked on the bed reading. He tapped me on the shoulder, and I looked up from my book. "I just wanted to tell you," he said, and smiled at me. "I think I'm falling in love with you after all."

I closed my book and rolled over into his arms. "I love you," I said, and was surprised by how natural it felt. It wasn't till afterward, in fact not until the next day, that this began to scare me a little. Was that really why I had split up with Kent, because I was in love with Jason? Was that why he and Jeannette were no longer lovers too? Was this what we had both been working toward all along, the two of us monogamously ensconced in a studio apartment together? It made me feel a little scared that we would end up by taking each other over, the way couples do. It was appealing all the same to think of it as love, and certainly I felt enough tenderness and affection toward Jason for love to seem like a reasonable word. I could hardly remember the days when we had been strangers, or rather, I could remember how he had looked, how I had lusted after his twenty-nine-inch waist, but I could not remember what it had really felt like not to know him.

One night when Jason and Jeannette and I were sitting around on the floor gobbling cherries out of a big paper bag, Kent called. I answered the phone, and when I heard who it was, I withdrew a little from the other two. Kent sounded upset.

"Listen, Anne, there's something bizarre going on," Kent said, talking very softly and very fast.

"What is it?"

"Margie's turned up here. She's in the bathroom right now."

"Margie? Where's she been all this time?"

"Visiting people. Listen, that isn't the point." Then his voice changed. "So anyway, how are you?" he asked in normal tones.

"What, did she just come out of the bathroom?" I guessed.

"Yes, that's right," he said jovially. "You just ask me whatever you want to know."

"She's not going back to Alan?"

"That's what it seems like," he said, still in that hearty tone. I tried to think. "Is she in bad shape?"

"Yes, just a little strange, you might say."

"Kent, has she actually moved in on you?"

"You got it!" he sang out, as if I had just won a quiz show. Jason and Jeannette were openly listening by this point. I grimaced at them.

"Does she—I mean, should she have a shrink taking care of her or something?"

"Well, I think that might be a little extreme."

"Kent, what about Curtis?" No answer. "Is he with his father?"

"Sure seems that way."

"Have you told Alan she's there? Does he know?"

"No, I don't think so. I did want to do just that . . ."

"But she said no?"

"Exactly."

"Kent," I said suddenly, "does she want to sleep with you?"

"Well, as a matter of fact . . . ," he said, still hearty, all-American.

"Oh, Kent! And what did you do?" No answer. "Did you sleep with her?" Jason and Jeannette were fascinated.

"Yes," Kent said, finally losing that expansive voice.

"Why?" I asked.

"A mistake," he said.

"What the fuck do you mean, 'a mistake'? You thought it was

someone else?" I was clowning a little for Jason and Jeannette, which was perhaps heartless of me, but I was overjoyed to discover that I felt no pain at the thought of Kent's having slept with someone else; I had minded a little about the nineteen-year-old, to my own dismay, and now I had been tested again with better results. I was also taking shameful advantage of the fact that with Margie in the room he couldn't yell at me. It was possible he didn't even want her to know it was me he was talking to.

"Very funny," he said.

"What do you mean, 'a mistake'?"

"It seemed necessary." I was sure Margie was getting suspicious. Kent's voice was now positively furtive.

"You mean she asked and you couldn't refuse?"

"Basically, yes."

"But you don't want her as a permanent fixture."

"Exactly."

"And what about your new girlfriend? Does she know?"

"No," Kent said. "I hope never."

"You hope she never finds out. So what can I do? Do you want me to stop by and see Margie?"

"Maybe not just yet."

"Shall I tell Alan? He must be worried."

"No, better not. I don't know."

"Well, look, if I can help, you know I will. But I think you should let me tell Alan. I mean, with Curtis and all, he must be out of his mind not knowing where she is."

"Okay," Kent said.

"Okay I can tell him?"

"Maybe that would be best."

"I won't tell him you told me. I'll tell him I saw Margie on the street. No, I'll tell him I called you and she answered. Okay?"

"Okay."

"Look, it sounds to me like you're getting mixed up in things that really shouldn't be your problem. You should stop sleeping with her for one thing, and I say that with no ulterior motive, I promise."

204/ A MATTRESS ON THE FLOOR

"Yes, I know, but it isn't so easy." Now he sounded irritated.

"Well, try. And I'll call Alan. Listen, how weird is she?"

"On a scale of one to ten? Eight."

"That tells me a lot."

"Listen," he said, "I'll talk to you another day, okay? I've got to go now, I have a friend here."

"Margie?"

"Exactly. Take care of yourself," he said, and we hung up.

Jason and Jeannette were naturally very eager to hear the story behind the phone call. We all three agreed that I should call Alan. I didn't think it was at all fair. Margie leaving him to worry about whether she was dead or alive, and then making Kent cooperate in keeping Alan worried. I thought, rather suddenly and unexpectedly, of the deaths of my own parents, of how it would have felt to hover in uncertainty for days instead of knowing immediately. Of course, what I knew immediately was that they were dead, while Curtis would find out at the end of his uncertainty that his mother was alive and well. Though surely Alan could keep away the worst of that uncertainty, even if it meant telling lies. It all gave me the creeps.

"Alan? This is Anne. Listen, have you heard from Margie?"

"Yes," he said, sounding puzzled. "I talked to her yesterday. She calls every day to talk to Curtis." So she'd just been stringing Kent along; she had been in touch with Alan all the time. What an unpleasant little game.

"So you know she's staying with Kent?" I said quickly, not letting myself think about the rights or wrongs of revealing this.

"With *Kent?* Are you sure?"

"Yes," I said. "I just talked to him—I mean, when I called, she answered the phone and I recognized the voice." I realized belatedly that I still didn't want to incriminate Kent, but Alan didn't even seem to notice what I had said.

"I thought she was staying at a hotel."

"I don't think so," I said.

"Are they—I mean, do you know, I don't mean to hurt you, Anne, but do you think . . ."

"I don't know," I said, sticking to my policy of not incriminating Kent. "You better ask her."

"I'm just—you know, we split up a couple of weeks ago."

"Yes, I heard. But I didn't hear why." I felt I was surely by this point entitled to hear the full story.

"So you and Kent are really through for good?" Alan said, sadly. I knew he was thinking, Number one, that's a bad omen, a relationship that splits and doesn't heal, and number two, so Kent is really on the loose.

"Looks like it," I said.

"Well," Alan said halfheartedly, "people have to grow, even if it hurts."

We said good-bye. Jason, Jeannette, and I were all fascinated and tried to figure out what would happen next. Jason's theory was that Alan would immediately storm over to Kent's apartment, bringing Curtis, and that Margie would be mightily pleased by all this drama and amid tears and flooding reconciliations would go on home with her husband and son. Jeannette thought it was more likely that Alan would try to get in touch with Kent and find out what was going on. She thought he'd be afraid to force a major confrontation. My own theory was that Alan would in the end do nothing, would just sit at home miserably and wait for Margie to take the next step, which she would do just as soon as she got tired of her current game. As it turned out, Jason was right, which may perhaps show that it takes a man to understand a man. I got all the details from Kent.

After he had talked to me on the phone, Alan dressed Curtis, who was already in bed. They got in the car and drove to Kent's apartment. Alan had the good luck to be let in downstairs by another tenant; he didn't look very menacing with the sleepy child in his arms. When Kent came to the door to answer the bell, Alan demanded, "Where's my wife?" Poor Kent, of course, knew it must have been my doing, but he just stepped aside and let Alan enter and discover, draped on the couch, his wandering wife. Kent's own feelings at this point were very mixed; he felt he had betrayed Margie, but on the other hand he hoped that Alan would take her away. Then there was the very touching reunion between mother and son. Alan cried, "Margie!" and Curtis woke fully and cried, "Mommy!" and Curtis was in Margie's arms and so on. Margie, to give Jason still further credit, seemed to enjoy the whole thing very much. At this point, Kent, trying to be discreet, slipped into the kitchen. When he came back a little while later, everything seemed to be settled. Margie was gathering her stuff together and Curtis was hanging on to her, and Alan took Kent aside and thanked him, man to man, for helping Margie through this difficult period. This was naturally a little bit uncomfortable for Kent, though when he tried to say something in reply, Alan made it clear that Margie had said that she had been sleeping on the couch; he told Kent not to worry, he was a friend, he was someone Alan trusted, he knew Kent had not been trying to do anything besides help Margie out. The two of them shook hands. Then the happy family left, and Kent, a little confused, a little guilty, extremely relieved, called me again with the story.

By then Jeannette had gone home and Jason was in the shower. Kent sounded tentative at first; he wasn't sure exactly how to react to what had happened. I told him that Margie had been in touch with Alan all along, and then Kent felt more completely irritated with her, relieved to have her gone. I asked about what had happened sexually. He was embarrassed but he told me.

The very first night she had turned up, Margie had seemed distraught and Kent tried to comfort her. She had told him that she and Alan hadn't been getting along at all, that they had actually been having physical fights, that by mutual agreement she had gone away to think it all over, but that she now found herself still more at a loss—the marriage, Curtis, her whole life, how could they patch things up, what happened if they didn't? Kent tried to comfort her, offering his own lately gleaned insights into the breaking-up process, suggesting that a little time apart had been a good idea, she and Alan would see each other again and perhaps come to a better understanding, they shouldn't be too hasty to break up because it hurt badly and afterward it was easy to regret.

After Kent told me he had said that, he paused.

"Do you ever regret it?" he asked.

"Yes," I said.

He took up his story again immediately, just as though nothing of any importance had been said. Anyway, he made Margie scrambled eggs and sent her off to take a shower and made up a bed for her on the couch. He swore to me that he had no designs on her, whatever attraction she had once held for him had long ago worn off, she was a friend's wife, she was herself a friend who had come to him because she was in trouble, and anyway, he had a girlfriend.

This I suppose could have been interpreted as a rebuke for me, a reminder of Kent's own principled fidelity, but I was immune to such implications. Besides, I knew that this particular pride went before a fall.

After he thought she was asleep on the couch, she simply got up, came into the bedroom, and joined him. She got into bed beside him and whispered to him that she needed to be hugged, she felt so lost and lonely. He hugged her, hoping she would go back to the couch. She put her hand on his crotch. He protested that this was a bad idea, she had a husband, he had a girlfriend. She whispered that she needed to feel wanted, that she was so unhappy, wouldn't he love her and comfort her just for one night? Who would it hurt? What was so terrible about coming together again for one night now?

And so Kent was seduced, foolishly allowing himself to believe in the "just for one night." What he got instead was Margie moping around his apartment all day, greeting him when he came back from work with a brave little smile, clinging to him at night, whispering that he was the only thing standing between her and total despair. Poor Kent.

"You were a sucker," I told him, feeling that the best thing for him to do would be to treat it somewhat lightly in retrospect.

"I certainly was," he said, with relief. "She is a dippy lady."

"But there's method in her madness. She got you taking care of her, lots of attention, and now she's gone back to Alan with some hot ammunition for next time they fight."

"You think she'll tell him that we were sleeping together?"

"Of course she'll tell him. If she doesn't think of some more complicated story which she thinks would upset him even more."

Jason was out of the shower by now, lying naked on the mattress. He was pretending to ignore me, massaging his balls in a sort of idle way, less sexual than simply luxurious, the joy of being out of clothes and clean from the shower on a hot July night.

"I have to go now," I said. When he heard me say that, Jason turned his head and leered at me. I stuck out my tongue.

"Listen, Anne," Kent was saying, "I guess I should thank you. You really took the right step, you got me out of a mess."

"My pleasure," I said. "You know what a busybody I am." Jason was getting an erection.

"I'd like to see you soon," Kent said. "It's been a while and I don't want to feel we're losing touch."

"Sure," I said. "I'd like that. To see you."

"Do you think it's time we met each other's—I mean, for me to meet Jason and you to meet Emily?"

"Well, no," I said, "I don't really think that's such a good idea. It seems like it might be a little sticky, especially for them." Jason was getting a little sticky.

"Okay, maybe you're right. Shall we just go out the two of us then? Some time next week?"

"Sure," I said. "I'll call you over the weekend, okay?" The dismissal in my voice, my eagerness to get off the phone, finally became too obvious for Kent to ignore, though he seemed to want to prolong the conversation. We hung up and I turned my attention to Jason.

"You want help?" I asked him, rolling over next to him. "Or are you doing okay just by yourself?"

"You neglect me while you talk on the phone to other men. What else can I do?" He grinned at me, that ridiculously sexy I'm-about-to-drive-you-wild grin, and then he proceeded to drive me wild.

20. Encounters

My uncle's book was a best-seller. I called up to congratulate him and, incidentally, register my latest change of address. I had felt very shy about doing this, after I hadn't told him about Jason's existence. Uncle Douglas sounded very happy; there was a big paperback sale in the wind, there was even talk of a series on public television. He took the news of my move without comment. I told him it was just temporary, I was still planning to find a place of my own.

It was a little strange for me to think of my uncle and aunt getting rich. Not that I had any idea how rich they were getting, but I assumed a best-seller meant a fair amount of money. I wondered whether they would take a trip, buy a new house? It was hard for me to picture them indulging themselves. One thing they did was send me a present; my uncle bought from my aunt one of those $170 long silk robes that constituted the upper end of the Boudoir Boutique merchandise and they shipped it to me. It was rose colored and the lapels were quilted. I was in awe of it. True, it felt marvelously luxurious next to the skin, but not exactly in a comfortable or reassuring way. I felt I had a responsibility to it, to pose myself and drape myself and do nothing plebeian while I was wearing it. Jason fell in love with it and wore it much more frequently than I did. He looked very beautiful in it, I thought. It came to a little way above his ankles, and he belted it close around his twenty-nine-inch waist and paraded around the room, an exotic prince, or maybe the court magician.

At work, Mark Riskin made a pass at me one day when we were discussing how the fluorescent testing was going. I was in his lab, which was fairly small, and there was a lab technician working over at the sink. The water was running and I didn't think she could hear what we were saying. Without preliminaries Mark asked me, "Listen, would you like to start going out with me?"

It seemed an odd way to put it, but perhaps the really odd thing was that he didn't seem the least bit embarrassed. In fact, I wasn't embarrassed either. "I'm sort of involved with someone," I said.

"Oh, okay. I didn't know." He didn't seem at all hurt.

And that was that. It was flattering in a certain way, but it was basically a tribute from someone who didn't appeal to me in the least. Thinking it over, I came to the conclusion that Mark had chosen me as a possible girlfriend because he thought that with me he wouldn't have to waste time on dates discussing anything but biology. I told the story to Jason, thinking there was no harm in adding to his sense of being one up on Viatech. He was amused. He didn't find Mark any more of a threat than he found Richie Grossman. Together Jason and I pretended to be Mark in bed with a woman.

"So did you read that article on synthetic enzymes?" That was me, playing Mark, because I had the vocabulary.

"Oh, honey, ohh, harder, harder!" That was Jason, falsetto.

"But as I was—oh!—saying about the enzymes—oh!—it seems they can now purify them—oh! oh!"

"Oh, baby, purify me!"

It was extremely silly. The nice thing was that Mark's offer and my rejection didn't make relations with Mark at all uncomfortable for me. He didn't refer to the subject again, and he seemed perfectly natural toward me.

When I told Charlotte that Mark had asked me out, she didn't take it lightly. She interpreted it as a threat to my achievements, to my position at Viatech. She was almost ready to have me complain.

I managed to assure her that Mark had put no pressure on me, that he was not in any way interfering with my work. I pointed out to her that when I had made a pass at Jason, all those months ago, I had been guilty of the same offense as Mark; at least in theory, Jason could have worried about what would happen to his job if he offended me. Charlotte enjoyed the parallel, but Charlotte, to put it mildly, did not see the point of Jason. She had trouble understanding why I had moved in with him. She thought it was strange that his old girlfriend was living right next door, was essentially part of the family. She suspected Jason of having sultan's-harem fantasies. I did not, of course, admit to her that I thought I had gone and fallen in love with Jason. In fact, we didn't discuss Jason very much, any more than we discussed her lover. I had taken to having dinner at Charlotte's apartment one or two nights a week; she didn't cook me anything as elaborate as she had the first time, but the food was always wonderful. She made cold soups and homemade bread and seafood salads and so on. This helped me keep some distance from Jason; he went out with his friends and I went to Charlotte's. But Charlotte and I didn't discuss our lovers. We talked about our pasts; she told me those psychiatrist-approved anecdotes she was so good at. And we talked about people at work. Charlotte's opinion was that I shouldn't underestimate Peter Chang; he might be an unpleasant person, but she thought he was the best scientist of my three teammates. She also thought that he had been the one considered most brilliant as a student; perhaps his soured fantasies were a real burden. Henry Madison she was more prepared to dismiss, though warning me that he did know his stuff, he sometimes caught people out very embarrassingly on errors that seemed to be trivial but turned out to undermine big pieces of research. As for Mark Riskin, whom Charlotte referred to as "your beau, Mark Riskin," she thought he was solid, not flashy. This surprised me a little; I had been seeing him as a man given to enthusiasms, partially because of his sympathy for me and my idea. No, Charlotte said, Mark was a patient and reliable and talented worker. He was quick to see the significance of anything he came across, but he did not tend to make sudden leaps. The problem that I had with this kind of conversation with

Charlotte was that it was obvious that she regarded my work with my team as nothing but a race. She was giving me advice: You can beat Henry Madison easily, as long as you watch your small points; you can put Mark Riskin in the shade if you give off a few bright flashes; keep an eye out for Peter Chang coming up from behind.

It bothered me, her grooming me as her entrant in the recombinant antibody stakes. I didn't really see the project that way, in part because I wasn't sufficiently enthusiastic about anyone's chance of doing something really important with it. But also, that isn't the way I like to work, in cutthroat competition to impress Richie Grossman. I expect credit for the work I do, and I don't mind pushing for the credit if I seem to be being passed over, but I don't like to judge every meeting in terms of who made the best impression and who got left in the dust.

To be perfectly honest, I also had some sense that Charlotte was using me to fight her battles vicariously. She wanted me to leave my teammates far behind and speed to an exalted position in the front ranks of Viatech, whatever that meant. I couldn't help feeling that she wanted me to vindicate all female scientists, which is something I had come across before and which had always made me uncomfortable. It's too heavy a weight for me; like everyone else, I take comfort in the idea that somewhere out there are female scientists so brilliant and so dedicated that they will vindicate us all, including me. I'm not prepared to be pointed to as the standard-bearer. I'm not that good. I'm high minor-league material but I'd be low major-league quality. There are people with instincts for the work, people who can, for example, magically make recalcitrant cell cultures start growing, people with scientific "green thumbs." I have a little of this, but only a little. There was no one at Viatech who I necessarily thought had more of it, and I felt quite able to compete there, but I didn't fool myself that I was a quantum jump ahead of the crowd. Charlotte would have none of this. It was my low opinion of myself getting in my way, it was my fear of competing with men, it was laziness.

But if I asked Charlotte why *she* didn't push to the fore, she just told me that she didn't really like science all that much, she probably shouldn't have gone into it in the first place, she was content now to do it for a living but that was all. I suggested that this was also an excuse, but Charlotte waved that aside with the serenity of the psychoanalyzed—I know more about my subconscious than you do, and more about yours too.

Oddly enough, when you consider that she professed to dislike science, the conversations with her I enjoyed most were more or less about science. That is, about our relationship to science, how we had gotten into it, how we had reacted to various kinds of research. It was a part of my life I had never really talked about with a close friend before, because I had never had a close friend who was a scientist. For Charlotte it was a somewhat more fraught subject, since she insisted she had never wanted to go into science in the first place.

"But Charlotte, there was never even a moment when it really really grabbed you? When you wanted to study it for its own sake, not just because of your father?"

Charlotte shrugged, as if unwilling to admit it. "Maybe back at the beginning, you know, when the real reductionists made it sound like if I only got the molecules straight I would understand everything there was to understand about life. You know, 'biochemistry is everything,' that sort of attitude. They never admit that the whole may be more than the sum of its parts, or that the parts could be anything bigger than molecules. It did have a certain appeal, especially for a person with a methodical temperament."

"I know," I said. "I also got sort of disillusioned with the reductionist biochemistry. You can't really use it as a way to understand how organisms work. But then I discovered DNA."

"Oh, did you do that? Boy, James Watson could at least have mentioned you. What a bastard."

Watson, of course, is the scientist who with Francis Crick figured out the structure of DNA in 1953. They won the Nobel Prize for it in 1962, and from Watson's book, *The Double Helix*, it is clear that they were racing for the prize from the beginning. Lots of scientists take exception to the tone of that book, and women scientists in particular tend to resent the comments Watson makes about Rosalind Franklin, a scientist who also studied the structure of DNA; there has been some controversy about whether some of her results were appropriated or exploited by Watson and Crick without her permission. Watson then added insult to injury by complaining in his book about her lack of femininity, her unwillingness to wear lipstick, and more.

"You know, I suspected all along that it was really you who discovered the structure of DNA," Charlotte said thoughtfully. "Watson just wasn't man enough to admit it, huh?"

"He never liked me—"

"Don't tell me, you didn't wear lipstick."

"Worse, I had flat-heeled shoes."

"My God, I'm surprised he condescended to steal your research."

"But you know, Charlotte," I said seriously, "the timing of their discoveries, Watson and Crick's, I mean, really affected me. I mean, when I was in college that was all still pretty fresh. A lot of my professors had spent part of their professional lives without knowing how DNA worked. It was being taught as the discovery of the century, as the most important thing in biology."

"And so, like good little biology students all over the country, you answered to the call."

"It really did seem a little like, excuse me, the secret of life. There it was, the thing that made life life, if you know what I mean, and also the thing that made each kind of life what it was. It seemed like the opening to everything."

"My goodness," Charlotte said, "you really were inspired."

"Well, even more so when recombination came along. Notice I didn't say, 'when I discovered recombination.' "

"What do you mean by 'came along'?"

"All the original furor was right around when I was beginning college. There were these conferences to discuss the dangers of recombinant DNA. I don't think I really understood what recombination was probably till I was in my senior year. Still, that was pretty close to the actual beginning of it all."

"And it knocked you over?"

"Sure. Don't you see? I had already decided I would go into genetics, there I was, thinking of DNA as this tiny secret molecule to be studied, I don't know, almost worshipped. All the secrets of everything alive. And then all of a sudden I find out that we can actually cut it into pieces and rejoin the pieces and find out what our new pieces are, what they code for. I almost couldn't believe it. I couldn't believe science was so clever."

I was a little embarrassed. I really had felt all those things back once upon a time, but they hardly figured in my day-to-day life and work anymore. I was now accustomed to the technology of recombinant DNA, I used it casually, I took it for granted. It was a little strange to hear myself speaking like a novice.

But Charlotte smiled. "That's the right way to choose a field," she said. "That's why you're so good at it."

And I did resolve to respect my own work a little more, or maybe not my own work exactly, but my field. I decided I should try to remember that it had once seemed the most amazing and important line of work, and that even if it had now become only a pleasant daily bread, somewhere within it were still the seeds of what had inspired my awe and excitement.

I was thinking a great deal during that period about how people felt about their work. It grew out of my earlier attempts to divide my acquaintances according to whether they had content or not. Perhaps there was such a thing as professionalism without content; into this category both Louisa and Felice fit very neatly. Then there was content without professionalism, and that was Jason. Maybe Kent as well, although I was inclined to feel that he should be given credit for both content and professionalism, but in his case the two were completely unrelated. And that left the fortunate few who had professionalism which grew out of their content. Jeannette. My uncle. Charlotte, whether she was willing to admit it or not; I knew she did good work. Me.

I did talk to Jason about the possibilities for him to at least give music a try. I was no judge, of course, but it sounded to me as if he had talent. He was also dedicated; he spent a great deal of time at the piano, though I couldn't tell whether he was just messing around or really practicing. I was accustomed to his music as background for almost everything I did in the apartment, including, once, a rather misguided attempt to fuck sitting up on the piano stool while he kept playing. We were both laughing too hard for it to be a valid test. Jason was not exactly defensive about his chances for a career in music, he was just not willing to take any practical steps as far as I could see. He was occasionally ready to fantasize—records he would like to cut, cities he would like to play in. He would sit at the piano, dressed as often as not in my pink silk robe, and talk an intro to me, as though I were a whole audience.

He played for me and for Jeannette, and for other people too, for friends who dropped by, for other dancers Jeannette knew who occasionally turned up to practice something with her. And everyone seemed happy to listen, everyone seemed to think he was good. But whatever the jump was to playing in public, he was unwilling to make it.

One night toward the end of July, Jason and I went to Central Park to hear the New York Philharmonic play in Sheep Meadow. We took along a blanket and a shopping bag containing a picnic supper. We got there fairly early and found a place a reasonable distance from the stage, close enough so that we could see the musicians and watch the conductor, but not so close that we would be in the really densely packed area, and we spread out our blanket. New York is a big city, of course, and there were an awful lot of people at the concert, but fate is fate, and Kent and his new girlfriend almost literally stumbled over us when they came looking for a place to spread their blanket. While he and I were exclaiming over the coincidence, she spread the blanket. I assumed that he would have preferred to go on and find a place a little farther away from us; I had been picturing the concert as a chance to lie in Jason's arms under the stars, and I was hardly eager to have Kent two feet away, and surely he would have seen it the same way. But Emily spread out their blanket, put down their shopping bag, and came over to meet me, all smiles. She was plump, maybe a little fatter than plump. She had a mass of dark curly hair, down almost to her waist, over which she wore a pink bandana. She wore a pink and white dress that tied around her under her arms with a drawstring and reached down to her feet. A muumuu, my aunt would have called it. Her shoulders were bare. She looked about sixteen. Kent, wearing jeans and a workshirt, looked quite good, but at least fifteen years older than Emily.

I liked Emily. But I am afraid I liked her with a sort of condescension, as though she were the endearing little sister of a friend. It was hard for me to think of her as my successor in Kent's life.

"I've heard so much about you!" she said to me, and then giggled. "Or maybe I shouldn't say that!" She spoke enthusiastically, always eagerly.

"That's okay, I won't ask you what you've heard," I said. I smiled. I felt more than a little uncomfortable, and so, I think, did Kent. But he, thank God, did not say to Jason, 'And *I've* heard a lot about *you*,' or something like that, and Jason also held his peace. We all agreed that it was a nice night for a concert, the sky seemed clear, we would probably be able to see the stars when it got dark.

Emily announced, "I hate not being able to really see the stars! That's one of the things I really hate about New York!"

There was a brief silence. Then Kent said, "Time to eat." They settled down on their blanket and began unpacking their shopping bag while Jason and I did the same on our blanket.

We didn't join up into a single group and start sharing food, neither did we quite turn away into two couples. We all kept catching each other's eyes and nodding cheerfully. I took a sort of mean glee in the superiority of our picnic supper: pâté and French bread and Camembert and olives. Kent and Emily seemed to have gone the organic route, which I assumed was Emily's influence, since Kent's idea of a wonderful picnic would be cold roast chicken and macaroni salad. Instead they had tahini and a rather dis-spirited-looking bean sprout salad and pita bread, and the whole effect was not promising.

We offered them some of our wine, and they accepted. The orchestra was tuning up. Jason and I packed our scraps and containers into the shopping bag and settled back to wait for the music. We kept the bottle of wine near at hand. Again I thought of how I had pictured myself lying wrapped up in Jason with the music around me, and I wished Kent and his nineteen-year-old vegetarian-poet girlfriend were off at the other end of Sheep Meadow.

We applauded the conductor, whom we were close enough to see, he lifted his baton, we were bathed in Beethoven. It was a lovely and slightly improbable combination, the music, the park, and, visible out beyond the trees, the row of skyscrapers along Central Park South. As the night grew darker, the lights around the park became less incongruous; the city itself disappeared except for the dots of light which suggested the buildings but without ferocity. They seemed no more surprising than the stars, which we could indeed see. I hoped Emily was satisfied.

In the brief silence after the first movement, Jason produced a joint, lit it, passed it first to me and then to Kent and Emily. Then he put his arm around my shoulders and I settled into him, carefully not looking around to see what the other two were doing. It was admittedly a little strange, the idea that Kent and another woman were possibly doing the same thing two feet away. I lay with my head pillowed on Jason's arm and looked up at the stars, and he pressed his body very gently against mine. When the symphony ended there was a moment of confusion for me, before I sat up and began to applaud along with everyone else. I had really been—I don't know if you could exactly call it outside myself—in some sense unconnected from the actual details of what had been happening.

It was in fact only later that night, when Jason and I got home, that I gave serious thought to what Kent had thought of Jason, what Jason had thought of Kent, and so on. I asked Jason, but he just shrugged and said Kent seemed like a nice guy, that girl was somewhat silly. One way or another, I found myself feeling a little bit sorry for Kent. I wondered if Emily would go on camping trips with him. I was sure that she at least professed a love for the mountains and the forests, for the great outdoors where you could see the stars. I wondered whether Emily, instead of being the conventional on-the-rebound opposite of the ex-girlfriend, me, was Kent's attempt to replace me with someone even more extreme than I in what he perceived as my mode.

That night something happened between Jason and me which had never happened before. In fact, we had not been wildly adventurous sexually; I don't mean that we had stuck to only one or two ways of making love, but there had never been any exotic explorations either. What happened that night was quite spontaneous. We had been making love for quite a while. I was on top of him. I had already come several times and we were both sweaty.

"Lie back," I whispered, pushing his hands down onto the mattress. "Let me. I'll do it all." His hands came back up to hold me. "No," I whispered, pushing them back, "you lie still." I was suddenly conscious that there was at least a small titillating element of cruelty in what I was saying. I moved on him and he moaned.

"You have to lie still," I told him, "keep your hands down."

"Tie them," he whispered, "tie them down."

I went and got the clothesline that Jason sometimes hung across the room when there was handwashing to dry. It was a little bit hard to tie his hands because there wasn't really anything to fasten them to, but finally I tied the cord to one wrist, passed it under the mattress and out the other side and tied his other wrist. His arms were held tightly out away from him at right angles; he looked crucified. I was a little horrified that that was the image which came to mind, even more horrified when vague images of torture seemed to be lurking behind it. And I was also extremely aroused by the whole process of tying him up, and so was he. I settled on top of him again, and began moving as slowly as I could, trying very deliberately to tease him. I enjoyed watching his arms pulling against the rope. I would in fact have gone on teasing him like that longer, except that I finally lost control of myself and in so doing allowed him his orgasm. Then afterward there was the curiously matter-of-fact business of untying him before I sank down in his arms and felt suddenly embarrassed.

I had always thought that he was more or less the dominant one

when it came to sex between us. I would have been much less surprised if it had been suggested to me that he would tie me up. Not
that anyone else ever had, or had ever even tried. I felt closer to
Jason at that point than I ever had before, I think, and I also felt a
little bit afraid, as though I saw for the first time that things were
moving much too fast between the two of us, that we were in danger, living together in this single room, of filling too many places
in each other's lives, despite any precautions we might take.

IV. Decorating

21. Housewarming Presents

Anne is now living in her own studio apartment, up on the West Side, not far from Columbia University. Oddly enough, it was Kent's new girlfriend Emily who found her the apartment. About a week after the concert at Sheep Meadow, Emily telephoned Anne to invite her to a party. Anne declined politely, saying she and Jason already had plans. Emily, sounding a little mournful, said that she hoped she and Anne could get to know each other. Anne said vaguely that that would be nice, it's just that everything is so hectic, I'm very busy at work, I'm thinking of looking for a new apartment. Aren't you living with Jason, Emily asked, and Anne said, Yes, but he has only one room, it really isn't a big enough apartment for two, I was only staying there until I could find a place of my own.

Anne wanted this message to get back to Kent; instead of emphasizing to him that she was completely established in another couple, she felt she would prefer to present herself to Kent as a little more independent these days. Good, let Emily tell him that Anne and Jason were not living together on a permanent basis.

But what Emily did was call back an hour later to offer tentatively that she had this friend who had suddenly decided not to go back to Columbia next year, in fact he was moving out to Los Angeles, and he had this really nice studio right off West End Avenue, his family had a lot of money so it wasn't just a cheap student apartment. And so, with a confused feeling that apartments opened up for her whenever she wasn't sure she wanted them, Anne went uptown, saw the apartment, and ended up taking over the illegal sublet without even notifying the official tenant, who was somewhere in western Canada.

So now Anne is living in an illegally sublet and resublet studio apartment on the Upper West Side. Emily seems to consider that finding the apartment has made her one of Anne's closest friends and is constantly dropping by. Jason, who agreed with Anne in principle that she should find a place of her own, seems a little disappointed now that it has happened, but he is also a frequent guest. Kent has never been there, though Anne suspects that Emily is always suggesting to him that he come with her. Charlotte hasn't seen it yet either, but Anne has promised to make her dinner as soon as she's properly settled. Anne has had the new apartment for only two weeks.

In all, she lived with Jason for a month, and perhaps she was crazy to interrupt an arrangement that was making them both so happy. But she could already sense that the realities of coexistence in such a small area were beginning to intrude. Two people in one room, never out of each other's sight unless one was in the bathroom. Every tiny bit of messiness committed by one of them constantly visible to the other. It had, in fact, seemed to Anne that unless she moved out fairly soon, her relationship with Jason would change for the worse, that it might end by failing. The thought of such a failure frightened her.

Anne is not used to being alone in an apartment. It feels strange, and more than a little bit terrifying. For one thing, unexpectedly, she is subject to physical fears. Before she can go to sleep, she checks that the door is locked, that the stove is off. Sometimes when she is in bed she gets up to check that there is no one in the bathroom, taking a deep breath and sweeping the shower curtain to one side. She checks her closet too. Her mattress is on the floor, so at least there is no under-the-bed. And then she checks the lock on the door again.

Anne's new apartment is not as large as Jason's, but it is pretty. There is a bay window and the ceiling is high. The walls are in good shape, white and not marked. The floor must have been beautiful once, polished blond wood, but the tenant before Anne scarred it badly. It needs to be resanded and rewaxed, and Anne is not quite up to that. Kent, she thinks, could do it and enjoy doing it. Her "kitchen" is very compact—stove, sink, half-refrigerator, cupboard—and it is not really divided from the room, just off in a corner. She had to clean it very thoroughly when she moved in. The last tenant sold her the double mattress and the small table and the three chairs for two hundred dollars; he left nothing else behind but dirt and a collection of wooden crates. Anne had at first meant to throw these out, but in the end had piled them in three columns of three to form a makeshift bookcase.

Anne has scrubbed the apartment; she bought glass cleaner, basin, tub, and tile cleaner, scouring powder, brushes, a broom, a mop, a dry mop, sponges, steel wool, a bucket. Now the apartment is immaculate. She has bought one fitted sheet, one nonfitted sheet, two pillow cases. The fitted sheet is a dull, dark brick red, the top sheet is gray, and the pillow cases are dark blue with a thin gray stripe. She has bought two plates, two mugs, two knives, two forks, two spoons, one pot, one frying pan, a package of paper napkins. The plates and mugs are heavy blue ceramic and come from a cheap household goods store not far from the new apartment. The silverware is from Woolworth's. And that, besides the cleaning supplies and some toilet paper and a small alarm clock, is just about it. Her books have not yet been distributed on the crate shelves. The room is clean but bare, as though someone conscientiously neat were moving out, had already moved out except for the last load, the mattress for the last night.

Anne makes lists, both mental and written, of the things she has to buy, wants to buy. A bath mat, a bedspread, more plates and silverware, a teapot, a coffeepot. A piece or two of furniture—a dresser or an armchair or a real bookcase—a record player, a tablecloth, a vase. Little things: a bottle opener, a vegetable peeler, a corkscrew, a sharp knife. Important things: pictures for the walls, a rug, plants. What is holding her back? She comes home from work every day empty-handed—not even a corkscrew. Jason bought her a bottle of wine the third night she was in the apartment, to celebrate, to show his goodwill, and fortunately it was California champagne, so they didn't need any equipment to get it open. And they drank it from the bottle. Buy: wine glasses, water glasses, ice trays.

What is holding her back? She is taking some pleasure in the austerity, in the sense of a life to be created, in the lists themselves. She is a little bit afraid of the decision represented by each and every item on each and every list, and as long as she has the small ones still in front of her, the larger ones do not seem too imminent. How can she choose a rug when she hasn't chosen a vegetable peeler yet?

Sometimes she feels that she is waiting for things to come to her. In fact, finally they begin to arrive. Emily brings her a rather unhealthy-looking geranium. Anne sets it on one of her crates over in front of the window, and the geranium revives and even tries a few red flowers. Emily, impressed, contributes a spider plant and a jade plant, which also go on top of the crate. Anne feels almost more grateful to Emily for the plants than she felt for the apartment. She is even willing to listen to Emily agonize about Kent, which she has up till now been reluctant to do. Emily sits cross-legged on Anne's floor and explains at length: She has to go away to Israel to see her parents in a week, she'll be away for more than three weeks, what if Kent finds someone else? Don't worry, Anne says, he cares about you, he's loyal. Emily confesses: What is really worrying her is that once she is away from Kent *she* will slip and cheat on him and spoil everything. Anne cannot understand why Emily needs her for a confidante. Doesn't she have any friends her own age? It is hard for Anne to accept that to Emily she is a source of expert advice: how to cope with Kent. But really, Anne says, after all, I didn't do such a great job of it. Kent and I split up, after all. Yes, says Emily, but you had so many good years together. I really respect that. I'd really like to have a lasting relationship.

Look, Anne says, you don't want to cheat on him, don't cheat on him; you cheat on him and don't want him to know, don't tell him. And still Anne feels a certain fondness for Emily, this plump child sitting on her floor, spreading her cotton skirt out around her, twisting her hair into tiny ringlets, going off eventually, no doubt to spend the night with Kent, leaving behind her, as often as not, a plastic yogurt container filled with homemade hummus or tabbouleh.

Anne finally telephones Louisa, who is eager to come over. She brings, of course, a housewarming gift: a big casserole made of enameled metal, white with green leaves on it. Anne can return it if it's something she doesn't need, Louisa says, and Anne is glad to assure her, she loves it. Anne is sorry to have nothing to offer her, just instant coffee and a bag of chocolate-chip cookies. Louisa admires the apartment, though Anne suspects that Louisa thinks it a pity that Anne is living in one room.

They catch up on each other's news; yes, Anne is still involved with Jason, and she occasionally hears from Kent, more often from his new girlfriend who is always dropping by. Louisa looks a little bit perplexed. What about Jim, Anne asks.

Louisa blushes. "It's going really well," she says. "We're really in love."

"That's great, Louisa." Anne doesn't ask what happened to the difficulties of a month or so ago, because Louisa has too convenient a memory to be bothered about things like that.

"How's Felice?"

"Oh, she's fine. She's just like always. Except there's a chance she might get a part in an ad for men's shirts."

"Great. I mean, she must be really excited."

"Yes," Louisa says, "I guess she is. I mean, this could be the real start for her."

Jason also gets into the act of bringing things to put in Anne's apartment. He contributes a bedspread, a little shyly, offering to take it away again if it doesn't please her. In fact, she loves it. It is an enormous patchwork quilt, a crazy quilt, pieces of cloth of every shape and size, also of every fabric. It is just big enough to cover her bed. Where did he get it? He and Jeannette found it at a flea market, it was torn and very dirty. They had it dry-cleaned and then Jeannette mended it, even added some new patches. Anne is overwhelmed, they would do all this for her. With the quilt spread over the bed, the room looks completely different, much more friendly. Anne can see that the quilt was pieced together by someone with no eye for conventional color combinations; patterns and colors are jumbled higgledy-piggledy.

"I would like to take this quilt as the metaphor for my life," Anne announces to Jason, after they have initiated it, made love on top of it, seen each other naked against it.

"Okay," he says, "I brought you a bedspread, now the least you can do is buy me a bath mat."

And amazingly enough, she does, she has one there for him on his next visit, a luxurious thick oval bath mat, shocking pink, and a matching bath towel for him. It is her way of saying thank you for the bedspread, which continues to enthrall her. She has trouble thinking of a way to thank Jeannette, finally buys her a six-foot-by-three-foot scarf of dark green silk with gold threads around the edges. Jason reports that Jeannette loves the scarf. You have to bring her to see me soon, Anne keeps saying, or else I'll come there. Come over, Jason urges, and Anne does, and they have a familial evening, the three of them, the way they did when Anne was living with Jason. Jeannette wears the scarf as a shirt, tied around her torso, the ends crossing and recrossing her front to tie in back. They eat yogurt and grapes and barbecue-flavored potato chips, which are one of Jeannette's weaknesses, and after dinner they push Jason's piano into Jeannette's studio and she dances while he plays.

And Charlotte, Charlotte also makes a contribution to Anne's new apartment. She marches into Anne's lab one day with a shopping bag full of cooking equipment and announces that they are all things she doesn't use anymore. Anne is to take them, and without any fuss. And so Anne acquires things to put in her kitchen drawers: a rolling pin, a measuring cup, two wooden spoons, a whisk. Also a colander and a pepper mill into the bargain. But Charlotte's contribution is even more than that; she invites Anne to come along on a trip to Macy's. Charlotte comes away with four linen napkins and an egg slicer, and Anne acquires three enormous cushions, a quantity of glasses and plates and bowls of various sizes, a coffeepot, and all sorts of other things, some of which surprise her when they emerge from her bags back in the apartment—a muffin tin?

Because she has to help carry all Anne's packages home, Charlotte gets to see Anne's new apartment for the first time.

"Who are you supposed to be, Saint Theresa? Couldn't you even afford one comfortable chair?"

"Charlotte, up till today I haven't been able to bring myself to buy wine glasses. I don't know how to thank you for doing all this with me today, it all seemed so easy with you there."

"Of course it's easy. Now come the important things. You need a rug and at least one armchair and a proper desk and some bookshelves and something to go up on these walls." And somehow just hearing Charlotte rattle them off like that, Anne is confident that she will go out and find them all.

Anne takes her three new matching cushions out of their bags and puts them on the bed and floor; they are covered in a heavy ridged fabric, browns and grays and a little sandy white. Charlotte goes to the sink and begins rinsing Anne's new glasses and dishes.

"Listen," Anne says, suddenly overwhelmingly happy, "this won't be the fancy dinner I promised you, but I could go out and get some stuff, we could have supper. Break in my plates."

"Go on," Charlotte says. "I'll finish unpacking your new toys."

Anne goes out, buys a corkscrew immediately, a bottle of cold white wine, cheese, bread, crab meat and olive salad. On the way back she stops, struck by a poster hanging in a store window. A Japanese print of mountains and tigers and, in the foreground, a fountain where several young girls are posed in carefree attitudes, as if the mountains cast no shadows, as if the tigers were cats. Anne goes and finds that she can buy it framed for sixty dollars, which, the man is assuring her, is marked way down, half price. All her money for the rest of the weekend, but Anne hands it over, talks the man into throwing in a picture-hanging hook which

will support the weight of her new acquisition. She struggles home
with the heavy package. Charlotte approves. Anne, of course, has
no hammer, but she does have a pair of wooden clogs and, after
much debate over the perfect position, Charlotte uses the bottom
of one of these to hammer the nail into the wall. And then there is
the print hanging and Anne opening the bottle of wine with her
new corkscrew and pouring it into her new wine glasses, and they
settle onto the floor. They lean back against the new cushions.

Charlotte offers a toast, "To homemaking."

"To domesticity."

And so when early the following week Kent finally comes to the
new apartment, it is nowhere near as bare as it was. When she
opens the door for Kent, he is standing next to two huge boxes.
He carries them in.

One carton is full of sheets, towels, and pots and pans from the
apartment they had shared. He insists that she take them. In the
other carton is Kent's bargain with his conscience: he has bought
Anne a stereo. He has also brought along about twenty records
which he thinks are her very favorites. If she will accept this, he
will consider the rest of the records, the stereo in the old apartment, the furniture in the old apartment, the whole package, to be
truly his. Unless of course there is something she particularly
wants, he concludes a little lamely.

Again Anne is touched. She watches Kent setting up the stereo,
she looks through the records, which are indeed well chosen, she
assures him that the furniture and the remaining records are his,
that he has chosen perfectly. He finishes connecting all the wires
and asks for a trial record. She gives him a battered Joni Mitchell
album, a survivor from early in her college days, if not from high
school. Then, as the music fills her room, the first music she has
had there, she is proud to be able to offer Kent wine, to finally be
equipped to entertain a little. She praises the sound of the stereo,
and he insists it isn't a very elaborate setup, no better than the one
they used to share. She suspects it is at least a little bit better.
They sit on the floor and she thanks him again.

Emily is leaving for Israel the day after tomorrow, he says.

He'll miss her, but he thinks it's good she's going to have some time with her parents. She pretends to be very independent, but really she's so young. She's sweet, Anne says, I like her. Do you, Kent says eagerly, do you really? You have to see through some of the silliness on the surface, of course, he goes on, but she's really very special.

Anne, looking at Kent, feels suddenly sorry for him and wonders if this is not treacherous. Is she trying to justify her own persistent sporadic attraction to Kent, pretending that he really should be rescued from Emily? From Emily, isn't that a bit ridiculous, rescuing someone from Emily? No denying, right this minute Anne finds Kent attractive. He has come to visit bearing music, he is sweet and familiar, much more familiar than Jason has ever been. Treacherous. How can she even think of unsettling the conscience of Kent, a man who cannot live comfortably with furniture that he considers slightly ill-gotten?

Honorable Kent. He gets up to leave and Anne thanks him yet once again for the stereo and he reaches out to give her a hug. Honorable maybe, but self-deluding; the hug is quickly dangerously near collapsing onto the mattress. It is actually Anne who pulls away.

"Look," she says, "it isn't so much because of me, but this may be a very bad idea."

"You're right. I know, I shouldn't have—" He shakes his head, but he is smiling. In fact, they are both smiling, pleased to know, perhaps, that their idle lusts are reciprocated. "But some other day," Kent says.

"Definitely," Anne says, and they kiss good-bye lightly. He leaves, and Anne turns the record over, wondering what that last remark of his bodes for Emily.

22. Opening Boxes

"I'd be grateful if we could keep personalities out of this," says Richie Grossman.

"Personalities have nothing to do with it," Peter Chang says furiously. "What I am saying is that stupid time-wasting suggestions keep being adopted, we all keep running off in wrong directions. Now, if most of those suggestions happen to come from the same place, well, that isn't personalities, that's just facts."

"And would you mind telling me," Anne breaks in, looking him in the eye though he has rather been avoiding her glance, "would you mind telling me if you have ever considered anyone else's suggestions but your own to be anything except stupid? You don't really give a damn where they come from—as long as they don't come from you they're bullshit!" She starts out speaking calmly, but her voice cracks toward the end. She is astonished to hear herself talking like that in a meeting, still more astonished that whatever inner reservoir of anger has propelled her this far is apparently going to keep her going.

"Your suggestions have absolutely no scientific validity. You know how to use a piece of apparatus and all you can think to do is turn it on whenever you can!" Peter is speaking directly to her now.

"I don't think this is getting us anywhere," Richie Grossman says.

"Look, you guys, cut it out," Mark Riskin says, more forcefully.

Anne is not listening. "And you, you don't know how to use that piece of apparatus so therefore you won't accept any research where it has to be used. Right? I hate to think where we'd all be if you hadn't been taught how to use a microscope!"

"I don't have to take this," Peter says. He stomps out of the room and there is a brief lull.

Anne finds that she is trembling. Why did she let herself get so angry? Why didn't Mark or Richie come to her aid? All she did to provoke this was to suggest at the beginning of the meeting that there were several possible applications for the fluorescence testing they have been working on, that it would be worth putting a little more time in to see how far they could take it. Richie seemed enthusiastic, Mark seemed interested, Henry Madison seemed at least not hostile. But Peter Chang started in immediately: We've already wasted so much time with this, can't we get back to some meaningful research?

"I'm sorry," Anne says to the meeting in general. "I guess I lost my temper."

"That's okay, Anne," Richie says. "I guess you were provoked, all right."

"I'm not crazy, am I?" Anne asks, looking at Mark. "He really was being unreasonable, wasn't he?"

Mark nods, but before he can answer, Richie announces that it might be better to end the meeting here and let everyone cool off a bit. "Anne," he says, "I'd like to talk to you for a minute."

When the others have gone, Richie tells Anne that Peter Chang is "on edge" these days, his wife is in the hospital for tests, they think she may have cancer. Admittedly, Peter is being difficult, but maybe Anne could try to be a little understanding?

"Sure," Anne says automatically, then, "Richie, why didn't you tell me this before?"

"I should have. It's my fault." Richie is prepared to be magnanimous, but it is a false magnanimity, Anne senses, he is really blaming her for getting angry at Peter.

"Did everyone else know this? I mean Mark and Henry?"

"I think so." Richie looks a little sheepish.

Anne is angry, but not angry enough to lose her temper directly at her boss. "I'll try to make it up with Peter. That's really terrible about his wife."

"Yes," Richie says, obviously glad to be off the hook. "It's just terrible. And they've got two kids, you know."

Actually Anne hadn't known; she had known there were children but only in a vague imprecise way, not how many or how old or what sex.

It is with great relief that she finally leaves Richie and goes back to her own lab. She is furious: How dare they all sit there knowing about Peter's wife and not do anything to stop the fight? How dare they not tell her? Bastards. Filthy bastards, and that includes Peter Chang; if his wife is in the hospital he's entitled to be worried and distracted, but not to use it as an excuse to scream out at Anne all the nasty things he's been thinking about her all along. Back in her own lab she is faced with Arthur Schenk, hardly a figure to make her feel more kindly toward male scientists in general.

Arthur is fussing around with a computer printout, annotating it with a fine-point red felt-tipped pen. He looks up as Anne comes in and she is suddenly sure that he has heard the whole story already. News travels fast. She leaves the room again, and runs into Jason, who is wheeling his little metal trolley around a corner. Anne stops, thinking it is perhaps safe to exchange a word—if nothing else, it might be comforting. But they have literally exchanged only one word—hi—when a door opens and a scientist about Anne's age comes charging out.

"Hey, listen," he says to Jason, "something is going wrong with my mice. You guys are putting too many in every cage or something. They're coming to me all scratched and bitten."

"I wouldn't know about that," Jason says, "I don't work in the animal room. I just bring you the animals." There is perhaps a slight truculence in his voice; Anne suspects that he is putting it on for her benefit. She is in no mood to be patient with the opposite sex, not even with Jason.

"Do you think you could tell whoever *is* in charge of the animal room that he must be crowding my mice? They wouldn't fight like this under normal conditions." The scientist turns to Anne.

"That's the trouble with this place, no one you talk to is ever the person in charge of anything. Everyone passes the buck."

"Look," Jason says, the truculence more evident, "I'm not passing any bucks. But I don't have anything to do with taking care of your mice."

Anne intervenes, thinking to herself that if she doesn't, the two of them may decide to settle their completely pointless dispute with pistols at dawn. "The guy you should talk to is that little Puerto Rican man with the beard," she tells the scientist. "He takes care of all the animals. And he knows a lot about them all too; if there's some special problem with your mice, he'll probably be able to figure it out."

The scientist considers. He is clearly not sure that he should agree to run his own errand, but on the other hand, a suggestion from Anne is not to be dismissed like a suggestion from Jason. Anne is at least his peer, maybe more; there are, after all, rumors that she may be brilliant, that she's the boss's protegée.

"Okay. I'll talk to him." He turns away without a word to Jason and strides off down the hall with great purposefulness.

"Turkey," Anne mutters.

"Thanks," Jason says, "thanks for getting that turkey off my back."

"Yeah, well, I guess I should keep walking."

"I can go your way. That won't be suspicious." He trundles his cart along next to her.

"Heard any rumors about me today?" Anne asks.

"No. What happened, you finally gave in to Richie Grossman? No, don't tell me, you had a three-way scene, you, him, and Mark Riskin."

In spite of herself Anne smiles. Jason is of course speaking very softly, there is no one in the corridor to see them together.

"I had a knock-down, drag-out fight with Peter Chang. He was screaming and I was screaming and he finally walked out. And then Richie asks me will I please stay after the other distinguished colleagues have left, and guess what he tells me?"

"That he and Mark Riskin are running off together and you're left out in the cold. I told you not to put much faith in them. In the end we Jews marry Jews."

"Richie tells me that Peter's wife is in the hospital, possibly with cancer, and that's why Peter's on edge, and everyone else knew it except me, and there I was fighting with the poor bastard and humiliating him, and now will I please go easy on him in the future." Anne's whisper is violent.

"Why didn't Richie Grossman tell you before the meeting?"

Anne forgives Jason for bristling a little bit about the mice. "Because—I don't know why. Because he's another turkey, they're all turkeys."

At this point they both see several people heading down the corridor toward them and they stop whispering. Jason says in a normal voice, "Here's my next delivery, ten mice coming up," and turns his cart into the next laboratory.

Anne considers going back to her own lab. But she is not in the mood for working, she is not in the mood for Arthur Schenk. There is the possibility of going to Charlotte's lab, but that will mean telling and retelling and discussing the story—perhaps she is not in the mood for that either. She goes into a small reading room where journals and reference books are kept. The room is, thank goodness, empty. She sits down at the gray formica-topped table and, after a minute, reaches to a nearby shelf and takes down a few of the more recent issues of *Science*. She browses through these, looking mainly at the biology articles but also the editorials and the advertisements. She looks carefully at the job advertisements; suppose she wanted to change jobs? There doesn't seem to be anything appealing.

She is beginning to feel genuinely sorry now for Peter Chang, though she is still unwilling to concede that his wife's illness gave him the right to say the things he said. Still, it must be hard for him. Should she mention Peter's wife to him, wish her well, and thereby establish that there are no hard feelings from this morning, even if, in fact, there are? Better perhaps just to go offer the olive branch with no mention of the wife, to say, I'm sorry I lost my temper this morning.

She does not, in fact, go in search of Peter immediately after lunch. Instead she hunts up Jason and nods at him, which he interprets, correctly, as a request that he come to her lab. He busies himself with some tubing that she loudly declares to be defective, and then, when Arthur is not looking at them, Anne whispers in Jason's ear, is he free tonight?

No, not exactly. That is, not till around eleven, maybe later. But he'd like to come see her then.

So Anne has something to look forward to. Now, if she is going to be tranquil enough to do any work at all today, the sensible thing to do is to go find Peter Chang, to make some sort of peace with him.

But he is not in his laboratory. The door is locked and no one answers when Anne knocks. She knocks again and a head pops out of the next door down. Peter's lab assistant, who also works part-time for Henry Madison in the next lab. She is a cheerful woman, about fifty years old, patient and motherly with her two scientists, thorough, careful, expert at her work. She does not look pleased to see Anne.

"Peter's not here," she says shortly. "He's gone home."

"Home?" Anne is suddenly horrified: His wife has died, something terrible has happened.

"Yes. He was a little upset and he decided to go home."

It is perfectly clear to Anne that Peter's assistant knows the whole story, blames Anne completely, is ready to make trouble for her if at all possible. Anne swallows. It seems worthwhile to try and pacify her.

"He and I had a disagreement this morning in a meeting," she says. "I guess we both lost our heads. I came to tell him I was sorry."

The assistant looks taken aback. Then she says, a little more kindly, "Peter's been under quite a bit of strain recently. He wasn't feeling very well and it seemed like a good idea to take the rest of the day off."

"Maybe I should leave him a note?"

The assistant thinks it over, nods, and comes over to unlock the lab for Anne. She stands just inside the doorway while Anne looks around for a pad and a pencil. Peter's lab is immaculately neat, which is probably because of this most excellent assistant, whose name, Anne now recalls, is Mrs. Schwartz. Mrs. Schwartz opens a drawer with the confidence of someone who knows for sure what every drawer and cabinet in the room contains. She hands Anne a pad and a blue felt-tipped pen. Anne, who feels intensely irritated by the whole scene, prints a note. "Dear Peter, I'm sorry I lost my temper this morning, I guess we both got a little angry, I think we should get together soon and try to work things out, Anne."

Mrs. Schwartz pointedly does not look at the note as Anne arranges it in the center of Peter Chang's workbench, weighing it down with a small bottle of distilled water.

"Okay," Anne says, "I hope he's feeling better tomorrow."

"Honey," Mrs. Schwartz says suddenly, as if coming to a decision, "can I give you a little advice?"

"Sure," says Anne, thinking, I'm not going to like this.

"You know, I've been hearing a good deal about you, what with one thing and another. I hear you have a great future in front of you, they say you're a very bright girl."

"Thank you," Anne says, thinking, Now comes the kicker.

"But if you'll just take a little advice from an old lady, you'd be a lot better off if you'd push yourself forward a little bit less. Listen to what some of the other scientists have to say. It doesn't always have to be *your* ideas that people work on. That isn't a good way to do research, honey. You have to be willing to learn from the others, from the people with more experience than you."

"I am willing to learn," Anne says, thinking, You knew you wouldn't like it, now swallow it and get away.

Mrs. Schwartz shakes her head sadly. "No, I see how it is, especially with you young girls these days, you have to be competing with the men, pushing right to the front just to prove you can do it. Now, I'm telling you, honey, that's not a good idea."

"I'm sure you're right." Anne gives her a smile which surely even Mrs. Schwartz can tell is completely false. "I have to be going now." And she leaves the room, so Mrs. Schwartz can look over the note to Peter in peace, and goes almost running to Charlotte's lab to tell her the story, laughing, but also not so far from tears.

"That woman is completely ridiculous," Charlotte says. "And she's always hostile to female scientists. Always. She thinks we should all be lab assistants like her and help these wonderful men do their wonderful work. Don't worry about any of it. Peter rants to her about how you're always interfering with his ideas and she interprets it in her own special way."

"I simply cannot believe she said those things to me! Pushing myself forward! You know how much I wanted to be on this dipshit team in the first place, I'd rather have been left alone. Do you think that's what Peter's been saying about me, I'm always pushing, I won't learn from my elders?"

"I think Peter says that about anyone who gets in his way, which turns out to be pretty much everyone who has any contact with him. I just think that sweet old Mrs. Schwartz minds it more when they happen to be females."

"Maybe I'll go home too for the rest of the day. I mean, if Peter's entitled to, then I am too, right?"

"No, don't. For one thing, there's his wife—he's allowed to be more upset than you are. For another, you should either have gone right away or not gone at all. No, you go back to your lab and do a little work. The afternoon will be over before you know it."

"I can't just go in there and work. I feel too furious. I'll end up murdering Arthur Schenk because he sniffles too much."

"He sniffles?"

"He has hay fever. Isn't that what you would expect, of course he has hay fever."

"That's a little unfair. I sometimes have hay fever myself."

"Look, I cannot go work in that lab for the rest of the afternoon. I wouldn't be able to concentrate."

"So who said you had to concentrate to do science? Come on." Charlotte steers her back into the corridor and walks her to her own lab. Arthur is still hunched over his computer printout. Charlotte greets him cheerfully.

"Hello, Arthur, how are you on this lovely summer day?"

Arthur responds with his ridiculous Southern gallantry. "Mighty well, thank you, and how is your lovely self?"

"Just as perky as could be, thank you," Charlotte assures him, and he smiles and nods, then returns to his printout.

"Come on, girl," Charlotte whispers in Anne's ear. "I'm going to stand here with my arms folded until I see you doing something constructive."

"For Christ's sake, Charlotte," Anne hisses back, "I'll do something."

"I'm sure you will, I'll just wait and watch you get started."

Anne is no longer sure whether she is irritated or amused. With exaggerated carelessness she assembles some materials, a lab book, a beaker or two, some pipets. She goes to the incubator room and comes back with a little petri dish of bacteria culture.

"Terrific," Charlotte whispers. "Real science. I'll be moving along."

And so Anne actually does get some work done for the rest of the afternoon. Maybe not brilliant work, maybe even a little slap-dash, and she does want to kill Arthur every time he sniffles, but it hasn't been a wasted afternoon. She leaves Viatech with a certain feeling of virtue. Tomorrow she will be generous with Peter Chang. She will avoid contact with Mrs. Schwartz. Tonight Jason is coming late in the evening, a treat. On the way home she stops in a record store. She means to buy herself just one or two new records; instead she buys the Beethoven symphony they heard in Central Park, Joni Mitchell's latest album, which Anne has never heard, and three records by jazz pianists she knows Jason admires—it will be nice to have that kind of music in the house again.

In her apartment she finds herself restless, not in the mood to listen to any of her new records. Instead of cooking for herself, she walks up to a new Szechuan restaurant nearby and eats there. It is not until she picks up her chopsticks that she sees that her hand is trembling. She is still furiously angry, at Peter, at Richie, at Henry and Mark, at Mrs. Schwartz. She feels betrayed, attacked, she feels that all of Viatech has turned on her, which is silly. She puts down the chopsticks. She closes her eyes, tries to take deep breaths, to calm herself so she can eat her dinner. Slowly and deliberately she picks up one of her pot stickers, dips it in soy sauce, bites off a corner. Fried dough and hot meat and soy sauce—she chews slowly. She feels calmer.

She walks home, the evening still light around her, the sidewalks giving back a little of the day's heat. She plays one of her new jazz records, decides to unpack a box that sat in a closet when she lived in Louisa's apartment, on the floor against a wall when she lived with Jason, and in her new apartment in a closet once more. In the box are the knickknacks and little things she decided to take with her when she left Kent, most of them either things that were hers from the beginning or gifts people had given her while she and Kent were together. She had not wanted to unpack the box before because she was somehow afraid that those particular objects would remind her most fiercely of the apartment she had shared with Kent. It makes her happy to see the familiar objects—an Eskimo stone sculpture, a conch shell from Florida, an inlaid box from India—in her new apartment. And soon there will be Jason, and he will like the new music.

In fact, he likes it very much. It seems to make him feel welcome and comfortable in the new apartment to an extent he has perhaps never felt before, despite the pink towel and bath mat she bought him. He lies on the floor with his head in her lap, listening to the new records. She watches his face, his closed eyes, his long lashes, and every now and then she bends her head down to kiss him. Perhaps she is still upset about what happened at work, but she is confident now that there is nothing intrinsically wrong at Viatech, except perhaps that it is full of scientists and they don't behave like reasonable human beings. But that, after all, is an occupational risk that Anne really ought to be accustomed to by now.

23. Drama

Peter Chang came in search of her the day after their fight, and they made up with the stiff formality of two people who both feel wounded and righteous. Not gracious or grateful, but at least they are on speaking terms. Anne has joined the conspiracy which she can now clearly see encircling Peter; he must not be upset, he must be coddled, understood, helped through this difficult period. It is very well meant, but it is somehow very inept. It would be better to tell him to take a week off, or else just to leave him alone.

But anyway, things are relatively smooth these days; Anne, with the knowledge and consent of Mark Riskin and Richie Grossman, is quietly pursuing her ideas. She isn't wildly excited about the work she's doing, but on the other hand she has come to admit that she was at least partially wrong in assuming that it was impractical for Viatech to take on this particular project. She still doesn't believe that it's going to turn out the way Richie hoped it would, that she and Peter and Henry and Mark are going to set the world on fire, but it's at least clear that a few patentable and profitable things are going to come out of their work.

It is three in the morning, and the phone is ringing. A string of possible disasters passes through Anne's mind. She snatches up the receiver.

"Anne," says Kent's voice, "thank God I got you!"

"What is it, what's wrong?"

His voice is hushed. "Anne, Margie's moved back in on me. She's asleep in the other room. I'm talking from the kitchen, but I can't talk loud. Anne, you have to help me figure out what to do."

"Explain to me what's going on."

"It's the craziest thing. She just rang the bell, and when I let her in she collapsed on me, she practically had hysterics. She told me Alan beat her up."

"She really says he beat her up?"

"Yeah, well, I asked her about that after she calmed down, and it sounds like they had a big fight and beat each other up a little. She said she kicked him in the stomach. And then she kept saying, 'Oh Kent, I need you so much,' and looking at me with big eyes. Anne, I'm going to go insane."

"Well, at least this time don't sleep with her."

"Are you kidding? I put her to sleep in the bedroom, and *I'm* going to sleep on the couch. If she touches me I'll call the police."

He pauses, then continues in a calmer voice, "Anne, I mean, I don't want to turn my back on a friend who really needs help. But I get this feeling that she's just using me."

"Of course she's just using you, remember last time when she was pretending that Alan didn't know where she was? And hasn't Emily just left for Israel? I bet Margie's been keeping track. I think you have to face the fact that for one reason or another she's decided to replace Alan with you, at least for the time being."

"Anne," Kent says, a little hesitantly, "could I possibly ask you to come over? I mean, I'd feel a lot better, just for tonight, if it wasn't just me and Margie. What if she does something crazy?"

"Well," Anne says, reluctantly, not eager to leave her apartment in the middle of the night, not eager to get involved with Margie and Alan. "Okay, I guess so."

"Get a cab," Kent says eagerly, "I'll pay."

"Don't be silly," Anne says. She hangs up, grabs clean underwear and a dress to wear to work tomorrow, her hairbrush, and stuffs it all into a shoulder bag.

When she gets to Kent's apartment, he has already arranged a sleeping bag on the living room floor for himself; the sheet and pillow on the couch are for Anne. Anne looks around the living room that is so much more familiar than her own apartment. She puts down her bag, gives Kent a hug.

They sit on the floor and lean back against the front of the couch. In whispers, keeping an ear constantly alert for the bedroom door opening, they discuss Margie: Is she genuinely nuts? Why doesn't she just leave Alan if she wants to, without playing all these games with Kent? Is it possible that she is in love with Kent? The intimacy—Kent and the soft late-night conversation—is as disturbingly familiar as the living room.

Finally they leave the subject of Alan and Margie. Kent asks how Anne is doing. Okay, she says.

"Can I just ask—I mean, I don't want to pry, but is it getting serious with Jason?"

"Oh, I don't know. I guess so. More serious than it was, anyway."

"It still hurts me sometimes when I think of you with someone else," Kent says, though he says it fairly lightly.

"Yes, I know. Sometimes I think of 'Kent and Emily' and it doesn't quite seem possible."

Surely they can say these things to each other so calmly only because it is four in the morning. Kent puts his arm around Anne's shoulders.

"Emily is important to me," he says, "but it's so hard to say what that means when we've only known each other a month or so. I mean, in comparison to years."

"Sure," Anne says.

"Poor old Alan. It seems so much worse when there's a kid involved."

"I know." They sit quietly for a minute or two, and then Anne suggests that they get a little sleep. "Kent, have you got something I could borrow to sleep in? I didn't bring anything."

He finds her a teeshirt. She changes in the bathroom, brushes her teeth with his toothbrush, thinking, Well, one has a certain privilege with an old lover's possessions. She comes back and lies on the couch, listening to the noises of Kent getting ready for bed. Margie, she thinks, is in for a small surprise tomorrow morning.

Kent turns off the lights, lies down on his sleeping bag. Anne has reached that point beyond tiredness that comes with staying up all night. After a while Kent whispers, "Anne?"

"Yes?"

"Come down here with me."

She does. They lie on top of the sleeping bag, too hot to go inside it. Kent hugs her.

"Thank you for coming over," he whispers.

Does he mean for coming over to the apartment or for coming over to join him on the floor? Anne's head feels empty. Experimentally, she closes her eyes and is amazed by the physical relief that brings; how silly not to have realized that her eyes were tired and wanted to be closed. Kent's hands reach up under her teeshirt—well, actually his teeshirt. Everything is happening very slowly, underwater. She does not open her eyes even once while they make love, and after they finish she lies back on the sleeping bag and thinks as she falls asleep that she really should move back onto the couch, she shouldn't sleep here next to Kent.

"She'll see us," Anne says, already almost asleep.

Kent reaches out and pulls the sheet off the couch, flaps it out into the air so that it settles gently down over Anne and himself. Then Anne is truly asleep.

"Come and get your goddamn girlfriend!" Anne and Kent are awakened by Margie shrieking into the telephone. "She's here naked in bed with her old boyfriend, or did you know that? Come get her, you bastard, come take her away!"

Anne is not at all sure for a minute where she is or what is going on. But Kent, quicker to wake up, quicker to function, has leaped up and run into the kitchen. Anne hears the receiver slammed down. Then Margie begins to scream at Kent: "You bastard! You motherfucker! You lousy fucking son of a bitch!" Her voice is breathless, as though a physical struggle is going on.

Anne gets up too, looks vaguely around for the teeshirt she was wearing, hears a thump from the kitchen. Kent and Margie seem to be wrestling. He is trying to hold her wrists and she is trying to kick him or knee him or get her hands free. She is wearing a perfectly ordinary blue nylon nightgown, and he, of course, is naked.

This cannot be happening, Anne thinks calmly, but even while she is thinking it, she is grabbing for Margie's knees. Together Anne and Kent half drag, half carry Margie out into the living room and force her into a sitting position on the couch. She seems to be a little less violent, so Anne releases her long enough to locate the teeshirt and put it on; it comes down over her hips so she feels at least marginally clothed.

She sees Kent's underpants, neatly folded on top of a pile of clean clothes for tomorrow, and passes them to him. Margie is now sitting rigidly still. Kent tentatively releases her, pulls on his underpants.

"Okay, Margie," Anne says at last, "I'm sorry it upset you to find me here." She speaks very gently, thinking, I am talking to a crazy person.

"Look," Kent says, also gently, "wouldn't you like to call Alan, just so he could come talk?"

"No!" Margie shouts desperately, then, surprisingly, she turns to Anne for help. "Don't let him send me back to Alan! He can't make me go back to Alan if I don't want to!"

"Of course not," Anne says, soothing, reassuring. "No one can make you go back to Alan if you don't want to and no one will."

The phone rings.

Anne goes into the kitchen to answer.

"Hello?"

"Anne?" It is Jason, of course.

"Hi, Jason."

"Anne? What's going on? Are you all right?"

"Yes. I'm really sorry she woke you up."

"Anne, who was that? It sounded like a lunatic."

"You remember Margie? That woman who moved in on Kent that other time and I called her husband and got him to come get her?"

"Yeah?"

"She showed up at Kent's place again tonight. And he asked me to come over and help him and then when she found me here she went crazy and called you."

"Are you sure you're okay?"

"I'm okay, but I don't know exactly what we're going to do with her."

"I could come over too if you think it would help," Jason says.

"No, I don't know how she'd react to anyone else. I'll tell you how it comes out when I see you later."

Anne goes back into the living room and sits down next to Margie on the couch, and Margie promptly buries her head in Anne's teeshirted bosom and begins to cry. Anne pats her head.

"There's no place for me to go," Margie sobs.

"That's silly," Anne says lightly, "there's lots of places. If you're sure you don't want to go back to Alan, you can get a hotel room, or an apartment of your own."

"Or you can go stay with your parents for a while," Kent suggests, and Anne thinks, Oh yes, the rich parents in California.

"It isn't fair for you to be here," Margie continues, without releasing Anne, "you moved out on Kent months ago. It isn't fair for you to come back while I'm here."

Kent starts to say something but Anne gets there first. "Margie, Kent didn't ask you to stay here. He's just letting you stay for a night while you figure out what to do next. But you can't just decide that you're going to move in." Is there actually any point in trying to reason with Margie? Just as she always sensed imbalance behind Margie's normalcy, Anne now suspects method and premeditation underlying Margie's hysteria.

"But I love him," Margie says to Anne, ignoring Kent. Definitely, there is a sly look in her eyes.

"Kent?"

"Yes, I love him. I've loved him for years. You don't love him any more, do you? You have someone else."

"But Margie, Kent isn't in love with you. Or with me. He's in love with someone else. And you can't just decide to move in and then make him go along with it."

"Last time I was here he slept with me," Margie says, watching closely for Anne's response.

"Margie," Anne says, "just because someone is willing to go to bed with someone else doesn't mean . . ." What is there to say?

"You fucker!" Margie dissolves into sobs. "You've gone and bought the whole line of bullshit. You're sitting there telling me that a guy can just fuck me and then leave me, no responsibility, no emotions. You're a traitor, that's what you are, you're a traitor and a whore!"

"I give up," Anne says to Kent.

"I'm going to call Alan," Kent says.

"No!" Margie screams, and sobs violently. Anne puts her arms around Margie, and Margie allows herself to be held and stroked while Kent dials Alan's number. But before Alan answers, Margie jumps up and runs over to cut the phone connection with her finger on the button. "Listen," she says, amazingly calm, "don't call him. I don't want to see him. If you'll lend me some money, I'll move into a hotel tomorrow, I promise I will." The idea seems to make her quite cheerful.

And so the remainder of that peculiar night is spent quietly, Margie actually falling asleep on the couch, Anne and Kent drowsing off in the armchairs.

24. Sheltering the Homeless

Anne hears from Louisa about Felice's big break; she's going to be in a magazine, she's going to model winter clothes. She's so young, Louisa says, I worry about her in that professional world.

"Felice seems pretty tough to me," Anne says. This conversation takes place in the same soup-and-salad place where Anne once took Louisa into her confidence about Jason. This is a carefully prearranged working girls' lunch, aimed at easing Anne's guilt over never seeing Louisa.

"She may seem tough, but I don't know if she really is. I'm not sure she's ever even had a boyfriend."

"Well, that's pretty good evidence of how tough she is right there."

Louisa looks puzzled. "I suppose," she says good-naturedly, clearly without any idea of what Anne means. "Poor Felice. I wish I knew someone for her."

"If her career is really about to get off the ground, she may not have too much time for romance in the immediate future."

"Oh, but Anne, that would be so sad. Because she really is a very nice person."

Anne hears from Jason about the drug bust at Sidney's. Cocaine; one mayoral aide, one fairly well-known singer. And Sidney's is closed for a while. Jason wasn't there that night, which is just as well, Anne thinks. She knows he has recently started going there again, and it makes her a little uncomfortable. Sidney himself, according to Jason, is insisting that the whole bust is merely going to be millions of dollars in free publicity. Jason isn't so sure.

As if inspired by Sidney's problems, he finally raises with Anne the question she has been waiting for since that night with Margie and Kent.

"Anne, I feel silly asking this . . . that night you were at Kent's you went there to help him, but I can't help wanting to know . . ." He trails off, looks at Anne expectantly. This conversation is taking place on her mattress; the two of them are naked on the quilt he brought her, resting after sex, or rather, knowing Jason, between sex.

"Jason, I've been to bed with Kent exactly twice since I stopped living with him."

"Oh. Well, I suppose I really have no right to let that bother me."

"It's hardly a wild ongoing thing."

"No, I suppose not." Jason manages to look wounded.

"Jason?"

"Yes?"

"How about you?"

"What about me?"

"Jeannette?"

"Oh." He is silent for a minute. Then he shrugs, resigns himself to the loss of his moral advantage. "Four times." He grins, more than a little sheepishly. "But we were drunk, or stoned . . ." His voice is parody, Anne picks up the tone.

"And it only lasted thirty seconds and you hated yourself as soon as it was over and you'll never do it again."

There is a short pause; they are embarrassed, in spite of themselves.

"Oh, well," Anne says, "two of a kind."

Much as she hates to admit it, she doesn't like the idea of Jason's reunions with Jeannette. It bothers her. It bothers her more than the idea of Kent and Emily. But she has forfeited her right to mind, or at least to complain, just as Jason has forfeited his. Truly, two of a kind. And what does that leave for them to do except shrug as if it doesn't matter and then make love again?

Anne hears from Kent that Margie has in fact moved into a hotel, that he has talked to Alan on the phone and Alan is also in touch with her. Alan is trying to talk her into seeing a shrink; he himself is already seeing one. Kent seems to be largely out of that tangle, for which he is grateful. "Do you think she was serious when she said that about being in love with me?" he asks.

"I don't know, but I don't really believe anything she says. Maybe it's my fault, maybe I'm being unfair, but I think she was just using that to blackmail you into doing what she wanted."

"But why would she have wanted that, I mean, to move in with me, if she wasn't in love with me?"

"I don't think it's really possible to follow her reasoning. She's not sane. I think she thought it would hurt Alan, and I suppose she must have had some kind of a thing about you. But you mustn't feel guilty about it. It seems to me that Margie wants some kind of cosmic attention, and she's willing to screw up other people's lives until she gets it."

This conversation takes place over dinner in an Italian restaurant near Columbia. Anne has resolved that she and Kent are not going to hop into bed together tonight, and she suspects that Kent feels the same way.

Something occurs to Anne. "Kent? You aren't paying her hotel bill by any chance?" Kent looks uncomfortable. "Oh, Kent, you shouldn't let her keep you involved like that."

"But she said she wouldn't take money from Alan. And I had to get her out of my apartment."

"So let her take it from her parents, I thought they were so rich."

Kent changes the subject, he has gotten a letter from Emily, she is enjoying Israel, getting along okay with her parents. Anne takes this as a signal of Kent's celibate intentions for the immediate future, and in fact, after dinner he walks her back to her building but doesn't even come in.

Anne hears from Charlotte about Peter Chang's wife. Actually,

Anne could have heard it from almost anyone at work, but she generally prefers not to discuss this particular subject. Charlotte tells her that his wife has turned out not to have cancer at all, it was just a benign something or other, Anne experiences a double relief—relief that his wife is okay and relief that now they can't say she was cruel to a man with a dying wife. Anne even thinks she senses at Viatech a certain impatience with Peter; he had them all tiptoeing around making allowances for him for weeks and it was just a false alarm.

"He's lucky he's a man," Charlotte says. "If he were a woman, everyone would be criticizing him for letting his personal life interfere with his work."

This conversation is taking place in Anne's lab. Arthur Schenk is probably listening, though he is pretending to be absorbed in some computations over on the other side of the room.

"Oh, Charlotte, I don't know if that's true. I mean, not when personal life means cancer."

"They might not say it, but if he were a woman that's what they'd be thinking."

Anne smiles at Charlotte, her friend, who has never had any patience with Peter. She makes up her mind to invite Charlotte over for dinner soon, even if it is intimidating to think of cooking for her.

Anne hears from her Aunt Letitia that her Uncle Douglas is off again, touring to publicize his book, which is still on the best-seller list.

"California, Nevada, the West this time," says her aunt.

"Oh, that's terrific."

"Who would have thought it, that's what I say. A book about physics, and all those people shell out twenty dollars."

"How's the boutique?"

"Booming, just booming. I tell you, Anne, Douglas and I are going to be rich beyond our wildest dreams. Between underwear and physics . . ."

This conversation, of course, takes place over the phone. I should visit her, Anne thinks. I should to go Chicago some weekend.

Anne hears from Felice that the shoot for the fashion magazine went well. From Jason that Sidney's is still closed and Sidney is beginning to sound a little less sure of himself. From Kent that Margie is thinking of going to California to stay with her parents. From Peter Chang that the whole project is doomed, they might as well follow up her ideas as anyone else's, it isn't going to come to anything anyway. This may actually be some sort of grudging apology, Anne thinks.

Anne invites Charlotte for dinner the following Thursday and spends a great deal of time worrying about what to cook. She is repeatedly tempted to cheat with gourmet-shop prepared salads, even main courses. The idea of cooking for Charlotte is frightening. Charlotte always cooks something "European," meaning French or Italian. Anne buys a Mexican cookbook. She won't try anything too ambitious, guacamole certainly, then maybe enchiladas stuffed with chicken and cheese, baked with green sauce. Is the meal too green? She adds a tomato salad. For dessert she is planning a dark chocolate cake she has made before; no point in taking too many risks. Sangria; she buys fresh oranges and lemons.

Anne ends up awestruck at her own dinner. She stares at the food she has produced, her fingers still burning from the peppers, which she did not remember to clean under running water the way the cookbook told her to. Anne and Charlotte eat ravenously. The food is very spicy; Anne underestimated those peppers in more ways than one.

After they have both eaten much too much chocolate cake, Anne shows Charlotte the results of a foraging expedition she made last Saturday with Jason, junk shops and antique stores in the Village. Jason had borrowed a car again so she could buy bigger things. First of all is a small wooden bookcase, waist-high, up on four little wooden claws. It won't hold too many books, but it's definitely an item of furniture. In a certain way Anne knows it is graceless and badly proportioned, junk furniture, not antique furniture, but she feels affectionate toward it, such a peculiar little mutant animal of a bookcase.

Charlotte, who likes antiques, not junk, says dubiously, "I suppose it's better than the crates."

"Look what else I got," Anne says, pulling two cardboard cartons away from the wall. Old issues of *National Geographic,* at least a hundred of them, from the fifties and sixties. Anne has been luxuriously reading through one issue every night. She loves the pictures, the unmistakable prose, "turning up its face to catch the midnight sun, this little flower . . ." Just to own all those old magazines gives her an insane pleasure.

"Clutter," Charlotte says, "you are deliberately accumulating clutter."

"You could call it that."

Anne thinks suddenly and sharply of her parents' house. They did not accumulate clutter, she thinks, and now it turns out that I do. And she tries to imagine welcoming her mother into this new apartment, cluttered or not, and is relieved to find that she can picture it, her mother is smiling, glad to be there.

Charlotte is shaking her head. "All the things other people finally make up their minds to get rid of."

"My real personality coming out."

"That may be truer than you think."

"Now I don't want to show you what else I bought."

"Come on. Worse than a hundred old *National Geographic*s?" Anne produces a strange dark-green teapot decorated with little gilt stars. Charlotte observes it silently for a moment.

"It has no lid." Charlotte's voice is flat.

"I thought I might put things in it," Anne says apologetically.

"Roses? Dried weeds? Or just paper clips?"

"I haven't decided."

"Ah, the creative process." Then Charlotte grins at her. "I hope you realize that the world is full of teapots without lids and bizarre little pieces of furniture and homeless magazines. If you're going to start taking them all in, you're going to need more than a studio apartment."

And from then on, Charlotte begins to leave little gifts in Anne's lab, knickknacks, pieces of china, all chosen for almost surreal ugliness, and Anne thanks her politely for each one and gives them all a home.

The next evening, Anne arranges her *National Geographic*s in chronological order. She doesn't actually have a complete set for any given year, but she finds that doesn't bother her. The magazines line up neatly along one shelf of her claw-footed bookcase. Anne is pleased with the way each issue lists its articles on its spine, so easy to browse along her shelf and choose, Switzerland, Kenya, anything she wants. A shelf full of choices. It is an exceptionally hot evening, even for August. Anne decides to go to the corner to buy a carton of ice cream. That, as it turns out, was a lucky thing to have done.

Back in her apartment, Anne considers an idea that has been tickling at her mind for a day or two. She takes out the pink silk robe her aunt and uncle sent her. Is there a way to hang it on the wall without damaging it? She places it neatly on a hanger, hooks the hanger on a nail in the wall. Nice, but not exactly what she had in mind. She ties a piece of string to the neck of the hanger, stretches it through one of the arms of the robe, tacks the other end of the string to the wall. She splays out the other arm too, then spends a number of frustrating minutes trying to use the same method to spread the skirt of the robe. Finally it is arranged to her satisfaction. She opens her carton of ice cream and sits back to regard her new ornament. A beneficent pink silk deity.

The doorbell rings several times. "Who is it?" she yells into the intercom.

"Anne? It's me! Alan!"

A minute later he is standing in the middle of her apartment, along with Curtis, who looks hot and cranky and somehow not well. Oh Christ, Anne thinks, why do I have to deal with this?

She smiles at them, a little weakly, tries to think what she can offer.

"Curtis, would you like some ice cream?"

"But you were eating right out of the package. I don't want to eat what you were eating."

"Look, this whole side is exactly the way it was when I opened the carton—I haven't touched this side. I'll put some of it in a dish for you." He looks unconvinced, but when she hands him some in a dish, he settles down on the floor and begins to eat.

"What's up, Alan?"

"Margie and Kent are having an affair." Alan looks ready to cry.

Oh God, Anne thinks, how do I get mixed up in these things? These people aren't close to me, don't interest me, how does my life keep getting tangled with theirs?

"I don't think so," she says weakly. She and Alan are sitting a little way away from Curtis, who is absorbed in his ice cream. Still, he can hear what they're saying.

"Yes, Anne, I'm afraid they are. Margie admitted it to me tonight."

"I think she might have been exaggerating."

"Oh, Anne, we have to face facts."

"Listen, Alan, I don't think this actually is a fact. But even if it were, Kent and I aren't together any more. It really isn't my business what he does."

Alan looks at her tenderly. "I know you better than that, Anne. You're such a caring person."

And what the hell does that have to do with anything? But all she says is, "Listen, I think Margie is, well, a little interested in Kent right now." Is that delicate enough? "And she's very confused and sometimes she sort of changes what's really happening into what she would like to have happening."

"Anne, she told me they were sleeping together. She told me tonight. And that other time she was staying with him, you know, when you called me and told me—well, they were sleeping together then too. And she says he's been begging her and begging her to leave me and come live with him." Alan's voice breaks. "That's the hardest thing, to have a guy you like and trust stab you in the back that way. It hurts almost as much as Margie walking out on me."

"Alan, I really think she's making this up. In fact I know. When she came to stay with Kent the second time, I went over and stayed there too. Kent isn't in love with her. I know he isn't. Margie is just, well, making all this up."

Alan looks confused but not convinced. "I don't know," he says, "when did this happen?"

"About a week ago."

"Well, since then maybe she and Kent really have started having an affair."

Anne wonders if this is indeed possible. She doesn't believe it. Kent wouldn't be such a fool. "I really doubt it," she says. "Look, why don't we call him up and you can talk to him about this? Because I'm really sort of on the outside, I mean, Kent and I are friends now but that's about it."

Curtis has finished his ice cream. He doesn't want more. He's tired, he complains. Why doesn't Anne have a TV?

"I think he's coming down with something," Alan says in a rather hopeless voice. It seems to Anne that Curtis and Alan both have a neglected look about them, as if they have been sleeping between wrinkled sheets and wearing clothes that could do with a washing.

"Curtis?" Anne says. "Would you like to lie down on my bed and take a rest?"

"No," he says, "I want my own bed."

"Come on, old man," Alan says, "I'll lie down with you." He takes Curtis in his arms and the two of them stretch out on top of Anne's quilt. Anne wonders if one of them is crying; they are hugging and shaking lightly in an odd way. Anne is touched and embarrassed. She decides to make iced tea for Alan and herself. How long will they stay? Anne boils water, measures orange pekoe into a teapot. She steeps the tea for a couple of minutes, then fills two glasses with ice cubes. Alan has left Curtis, who is apparently asleep on the bed, and comes to join Anne. Anne pours the hot tea over the ice cubes and hands Alan his glass of already icy cold tea.

They go and sit against the wall, away from the bed. Anne turns out the overhead light and switches on her architect's lamp, adjusting it to shine on Alan and herself. "I think the best thing to do would be to call Kent," Anne says.

Alan shakes his head. "I couldn't talk to him."

"But Alan—" What is there to say?

"You see, Anne, we've been having some problems, just between us, but I don't think they were anything we couldn't work through together. Margie was just feeling suffocated because, you know, she didn't get to see many people, she was home all the time. You can understand that."

Can it really be something so obvious? "Is that really what you were having problems about?"

"Well, I think so. She says that it was just the strain of the two of us living together, that I began to get on her nerves. You know, she's very sensitive. She had a sort of breakdown when she was about fifteen. But see, the thing is, she said she wanted to, you know, not live with me, but I think all she needed was some interests outside the home."

Anne's sympathies veer momentarily toward Margie; suppose she really was just sick and tired of Alan and he kept insisting on trying to shape her life into a modern parable on the position of women?

"The problem was," Alan continues, "she would lose control of herself. We would have these terrible, horrible fights."

Anne is beginning to be suspicious of Alan. All this sincerity. Isn't he just being a little more roundabout in his methods of putting Margie completely in the wrong? Oh well, as they say, fault on both sides, no doubt.

She crunches an ice cube, now just a tiny piece, and she wonders how to get Alan out of her apartment, back into his own life. Call Kent herself? Ask if he knows where Margie is?

"Kent," Alan says sadly, as if answering her thoughts. "I just can't believe she's involved with Kent. He was such a good friend, you know? I never even thought about him having been involved with Margie once upon a time."

"That wasn't very serious," Anne says.

"I see they told us both the same story." Alan shakes his head mournfully.

"Alan, I really don't think it's a story. I think Margie is very upset and behaving in a very peculiar way. Maybe it's another breakdown. If you ask me, she should be getting some kind of help. And Kent is mixed up with it only in her mind."

"No, Anne, I have to try to come to terms with it. And I'm afraid you have to come to terms with it too—maybe I can help you." Alan meditates for a minute, as though coming to terms with it right then and there. He shakes his head. "The one thing I really can't accept at all is the idea of Kent as Curtis's stepfather. Curtis living with Margie and someone else."

Anne begins to wonder if Alan is crazy too. And poor old Kent, if he heard this, what would he think? "Alan, this is so insane. All you have is Margie's word for it and I'm telling you that you can't trust that. At least could we call up Kent?"

"Oh, Anne, you're just like I was, you want so badly not to believe it. I understand how you feel, darling, really I do."

Darling? "No, Alan, I don't think you do."

"Be brave, Anne darling, we have to help each other be brave." And with that he wraps his arms around her and kisses her passionately. Anne is wriggling to get out of that embrace; she wasn't expecting it, it takes her a minute to marshal her forces.

"Alan, cut it out. I mean it, stop it." She pushes him away more forcefully, hampered by trying not to wake Curtis, thinking, two of a kind, you and Margie, two of a kind.

"Don't push me away, Anne, we need each other right now," Alan gasps, trying to push her down onto the floor, his hands kneading at her breasts.

"I don't need you, not right now and not at all!" She pulls away and stands up. "I don't want this, Alan, I'm not joking!"

He stand up too, very embarrassed, as well he should be. Anne is ready to tell him to take his kid and go, when he suddenly bursts into loud tears and she finds herself opening her arms to him after all, though only for a moment, patting him on the back, steering him to the bathroom and telling him to go in and wash his face. While he is in there, she calls Kent.

"Listen," she says abruptly, "Alan is here. He says Margie told him tonight that she's having an affair with you, and he's very upset about it."

"Oh Christ," Kent says. "Meanwhile, she's here."

"What?"

"She just showed up here tonight and asked if we could talk. It's all okay, she'll be going home soon."

"Should I tell Alan she's there? He can come get her or something."

"Christ, Anne, don't I have enough troubles?"

The water stops running in the bathroom and Alan emerges. "Is that Kent?" he demands, and when Anne nods, Alan grabs the receiver. "Is Margie there?" he screams, almost hysterically. Curtis wakes up and calls out, "Daddy?"

"Alan?" Anne can hear Kent's voice coming through the receiver. Then Margie's voice, shrill and triumphant as she screams into the phone, "Here I am, Alan, you bastard! I'm with Kent, that's where I am!" Confused noises come from the receiver and then Alan slams it down.

"You heard? She's there."

"Yes, but I still think you don't understand . . ."

"Fuck that! Just fuck that, Anne! Don't tell me what I don't understand. Thanks for all your help!" The door slams behind Alan almost before Anne realizes that he is leaving.

She stands by the phone for a minute, stunned. Then it occurs to her that she has to call Kent and warn him that Alan may be on his way over. She calls, but no one answers; Anne has a vision of Kent busy holding Margie down, no free hands, Margie hysterical.

Then Curtis, sitting up now on the bed, says in a trembling voice, "Where did my daddy go? I don't like this bed. I want to be in my own bed."

25. A House Call

The overhead light is on again; Curtis sees monsters in the semi-darkness when it is off. The remainder of the ice cream has been consumed. Anne has reassured him, Your daddy will be back soon, but she cannot answer Curtis's devastatingly specific inquiries: when? in half an hour? in an hour? She sympathizes with his fears, she imagines that he is remembering how his mother went away and is now afraid that his father has gone too. Poor Curtis, left alone with Anne, whom he perhaps associates with other frightening moments, left alone in a place where the bed is on the floor and the kitchen is in the living room and there is a pink bathrobe hanging on the wall. Poor Curtis.

But poor Anne too, surely. Not an expert with children, in fact pretty ignorant. Curtis keeps complaining that he feels hot, and his forehead is burning to the touch. Is he really sick? What should she be doing? How dare Alan do this to Curtis?

Again she dials Kent's number, again no answer. I don't feel good, Curtis is saying. Where's my daddy? I'm so hot. Anne tries distractions, a pile of *National Geographic*s, some ice cubes to suck. Success; he turns the pages of the magazines slowly, occasionally asking her where a certain picture was taken, and she senses in him the impatience of a child just about to read, a child to whom reading will be important. The ice cubes crunch companionably between his teeth, between her teeth, and she recognizes that he is making an effort, that he is playing guest, that he is controlling himself. Four-year-old gallantry. She hugs him, and he whispers, almost helplessly, "Anne, I really don't feel good."

Again she puts her palm on his forehead. Surely this is too hot to be nothing. What can she do, whom can she call? Who could be a comfort? Charlotte, she finally decides. Who else is there, anyway?

Charlotte answers the phone and Anne senses almost immediately constraint in her voice. She is talking as though there is someone else in the room listening. Of course, Anne realizes, the lover must be there tonight. But by this point, Anne is beyond worrying about disrupting Charlotte's love life. What if something is really wrong with Curtis? She explains to Charlotte what is going on, an edge of hysteria in her own voice.

Charlotte tells her to hold on, and there is a new voice on the phone, professionally reassuring. What is Curtis's temperature, exactly? Anne doesn't have a thermometer? Okay, calm down. They'll be over in fifteen minutes.

Anne hangs up, tells Curtis that a doctor is coming. "To the house?" he asks.

"Yes, and one of my friends is coming too."

He thinks it over. "I don't know," he says finally, "everything about tonight is strange. You know?"

"Yes," Anne says.

"My mommy," Curtis says, "my mommy is thinking."

"Thinking?"

"Yes, she took a vacation just to think. She needed to think."

"Everybody needs to think sometimes," Anne says helplessly.

"She bought me an invisible man."

"That's terrific."

"You know what that is?" Curtis sounds suspicious.

"Oh yes, I used to have one too." Actually it was her cousin's, but she wants Curtis to feel how enthusiastic she is. Actually, as a child she couldn't stand to look through the clear plastic skin at the colored veins and arteries and organs, but now, from her pinnacle as adult and biologist, she can approve.

"When you were a little girl?"

"I guess I was a little bit older than you. But I remember what a great thing it was. Later, when I had to learn about the circulation of the blood in college, I thought about my Visible Man and how the veins and arteries traveled everywhere in his body and that helped me picture it." Actually, when she was home from college one Christmas she spent an hour playing with the Visible Man. And it did help.

Curtis is silent for a minute. "Tell me about the blood," he says, finally. "The blue ones are veins and the red ones are—"

"Arteries," Anne says. "They're red because they carry all the fresh new bright red blood away from the heart, and the veins are blue because they carry all the old tired used-up blood back to the heart, and in the heart and the lungs all the old tired blood gets turned into new fresh blood and sent back out through the arteries again."

"If you cut yourself and it was a vein, would the blood be blue?"

Anne has a feeling that he has asked this question before, that he is testing her. "No, it's just a darker red, really. Do you know where your heart is?"

He puts his hand approximately over his heart. She helps him find the beat and then the pulses in his wrist and neck. Curtis seems fascinated by this new revelation about the rhythm of his body. They find her pulses too. It seems to her that his are very fast indeed. Why doesn't Charlotte come, with her doctor?

Actually, they are there very soon, having stopped along the way to buy a thermometer, a bottle of children's Tylenol, and an enormous bottle of 7-Up.

"The idea is to give him lots of liquids," says the doctor.

The doctor, Charlotte's lover, is astonishingly beautiful. She is tall and slim with glossy black hair that hangs to her shoulders. Her clothes are simple—linen slacks and a cotton shirt—but there is something pampered and luxurious in her appearance. Also something very reassuring and professional as she feels Curtis's forehead, pops the thermometer in his mouth.

Charlotte has introduced her as Blair. "Blair," Anne says tentatively, "thanks for coming, it's such a relief to have a doctor here."

Blair looks up from superintending Curtis's thermometer. "Ac-

2

tually this is pretty far from what I do as a doctor," she says. "I think I can be of more use as a mother."

"What is your medical specialty?" Anne asks.

"Cancer," Blair says crisply, in the tone of someone who is well used to all the various responses people make to that word; accordingly, Anne makes no response. Curtis looks up around his thermometer, interested; he has heard that word.

Blair looks at the thermometer and reports that Curtis's temperature is in fact a little high. He immediately wants exact figures. A hundred and two, she tells him. A little bit woefully, he then has to ask what normal is; he has forgotten since the last time he had a fever.

When she feels for his pulse, he is able to report to her that he and Anne found it, that they found the one in his neck, too. Blair adds the one in his ankle to his repertory.

Then she looks up and says to Anne, "I think this is the proverbial 'bug,' I think it's some kind of twenty-four-hour virus. The best thing to do is to keep giving him liquids, and try to keep him resting."

Curtis is given Tylenol, then a glass of 7-Up. His spirits seem much better. Anne makes iced tea once again, for herself, for Charlotte and Blair. They keep Curtis company while he drinks his 7-Up, and then when he looks a little sick and says he has to go to the bathroom, it is Blair who scoops him up and carries him in, moving always with that complete assurance which makes Anne very reluctant to have her and Charlotte leave.

"She's wonderful," Anne says to Charlotte, while the other two are in the bathroom. "She scares me a little."

"Yes," Charlotte says. She changes the subject. "What on earth is going on with that boy's parents?"

"I don't know, and I understand least of all why Kent and I have to be so involved. Really, it makes no sense to me at all."

"He seems like a nice kid."

"He's a terrific kid," Anne says, surprising herself by her own vehemence. "He's worth both his parents put together and then some."

"It's good you feel that way. I mean, if they're going to drop him in your lap like this."

"But think how he must feel about it. And being sick too."

Blair and Curtis emerge from the bathroom. "Well now," she says, "do you think you might like to get a little rest?"

His face crumbles. He obviously does not want to be abandoned. "I'm too hot," he says.

"How about if I give you a sponge bath? Would you like that?"

"A bath?"

"Sure, it'll make you feel better. Come on, back into the bathroom." And back into the bathroom they go.

"These insane nights," Anne says, "first over at Kent's with Margie, now this. And now I've gone and interrupted *your* night—I'm really sorry."

"Don't worry about it. I'm glad you and Blair got to meet each other, regardless of the circumstances."

"She's wonderful," Anne says again.

"I know. It's easy to fall in love with her. Curtis already has."

Splashes come from the bathroom. Anne and Charlotte crowd in and find Curtis naked in the tub, Blair swooping water up over him. Curtis looks happier than he has looked all evening.

Blair suggests that Anne find something Curtis could sleep in. She whisks him out of the bath, dries him with Jason's pink towel, and dresses him in the teeshirt Anne has provided. Then she installs him on Anne's bed, gives him another glass of 7-Up, and patiently answers his questions.

"Do you have any children?"

"I have three children."

"Where are they?"

"In Connecticut."

"But you don't live there anymore with them?"

"Of course I do. I live there all the time except for two days every two weeks when I come here to New York for my job."

"But then you go back to your children?"

"Yes."

Poor Curtis. And poor Charlotte, who also has to listen to this.

Charlotte who knows that Blair is what she wants but can only have her two nights every two weeks. Like knowing that science is not what she wants and having it all day. Charlotte is not happy. The richly detailed life, stable and carefully thought-out, does not actually leave her a happy person. But somehow, happy and unhappy are not the important categories for considering Charlotte and her life. Charlotte has accepted certain constraints, not only accepted them but built upon them, with care and deliberateness and even, Anne thinks, with honor.

Curtis is lying back against the pillows sleepily, and Blair carries his glass back to the sink. She tells him to just rest for a while and obediently he closes his eyes. Anne thanks her for coming. Nothing seriously wrong with him, Blair says, and he's unsettled because of the business with his parents. You better hope they don't come bursting in here as soon as he goes to sleep.

"But I have to go to work tomorrow," Anne says. "What will I do with him?"

"I'm sure they'll remember him by tomorow," Blair says. "But for now, the best thing you can do is to give him liquids to drink, help him fall asleep. Give him the children's Tylenol every four hours if he needs it."

"Okay," Anne says. "I shouldn't keep you two here. I'll manage." Actually she isn't at all sure she will manage. Anne offers to call a cab, but it turns out they came in Blair's car. And off they go into the night.

Curtis is almost asleep. "Where did the doctor go?"

"She went back home to go to bed, because she saw that you were doing fine. All you have to do is go to sleep too, and when you wake up, you'll feel much better."

"She went *home?* To Connecticut?"

"No, she's staying with that other lady while she's here in the city. Come on, Curtis, you shouldn't be talking. You should be going to sleep."

He is silent for a moment. "Anne?"

"Yes?"

"Would you hug me good night?"

Anne remembers how Alan helped Curtis fall asleep earlier in the evening. She does the same thing now, lies down next to him and puts her arms around him. His body feels so tiny and so hot that she is again terrified for him; can he really be safe, can it really be nothing serious? His breathing is a little labored, but he does fall asleep. Anne is almost asleep too, but she makes herself get up and check the door, the stove. She brushes her teeth and changes into a nightgown. Then she gets into the bed and finds it difficult to fall asleep and difficult to control her thoughts while she lies awake. First she is imagining Curtis sicker, even dying, thinking of how frail he seems, how he was lost in the woods and completely defenseless.

It's odd, Anne thinks, that she has personally never regarded as imminent the dilemma of whether to have children. And yet, here she is, twenty-nine years old. Is this all part of that refusal to grow up which Kent was always accusing her of? Kent, of course, wants children. And so does she, she supposes. At any rate, she has never thought of deciding not to have children.

Anne knows her mind is drifting. She thinks of Charlotte and Blair, of Blair's children, who are no doubt exquisite and perfectly trained. She thinks of Alan and Margie and decides not to bother calling Kent again. Let him handle it, Anne is tired, she's done enough. What if they don't turn up by tomorrow morning? She pictures herself with Curtis established in her apartment—surely there is some kind of nursery school or day-care center in the neighborhood. She will drop him off every morning, come home in the afternoon with groceries for supper, pick him up, or maybe pick him up first so they can go shopping together. She will buy him some new clothes, little shorts and shirts and socks. She imagines a big box of toys in one corner of the apartment.

She feels very tender toward Curtis now. So what if there is no genetic tie? What does that matter? So his genes come from Alan and Margie, Anne thinks, sleepily, picturing little chromosomes, will there ever be a child with hers? She thinks about the bacterial chromosome, which is shaped like a loop. And, thinking about chromosomes, she finally does fall asleep.

She and Curtis are both awakened about six in the morning by the insistent ringing of the front doorbell. Alan again; Anne buzzes him in. She opens the door to find not only Alan but also Margie, who snatches up Curtis. Thinking of that day when Curtis was lost in the woods, Anne says to herself, I always seem to be presiding at family reunions. Curtis is awake and cranky but also already clinging to Margie. Anne hastily explains that he isn't well, a doctor was here.

Alan and Margie both thank Anne repeatedly, but with a strange lack of conviction, as though they really are convinced that the rest of the world is there to play supporting cast to their drama. They exit again into the early morning, leaving Anne to collapse back onto her bed and fall asleep, this time immediately, until her alarm goes off.

Three days later, Kent reports to Anne that though Alan and Margie are still "having problems," they think they can work things out. A week and a half later, he reports that they have flown out to California to stay with her parents for a while. Alan has taken a leave from his job. In California, on the big estate where Margie's parents live, Alan and Margie hope they will be able to get away from the tensions of the city and really work on their relationship. At least, Anne thinks, it will be nice for Curtis to have a big piece of California to play on, and to be spoiled by his grandparents.

26. Gifts

Rumors travel fast at Viatech. There are various pathways and they intersect in various ways; people who have not yet heard a given rumor usually know that there is one in the offing, that it will reach them soon. Anne knows that there are perhaps going to be layoffs, support people at least, maybe researchers too; and then she knows that Arthur Schenk has been fired.

She has heard it from Charlotte, and she doesn't completely believe it, but then she comes into the lab and finds Arthur sitting dully at his bench, staring off into space.

"Good morning," he says to her.

"Hi, Arthur."

"It seems I have lost my job here," he says, his accent lingering on the words with self-pity. "It seems my services are no longer desired at this illustrious company."

"I'm really sorry, Arthur. But you'll find something else, I'm sure."

What else can she say? Essentially she agrees with whoever fired him, but still she feels sorry for him sitting there all alone.

"They're cutting back generally," Arthur continues. "That's what they told me. They're running into money troubles and they're going to have to cut back."

As Arthur perhaps intends her to, Anne feels a certain cramp of fear: Is this the beginning of a general failure? Is Viatech in serious trouble?

"Oh well, I don't guess you have very much to worry about," Arthur says. "You seem to be doing just fine." There is no hostility in his voice. He is just bewildered.

"I've just been lucky lately."

"No, I think you must have a real talent for this. I didn't see it at first, I have to say, and at one time I didn't think you'd last another month."

"Why not?"

"When you were carrying on with that lab tech I figured you couldn't really be serious about your work here. I thought you were just playing games."

Anne is shocked. To hear him say it like that, so casually—how long has Arthur known? Does everyone know? "How did you know that—about me and the lab tech?"

"I just put two and two together. Not really very hard for someone who shares the lab with you."

"Did you tell anyone? Has everyone known all along?"

"I didn't tell a solitary soul," Arthur says, with an odd dignity. "That wouldn't have been my business to do."

"Oh, that's good. I mean, thank you." Anne is wondering if others have guessed.

Arthur is the only researcher to have been fired, at least so far. Everyone knows that he feels wronged. Everyone knows that he is not even trying to finish up the work he was doing. Everyone also knows that after he leaves, Anne Montgomery is going to get to hire a new skilled lab technician and use the whole laboratory for her own research. Viatech is cutting back, so they won't be hiring another Ph.D. But Anne will have this new skilled lab technician plus the one whose time she has been sharing with Arthur, and this is another mark of favor, of the faith that Richie Grossman has in her.

Charlotte insists on viewing the firing of Arthur Schenk as a personal victory for Anne. Her attitude suggests that by dint of hard work and general brilliance, Anne has contrived to rid herself of an annoying labmate. Anne, who can't help feeling sorry for Arthur, is more than a little uncomfortable with this. At the same time, she keeps thinking of how luxurious it will be to have the lab all to herself, to spread her things out, to relax over her work without worrying that Arthur's eye is upon her. To replace the annoying and unappealing presence of Arthur with a pretty plant.

To fuck during working hours every now and then, Jason suggests. Jason also seems to be a little bit awed by the way people at Viatech are talking about her. He assures Anne that no one knows that he is involved with her; otherwise they would never discuss her in front of him, even to say flattering things. Anne senses that Jason is feeling somewhat threatened; though the successes that he and his friends aspire to are flashier than having one's own lab at Viatech, still he cannot help absorbing the opinion that Anne is doing brilliantly. And brilliance is brilliance, success is success. Anne remembers something Jeannette said to her while Anne and Jason were living together: He likes women with vocations, look at you and me.

Rumors continue to circulate at Viatech: Richie Grossman is thinking of dissolving the company. Some research group is on the verge of a big breakthrough. There isn't any real problem, things are tough all over. Richie is about to lay off half the personnel. At a meeting of Anne and her teammates, Richie comes right out and says, "I hope none of you guys are letting these scare stories scare you. I mean the ones about how the whole company is about to fold, just because we're getting rid of some dead wood. I don't want any of you people hunting around for new jobs. This team is really producing."

In fact, the project, while nothing like Richie's original grandiose plan, is going well enough. It isn't nearly as bad as she once thought it would be, and it seems to be doing her a lot of good professionally. No, Richie Grossman isn't a complete fool by any means. And neither is Mark Riskin and neither is Peter Chang, though she isn't so sure about Henry Madison. So if Richie is indeed to be trusted, if the company is not failing, Anne can look ahead into the coming fall and winter with some degree of pleasure and security.

One evening Louisa calls, just back from a weekend in one of the Hamptons. Anne invites her over, thinking that with her it will be possible to exult more openly than with Charlotte or Jason.

Louisa arrives, exclaims over the apartment—Anne's done so much with it, that robe on the wall is such an original idea, where did she find that teapot? Anne has collected more large pillows on the floor, though Louisa, like Charlotte, is someone who really prefers a couch. There is cold white wine to drink, and Anne has already asked for news of Felice before she notices what Louisa is coyly waving in front of her, waiting for her to notice.

"Louisa—are you engaged? My God, is that what that means?"

Louisa examines the diamond ring as though she has never seen it before. "Well," she finally admits, "last weekend Jim asked me when we were walking along the beach, and oh Anne, I was so surprised when he took this little box out of his pocket."

At least Louisa has had the proposal she deserved, right out of an advertisement for engagement rings in a women's magazine.

"Oh, Louisa, that's so wonderful. When are you planning to get married?"

"I think maybe in October or November."

Anne is taken aback; that seems so soon. It is almost September now. She was imagining that the engagement would last at least until next spring, maybe till June, surely the appropriate month for Louisa's wedding.

Louisa is going on about the wedding; they're going to have it in Minnesota, of course, and she's already told her parents about it and they're just thrilled, and naturally she wants Anne to come.

"Do you think it's okay for me to wear a white dress?" Louisa asks, giggling, naughty, as though Louisa would ever consider wearing anything else at her wedding.

"Why, aren't you a virgin?" Anne asks, obligingly, and Louisa bursts into more emphatic giggles.

And they will be moving out to the suburbs, she isn't sure yet which suburb, and she will keep working until, of course—she smiles. Yes, Louisa will have babies. How soon, Anne asks. Immediately?

No, Louisa doesn't think so. After all, it wouldn't do any harm for her to go on working for a year or so to help pay for the house. But soon. The happy ending, the exact happy ending that anyone would surely have predicted for Louisa. And she deserves it.

Now Anne tells Louisa a little about her own success at work, and Louisa is thrilled for her. "Who could believe I could have a cousin who was such a brilliant scientist?" Louisa says.

Next Emily turns up, back from Israel. She telephones to ask if she can stop by. She is the first person to be really knocked over by the way Anne's apartment is looking these days, to walk around picking specific items out of the clutter that is rapidly accumulating from all Anne's visits to junk shops and bargain basements. And she has brought a gift, a set of elaborately woven embroidered camel bags that she bought in the Arab market in Jerusalem. They are supposed to fit over the hump of the camel. Together Emily and Anne stretch them out across the wall, tack them into place. Anne is becoming aware that she will not, in the end, have an apartment with individual things hung on the wall, set in white spaces of background; in the end the walls will also be cluttered.

Emily looks tanned and healthy in a long orange caftan that she also bought in Jerusalem and a heavy amber necklace.

"So how was Israel?"

"Oh, it was so neat. I can't describe it. I wrote a cycle of poems about it and when I get them all finished, you know, polished, I'll show them to you."

Emily runs on about how strong the ties are that she feels to Israel, how she even got along with her parents while she was there, how someday she'll go back and stay for a long time.

"Forever?" Anne asks.

"Maybe. I don't know. I don't know if I could really do what I want to do if I lived there, though."

"And what is it you want to do?" Poetry, Anne is thinking, or living in the country; Emily's reply is unexpected.

"I think the most important thing I want to do is create a sort of family around me, of all the people who are important. My role models and my lovers and people who love me and people who model themselves on me. See, I think that nowadays people get so separated from their real families that they have to build new ones. And if I went to live in Israel, I'd just be moving back with my parents, back into my original family." She pauses, thinks it over. Then she says, very shyly, "I'd like to have you in my family, Anne."

Anne smiles. "Thank you," she says, and feels tremendously touched.

After Emily leaves, Anne finds herself thinking about family. Normally you don't choose the family you grow up with, but you can choose, at least to some extent, the family you will create around yourself. But Anne, of course, did choose the family with which she finished growing up. In retrospect, one of the reasons that the death of her parents seems to her particularly terrible is that it removed from her life that all-important unchosen connection.

As if in response to these feelings about family, things start to happen to Anne, little things, but somehow significant. She gets a letter from Curtis. Not exactly a letter, but a picture he has drawn which Alan or Margie has obligingly sent on. The picture is a human figure with red and blue lines all over it as if it were trapped in a spider web. The circulation of the blood. Curtis's name is signed laboriously in one corner. Anne stares at the picture for a long time, feeling that there is a message in it. That afternoon after work she goes to a frame-it-yourself place and mounts the picture behind glass with a thin chrome frame. She hopes, as she hangs it on the wall, that someday Curtis will be in her apartment again and she can show him what respect she has accorded his picture.

If she could really choose a family now, she thinks, she might choose Curtis. She would teach him about how the body works, she would get books with good pictures in them, and she would learn how to take care of him. Margie and Alan do not deserve Curtis, Anne thinks, all they can do is use him in their stupid games. But she forces herself to be fair; they have raised him to be the interested gallant child that he is, they deserve credit, they deserve their son. And for his sake, Anne must hope that they patch up their marriage out there under the California sun. Anne pictures Emily with children, children who are fed on hummus and tabbouleh, children who have poems written about them. Would that really be such a terrible fate for Kent, to be the father of those children? But Anne cannot picture it. She has grown fond of Emily, she wishes her well in life, with her poetry, with her family, but she doesn't really believe in Emily as a long-term companion for Kent.

In Anne's mind there is a connection between what Emily said and her own purchase, a couple of days later, of a number of old photographs in a store near Jason's apartment. The photographs are the kind that are printed like postcards, family shots from before the First World War. Solemn-faced children, slope-bosomed mothers, mustached fathers. Little girls in sashed white dresses, little boys in shorts. And always the rigid expressions, as if they knew that seventy years later a stranger would be buying these pictures, as if they are unwilling to allow their faces to give anything away to the casual purchaser who will carry off their family portraits to hang them on the already overcrowded walls of a studio apartment on the Upper West Side. Anne assembles a gallery of these postcards, a space of wall given over to the carefully posed photographs of strangers.

And there is another thing which happens which seems also to bear on the subject of family. This is something that happens at work, a gift Charlotte gives to Anne. Arthur Schenk is about to leave, and though Anne knows that he has not found another job, and although she feels sorry about this, she wants him to leave because she is already planning the reorganization of the lab; now that she has finally started working on her apartment, she is eager to revamp all the rooms in which she finds herself. She is going to hang things on the walls, she is considering a few plants, maybe a row of nonscience books.

Occasionally in the midst of her planning she thinks of the rumors that Viatech is in trouble and she feels much more personally threatened than she has felt before by the possibility of the company failing. Once she has her own lab, she will probably feel she is safeguarding her home by looking for valuable scientific properties for Viatech to patent. Very well, so she'll work better, so everyone will be happy. Sometimes these days Anne does feel that she has real flair for what she does, more than she has been willing in the past to give herself credit for.

The present from Charlotte is left on her lab bench one lunch-time. The wrapping paper is exceptionally beautiful, dark gray with little gilt crowns, and Anne saves it, thinking that perhaps a little square of that would look nice up on the wall of her apartment. Think of a patchwork quilt of a wall, little scraps of paper pieced neatly together; would it give off the same glorious feeling of random harmonies that her quilt gives? The present from Charlotte is a small book, clearly old, second-hand, bound in light-brown leather. *The Tenant of Wildfell Hall* by Anne Brontë. There is no card with it, but of course when she sees the name of the author she knows who it is from. Again, Anne feels, there is a message here, just like the picture from Curtis, the camel bags from Emily. Emily! The other Brontë sister; she will have to tell Charlotte. Unfortunately, Charlotte is almost certain not to like Emily, no point in introducing them. Still, even from a distance the pattern is a pleasing one. But the message? She will have to read the book. She opens it to the first page and is immediately struck by the first sentence, which itself seems to suggest something very important about herself and Charlotte. "When we were together last, you gave me a very particular and interesting account of the most remarkable occurrences of your early life, previous to our acquaintance; and then you requested a return of confidence from me."

27. Messages

It is a sunny Saturday morning early in September. Anne and Jason are wrestling with a heavy desk which Anne has just bought, thirty seconds ago, for a ridiculously large sum of money in a dim little antique store. Well, maybe it isn't a ridiculous amount of money for an antique desk, but then again it isn't a very large desk, heavy though it is. Once she had fantasies of wide blond wood surfaces and now she has a small, almost square dark wood table, with—strangest of all—a square of marble inlaid in the center of the top. Smoky gray, heavily veined marble. The man in the store, with the air of someone who didn't believe his own stories, had suggested that the desk had once been used in a kitchen, maybe for rolling out pastry.

Anyway, Anne now has this desk, which is heavier than it looks, and she and Jason are lugging it down the street, keeping an eye out for one of the big old Checker cabs that might be able to fit the desk in the back seat.

"Why couldn't you have bought this the day I had the car?" Jason asks.

"This is a wonderful opportunity for you to show me your muscles," Anne says, her sweaty fingers slipping a little on the edge of the desk. They are pleased with each other.

They were so excited by her buying it that they didn't even think about getting it home, they just picked it up and carried it out of the shop in the initial jubilation of realizing that it belonged to Anne. On this desk, she is thinking, she will write a letter to Curtis, to ask how he is doing in California. She will write to her Aunt Letitia to tell her how thrilling it is to see her uncle's book on the best-seller list every Sunday. She will work on plans for her research, the research she will do in the lab that is all hers now that Arthur Schenk has finally dropped out of sight. Her architect's lamp will clamp anachronistically onto the edge of the desk, she will write with her arm lying against the cool marble.

"Hey!" Jason has spotted a Checker. The driver is a young woman with long blond hair and a richly embroidered workshirt. She admires the desk, she efficiently helps them wiggle it into that big back seat. Anne and Jason crowd into the front seat and they sail on uptown.

"I really think I'd enjoy being a cabdriver," Jason is saying.

"It's fun most of the time," the woman says. "You just have to be careful."

"I can imagine," Jason says. "But I really think I'd like it. I like driving in the city, most people hate it."

"I know what you mean. I like it too, gets out all my aggressions."

Anne is thinking about a job for Jason. Will he ever bring himself to give music a real try? Does it matter, as long as he is content, as long as he is slim and beautiful, as long as he is wonderful in bed? What more does she want of him? She presses her thigh against his and he returns the pressure, and she thinks that she will keep urging him, at least once in a while, to try playing the piano professionally. She will be careful, she doesn't want to make him resentful, but you never know, he could suddenly agree, he could try it, he could succeed.

They reach Anne's building and shove the desk out onto the street. Anne gives the driver a huge tip, and she thanks them and wishes them good luck as she drives away. Anne and Jason maneuver the desk into the elevator and then into Anne's apartment, and finally there it is, one of the chairs drawn neatly up under it, the lamp attached.

"It's beautiful," Anne says. "I love it."

"I love you," Jason says, and they go and take a shower together to wash off the dust and sweat of getting the desk uptown.
She watches the water running off the smooth planes of his body,
then soaps him all over. Will they survive together, she and Jason?
Already there is something complicated between them, something
with different textures at different moments. Hard to believe it
started with simple lust, with her staring at his twenty-nine-inch
waist. Not that lust doesn't still play a part, she thinks, soaping his
ass for the third time. Do they either of them want the relationship
to last forever, do they want that kind of romantic success? They
don't discuss it. They have no history together. How long since
they first slept with each other? About five months now. Is he family, by Emily's definition? Probably, and yet sometimes it seems to
her that they are almost strangers, such a short connection, such a
quickly told story.

Out of the shower, drying each other, the pink towel for him,
the baby-blue towel for her, her hair damp against the quilt as they
finally do make love. They make love for a very very long time;
the connection between them is old enough for this, they know
each other's pace, they read each other's signals, they postpone
frenzy until the moment for it is almost past and then slide into it
and let it carry them away. At this, at least, they are inarguably
skilled. At piano playing, maybe, probably, maybe not quite
enough, maybe enough if the drive were there too. At science,
maybe, probably, maybe more than she thought, maybe it's all just
a question of lucky breaks. But when it comes to the two of them
fucking on a patchwork quilt on a sunny September day, well,
then they are champions. And that is not nothing.

"I think the summer is ending," Anne says, feeling a slight
breeze come in through the window and dry her sweat. "Today
does feel a little like fall."

Jason grins at her, teasing. "Well, in that case I guess our summer romance is just about over."

"You're going back to your winter girlfriend?"

"Well, you know, you beach chicks are all very well for sum-
mertime—"

They can make these jokes, after all, because they both believe that they will go on together into the fall, into the winter, maybe beyond. Jason on a cold December night, Jason under the blankets. Anne feels suddenly very happy. She thinks without tension of the work she will do at Viatech this fall, this winter. Maybe I *am* a hotshot, she thinks, or if I'm not, maybe I can go on fooling everyone.

Jason gets up and puts on one of her jazz records. He pauses in front of the pink robe hanging on the wall.

"Do I never get to wear this ever again?" he asks.

So she gets off the bed and takes down the robe for him, leaving the tacks and the string up on the wall so she'll be able to put it back later. Jason wraps himself up, and Anne lies back on the quilt again and watches him putting on the record and then prowling around her refrigerator for something to eat.

Why is she always looking for a message? Stop worrying. There is work, there is Jason. Those will both last at least for a while. And Charlotte, her friendship with Charlotte will last. What about Charlotte and Blair? That too will last, Anne believes; Charlotte will go on not being completely happy with it, but she will go on accepting it and the two of them will continue letting their lives touch two days every two weeks. Yes, Charlotte and Blair will go on.

And Louisa and Jim? Anne wants to believe that they will survive. She wants Louisa's life to be solved, she wants Louisa to feel like a success. Let her be married in white and go off to the suburbs and look back fondly on her crazy career-girl days. Louisa and Jim will make it, Anne tells herself.

Jason returns to the bed with a bag of sunflower seeds.

"I didn't know you were into this sort of thing."

"Emily brought them."

Anne and Jason sit up so they can spit the shells out the window, a very irresponsible thing to do.

"Why, from this height," Jason says, "a falling sunflower seed could kill someone."

And Emily and Kent? Well, no, Anne doesn't believe they're

going to make it together for very long. With luck, they'll leave each other with nice memories. But Anne doesn't believe they have enough between them to keep them going. What does that mean? How much do Anne and Jason have in common? Sex, but there's no telling whether Kent and Emily may not have that too. But no, Kent is an experience for Emily and Emily is an experience for Kent, and Anne doesn't believe that in the end they'll have been much more than summer experiences for each other. Furthermore, she suspects that Kent is now genuinely due for one of those distinctly "grown-up" professional types. And Emily? Emily will find a student-artist of some sort, Anne predicts, and then feels bad, prophesying the end of Kent and Emily so calmly.

Margie and Alan then. And let's face it, Anne doesn't really believe they're going to make it. Can a marriage survive after such blatant cracks have appeared? And poor Curtis will end up with one of them or the other trying hard to like them both, trying not to blame them for not liking each other.

"What are you thinking about?" Jason asks her, genuinely curious, serious.

"I'm trying to decide whether all the couples I know are going to survive together or not."

Jason thinks that over. She expects him to ask, Well, what did you decide about us, or something like that, maybe lightly, as a joke, maybe nervously, seriously. But instead he says, "How can you ever understand what goes on between two other people? Think of the people who make it together, and then think of the people who seem like they should and just can't."

"It's true," Anne says, thinking that she doesn't understand what is going on between herself and Jason half the time—how can she be predicting for two other people?

Predict friendships, then. She will stay friends with Charlotte, also with Kent. Louisa, she suspects, she will lose when Louisa marries. And Jeannette she will lose if she ever loses Jason, and Felice seems to be gone already, if she ever really was a friend, and Emily will disappear if she breaks up with Kent. Or will she? Maybe Emily really is family. Margie and Alan, as far as Anne is

concerned, are gone already—except that if they come back to
New York she would like to see Curtis.

"Still predicting?"

"I'm doing friendships now."

Again, he doesn't ask for specifics. Instead he gets up and
moves around the room to the soft jazz in the background. Pink
silk, Anne thinks, I have a lover wrapped in pink silk. He brings
her a glass of cold white wine.

"In the winter," he says, "I will make you hot cocoa at night."

She understands that this is his way of saying that he will be
around, that this is in fact his response to what she said about deciding which couples would last.

"And in the spring," she says, "what will you do for me in the
spring?"

"Bring you daffodils and strew them upon your naked body."

He goes over to the new desk, adjusts the architect's lamp to a
more pleasing angle, then stands back and looks around the apartment as if registering for the first time the abundance of objects,
old magazines, bits of extremely peculiar china.

"So this is what the house of a scientist looks like," he says. He
is teasing, of course, but again Anne finds herself almost leaning
forward, listening for the message.

"I never knew this was what my house would look like," she
says honestly.

"I wouldn't have guessed it either. But now that I see it, it
seems to suit you. It shows what a fascinating woman you are."

"Or do you mean what a weird woman I am?"

"Maybe. Anyway, all scientists are weird." He is quoting her
own line back at her. Anne smiles: Is that the message?

Jason picks up a pile of old *National Geographic*s and settles
himself against a cushion at the foot of the bed. They are not in
any hurry to do anything, Anne and Jason, they can lie around
naked or in pink silk robes and read old magazines. Or he can read
while she sorts and re-sorts the people to whom she is connected.
Which of them belong in what Emily would call her family?

Anne strokes the pink silk across Jason's shoulders. Beautiful Jason, beautiful pink silk. If she and Jason had a child together would it look like Jason? Would it get his ass?

"Why can't recombinant DNA research stop fooling around with antibodies and work on something important, like how to give children your beautiful ass?"

He looks up from his magazine, a little surprised. "My ass?"

"I'm crazy about your ass, didn't you know? That was the first thing I ever noticed about you."

"What about it?"

"I just think it's beautiful, that's all."

"Oh yeah?" He gets to his feet, looks around as though trying to make sure that no one is watching, and then turns his back on her and flips up the robe. Anne applauds, wishing she knew how to wolf whistle.

"And if you're very very good, maybe I'll let you touch it later," he says, sitting down again.

So what is the message then? Recombinant DNA, pink silk, Jason's ass, weird scientists? Anne grins. She feels very good, as though she has just showered and made love, as though she has just bought a beautiful new desk on which she will write letters and read articles, as though next to her on the beautiful patchwork quilt in the luxurious pink robe is a man with a beautiful ass, not to mention his many other excellent qualities. And how can she be expected to understand what goes on between other people when she never understands exactly what is going on between other people and herself, when she is always listening, a beat too late to catch the message which has already gone by?

"So I'm going to be your next experiment," Jason says. "You know, some things lose all their magic if you analyze them too closely."

"That's not a very scientific approach."

"Scientists are weird," Jason says again, very definitely.

Anne lies back against her patchwork quilt. A new desk, a pink silk robe, autumn beginning, and somewhere, a little more distant, the hum of the incubators, the bacteria growing and doubling in their incubators. And their messages, at least, she can read.